Ednah Dow (Littlehale) Cheney

Life of Christian Daniel Rauch of Berlin Germany

Ednah Dow (Littlehale) Cheney

Life of Christian Daniel Rauch of Berlin Germany

ISBN/EAN: 9783743313699

Manufactured in Europe, USA, Canada, Australia, Japa

Cover: Foto ©Raphael Reischuk / pixelio.de

Manufactured and distributed by brebook publishing software
(www.brebook.com)

Ednah Dow (Littlehale) Cheney

Life of Christian Daniel Rauch of Berlin Germany

LIFE OF

CHRISTIAN DANIEL RAUCH

OF

BERLIN GERMANY

SCULPTOR OF THE MONUMENT OF QUEEN LOUISE, VICTORIES
OF WALHALLA, ALBERT DURER, FREDERIC
THE GREAT etc.

DRAWN FROM GERMAN AUTHORITIES

BY

EDNAH D. CHENEY

AUTHOR OF "GLEANINGS IN FIELDS OF ART" EDITOR OF "MICHEL ANGELO'S POEMS" etc.

BOSTON
LEE AND SHEPARD PUBLISHERS
10 MILK STREET
1893

TO

ANNE WHITNEY

SCULPTOR

To you, true daughter of Art, my thoughts have often turned while I tried to bring out the noble life of this great man, who believed in Art as the expression of the highest in Humanity.

You share his Faith and his Devotion, and to you, as to him, Art has been an elevating vocation which has made you every year higher, wiser, and sweeter.

May I dedicate my earnest though imperfect work to you, with the deep respect and affection for yourself and admiration for your work which a friendship of many years, cemented by holy memories of the one who brought us together, has established in my heart.

EDNAH D. CHENEY

Jamaica Plain, *June 27, 1892.*

PREFACE

In the autumn of 1877 I visited Berlin, and for the first time saw the statue of Queen Louise, by Rauch. It was a revelation to me in modern art, and I felt the joy of the discovery of a new star in the heavenly galaxy. So simple without weakness, so pure and sweet without affectation, so noble and so modest, I accepted her as the queen of modern womanhood and the ideal of artistic representation. When I turned to the statue of the king, and found that this artist did not depend upon the exquisite sentiment of his first subject for his results, but out of far less promising material had gained an even greater artistic success, I felt that here was indeed a power, and, still more, a trained and educated power, that must help forward the progress of art.

When I spoke of him to an American sculptor of fine intellectual culture, as well as artistic feeling, and found that he did not know him even by name, I felt a great desire to introduce Rauch and his works to the better knowledge of my countrymen, who are in that formative stage of art when such an influence is most precious.

Since that time the great political movements in Germany have kept her people and country so much in our thoughts, and the stream of travel in the direction of Berlin has so much increased, that I have no doubt that this artist is far more widely known than he was then ; but I am equally sure that those who know a little will desire to know more, and I have therefore hoped to do a service in introducing him to an American public, so many of whom have had, or will have, an opportunity of seeing his original works.

During my brief visit I spent what time I could at the Rauch Museum, and in seeing the monumental statues, and tried to obtain some account of his life. A very interesting address made at the commemoration of the centenary of his birth was all that I could then find.

It was with great delight that I learned after my return home of the publication of the first volume of Dr. Eggers's "Life of Rauch," which I at once ordered. This work was projected by the brothers Eggers, both of them artists of high reputation, and friends of Rauch in his later years. By the death of Friedrich Eggers the whole work was left in the hands of his brother Karl. The publication of the later volumes was delayed by the acquisition of a large quantity of new material, consisting of letters to Goethe and others, and necessitating an entire revision and re-arrangement of the manuscript already prepared. The succeeding volumes followed slowly; the second was published in 1878, the third in 1886, the fourth in 1887, and finally the fifth, which is hardly a part of the narrative, but rather an illustrative appendix, appeared only in 1891.

During all these years, as far as other claims would allow, it has been my pleasant occupation to study this . life, and to make real to myself the character of this man ; and as the image of him grew clearer in my own mind, so did the purpose to try to present him to my fellow-countrymen in his "very habit as he lived."

I am almost entirely indebted to this biography for the material of mine ; indeed, it would have been folly in this distant land to have attempted to go behind a work so carefully executed with every advantage, and seek to make an original book. A full translation would have been too large a work for a publisher to venture upon, and I have therefore done as I felt that I could, gathering up the facts into my own mind, and striving to reproduce them in a popular form. When I again visited Berlin, in 1891, it was with this purpose in view and partly executed; and I received from Dr. Eggers permission to make such use of his work as I had proposed.

I wish here to make to him the fullest and most grateful acknowledgment not only for this permission, but for the excellence and fulness of his biography, which has left so little to be desired. I availed myself, however, of every opportunity within my reach to obtain independent impressions of Rauch's personality and work, and was fortunate enough to meet one person who had known him in youth, and another who had a hereditary knowledge of him, besides gathering the general impression of feeling in regard to him, and again seeing his works.

I have found great difficulty in following any strict chronological sequence in presenting the facts of Rauch's life. As one of his great works often occupied him for many years, and others were in different stages of progress at the same time, it seemed better to take up each as a separate theme, and describe the whole course of its production, from its beginning to its close. I have, however, endeavored to give so many dates as to keep the epoch of any event easily before the mind, and show the onward march of time.

I have made one addition to the life drawn from other sources; viz., the chapter on Queen Louise. It is through her statue that Rauch is more generally appreciated by travelling Americans than by anything else, and yet this woman is not so well known as she should be, and as she is destined to be in coming years; for Germany to-day reveres and loves the mother of her emperor, and, as he said, "the founder of German Unity," far more than even in her lifetime. I have, therefore, given a sketch of her life, which of course Dr. Eggers did not think it necessary to do for a German public.

While I have thus freely used his facts, statements, and opinions, often being obliged to condense them very much in order to bring five large volumes into the compass of one small one, and also to translate very freely, I have put into quotation marks the direct extracts from Rauch and others, and also any sentences of Dr. Eggers which I could translate pretty literally, or which seemed especially good in expression, or for which I preferred to have his direct authority. If I am accused of plagiarism, I can only admit the charge by the wholesale. It would be entirely impossible for me to say what part of the book is my own thought, or what was suggested by another. I have so made it my own by long possession, that I feel like the mother of an adopted child who thinks his virtues are inherited from her. I have given no statement which I did not believe, and have uttered no opinion which I am not willing to maintain ; and if the book only interests the reader in my subject, he is perfectly free to give the merit of it where he thinks it is due.

If I shall induce any one to study the original volumes of Dr. Eggers, and, above all, the sculpture of Rauch, I shall have done him a service which I am sure will atone for all my deficiencies.

CONTENTS

LIST OF ILLUSTRATIONS

LIFE OF CHRISTIAN DANIEL RAUCH

CHAPTER I

BIRTH AND CHILDHOOD. — LIFE AT COURT
1777–1804

THE little city of Arolsen, not far from Cassel, was in the eighteenth century ruled over by Prince Friedrich, a man of high culture and strong character, who loved science, and cared much for the improvement of his people. His "Kammerdiener" was named Johann Friedrich Rauch. From the papers of this person, we learn that his prince sent one hundred and thirty soldiers to aid George III. in prosecuting our Revolutionary War. His Kammerdiener apologizes for this transaction of his prince, and says that he was very careful that the agriculture of the country should not suffer from it.

In this letter we also find the first mention of our hero, January 18, 1778.

The family then consisted of three sons. The oldest was fifteen and the second son twelve years old. Next to them there had been two daughters, who were now both dead. The youngest child, then a year and six days old, was

CHRISTIAN DANIEL RAUCH, *born January* 2, 1777.

This date at once indicates at what an important epoch in the history of both Europe and America he lived, and how a biography of him must represent, from an individual standpoint, many of the most striking political and intellectual influences that have made the present condition of the Christian world.

The father, who had been a soldier, and had become a court-servant, was noted for his strict order and integrity, and also for the punctuality and fidelity with which he fulfilled the duties of his little office. These traits reappeared in his son. His mother was the daughter of a mason, and this fact also may have influenced his tendencies.

The children were brought up in the strictest simplicity. Until his twentieth year, Christian did not know the luxury of an overcoat in that severe climate. At home he wore a "Gatten-jacket." As this garment was especially convenient for sausage-making, it was called the "sausage-jacket." He grew rapidly, was vigorous, and had a fine appetite. If he was sent to the apple storeroom, he filled his pockets and sack with apples for his own eating. His mother was aware of the trick, but said nothing, "they tasted so good to him."

According to his own statement, he was not the finest of the children. "His eldest brother," he says, "was the handsomest and the best." He died when Christian was only a few years old. His death-bed was surrounded with African marigolds, and Rauch could never bear the sight or odor of these flowers, so forcibly did they recall this early sorrow. A younger brother, "beautiful as a picture," as Rauch was wont to say, died in Poland; and only one, Friedrich, who became court-gardener in the princely garden of Herrenhausen, survived to full maturity.

Rauch's education up to the age of fourteen was very narrow. The Old and New Testaments, the Catechism of Martin Luther, and the "Book of Saints" were his only books of study. An old atlas, used by the choir leader to raise his seat, gave him his first ideas of geography.

He learned French from two old mechanics in whose workshop he delighted to play, and a French emigrant whom his parents invited to their house for his advantage. In his ninth year he was obliged to attend regularly to his French lessons, and he found this early knowledge of French very useful to him. He attended church service, with singing and preaching, and also Sunday-school on Sundays and on Tuesdays and Fridays.

He was so bright and studious as to attract the attention of the prince, who looked over his exercises, and once gave him a pair of new silver shoe-buckles as a reward for a clever composition. His brother Friedrich aided and encouraged him, and brought him books to study.

"The teacher says so," was a frequent formula of the conscientious child. One rainy day, when walking with his father, he took pains to walk exactly in his father's footprints, and as with his short legs he was obliged to spring from one to another, he spattered mud over his father's stockings. His father said, "What nonsense is this, youngster?" — "Father, the teacher says, 'Children must walk in the footsteps of their elders.'" This was not a joke, but a literal fulfilment of a duty, as was always so characteristic of the man.

Another anecdote illustrates his simple belief. An old linen weaver came every spring and set up his loom, and stayed with them. He slept in the same room with Christian, who found him an agreeable companion, one who answered all his questions.

As the Passion of Jesus was read in school at this time, the boy became so absorbed in it, that he imagined that the scenes of the Crucifixion were actually taking place in Jerusalem. He believed in the resurrection, and, thinking that it must spread a glory over the whole earth, he waited anxiously for Easter morning. "It is going on now," he called out suddenly, raising himself up in bed. "What is going on?" said the old weaver, waking up. "The Resurrection of the Lord!"—"Oh! youngster," cried the weaver, "that was over long ago. Go to sleep!"

His father's position enabled him often to visit the princely apartments. There hung pictures and prints which fascinated him, especially "The Death of General Wolfe," one of the best pictures of Benjamin West, finely engraved by Woollett in 1776. A bust of the Apollo, four feet in height, and busts of Frederic the Great and of Goethe also interested him. He had access to the workshop of the sculptor Valentin, and having made acquaintance with his apprentices he saw their work, and noticed especially a marble chimney-piece for one of the castles. Valentin had much to tell of London and the glories of Westminster Abbey, which the boy never forgot.

According to German custom, when the boy was of suitable age — thirteen years old — he was confirmed in the church, and was then to choose his life-work. Christian himself had no doubt what it should be, but it required some entreaty on his part before it was agreed that he should be apprenticed to the court sculptor in Helsen. This took place October 17, 1790. The contract was for five years. As he boarded with his parents, he had to walk five miles daily to his work-place. The work consisted mostly of funeral urns, chimney-pieces, sandstones for graves, and ornaments of wood for picture-frames.

Christian fulfilled his five years' apprenticeship, wandering between Arolsen and Helsen, working earnestly, and looking dreamingly forward into the future. His first glimpse into the outer world was gained by a trip on foot to Cassel with his comrade Wolff. Here he first saw an antique marble statue, but he was much more moved on visiting the atelier of Ruhl, where he saw active, progressive work. Ruhl had just returned from Rome, and brought with him fragments of ancient art, and designs for new work. He told much of living artists, especially of Canova, and the boy saw the process of modelling a lion in clay.

In every little court of Germany at that time was to be found a prince who imitated Louis XIV., and tried to surround himself with French influences and ornament. Such a man was Count Friedrich II. von Hesse. He was the founder of an academy which did service to art. When Rauch's apprenticeship was ended, he came to Cassel to be under the especial instruction of Ruhl, who was the life of the academy. He arrived there in September, 1795, with three French "laub-thalers"[1] and a lucky penny in his pocket. For his work as helper in wood, and then in stone, he received one "laub-thaler" per week. In the evenings he went to the academy, and modelled in clay after the living model, by which he gained a silver medal.

In four months' time Christian was thrown still more on his own resources by his father's death; but his brother Friedrich, the Schloss-castellan of Sans-Souci, supplied his place as far as possible, sending him books, and directing the course of the young sculptor.

But this support was soon withdrawn. In January, 1797, the painful news came from Potsdam of the dangerous illness of Friedrich. Christian hastened to Potsdam only to find his brother in his grave.[2] He took his papers to carry to the king, who had felt great sympathy for the young castellan, and wished to see his brother. The beautiful young sculptor charmed the king, and he offered him aid in his art. But the Kammerdiener Rietz, to whom the matter was left, wished to engage him in the personal

---

[1] The laub-thaler was an old French coin with a wreath of leaves upon it, and hence its name. As it had gone out of general circulation, it was often used as a lucky penny.

[2] For the grave of this brother, Rauch designed the statue of Hope, which was one of his last works. It was left unfinished, and was placed over his own grave.

service of the king, and represented to the youth that he would have to struggle long and hard as a sculptor, while a place at court would at once enable him to support his mother and younger brother. Therefore Rauch entered into the personal service of King Friedrich Wilhelm II. February 7, 1797.

The king having been ordered to try the baths of Pyrmont, Rauch, who knew the locality well, went thither to make arrangements for him, and was allowed to spend a week with his mother, for the last time, as it proved, although she lived thirteen years afterwards.

On the death of the king in the autumn, Rauch had much leisure for his work, but he remained in the service of Queen Louise, the wife of the new king, Friedrich Wilhelm III. He used all his spare time for study ; and it is said that the queen even allowed him to draw while waiting in her antechamber. At this time Berlin afforded him rich opportunities for study. The plans of Frederic the Great in founding an academy, and inviting men of talent and distinction to his capital, had been followed by Friedrich Wilhelm. Best of all, Schadow, then only twenty-four years old, had been called back from Rome, had been made director of the Royal Atelier of Sculpture, and had received a commission to finish a monument for "den Grafen von den Mark."

From this time dates the project for the statue of Frederic the Great, which the army had wished to erect even before his death, but which Friedrich Wilhelm II. preferred to erect at his own cost. Schadow, at the king's desire, had made a model in Greek costume, and the disputes in regard to classic or modern drapery had already begun ; but little did any one think that the artist who was to complete the monument was then spending his precious days in the queen's antechamber.

Only in the evenings could Rauch attend the studies of the academy, or the lectures of Hirt and Rambach, but he worked unweariedly in every moment of leisure that he could command. He accompanied the youthful royal pair on a visit to Silesia and Posen. They were everywhere greeted with the warmest enthusiasm. The simple citizen's life of this happy couple might seem to allow much time to Rauch, but the frequent changes of residence left him little opportunity for study ; and he became impatient at the want of satisfaction for his strong desire for progress in his art. With his intense love of work, this easy service was very irksome to him.

In 1798 he petitioned the king for a small pension, with opportunity to give his time to study. The king refused to exchange his salary as " Lakay " for two-thirds of the sum as an artist, suggesting that, as he was situated, he had sufficient opportunity to perfect himself in art.

In 1802 the Emperor Alexander of Russia came to Prussia, and formed the well-known league of friendship with its king. Rauch was appointed to the special service of the emperor, who gave him forty ducats for his attendance. On his return journey he saw Warsaw for the second time, and met the artists there more intimately. Meantime his unwearying friend, Baron von Schilden, had secured for him six months' leave for study in Dresden. In addition to the emperor's gift he received ten *Friedrichs d'or* from the king, — a sum we need not despise when we remember how frugal the king was in his own household, and in gifts to his own children.

In this year the first work of Rauch was exhibited. The Sleeping Endymion and Artemis, as well as some busts, were shown in the academy.

Through the winter he continued in the service of the beloved queen, but felt discontented that he was not following the right path. This early court favor, which would have seemed the height of good fortune to many men, was almost the only hindrance which Rauch had to struggle with in his artistic career ; and, since his mother and young brother depended on him for support, it could hardly have been won for them, at less cost to his artistic life, in any other way.

But the next summer brought to him an influence which made him feel more imperatively the necessity of following out his own path.

Schadow had paid little attention to Rauch, considering him only as an amateur, and believing that if he had any real artistic power he ought to have shown it at an earlier age, since he himself at twenty-four was already court-sculptor, while Rauch only exhibited his first work at twenty-five. As soon, however, as he perceived the real earnestness of the young sculptor, he sympathized warmly with him, gave him a large relief to model after a sketch, and in the autumn commissioned him to put it in plaster. The subject of the sketch was "The Physician Giving Help on the Battlefield." The classical tendency is very strong in this work, and one might imagine it a scene from the "Iliad." Besides the regular pay, Schadow gave Rauch a gratuity of a hundred thalers for this relief, which made Rauch very happy. He felt the joy of earning in his own true line. Even the service of the lovely queen was joyless in comparison, and again and again he sought to be released from it.

But his request was always refused on account of his charming personality, for others did not suspect the greatness in him, which was yet unknown to himself. He made one more effort with the king, and at last, January 31, 1804, the long-desired release was granted. A pension of one hundred and twenty-five thalers and twelve groschen was allowed him, with permission to go to Rome and spend it there. Thus his full desire was gratified ; for all his longings turned to Italy. Baron von Schilden offered him two hundred thalers for his journey to Rome, and as a return Rauch modelled a bust of the baron, for which he received one hundred thalers more. A young Count

Sandretzky had expressed the wish for the company of a young artist on his journey to Rome, and it was decided that Rauch should accompany him, going to Dresden on the first of August. The court passed the summer at Charlottenburg, and Rauch was allowed to model the bust of the queen. According to his own judgment, this work was somewhat dry and stiff, although it had true and good points.

The young traveller had already begun to keep a diary, as he continued to do all his life, but it was usually more a record of observations and facts than of feelings; but as he started on this eventful journey he looked back over his youthful life and made these notes in pencil.

"I left Schwalbach with peculiar reflections. I was here in March, 1793, at the beginning of the second campaign of Prussia against the French. I met my brother on the march hither near Wickert, and made the march to that place with him; slept one night there, and then, having seen my brother less than twenty-four hours, I travelled back in storm and snow over Wiesbaden to my parents. I was then a little more than sixteen years old, and beginning to learn sculpture. The future lay in the dark distance before me. All was expectation: this tumult of strife before me, never before seen; the crowds of discontented people; the devastation of war, then incomprehensible to me; the throng of people, which formed like lines on foot and horseback on all the roads, amazed me. One·saw this scene from every hill, the fearful Mainz always before the eyes. All this made me sick, although I was sound in body. At Wiesbaden, where I slept the next night, I became homesick, and I hurried with all my force towards home, where my parents and friends expected and received me. Perhaps I tell this little digression without connection, but it escaped me without my will, and my last word was 'reflections.'

With these I left this morning the misty Schwalbach, which brought back again all the ideas and wishes with which I then travelled this way ; and I now compared them, thanking Heaven and blessing my parents that what I longed for eleven years before (it always seemed to me as if my innermost wishes would be gratified, but I could not count upon it then) was brought to me in all its fulness at this moment, when I was hastening to glorious Rome, — my goal, the goal of all men who love the noble, especially the goal of artists and poets. I have the joy of which hundreds are worthy, and yet they cannot reach it.

" Grateful and happy, I stood upon the height and looked over the broad Rhine valley. The Rhine streams through this beautiful meadow about green islands which seem made for his pastime, or as if he made them himself. Above, perhaps in the region of Mannheim, one sees it in a long stripe as it bounds the horizon, and through this distant opening it seems to rush towards one. Mainz has something fearful to me, it lies so big, so strongly fortified there, watching the Rhine ; there is something commanding in this part of the landscape. The cathedral, the castle, the specially large buildings, have a decided blood-red color, and this is fearfully mirrored in the water. The long bridge of seven hundred and thirty paces appears from the road like a little string of pearls binding both shores together. .

CHAPTER II

ROME. — RETURN TO BERLIN
1804-1810

AUGUST was approaching. Rauch's friends feared that the young count would fail to accompany him, but Rauch felt sure of him, because, in ten minutes' conversation, he had found in him so much confidence and sympathy. The count was awaiting him in Dresden, and they visited the gallery together. They left Dresden the fifth of August, passing by Weimar, Gotha, Eisenach, Frankfurt, and Mainz; then down the Rhine, travelling by boat, by carriage, or on foot, with extra post as opportunity offered or the humor prompted them.

Rauch's diary has preserved for us a most interesting and precious record of his experiences and thoughts.

At Ludwigsburg he first saw a monument of Dannecker's, and soon afterwards became acquainted with him. He speaks thus of the now world-renowned Ariadne: "Dannecker has modelled a life-sized nude Ariadne riding on a tiger;[1] she is so boldly outstretched that, while taming this wild beast, she seems to be pleasantly carried along with it!"

He shows in his journal the keenest sensibility to the beautiful natural scenery of the Rhine, and no less to the interesting historic associations, as well as the rare objects of scientific interest, like the beautiful crystals. Always

---

[1] Rauch calls this animal a tiger, but opinions seem to differ in regard to it, and it is commonly called a panther. I do not know of any classical authority to establish the point.

and everywhere he had his eyes open, and was never weary
of observation and study.

The journey through all the magnificence of Switzerland
is described in glowing colors. He noted everything, the
mountains, the trees, the flowers, the old monuments, and
the merry dances of the people. But he felt so deeply,
almost painfully, the awful sublimity of the Alpine heights,
that the smiling beauty of the valleys and the home-life
of the peasants was a relief to him. At Geneva they
rested a fortnight, and the count began to model under
Rauch's direction. Rauch himself made a sketch for a
Genius of Death, in which he unintentionally made a striking likeness of Frederic II. the Great ; he also sketched
Ariadne lost in grief. He thought of carrying out this
idea in Rome, but nothing remains of it. The travellers
passed into France by Lyons, and on the sixteenth of
October Rauch visited the atelier of Chinard, of whom he
speaks with generous but discriminating praise. "On the
whole," he says, "the mixture of old French and modern
Greek style is mingled in his work in a somewhat curious
manner, but one sees in it the industrious artist full of .
talent. I have never seen better executed busts. His
atelier is excellent. It was formerly a church, which stood
in the Revolution. It was a pity that we did not see him.
He was absent in Bourdeaux."

At Nîmes, Rauch first saw one of the monuments of
that classic antiquity whose spirit he had imbibed so fully.
" October 18 we saw in Nîmes the splendid theatre, this
immense building ! For the first time I greeted with reverence a work of the genius and the hands of Roman
greatness ; it was always my childish wish to see the Col-
iseum ; here I see the daughter ! Timidly, as becomes a
child of nobody, of misery, I stand there with open mouth,
and nod to my neighbor : Yes, yes, that is true, that is a
building ! That is very beautiful ! The count has the
good idea that one might, with right good profit, give up

a whole life to be a Roman only for four weeks : I believe it with a good conscience, without fearing repentance." This almost boyish enthusiasm for antiquity lasted all through his life. ·" Then we went to the so-called Maison Carrée, a very poor name for a very fine temple. It corresponds completely to the idea of joyous holiness, a canon for beautiful, light, pure architecture."

At Marseilles, Rauch gives vent to his enthusiasm for the sea and the noble ship, "so built that the sea cannot destroy it, only iron and rock." But a day or two afterwards he saw the reverse side of sea life, for he was "*ganz teuflich*," seized by sea-sickness, and at no price would he stay on the rocking vessel. He preferred to seek an old house, three-quarters of an hour away, there to eat a supper of bread and oil, with bread perfumed with spoiled olives, and to make his night-quarters in a bed three steps high from the ground, and on straw that had lately been trodden by the cattle. "We would have slept with all that as in Abraham's bosom, but the rats must hold a festival, which they do once every year, for I never heard leaps and tones of such a wonderful kind from these people."

December 2, at two o'clock in the morning, they arrived in Genoa, in beautiful, clear moonlight, so that he says, "The palaces and churches of polished marble shone out like the eyes in a peacock's tail."

After describing the splendid buildings and porches, he writes, "This was not all that made it so imposing, but the plan, the thought, the construction, the relation of the single parts to the whole. One does not look for the Greek style in it, but for the old time of the kingdom, the broad consciousness of power and freedom, when Andrea Doria ruled the sea, and each looked up with envy to the higher power ; so one sees here the strife of rank — every one is prince. Quite lost in these monuments of former greatness, I enjoyed these impressions, which the 'Superb Genoa' will always keep for me. From my childhood the name of Genoa was for me bound up with the mystic, the sublime. The actual has often shown me my impressions were wrong, but not here. Indeed, my Genoese are no longer in the long halls and secluded streets of Genoa, but her whole I, her character in special, speaks plainly in these surroundings which she created around her. Exactly as the Greeks and Egyptians speak in their temples, so do the Genoese in their palaces." This extract shows with what living imaginative observation the young artist looked at everything.

On the twenty-third of December, 1804, he attended a great ball in Genoa, in honor of the coronation of Napoleon I. as emperor. Everything was in great splendor, only guests failed. At eight o'clock, although the invitation was for seven, not a dozen guests had arrived. "Was a slight rain the hindrance?" he asks, "or did the invited not care to join in festivities on this occasion?"

The travellers hoped to pass New Year's Day, 1805, in Milan, but they were so much delayed by the bad travelling that they reached there only on the second. The beautiful cathedral was not then finished, but Rauch admired its great extent and richness. "The first thought inspired," he says, "is rest."

He speaks with enthusiasm of the "Last Supper" of Leonardo da Vinci, which is injured, "but not enough to prevent one's finding in it all the great essentials of art." "Only a few times in my life," he says, "have I had much satisfaction in pictures, and never, I believe, any like this." The concentration of interest of all the characters in the scene passing before them impresses him deeply.

At Parma the loveliness of Correggio gives him delight. In the convent of San Paolo a French painter was copying the groups of boys looking through the windows, and Rauch had an opportunity of close study from the scaffolding. He says, "Correggio never could have produced anything more lovely, more charming, nor even Raphael; but how dangerous for a convent ! "

Rauch entered Rome, not only secured against outward want by the pension granted him by the king, but amply prepared to enjoy and learn from everything, by his previous study and observations. From the beginning of his artistic career his longings had turned thither, and he had so prepared himself for acquaintance with its treasures that he need lose no time in beginning his work. He arrived at Rome at a favorable time for art. The German revival, which began twenty years before Rauch's birth, was now in full flower. Lessing and Schiller had done their work in poetry and criticism. Germans were taking the lead in sculpture at Rome. Winckelmann had opened anew the study of Greek antiquity. When Gottfried Schadow was in Rome, from 1785 to 1787, he often found himself alone in the great galleries of sculpture, in spite of the great number of artists in the city who might have been expected to be attracted by them. The French David, in 1784, was devoted to the classic in his way, and he held modern Rome inthralled by his picture of the "Oath of the Horatii and Curatii." "David and his school," says Dr. Eggers, "is a back-grasp into the Roman world, with that theatrical accent brought out which is alike characteristic of old Rome and of modern France." Then Carstens, and others who had seen the Greek with more sympathetic eyes, followed in the same path.

Rome was undisturbed by the stormy scenes of the French Revolution, and afforded a quiet spot for the unfolding of art. Karl Ludwig Fernow had introduced the philosophy of Kant with enthusiasm to Rome, and thus Rauch became interested in the great master of thought, whose monument he afterwards erected in stone.

Many other important influences were at work. The young Rumohr had just made the first of his five Italian journeys which led to those "*Forschungen*" which must count as the foundation of the German study of art found in Hegel's "Philosophy" and Kugler's "History of Painting." Among the Catholics was D'Agincourt, who had written a history of the art of the Middle Ages. Protestantism had also its representatives. "August Wilhelm von Schlegel, Tieck, and his brother, who was devoted to Greek forms, formed with Madame de Staël a distinguished company."

But the person who united most perfectly this society, "the like of which," says Dr. Eggers, "was never seen in Rome, either before or since," was Wilhelm von Humboldt, whose noble personality drew around him all that was most learned and artistic from every land.

He went to Rome in 1802 as resident minister of Prussia, an office which clothed him with a certain authority, although it involved no pressure of business. Full of learning, liberal and moderate in religion, and loving Rome as the Romans did, no minister had ever been so beloved by all classes of people. Fate willed that even a dearer tie bound him to the classic soil, since his beloved eldest son was buried in Roman ground. His wife, full of every womanly charm, joined in his studies, while she cared diligently for his comfort; and her wide correspondence with many of the best artists of her time shows her deep and intelligent interest in art, as well as her motherly kindness.[1]

While Humboldt was busy in collecting a museum of casts to remind him of Rome in quiet Tegel, his wife employed the painters; for this happy couple were complements of each other, as his nature was inclined to plastic art, and hers to painting and music. From splendid receptions, where princes and cardinals were present, to the simplest artistic reunions, the most charming society was

---

[1] Yet later, one New Year's time, when Rauch was in Berlin, Frau von Humboldt had filled his bureau with fine linen shirts, so that he declares the drawers do not shut so easily as before.

found at this house, and all its delights were brought to their height when Alexander von Humboldt returned from America. All hung on his lips as he described the wonders of a newly discovered country in his mingling of scientific and poetic speech.

Into this charmed circle Rauch was welcomed most cordially, this family becoming as dear to him as his own. The relation of unbroken love and intimacy remained unchanged to the latest day of his life. Could the inheritance of a kingdom have been so helpful to a young artist? As Wilhelm von Humboldt studied language, and found in it the means of expression, so Rauch made plastic art the vehicle for every thought and feeling.

Rauch assisted Humboldt in making his collection of casts, and took charge of his house and grounds when he was in Albano. He instructed the children in drawing, and here showed those admirable powers of teaching, rather by examples and facts, than by words, which came afterwards into play with the numerous pupils in his atelier.[1]

While Thorwaldsen, in his devotion to classic art, had at once begun to express himself in works in direct imitation of the antique, Rauch felt it to be a necessary preparation for his future career to study the antique thoroughly, and, as it were, to assimilate its life, that he might reproduce it in relation to his own time. This course marked a strong characteristic of his art, which was so filled with the past and so true to the present. The celebrated scholars Zoega and Welcher were his

---

[1] A funny incident will illustrate his methods of discipline. He thought that the children were too devoted to their dolls, of which they had a numerous family, and one morning they found them all hanging to the bell-rope. The children felt deeply for the ignominious suffering of their family through the night, and sought revenge on their master. They put a dozen eggs into his bed under the sheets, and watched eagerly in the morning for their teacher's coming. To their surprise, he came in with a basket in his hand, saying that he had a gift for the most industrious. Their faces lengthened when, at the end of the lesson, he brought out the eggs, which had given him as bad a night as he had the dolls.

guides in these studies, and he was busily engaged in making collections, and in drawing for himself and Humboldt. Finally he decided to make an attempt at an original work, and he modelled a relief of Jason. It remained long unfinished in Thorwaldsen's studio, and may now be found in the Rauch Museum. He also made some busts, especially one of Queen Louise, which led to his first great work.

The stirring political events in Europe, which affected Prussia so deeply, obliged Wilhelm von Humboldt, who had never meant to leave Rome, to return to Germany, to give his aid in defence of the Fatherland. In the autumn of 1808 he went thither, taking only his son Theodore, and leaving the rest of his family in Rome. Rome had become a French state, and Rauch received an appointment to select works of art for an exhibition. Amid all the political excitement, Wilhelm von Humboldt did not forget the friend he had left behind, but succeeded, to the astonishment of many, in procuring a cabinet order increasing his pension from one hundred and twenty-five to four hundred thalers. Humboldt expresses his delight at this success, and also his pleasure in Rauch's restoration of an ancient bass-relief.

Frau von Humboldt kept Rauch's twenty-third birthday by a delightful reunion of artists, where Zacharias Werner declaimed and sang, and Jagemann blew on the horn melodies which Thorwaldsen was heard repeating in the workshop. The "incomparable Li," as they called Frau von Humboldt, exerted all her powers to make the evening delightful.

In March, Rauch went with Frau von Humboldt to Naples. He found the living art miserable. "One would think the artists were only joking," he said; a severe criticism from Rauch, to whom art was ever the most serious vocation.

This year brought to him and to Prussia a heavy loss. On the thirty-first of July came the news of the death of Queen Louise. Rauch completed her bust, and ventured to send it to the king on the seventh of September. Here begins the story of the celebrated monument by which Rauch is best known to American travellers, and perhaps to all the world. As its history runs over several years, I shall leave the subject now, and bring it into a separate and connected history.

Wilhelm von Humboldt was appointed Minister to Austria, which led to his wife and family leaving Rome and joining him in Vienna in 1810. The loss of the home which had afforded him so many happy hours made a great change to Rauch. He accompanied the family to Florence, where the presence of Thorwaldsen afforded some relief to his loneliness. He needed all this consolation, for it was indeed a great loss, which changed all his life at Rome. He almost tired Thorwaldsen out, driving from gallery to gallery to drown his grief. All his affections clung around the rooms in Trinità del Monte, and all others seemed strangers to him in comparison with the beloved family. His thoughts follow them to Vienna, and, when he hears that they are all re-united there, he exclaims, "How much joy in one day, in one family! What is a wedding-day compared to it?" These words give us a glimpse of the strength of Rauch's affections, which he was rather chary of expressing.

Humboldt's letter (which is spoken of elsewhere), recalling him to Berlin, fell like a bombshell into Rauch's heart, which was so full of his work in Rome and the garden which he was taking care of for Frau von Humboldt. He had sat so steadily at his work on the Jason, that the thumb of his right hand was disabled. But now the model was finished in all its folds, even to the smallest details.

But Rauch had no choice but to leave it all. The long-expected sons of Schadow arrived, and he left to the sculptor Rudolf his atelier, and his dwelling-house to both of them. He gave his relief to the moulder to make an impression, to keep until he could take it up again from the beginning.

He left Rome on the second of February, and passed a happy week with the Humboldts at Vienna. He found the lady of the house in better health and more delightful than ever, while Humboldt himself had become more earnest and thoughtful, and even older. It was no wonder ; he had learned to take the sufferings of his people to his head and heart, and was for a short time relieved from his diplomatic activity.

Rauch had been absent from Berlin six years. They were student years in every sense of the word. In the society of the most cultivated men of his time, absent from the exciting political disturbances of his country, freed from pecuniary care, he enjoyed one of the greatest of mortal privileges, that of carrying out his own life in freedom. Now his work was to begin.

The meeting with his early benefactor, Friedrich Wilhelm III., was full of both joy and pain, since during his absence the king had lost half his kingdom by the peace of Tilsit, and half his life through the death of his wife. The king was too much overcome by emotion to speak of the commission he had given to Rauch. The artist found the king's countenance ennobled by these deep experiences, and was struck by his beauty and his frank, manly bearing as never before. Perhaps at this moment arose in his mind the ideal of a true king, which he has so beautifully embodied in the statue made many years later.

Next to the welcome of his bereaved king, he felt the kind greeting of his master in art, Schadow, who offered him a place in his home and his atelier.

Rauch was now settled at Charlottenburg, in order to

begin the work for the full-sized monument of the queen. He had his workshop in the spacious castle. From it he looked into the large garden remarkable for its beautiful trees. "There," says Dr. Eggers, "in his leisure hours he walked with his little daughter, whom fate had sent to him; there, after the refreshing rains, he enjoyed the luxury of the North German summer."

This brief mention is all that the biographer gives of the relation which brought to Rauch his "adopted daughters," who became to him a great joy and comfort for the rest of his life. Although there are various rumors still afloat in regard to this connection, they differ so widely that I cannot venture to give any of them as reliable, and I must leave the subject under the kindly veil of mystery which has always shrouded it.

While we cannot approve the action of Rauch, if, as conjectured, he formed such a tie without legal sanction, it was too common an occurrence at that time to incur severe censure; and the whole testimony is that he did everything to atone for his fault, by the adoption of the children, whom he fondly loved and carefully educated. The universal affection and respect felt for him led to their full reception in the distinguished society in which he moved; and, as we shall see in the course of our narrative, he was exemplary in his relation as a father, and his daughters returned his affection and repaid his care.

From his pleasant retreat at Charlottenburg, Rauch kept up an active correspondence with the friends he had left at Rome, with his dear ones at Vienna, and with Lund at Stockholm. Unlike most artists, Rauch was an excellent correspondent, and his letters, written in a free, vigorous style, give us vivid pictures of his life and thoughts.

When the king consented to Rauch's return to Rome, to put the model of the queen's monument into marble, he made diligent preparation for his journey and his studies

there.   He filled up the hollow of the model of the statue
with Greek translations, which he bought for twenty-
seven thalers.   He longed for the sunshine of Rome.
He had contracted a fever from working in the damp, cold
room of the castle, and Kohlrausch, a friend of Humboldt,
took care of him.   In the days free from fever he made
two busts, one of the Countess of Brandenburg, in which
he took little satisfaction, as she had a cold, expressionless
face, while he worked with enthusiasm on that of the
king, whom he greatly admired.   This bust in plaster was
freely sold, and he was now obliged to make one of the
Princess Wilhelm.   But being again attacked with fever,
the king sent him to his physician Hufeland, who decidedly
advised his departure.   It was arranged that Rudolf
Schadow, who had returned to Berlin for a while, should
be his travelling companion, and a carriage was bought
for the journey.

He took leave of the king beside the monument, and at
this time proposed that a pair of white marble candelabra
might be placed at both sides of the statue, to which the
king assented.   He was all impatience to start, but found
the truth of Frau von Humboldt's saying, "*Reisen leidet
immer Aufschub.*"   They did not get away until January
4, and did not reach Vienna until the fourteenth.   Schadow
was invited to stay with him, and they passed two happy
weeks at the Humboldts', where he had to renew his
acquaintance with the children, who had grown apace.

He went also to Munich, invited by the crown prince.
The Crown Prince Ludwig was then twenty-six years old,
and already devoted to art.   He had begun to make collections of antiquities, and he wished the assistance of
Rauch in securing them, as he feared the competition of
" the rich English."   He also wished him to make several
busts ; and Rauch took with him to Rome models of Van
Dyck, Snyders, Tromp, and Hans Sachs.   Rauch won the
friendship of the crown prince, who kept up a constant

correspondence with him. He also rejoiced in an intimate acquaintance with Schelling. Still, he felt keenly the separation from the Humboldts, and the uncertainty of seeing them again ; and it was not until he arrived at Florence that the old charm of Italy began to work upon him. Schadow went on to Rome ; but Rauch went to Carrara, where he spent the whole day in mountains and quarries, seeking for stone suitable for his work. He decided to stay in Carrara through the summer, to block out the statue and sarcophagus there, and so send them much lightened to Rome.

He was full of excitement in Rome, revisiting old places, greeting old friends, and noting the changes which even a year of absence had produced. All Rome was then excited over the expected coming of the Emperor Napoleon. Rome would again be the seat of empire, and rule the world. The Pope must depart. "Long live the emperor who will come and live on the Quirinal !" was the cry. The artists were full of zeal to decorate the palace for the residence of his Imperial Majesty ; and even Thorwaldsen, who had been ill and miserable, worked himself well over his great bass-relief, " The Procession of Alexander."

Rauch was entirely out of sympathy with this feeling, looking upon Napoleon as the arch-enemy of his fatherland. He regarded the shows only with an artistic eye, finding much opportunity for observation and study. While waiting for his restored models to dry, he made a bust of Thorwaldsen, which his friend liked so much that he put it in marble. The crown prince Ludwig of Bavaria kept up a lively correspondence with him, and could buy nothing for the future Glyptothek without his advice. He was also to have all the busts he had modelled for the prince put into marble. On the thirty-first of July he left Rome again for the quarries of Carrara. At that time Carrara seemed a place of banishment from Rome, for the artists did not generally work there. Rauch proposed, however, to have all the busts for Prince Ludwig cut at the quarries ; and he even suggested to the king to have all the mausoleum made in Carrara, as he found better workmen than in Rome. Here, to his delight, were both Tieck and Bartolini. He also proposed to cut a sitting statue of Humboldt's second daughter, Adelheid, of which he had made a model on a former visit to Rome. He delights in this work, and sends to Vienna for an exact profile, as, although he remembers her face well, she has changed in the ten years since he has seen her.

For this, as for the queen's statue, he can hardly find marble pure enough ; but at last he selects a suitable piece of Erestola, and on the fourteenth of September the first point in the stone is made.

During his stay at Rome at this time Rauch felt much annoyed by the tendencies of the artists towards Catholicism. When he came into their society, formerly so pleasant, and wished to hear the news from beyond the Alps, "the mad Zacharias Werner took the word, and when he was through with his crosses on the platter, plate, bread, breast, and brow, talked incessantly of the miracles of Monsignor Manocchi."

The company at table, except Rudolf Schadow, and Thorwaldsen, who talked little, held the Church Fathers closely to heart, and the most unpleasant things were said against the faith in which Rauch had been piously brought up, by those who had foresworn this faith only a few weeks before.

From such troubles he turned to work as his great consoler. He kept a constant oversight over all that was doing in Carrara, inquiring about every part, and knowing to what workman it was committed. He wrote regularly once a week, and these letters are filed in perfect order, and if one is out of the regular time it is marked "extra." He was thoroughly exact and orderly in all his accounts.

It is to these traits that he owed the freedom from pecuniary embarrassments and other petty cares which have despoiled the lives of so many artists. It is good to see that order and exactness are not inconsistent with genius.

If it had been possible to put the affairs of Rome and Germany into order with a chisel, Rauch would have been the man to do it, and he would have been at peace, but as it was, he was full of unrest.

In his letters to Tieck he constantly mixes up sculpture and politics, and one might gather the whole history of the German uprising for freedom from his letters. This lively correspondence attracts the attention of the French police. He is arrested and taken to prison, and his correspondence examined and sealed up. He is held only twenty-four hours, and his papers are returned, except the correspondence with Bussler in regard to the queen's statue, which has never come to light.

But good news soon came from Berlin to make up for this annoyance. Schadow writes him the most glowing descriptions, first of the battle of Grossbeeren, and then of the glorious victory of Leipzig. "I never had such joy in my life!" he exclaims to Tieck. "If you were only here, that we might rejoice together over our happy lot; for every day brings something newer and better, for freedom is the highest blessing." He pities his friend that he must spend the long evenings alone there in Carrara, when the seven stars and the clear moon are shining on such beautiful things on the surface of the earth.

In spite of his care in sending letters under cover, he is again arrested by the police, and ordered to quit Rome within twenty-four hours; but by the intervention of Canova, a deputation of French artists, with the director of the academy at their head, procured him permission to remain.

These events made his residence in Rome very dreary, and, much as he feared the solitude of Carrara, he longed to go thither to get through his work. He beguiled his anxiety with reading, especially Roscoe's " Leo X.," and the memorials of that great time ; and M. Angelo's works, which he had formerly been too much absorbed in Greek art to attend to, now began to occupy him. Excavations were also going on in Rome, and the Barberini Faun and other statues were purchased for Prince Ludwig.

Canova and Thorwaldsen were producing their best works, and Rauch speaks of Canova's Three Graces as " happy and original in composition, living and naïve." He is also especially interested in Thorwaldsen's Procession of Alexander, which he considers the best thing in this art in modern times. These distinguished sculptors were equally pleased with his work, and proposed him as a member of the senate of the Academy of St. Luke.

January 19, General Pignatelli took possession of Rome in the name of the King of Naples. Rauch would have preferred that the Germans should be the liberators, yet he was delighted to be freed from the French rule. The winter was pleasant, without snow or ice, and he says, " Everything is green like our hopes."

On his way to Carrara, February 12, he was attacked by robbers, but escaped at the cost of nine Roman scudi. He was so deeply interested in current events, that his walls were hung with military maps, which he now enjoyed more than the pictures of Raphael. Great was his delight, therefore, to receive from Prince Ludwig a commission to make a bust of Blücher, the hero of the day. As this was to be from life, however, he had to defer it until he could leave Italy. He expressed his feelings by modelling a bust of the king crowned with laurel. He was anxious to hasten to Berlin to meet the statue of the queen, but many unfinished works tempted him to delay. He employed seven workmen, and would have liked many more. It was a perpetual joy to him to design his works and put them immediately into marble. When at last he left Carrara, he chose the quickest way, by the mule-drivers' route over Pontremoli. He enjoyed the scenery, and hoped to see it again with friends; but now he hurried on, not stopping even at Vienna, although the Congress was sitting there, and Prince Ludwig was very desirous to see him. He was anxious to be in Berlin to meet the king on his return from the Congress.

CHAPTER III

QUEEN LOUISE OF PRUSSIA

Born March 11, 1776.   Died July 19, 1810

THE name of Rauch is so indissolubly connected with that of Queen Louise of Prussia, not only by his countrymen, but by all Americans who visit Berlin, that no one interested in the sculptor can fail to desire more knowledge of the heroic queen, the gracious and beautiful woman who was not only his early benefactress, but the inspiration and subject of his most beautiful, if not his greatest work. Therefore, before giving an account of this justly celebrated statue, I propose to offer a sketch of the principal events in the life, and the leading traits in the character, of Queen Louise of Prussia.

We should be obliged to go far back into the history of the various provinces of Germany to trace out fully the heredity of this princess, for she united in her ancestry the leading families of Sigismund and Hohenzollern.

She was the sixth daughter of the Prince, subsequently Duke and Grand-Duke, Karl von Mechlenburg-Strelitz.

Her mother was Princess Frederika Karoline Louise von Hesse Darmstadt.

Her father was at the head of the Hanoverian army of his brother-in-law, the King of England, and furnished to his assistance those hated Hessian troops whose employment our fathers resented so bitterly.

An early portrait of the mother is preserved, in which the traits of the daughter may be traced.

Her great ancestor, the Elector Frederic William, who founded the kingdom of Prussia, welcomed the Protestants, who were driven out by the edict of Nantes, so that Berlin became nearly half French. The elector married Louise of Orange, who built and adorned Oranienburg, one of the favorite residences of Queen Louise.

Louise, the third surviving daughter, and the sixth child of the family, was born in the palace in the Leinestrasse, Hanover, March 10, 1776. She was baptized Louise Augusta Wilhelmina Amelia.

Three years younger than herself was a brother, who became Rauch's steadfast friend, George, Duke of Mechlenburg-Strelitz. The lovely child grew up in a sort of earthly paradise, in a home adorned with beautiful gardens and fountains, statues and vases, according to the stately but artificial fashion of the day. Sorrow soon came into her Eden, however, for she lost her mother when only six years old. She was devotedly attached to her, and drooped so much from her sorrow, that she was sent for a short visit to her maternal grandmother, the widowed Princess of Hesse Darmstadt. In 1784 her father married the sister of his wife, the Princess Charlotte Wilhelmine Christiane. She lived, however, only a short time; and after her death the Duke decided to leave Hanover and reside at Darmstadt.

Here the young girl was much under the influence of her grandmother, a woman of remarkable character and ability.

When Louise was only nine years old she first met the poet Schiller, who came to Darmstadt to see the wife of Goethe's friend, the Duke Karl August of Weimar. He read the first act of Don Carlos to the princely circle.

The young princesses at this time lived very simple, healthful, and happy lives. We are told that they were in the habit of making their own silk shoes.

Louise had a pretty face and figure, a fair complexion,

with a soft color in her cheeks, and a lovely light in her open blue eyes.

Her first governess was Fräulein Agier, who was dismissed as being too severe, while Mademoiselle Gelieux gave great satisfaction, and helped to form the pleasing manners of the princess.

The French influence was very strong in Louise's life, and French was always her familiar speech ; but this fact did not overcome her patriotic feeling, and she is often called "The German-hearted Queen." She took great pains, in later years, to acquire full command of the German language.

Her governess sought to cultivate her heart as well as her head, and led the princess to seek out the poor and the suffering, to sympathize with their sorrows, and to comfort their distresses. She was carefully instructed in the Lutheran faith, to which she always remained constant, and was warmly attached to one of her teachers, the Rev. Andreas Frey. A little anecdote of her girlhood shows how early she learned to consider others before herself. She visited Strasburg, and was so much delighted with the noble cathedral that she wished very much to go to the top. Her governess did not forbid her doing so, but said, "It will be very fatiguing for me to go up, but I cannot let you go alone." The princess yielded to the feeling of her governess, looked wistfully upward, but did not ascend.

When Louise was fourteen years old a great event occurred at Frankfort, September 1, 1790. She was present at the coronation of Emperor Leopold II. The part of the city allotted to guests from Hannover included the street called the Hirschgraben, in which stood the house of Frau Rath Goethe. She was now a widow, and her only son, Johann Wolfgang, the great poet of his country, was naturally the joy and pride of her heart. It was arranged that the princesses Louise and Frederika should

be sent to her house, at which the dear old lady felt highly
honored. The young people enjoyed their stay with her
very much, for she allowed them to eat salad and eggs of
her cooking, and to pump water in the yard to their hearts'
content, preferring to incur the indignation of the governess, rather than deprive them of girlish pleasures.
Here Louise also probably first met Von Stein, the statesman who afterwards proved a true friend. It was while
the princesses were staying in Frankfort that their brother
made the call on Frau von Goethe, thus comically described
by the wild Bettina von Arnim.

She writes to Goethe in her quaint English : —

"A few days ago I went in the evening, and the maid
admitted me with the remark that she (Frau Goethe) was
not at home, but must come directly. In the parlor it was
dark. I seated myself at the window, and looked out
over the square. It was as if something scratched. I
listened, and believed I heard breathing ; I became uncom-
fortable. I again heard something moving, and asked,
'Jack, is that you ?'[1] Quite unexpectedly, and very deject-
ing for my courage, a sonorous bass voice answered out of
the background, ' Jack it is not, but John,' and therewith
the '*Ibique malus spiritus*' cleared his throat. Full of
reverence, I would not from the spot: the spirit, too, only
gave proofs of its existence by breathing and once sneez-
ing. Then I heard your mother; she stepped forward,
the scarcely burning, and not yet fully lighted taper behind,
borne by Betty. 'Art thou there ?' asked your mother,
as she took off her cap to hang it on its nightly pedestal ;
viz, a blue bottle. ' Yes,' we both called out ; and out of
the darkness stepped a be-starred gentleman, and asked,
' Frau Rath, shall I eat bacon-salad and omelet with you
this evening ?' From this I concluded, quite correctly,
that *John* was a prince of Mechlenburg ; for who has not
heard the pretty story of your mother ; how, at the corona-

---

[1] Frau Goethe had a tame squirrel which she called Jack.

tion of the emperor, the now queen of Prussia, then a young princess, and her brother, looked at Frau Rath as she was about to eat such a dish, and that it so excited their appetites that they together demolished it, without leaving her a leaf. Now the story was told with much enjoyment, and many another beside : how she procured the princesses the pleasure of pumping to satiety at the pump in the courtyard, keeping the governess, by all possible arguments, from calling the princesses away ; and at last, because she would not listen to her, used force, and locked her up in a room. 'For,' said your mother, 'I would rather have drawn upon myself the worst consequences than that they should have been disturbed in their innocent pleasures, which were granted them nowhere except in my house ; they said to me too, as they took leave, that they should never forget how delighted and happy they had been with me.' I could fill several sheets more with all such sorts of recollections."

Jean Paul Richter describes a visit to a hunting castle of the duke, and a charming wild country walk with the ladies and two bright children. Louise was at that time sixteen. She was like her sister Charlotte, and had the same loving blue eyes, but the expression changed more quickly with the feeling of the moment. Her soft brown hair still retained a gleam of the golden tints of childhood, and her fair transparent complexion was in the bloom of exquisite beauty. She was tall and slight, and graceful in all her movements. Jean Paul dedicated his Titan to "the four princesses of Mechlenburg."

The young princesses remained a while with their grandmother at Hildburghausen. The home, otherwise so happy, was, however, full of anxiety on account of the condition of the country ; for Dumouriez had repulsed the army of Brunswick, and the French emigrants and many of their own relations were in danger.

A temporary cessation of hostilities encouraged the

grandmother to return with her young charges to Darmstadt, and she was invited to visit the Landgrave of Hesse,
and present the young ladies to the King of Prussia and
his sons.   It proved a memorable day.   The crown prince
and his brother were captivated by the princesses of
Mechlenburg, and the king invited the elder princess and
her granddaughters to sup with him.

The feeling aroused in the crown prince was as deep as
it was sudden.   After the queen's death, he said to Bishop
Eylert, " I felt, when I first saw her, ' 'Tis she or none on
earth.'   That expression is somewhere in Schiller, I forget where, but it exactly describes the emotions which
sprang up in my heart at that moment." [1]

Louise had seen a very attractive picture of the crown
prince, and of course had heard much of him.   He was
then in his twenty-third year.   He was well-proportioned,
tall and slight, and his bearing erect and soldier-like.   In
youth he showed a fine character, of a decided stamp, and
Frederic the Great said of him, " *Il me recommencera.*"
He was a favorite with his uncle, and the young man
never forgot the parting interview in which the dying
king foretold the troubles that were coming on his country, and exhorted the young prince to stand fast by the
" True and the Right."

The attachment which had sprung up between the
Crown Prince of Prussia and the Princess Louise, and
between his brother and her hardly less beautiful sister,
grew and ripened, and fortunately met with no opposition
from the king.   It was a case of true love running
smooth, even rarer among crowned hearts than in humble
life.

The double betrothal was brilliantly celebrated April
24, 1793.

The princes returned at once to their military duties.

---

[1] " Und klar auf einmal fühlt's ich in mir werden,
    Die ist es, oder keine sonst auf Erden." — *Braut von Messina.*

The crown prince rejoined his regiment before Mayence, and, the Prussian headquarters being then at Bodenheim, the king invited the young brides to dine with him, and took them to visit the camp before Mayence. Darmstadt was within an easy ride of the camp, and the young soldiers could often have a vacation, which was sometimes made delightful by a quiet picnic in the woods at Gross Gerau. Goethe, then in his forty-fifth year, was with the troops, and he wrote in his diary of May 29, 1793, " Towards evening a lovely spectacle was offered to me. The princesses of Mechlenburg had dined with His Majesty the King at headquarters in Bodenheim, and afterwards visited the camp. I fastened myself into my tent, and so could narrowly observe the noble company, who walked up and down at ease directly before it. And truly, amid this tumult of war, one could take those two young ladies for heavenly apparitions, whose impression upon me has never been effaced."

On the eighth of November, 1793, the King of Prussia returned to Berlin, and a month later called his sons'from the field, that they might prepare for their weddings. During the absence of the crown prince, his palace had been prepared for the reception of the bride. The Prince of Mecklenburg left Darmstadt with his daughters and their grandmother December 15. They were just a week on the journey to Potsdam, where great preparations had been made to receive them.

Among the various decorations of welcome that greeted the bride, as she passed "*unter den Linden*" to her home, the most touching was that of the descendants of the French Protestant *Emigrés*, who greeted her in their own language. One of the little girls came forward, and spoke and looked so prettily, that the princess, on the impulse of the moment, stooped and kissed her as she took the flowers from her hand.

"*Mein Gott!*" exclaimed the master of ceremonies, "what have you done?"

"What!" exclaimed the astonished princess, "is that wrong? May I never do that again?"

This natural feeling won all hearts. "She will not only be our queen," said the people, "but our mother."

A characteristic story is told of the old king. He was dissatisfied that the invitations to the festivities had been mostly given to the nobility, and he said that he wanted to see some burghers' wedding-suits. So the next day he ordered that no cards should be given out, but that everybody who had a whole coat should be admitted. Consequently, there was such a pressure that the somewhat corpulent king could not get through the crowd without turning sideways, which he did, calling out at the same time, "Never mind, my friends. To-day the wedding father is no bigger than the bridal couple." On this journey, the grace with which Louise received all attentions, and the charm of her manners, laid the foundation of that love and respect which she never lost.

The wedding took place on Christmas evening, 1793. About six o'clock the family assembled in the apartments of the queen, where the diamond crown of the Hohenzollerns was placed on the head of Louise. Never did it rest upon one more worthy!

The princely couple were wedded in the grand saloon, according to the ceremonies of the Lutheran Church. The people wished to illuminate the city, but the prince begged them instead to give the money to the widows and orphans of the soldiers. It is delightful to record the simple home-life of this happy pair, in striking contrast to the European courts of that period, and even to that of the reigning king, whose licentiousness was notorious. He was much pleased with his new daughter, and was uniformly kind to her. On her birthday he presented to her the palace of Oranienburg, which became one of her favorite residences, and then asked her if she had any wish ungratified. She replied that she was so happy herself that she would like to make others so, and wished for a handful of gold to give to the poor. "And how large a handful would the birthday child like to have?" asked the king. "As large as the heart of the kindest of kings," answered Louise.

Both the prince and princess disliked the formal etiquette of the court to which they were obliged to submit, and the prince used to say that when his wife laid aside her jewels she was a pearl restored to her pristine purity. One day, taking hold of both her hands, and looking into her blue eyes, he said, "Thank God you are my wife once more!" — "Am I not always your wife?" she replied. "Alas! no; you must often be only the crown princess." They read and studied a great deal together; and she delighted in the works of the great living authors, Schiller, Goethe, and Schlegel.

Contrary to royal etiquette, they used the tender " Du " in addressing each other, which the prince justified by saying, "You know what you mean by 'Du,' but when you say 'Sie' you have to think whether it is a big S or a little one." The good Voss, the well-beloved "Oberhof-meisterinn," was shocked at this familiarity, but the prince playfully thwarted the rules of the "Dame d'Étiquette," as he nicknamed her.

The crown princess lost her first child in consequence of a fright, but on October 15, 1795, she gave birth to a son, who was, with much ceremony and many sponsors, christened Friedrich Wilhelm. He became Friedrich Wilhelm IV. of Prussia, and reigned until 1861.

Finding the palace of Oranienburg too stately and grand, the prince bought a very simple residence at Paretz, where Louise loved to live in quiet enjoyment with her family. She maintained the most affectionate intercourse with her sister. Schadow made a marble group of the two beautiful women, which is now in the Hohenzollern Museum. Louise happened to have a swelling in her throat, and Schadow wound a scarf so gracefully around her head and throat to conceal it, that the ladies of Berlin adopted the fashion. Louise sympathized deeply with her sister on the death of her husband, Prince Louis, who was a great loss both to her and his brother. She took her widowed sister to her own home, and gave her every protection and comfort.

The second son was born March 22. He became the King of Prussia and the Emperor of Germany, who was so well known to us by his long and prosperous reign.

Soon after the queen-mother died, and the king fell into a miserable illness, which was a severe trial to his daughter, on account of the wretched state of his mind. He had been very kind to her, and yet she could not be blind to his faults. He died November 16, 1797. His reign was neither honorable to himself nor fortunate for Prussia, although he had many popular qualities, which won affection from his subjects.

Louise's husband, who was proclaimed as King William III., succeeded to no throne of ease. The nation was demoralized by bad government, by war and defeat, and by licentiousness in the court. Frederic the Great had left a large sum in the treasury, all of which Friedrich Wilhelm II. had spent, and added a large debt, which rested heavily on the young king. The young couple at once recognized the duty of restoring the treasury of the kingdom, and resolved still to live on the revenues of the crown prince.

It would lead me too far if I were to enter into the political difficulties that beset the king. According to the testimony of Von Stein, he was to be honored for his sincere moral and religious principles. He was devoted to his country, and he felt the responsibility of his position. His uprightness, warm affection, and benevolence, are shown in his relations with Rauch, as well as in his devotion to his wife; but he did not possess the powers of mind and the firmness of will to guide Prussia steadily amid the perils of the time. Germany always blames him that he did not at once join her other princes in withstanding the encroachments of Napoleon, instead of trying to maintain a neutral ground. He did not love war, although his record as a soldier was honorable; and he desired to keep peace, in the hope of bringing back industrial prosperity.

Louise willingly entered into all his plans of economy and reform, but her sympathies were with the patriotic party; and she rejoiced when at last her husband joined the league against Napoleon. The time was not well chosen, and, the king being ill represented by his ambassador, his conduct appeared vacillating and unworthy.

The resolution of the king to live on the revenues of the crown prince until his predecessor's debts were paid, caused the royal couple to continue to live the simple life which both enjoyed. They entered into all the pleasures of the Christmas-tree, and often walked unattended "*unter den Linden.*" Old men remembered the charm of voice and manner with which the queen had spoken to them as boys, when they ran carelessly against her in their boyish sports. The Berlin ladies wore miniatures of the king and queen as ornaments; and every publisher wished to reproduce their likenesses.

Louise's first joy in becoming queen was that now she could dispense her benefits more freely; but her charity brought her into pecuniary difficulties. Her allowance of a thousand ducats a month had not been increased when she became queen. She found it impossible to meet the many demands upon her, and she consulted the privy councillor, asking him to represent the matter to the king. When it was suggested that she would impoverish herself by her charities, she replied that with her best friend, the father of the land, she must be its mother also. "I must help wherever there is need." A few days after she found a drawer of her desk refilled with money, and she asked the king what angel had put it there? "The angel is Legion," answered the king, smiling, "and I know only one; but you know the beautiful saying, "He gives to his friends while they sleep."

When the king and queen made a tour through Prussia the next summer, Louise won all hearts by her constant consideration for others' feelings. To her surprise, the inhabitants of the lately conquered Warsaw hastened to testify their allegiance and express their affection. The amber workers of Dantzic presented the queen with a beautiful necklace, and she wore it all the time of her stay.

When her carriage was overturned by the carelessness of a coachman, she softened the rebukes of her friends, saying, "The accident has frightened the people more than ourselves."

The queen's love of simplicity was shown in her dress. She never appeared in splendid costume, except when the dignity of the state required it. A lady of the period writes, "I never saw her dressed otherwise than in light muslin, with her beautiful light curled hair simply adorned." When entering a town one day, nineteen children met her, strewing flowers. One of them carelessly said, "The twentieth was left behind, she was so ugly." The queen immediately begged that she be sent for, and allowed to join her companions. The miners at Waldenburg spoke of her twenty years afterwards with enthusiasm, and one steersman showed the two ducats she had given him, which his wife had set for a necklace.

At Weimar she met Herder, whose poetry she admired. Her daughter, Frederika Louise Charlotte, was born July 13, 1798. This princess married the late Emperor Nicholas of Russia, and died in 1861.

The royal pair enjoyed with their children the country

life at Paretz, where they laid aside their grandeur and dined at harvest time with the farmers' sons and daughters. The queen gratified them by wearing her court dress, which they considered a mark of respect. She always sought out the neglected ones for her favors. Being asked if she did not find it dull at Paretz, she made the characteristic answer, "I find it very pleasant to be the Lady Bountiful at Paretz." Brought up in aristocratic circles, she did not question her position, but had learned from the new tendencies of the time, respect and sympathy for all classes. The king was silent and grave, the queen light-hearted and full of vivacity. She was more French than German, loyal as she was to her country and people. Her intellect was clear and well-trained, and she was far-sighted, and full of deep thought as well as generous feeling.

She often gave way to an affectionate impulse, and would take an ornament from her own person and bestow it on one with whom she had had a pleasant conversation. Goethe's mother long kept a necklace which Louise had given her in remembrance of such an hour. It was said of her that she was as pleasing to her own sex as to the other. She was fond of dancing and social enjoyment, but, happy in her married life, does not seem to have had a trace of coquetry in her nature. She received many of the celebrated poets, and gave them discriminating praise, and often a precious gift of remembrance. She was so thoughtful of others, even in trifles, that she bade the old councillor of war come to her in boots, and not appear in stockings, which she feels sure is not good for him.

She carefully abstained from interfering with politics. The king was sensitive as to his prerogative, and if she was asked to prefer a request to him, she would answer, "There is no need to take indirect means with him to gain what is just and right." The centenary of the kingdom of

Prussia was celebrated in 1801, and at this time Louise made the acquaintance of the Princess of Mechlenburg Schwerin, by birth a Russian, which ripened into a warm friendship, and did much to promote good feeling between the royal families of Russia and Prussia.

The queen took a deep interest in the education of her children, striving to put it on a more thorough basis than the fashionable habits of the time. Her religious feeling was simple and beautiful, and in her attendance at church she set aside as much as possible all distinctions of rank. She was very much grieved when the "Oberhofmeisterinn" once severely rebuked a respectable woman who by mistake entered the royal pew. She always attended the old Lutheran Dom-kirche, which is remarkable for its plainness. Her son, the old emperor, would not allow it to be altered or removed, but the present emperor is about to erect a new and handsome edifice in its place.

But while the domestic life of the royal pair was thus happy, and their relation to their subjects trustful and affectionate, the affairs of the kingdom were fast getting into a state of confusion and danger. Friedrich Wilhelm III. was one of those men unfortunately set in a place too large for him. He tried to maintain neutrality when all Europe was in collision, and safety lay only in a strong position strongly held. The queen is said to have sympathized heartily with the patriotic party, who urged him to draw the sword ; and undoubtedly Napoleon was correct in ascribing to her a great influence in the country. Finally, when the open violation of neutrality in the campaign of 1805 forced the king into more active measures, to the delight of the queen, he joined hands with Alexander of Russia in a league against Napoleon. This league was pledged in a somewhat melodramatic manner. When the king and the czar visited the tomb of Frederic the Great at midnight, the czar kissed the coffin of the great Frederic, and struck hands with his successor across it. Napoleon laughed at this alliance a year later, but it bore fruit in the end.

It is said that on her oldest son's birthday, in 1805, when he first received his hat and sword from his father's hand, and put on his uniform, the queen said, " I hope, my son, that on the day when you first put on this coat, your first thought will be to avenge your unfortunate brothers."

The king had the great misfortune to have bad councillors when he most needed brave ones, and " he trusted the cowardly Haugwitz with the important mission of conveying his decision of peace or war to Napoleon." This weak diplomatist put off the execution of his task until after the battle of Austerlitz, and then entered into negotiations with the conqueror, instead of making a declaration of war. No wonder that the proud emperor was not conciliated, but made new and humiliating demands upon Prussia! When the king at last decided upon war, it was under the most unfavorable circumstances. Napoleon longed to crush Prussia at a blow; and the day of misfortunes, the double battle of Jena and Austerlitz, enabled him to enter Berlin as conqueror October 14, 1806.

At this time the queen's health was much broken by grief for the death of her youngest son, Prince Ferdinand, as well as by her terrible anxiety for the country. She was advised to go to the baths of Pyrmont, where she enjoyed the society of her father and brother, and the Princess Marie of Russia. Schadow made a statue of the little year-old prince, which is now at Charlottenburg. Although it is denied that the queen had any part in directly bringing on the war, she took a deep interest in it, and was officially recognized as belonging to the army. The " Anspach Baireuthschen Dragooner Regiment " received through a cabinet order the name of the " Dragoon Regiment of the Queen." She rode beside the king, wearing a spencer of the regimental colors, which is still preserved as a relic by the troops.

Napoleon is said to have allowed most bitter and scandalous things to be said of her in the public prints, which only endeared her all the more to the people. The distinguished Viennese Ambassador, Gentz, expressed himself as much astonished at the intelligence and strength of judgment which she showed in regard to the political situation, as well as at her courage in looking clearly at the dangers around them, and the deep feeling she showed for the Austrian family and all the victims of the war. She was actually travelling in full march towards the enemy, who could be distinctly seen, when the Duke of Brunswick insisted on her return to Weimar, and gave her a squadron to escort her. An attempt is said to have been made to capture her, at whose failure Napoleon expressed great regret. As the army cheered her on her departure, already the terrible cannon of Jena were sounding. She left Weimar on the thirteenth of October, and had a hard journey over mountain-passes, while her heart was racked with anxiety. They had no means of getting correct intelligence. "I journey on between the mountains of hope and the abysses of despair," she said.

When she drove into Brunswick on the fifteenth, her nerves were so shattered that she could not give a clear description of what had occurred. On the fourth day, when she reached Brandenburg, she met a courier sent by General von Kleist, who gave her the full disastrous intelligence, "All is lost! The French are rapidly advancing! You must flee with your children; the whole kingdom is in danger." She reached Berlin that evening, and found that her children had already been sent to Schweldt on the Oder.

Her physician, Hufeland, accompanied her to Schweldt, where she found her children safe and well; but she was terribly moved on meeting them. She soon after joined the king at Custrin.   He and his brothers were all wounded.   The queen suffered many serious privations on this journey, but they were nothing in comparison with the anxiety she endured.   In one of her own note-books she wrote Goethe's words, —

> " Wer nie sein Brot mit Thränen ass,
>   Wer nie die kummervollen Nachte
> Auf seinem Bette weinend sass
>   Der kennt euch nicht, ihr himmlische Machte ! "

She remained true to herself through all these troubles, and the sympathy of the people was ever dear to her. When she accompanied her husband on a tour of inspec-tion of the walls of Custrin, and the commandant watched her as with bowed head she walked on in deep and anx-ious conversation, he pledged his faith that he would defend the walls to the last extremity.

The situation was indeed appalling.   Magdeburg had surrendered to the enemy, and every Prussian fortress between the Weser and the Oder was in his power.   The excitement caused by reports of slanders against her, said to have been purposely circulated by Napoleon, com-bined with the fatigue of her journey, and her distress of mind, brought on a nervous fever, from which she was in imminent danger for two weeks.   Scarcely recovered, she continued her flight from the conquering army, even to Memel, on the eastern boundary of the kingdom.   The low, flat isthmus on which Memel lies is most unattract-ive, according to her Hofmeisterin's description : " We spent three days and nights on the journey, our road partly covered by the stormy waves of the ocean, partly by the ice.   The nights were passed in the most wretched quarters.   The first night, without nourishing food, the queen lay in a room whose windows were broken, and where the snow blew upon her bed."

In the New Museum at Berlin is a beautiful picture representing the arrival of the queen at Memel.   The young queen and her devoted attendant have left their poor carriage and are seeking refuge from the snow in the miserable house which could alone give them shelter. The beauty of the queen is somewhat concealed by the very unpicturesque bonnet which she wears, but the old Hofmeisterin is a very interesting figure. The features resemble closely the actual portraits of her, while the expression and action express courage and endurance and devoted attachment to her mistress in her fallen fortunes.

The king soon joined the family at Memel, and the military situation became somewhat improved by the union of the Prussian and Russian armies, while the French experienced some severe reverses. Louise was cheered by accounts of the heroic deeds of Prussian officers; but the hopes thus raised were not soon realized.

The greatest trial of the queen's fortitude came from the calumnies of her enemies. She severely scrutinized her conduct, to see if she had given any occasion for them, and even wondered if she had been wrongly contending against fate in opposing the French. The visit of the Emperor of Russia, and his promises of firm alliance, gave her much comfort. It is said that Prussia might have made favorable terms with Napoleon at this time, if the king would have given up the Russian alliance.

From April 12 until the first of June, 1807, the queen remained at Königsberg with her sister Frederika, the Princess of Solms. She lived a very quiet, earnest life here, with no entertainments, devoting herself to the comfort of those about her, and to earnest study and thought. During this residence she became intimately acquainted with the court preacher, Bishop Borowsky, and with Scheffner, and other disciples of Kant, and her mind was full of great questions. The old Scheffner writes, " I have seen in no woman's face a freer, purer look, a more joyful, almost childish frankness." Among the circle around her tea-table was often the celebrated General Blücher, of whom Rauch made one of his greatest portrait statues, the "Marshal Forwards," as he was popularly called. All the company engaged in pulling lint for the hospitals; but the general tucked his bit of lint into the sheath of his sword, while he told stories of his battles, until the queen detected him, and laughingly reproved him, and at his request allowed him to take his stint home to be finished.

She returned to Memel early in June, where she was received by the people as a mother.[1] She soon afterwards learned of the battle of Friedland, and the establishment of the head-quarters of Napoleon at Tilsit. But the keenest blow of all was the intelligence that the Emperor Alexander had formed a separate truce with Napoleon, leaving Prussia and her king at his mercy. Yet in a noble letter to her father, written June 17, she shows the courage of her heart, and the religious foundation on which it is based. She is firm in her conviction that they have acted with honor. "Only wrong on our part would bring me to the grave. That will never take place, for we stand too high."

The truce between Russia and France came to an end June 21, 1807, that with Prussia four days later. Alexander met Napoleon at Tilsit, and the two emperors entered into alliance. The city was declared neutral, and each of the three monarchs had his own guards.

And now we come to the most trying event in Louise's life, and the one by which she is most generally known, — her interviews with Napoleon, and her effort to procure from him more favorable terms for Prussia, in the peace for which the Emperor Alexander was negotiating. Ap-

---

[1] A German friend has given me an interesting account of a family who received the queen into their home in Memel, when she was in the greatest distress. One of the sons of this family has lately come to Boston to pursue his art of designing in terra-cotta. He is now engaged on sculpture for the exposition at Chicago.

parently much romance has gathered about these interviews, and it is necessary to read the accounts with the remembrance of the characters of the actors, and the prejudices of the narrators, to understand fully the spirit of all parties.

It is said that Napoleon had treated the king, whose amiable but vacillating character did not command his respect, with studied indifference. When Louise's husband sent for her to come to Tilsit, to try with her womanly tact to obtain better terms from Bonaparte, she was almost beside herself with grief. In her diary she says, "God knows what a struggle it cost me; for although I do not hate the man, yet I look upon him as one who has made the king and his land wretched. I admire his talents, but I do not like his character, which is obviously treacherous and false. It will be hard for me to be polite and courteous to him; but just this hard thing is required of me. I am accustomed to make sacrifices."

She took careful instructions in regard to the impending questions from the minister Hardenberg, whose dismissal Napoleon had just obtained.

Under the escort of French dragoons, on the afternoon of the eighth of July, 1807, Louise reached the dwelling of the king at Tilsit. A quarter of an hour later Napoleon drove up to the house, where he was received by the Oberhofmeisterin von Voss and the Countess Tauentzein. He was very polite, talked a long time with the queen, and then drove away. At the dinner at eight o'clock, which early hour he had appointed out of consideration for the queen, he was in good humor, and talked much with her. She returned in good spirits, sanguinely believing that she had attained her purpose, and would obtain favorable conditions of peace.

One of the answers she is reported to have given was to his question, "But how could you ever begin war with me?" — "Sire, even if we had been imposed on in other respects, could the glory of Frederic the Great deceive us in regard to our powers ? "

Another account says that " she made a most favorable impression upon Napoleon, and pleaded eloquently for Prussia and her husband, and finally, even with tears, for the restoration of Magdeburg. The emperor was moved, but unfortunately the king entered, and the charm was broken."

Napoleon himself said, " She constantly led the conversation ; returned at pleasure to her subject, and directed it as she chose, but with so much skill and delicacy that it was impossible to take offence." He is also reported to have said, " She was the most admirable queen and most interesting woman he had ever met."

Talleyrand is said to have reproached Napoleon, " Sire, shall posterity say that you have given up the fruits of your victories on account of a beautiful queen ? "

Talleyrand gives his own version of this interview : —

" This failure," he says, " might be justly apprehended after the coarse question Napoleon asked the Queen of Prussia one day : 'How did you ever dare go to war, madame, with such feeble means as those you had ?' — 'Sire, I must confess it to your Majesty, the glory of Frederic II. had deluded us as to our own power,' was the queen's reply.

" The word 'glory' so happily placed, and in Napoleon's drawing-room at Tilsit, too, struck me as superb. Afterward I so frequently referred to this noble reply, that the emperor said to me one day, 'I am at a loss to see what there is in that saying of the Queen of Prussia that you consider so fine. You may as well talk of something else.'

" I felt indignant at all I saw, all I heard ; but I was obliged to conceal my indignation. Hence I shall ever feel grateful to the Queen of Prussia, who was a queen of other days, for taking kindly notice of my sentiments. If, among the scenes of my past life that I conjure up, there are several which are necessarily painful, I at least recall with great gratification the words she vouchsafed to address to me, spoken almost in confidence, on the last occasion that I had the honor of accompanying her to her carriage: 'Prince of Benevento,' said she, 'there are but two persons who regret that I should have come here; and those two are you and I. You are not displeased, are you, that I carry that opinion away with me?'

"The tears of emotion and pride which filled my eyes were my reply."[1]

Walter Scott, in his "Life of Napoleon," represents the queen, of whom he speaks in the highest terms, as seeking the interview with Napoleon of her own accord, and as herself introducing the reference to Frederic the Great without question of the emperor.

It is evident that Napoleon felt the charm of her presence, and admired her character, treating her personally with great respect; but he was not one to be turned from a settled purpose by a passing fascination. He declared that all was already arranged with the Emperor Alexander. At a subsequent dinner he appears to have been less gracious; and, although he presented her with a rose, he was deaf to her suggestion, "With Magdeburg," as she accepted it. She appears to have expressed very frankly to the emperor her feeling that she had been deceived.

A bitter thing it must have been to this high-spirited and noble-minded woman to sue, and sue in vain, to her husband's enemy; and the temperance with which she speaks of him brings out her nobleness. Rebuking her ladies, she said, " We cannot lighten our sorrows by hating the emperor, and malicious thoughts can only make us more unhappy."

The terms of peace were concluded between the two emperors and the king on the ninth and tenth of July. The

[1] From " Memoirs of Talleyrand " in *Century* of February, 1891.

Elbe was established as the boundary of Prussia. While the queen felt the full bitterness of this impoverishment of the kingdom, she yet expressed her satisfaction that the king had acted with honor, and had yielded only to inevitable necessity; and she felt that the result would be beneficial to Prussia. She said " Magdeburg would be found written on her heart, like Calais on Queen Mary's."

The pecuniary burdens laid upon the towns were so onerous that it is said some of them have not been discharged to this day. Louise gave up her jewels and most cherished treasures, and the king parted with the heirlooms of his family, to make payment for his subjects. She also persuaded the women of the nation to give up their ornaments; and every woman who gave up all received as a token an iron ring, which was worn as the proudest ornament. The iron cross was also used as a decoration of honor, for want of more costly material.

The queen never appeared more gracious and lovely than in this time of humiliation. Her daughter was now old enough to assist her in the simple hospitalities of the home at Memel, and her domestic happiness was almost great enough to make up for her public trials.

By her constant sympathy with the king, she now appears to have taken a more decided part in public affairs; and in influencing him to intrust the "restoration of the fallen state," as her biographer states, "first of all to Baron von Stein, the man whom posterity, as well as his own age, honors as the restorer of Germany," she certainly did her country noble service. He had foreseen the evils which came to the state, and endeavored to warn the king; but evil counsellors had procured his disgrace, and his services were lost to the country. Alike great by his ability and his character, he did not refuse the recall of the king in his distress; and though hardly recovered from a severe fever, he hastened to Memel to do his utmost for the fallen state. Louise looked for his help with the greatest eagerness. When, in September, it was reported that France threatened still severer measures, she broke forth in despair, "O my God, why hast thou forsaken me?" and immediately added, "Why does Stein tarry? He is my last hope." In a later letter she says, "Stein is coming, and with him I begin to see light." Stein justified her confidence. His statesmanship was broad and liberal, and he began such far-reaching reforms as the emancipation of the peasants, municipal regulations, etc., which gave confidence to the people of Prussia, and led to that united effort in which alone their strength lay. Louise was an efficient co-worker with the reformers. Her German biographer says, "It was she who smoothed the ways at court, and helped to overcome the difficulties, obstacles, and prejudices with which they had to contend." "I implore you," she wrote to Von Stein, "have patience during the first months; the king will certainly keep his word. I implore you, for the sake of myself, my children, my country, have patience."

A remarkable trait in Louise's character is the illumination which her mind gained from her affections. Her trustful love for her husband brought out the best in him, and enabled her to sustain him with her own higher courage. She confirmed him in his liberal sentiments, while she tempered the fiery zeal of Von Stein, whom Scharnhorst compared to Blücher, as being "wholly without the fear of man," and who frequently offended personal feelings and disregarded the usages of the court. Through the terrible days that followed, when the French stripped the capital of everything, even of its cherished works of art, Louise relied upon the great councillor, and would not despair. When again, with the support of Russia, it was thought advisable to try to influence Napoleon, the queen set aside all thought of self, and wrote him a letter; but it had no effect. At last Napoleon ordered the evacuation of East Prussia, and she was able to escape from Memel,

whose humid climate was wrecking her health, and go
to Königsberg in 1808. The royal pair did not leave
Memel without expressing their gratitude for the affection shown them there, and they were received with festive joy at Königsberg. The queen's youngest daughter,
Frederika, was born February 1, and the "Estates of
Prussia" became her god-parents, a touching expression
of the affectionate tie between the down-fallen king and
his afflicted people.

For a time, apparently exhausted by the long struggle,
Louise lived mainly, and very quietly, at Königsberg. She
was very much interested in the historical lectures of
Professor Süvern, of which she asked the manuscript for
private reading. She asks her old friend Scheffner for
explanations with the simplicity of a girl. "Will you tell
me just what hierarchy means? I have no clear idea of
it. If I understand right," she says, "the German age
(*Zeitalter*) was broken up because men followed their feelings and fancy more than they obeyed reason, which, as
one says, judges more correctly." She also asks him to
put the dates at the beginning of the periods of which the
lectures treat.

She wrote, "I have good books, a good conscience, a
good pianoforte ; and thus one can live more quietly amid
the storms of the world than those who stir them up."

But the rapid march of events soon broke up this
peace, and brought conflict not only into the country, but
into the band of patriots with whom the queen sympathized. The overthrow of the Bourbons in Spain made
every court in Europe tremble. Such statesmen as Stein,
Scharnhorst, and Gneisenau favored a bold policy of close
alliance with Austria, and a determined resistance to the
French emperor ; but the king, under the influence of
Russia, and without consulting Stein, ratified the disastrous treaty of Paris, and bound Prussia to take the position of an auxiliary power in the wars of France. Stein

asked and received his dismissal. Napoleon hurled at him a sentence of outlawry, which drove him first to Austria, and then to Russia, where he was able later to do his part in the deliverance of Germany and Europe.

It was a relief to the queen when the French evacuated Berlin, although they still retained the strongholds that commanded it, and many suspected a plot to get the royal family completely in Napoleon's power. He wrote courteous but formal letters to the queen, giving her permission to live where she pleased, and congratulating her on her return to Berlin. She has been blamed for not taking the part of Stein more thoroughly in these difficulties, and for accepting the invitation of Alexander to visit Petersburg against his advice. But we must remember that she was not an independent sovereign, able to act in her own right, nor had she the freedom of a private citizen; she was bound to support the king's policy when she could not change it, and she saw in Russia the last support of his crown.

The king and queen were welcomed to Russia with every attention. Thirty-two thousand soldiers lined the way to the winter palace. The king rode with the emperor; the queen followed in a state carriage drawn by eight horses. She wore a sable fur robe over white satin. Her old Oberhofmeisterin Voss and the Countess von Moltke accompanied her. The visit to Petersburg was full of gayety, and she received the most flattering attentions from the imperial family, but they could not dispel her melancholy. "I have returned as I went," she wrote. "Nothing will blind me any more, and I say again, 'My kingdom is not of this world.'"

One thing that did please her was a visit to a school for young girls, founded by the empress, which she hoped one day to copy in Berlin. She did not live to carry out her plans; but on the anniversary of her death the "Luisenstiftung" was dedicated, and her oldest daughter appointed patroness of the school, in memory of her mother.

She was much interested in Pestalozzi, and said "if she were her own mistress she would get into a carriage and roll away to him in Switzerland, in order to thank him with a pressure of the hand and tears in her eyes." She also took a great interest in the popular movements in the Tyrol, and speaks with warm admiration of Andreas Hofer. She delighted, too, in Schiller's "William Tell," and was full of zeal in the cause of freedom.

Her religious feelings were very strong, and she looked with hope to a reawakening of religious life among the people. On the twenty-ninth of September she gave birth to a son, who was baptized by the name of the Markgraf Albrecht.

Eagerly as the queen had longed for a return to Berlin, now that it was near, and she was coming with shattered health and sorrowful memories of the terrible changes that had taken place, her soul seemed sick even unto death, and sad presentiments oppressed her. The royal couple started on the fifteenth of September, and on the twenty-third were met at Waisensee, the next village to Berlin, by a deputation from the city. Young maidens strewed flowers before the richly decorated house prepared for their early meal. The Berlin people sent her a handsome new carriage lined with her favorite color, lilac. She expressed her pleasure that the first use she should make of it was to re-enter the capital. Her sons with their regiments formed her guard. On the twenty-fifth the king and queen appeared at the opera, and were greeted by a thousand voices singing Werner's "People's Hymn," which closes, —

> "Troste die Königin,
>   Rein ist und schön ihr Sinn,
>   Lass ihr aus Thränensaat
>   Frieden erblühn."

The following spring the queen suffered much from a wasting fever, and from the dangerous sickness of her daughter, as well as from anxiety about the threatening condition of public affairs.

For years Louise had desired to pay a visit to her father in Strelitz. She now decided to go thither on the twenty-fifth of June, to stay about eight days, the king having promised to follow her on the twenty-eighth. Her companion tells us, "The queen was very cheerful on the journey; but when we approached the frontier of Prussia Mechlenburg, a mysterious melancholy came over her, but she quickly composed herself, and it passed off." She was warmly welcomed by all her family, even by her venerable grandmother; and when her husband reached her, June 28, she wrote, and they were her last written words, "I am very happy to-day, dear father, as your daughter, and the wife of the best of men."

The queen was taken sick the same evening, but the physicians did not apprehend immediate danger, and, summoned by urgent business of the state, the king left her, July 3; and, being himself taken ill at Charlottenburg, he saw the queen again only in the last struggle with death. She felt this absence deeply, and held a letter from the king close pressed to her heart. She suffered keenly, especially from difficulty of breathing, often calling for air. She was still patient and affectionate, and tenderly recognized her husband and children when they came to her. I will not dwell longer on the sad scene. About nine o'clock she raised her eyes to heaven, and said, "I am dying. O Jesus, make it easy!" and passed to sleep.

At the dark pine forest on the frontier, a Prussian escort received the remains of the beloved queen. As the melancholy procession passed through Berlin, the lamentation was universal. The funeral services took place on the thirtieth, in the cathedral.

In the plantation behind the castle at Charlottenburg

was a summer-house in the form of a Greek temple.   The
queen loved the spot, and the king now deemed it sacred to
her.   Her remains were placed here December 23, just one
year after her return to Berlin, and seventeen years since
she came thither as a bride.   Only thirty-four years of
age, this lovely woman might seem to have hardly passed
her youth, but most truly could she say with Thekla, —

> " Ich habe genossen das irdische Glück,
>   Ich habe gelebt und geliebet."

The following remarkable letter to her father gives us
a clear insight into her thoughts and her family relations.
It is also very interesting to note the breadth of her political views, and how fairly she weighed the character of her
great opponent.

"With us it is all over for the present, if not forever.   I look for nothing more during my life.   I have resigned myself; and in this resignation,
this submission to the will of God, I am now tranquil and at peace; if I do
not possess earthly happiness, I have what means more, — spiritual blessed-
ness.   It becomes more and more clear to me that everything had to come
as it has.   Divine Providence is unmistakably introducing a new order of
things into the world; there will be a different arrangement, since the old
order has outlived itself and is falling to pieces.

" *We have fallen asleep on the laurels of Frederic the Great*, who, as the
master of his century, created a new epoch.   We have not kept pace with
the age, therefore it has left us behind.   No one is better aware of this than
the king.   I have just had a conversation with him, in which he repeatedly
said, as if speaking to himself, ' This also must be changed among us.
Even the best and most maturely considered plans fail, and the French
Emperor is at least more cunning and astute than we are.   If the Russians
and Prussians had fought as bravely as lions, even if unconquered, we should
nevertheless have been obliged to quit the field; the enemy would have had
the advantage.   We may learn much from Napoleon, and what he has
achieved will not be lost upon us.   It would be blasphemy to say that
God is with him; but evidently he is an instrument in the hands of the
Almighty to bury the old era, which no longer has any life, and which is
almost overgrown with excrescences.

" Better times will certainly come.   Faith in the most perfect being is a
guaranty of this.   But only through goodness can the world become better.
Therefore, I do not believe that the Emperor Napoleon Bonaparte is safe
upon his throne.   Only truth and justice are strong and secure.   He is only
politic (that means worldly wise), and he does not conform to eternal laws,

but to circumstances, as they happen to be. With such a policy he stains his government with many deeds of injustice. His intentions are not good, even if his cause is good. In his boundless ambition he thinks only of himself and his personal interest. We must admire him, but we cannot love him. He is dazzled by his success, and he fancies himself able to accomplish everything. Moreover, he has no moderation, and he who cannot preserve moderation, loses his balance and falls. I have a strong faith in God, and also in his moral government of the world. This I do not see in the rule of might; therefore, I have the hope this present age will be succeeded by a better one. All good men hope for this and await it, and one must not be misled by the panegyrists of present heroes, whom they esteem great. What has taken place is unmistakably neither final nor abiding, but only the opening of a path to a better end. This end appears to be at a great distance; we probably shall not see it, and shall die before it is reached. As God wills; all as he wills: I find comfort, strength, courage, and serenity in this hope which lies deep in my soul. Life is but a passage, yet we must go through it. Let us care only for this, to become each day riper and better.

"Here, dear father, you have my political creed as well as a woman can construct one. It may have gaps, but I shall not suffer by that. But pardon me for annoying you with this; from it you can at least see that you have a pious and attached daughter, and that the principles of Christian piety, which I owe to your teachings and your godly example, have borne their fruits, and will bear them as long as I live."

The sentiments of hope and forbearance in this letter may not seem so remarkable to us, who have seen her hopes realized; but when we remember that it was written in a season of the greatest national humiliation, as well as personal loss and suffering, and that she is speaking of the great conqueror, through whom these tremendous evils came, we cannot but admire alike the sagacious foresight, the wise liberality, and the temperance with which she spoke to one to whom she could pour out her full heart.

As Louise is not less interesting to us as a wife and mother than as a queen, I will give the conclusion of this letter, in which she so naturally tells her father of her home and husband and children : —

"Gladly will you hear, dear father, that the calamities that have befallen us have not forced their way into our wedded and home life; they have rather strengthened it, and made it even more precious to us. The king, the best of beings, is kinder and more loving than ever. Often I think I see in him the lover and bridegroom, always showing more by his actions than his words; I see the watchfulness that he has for me in all points. Only yesterday he said to me in his plain and simple way, looking at me with his true eyes, 'Thou dear Louise! Thou hast become to me in misfortune still more precious and beloved. Now I know from experience what I have in thee. It may storm without, if only it remains fair weather in our wedded life. Because I love thee so, I have called our latest born little daughter Louise. May she become a Louise!' This goodness moved me to tears. It is my pride, my joy, and my happiness to possess the love and approval of this best of men; and because I heartily love him in return, and we are so united that the will of one is also the will of the other, it becomes easy for me to preserve this happy union of sentiments, which has become closer with years. In a word, he pleases me in all points, and I please him, and we are happiest when we are together. Pardon me, dear father, that I tell this with a certain boastfulness. There lies in it the artless expression of my happiness, which interests no one in the world more deeply than you, dear, fond father! How to treat others; that, too, I have learned from the king. I cannot talk on this subject; it is enough that we understand each other. Our children are our treasures, and our eyes rest upon them with satisfaction and hope. The crown prince is full of life and spirit. He has superior talents, which are happily developed and cultivated. He is true in all his sentiments and words, and his vivacity makes dissimulation impossible. He learns history with especial success, and the great and the good attract to them his imaginative mind. He has a keen appreciation of what is humorous, and his comical and startling ideas entertain us agreeably. He is especially attached to his mother, and he cannot be purer than he is. He is very dear to me, and I often talk with him of how it will be at some future time when he is king.''

This son became the brilliant Frederic William IV., who said, "The unity of Germany concerns me deeply ; it is an inheritance from my mother." But he did not live to see it accomplished, and it is the second son of Louise, therefore, the Emperor William, with whom we almost feel a personal acquaintance, who interests us most deeply. The mother goes on to say of him, —

"Our son William will be, if everything does not deceive me, like his father, — simple, upright, and wise. Also, in his outward appearance, he bears the greatest resemblance to him, only he is, I think, not so good looking. You see, dear father, I am still in love with my husband.''

The prince was then eleven years old. What a reward it would have been to his mother for all her sufferings, if she could have foreseen the long life of this son, the unity of Germany accomplished under his reign, and, above all, the love and confidence with which he was regarded by the people!

The queen goes on to speak of her other children, and of how well it is for them to have seen thus early the serious side of life. "It is especially salutary," she says, "for the crown prince that he became acquainted with misfortune while crown prince."

And later she writes, —

"Even if posterity does not mention my name among illustrious women, yet, when it learns the sorrows of the time, it will know what I have suffered through them, and will say, 'She endured much, and she remained patient in the midst of suffering.' Then I could wish that at the same time they might say, 'She gave birth to children who were worthy of better times; she endeavored to lead them onwards, and at last her care has borne rich fruit.'"

Her prayer was not "dispersed in empty air."

The character of Queen Louise of Prussia was clear, simple, strong, harmonious, and tender. She had an exquisite regard for the feelings of others, in every situation of life, which made the peer and the peasant alike revere her as a superior, and love and trust her as an equal. The severe influences of a Lutheran training, the intellectual depths of a German brain, and, above all, the rich experiences of her short life, passed in a period when great ideas were everywhere struggling into action, and her full range from the queen's throne to the dependence of a wandering fugitive, gave her a firmness of purpose, a vigor of action, and an insight into the meaning of events, which surprised those who had first been charmed by her winning feminine grace and courtesy.

She had the rare good fortune not to lose the blessings of private life in attaining her exalted station, and that happiness kept her brave and sweet in all trials. Her influence upon her husband's career was always helpful; and although her own sense of the proprieties of her position, drawn from the teachings of her youth, prevented her from influencing the king as strongly as she might have done, and urging him to a course which might have saved much humiliation and sorrow, she yet did much to preserve for him the respect and affection of his people, and to make united action possible when the hour struck. Napoleon, whose sagacity was not often deceived, felt her power, and knew that her voice against him was worth "a thousand armed men."

Many portraits of Queen Louise are preserved in the Hohenzollern museum at Berlin. They differ very much in position, dress, and even expression; but they all represent the same delicately rounded outline, full blue eyes, small nose, and finely rounded chin, and soft fair hair, and all confirm the accounts of the fine intelligence and grace of her expression. Domestic relics, among which are the cradle of her children, her Bible, and specimens of her childish work, show the simplicity of her life. Elsewhere will be found a history of the beautiful statue of Rauch, which has done so much to preserve her memory.

"After death comes the resurrection." Louise is better known and more beloved to-day than even in her lifetime. Then she was the Queen of Prussia, now she is the mother of a line of German emperors who have established the unity of Germany, and made the country for whose humiliation she wept a power and an honor among nations. All Germany claims her now as its mother, and is true to its claim in giving her honor and loving reverence.

How gladly would she have accepted such testimony as this from the biographer of her great-grandson, the present emperor: "It was Louise who ingrafted a humane spirit upon the rough drill-sergeant body of

Hohenzollern education. She made her sons love her; and it seems but yesterday since the last of these sons, a tottering old man of ninety, used to go to the Charlottenburg mausoleum on the anniversary of her death, and pray and weep in solitude beside the recumbent marble effigy of his mother, who died in 1810. The introduction of filial affection between parents and children dates from this Queen Louise, and belongs to this century. Before this, it was the rule of the heirs of Prussia to detest their immediate progenitors."[1]

In 1880 the statue of Queen Louise by Encke was erected in the little island of the Thiergarten, sacred to her memory. I was told by a well-known connoisseur that this statue is the most faithful likeness of Queen Louise, the one by Rauch being much idealized, and that when it was dedicated he stood near the old emperor, who was heard to say with emphasis, " This is my mother !" He could truly say, " I respect the Unity of Germany ; it is a legacy from my mother."

[1] " The young Emperor William II. of Germany; a study in character development on a throne," by Harold Frederic. London, 1891.

CHAPTER IV

STATUES OF QUEEN LOUISE

1810-1827

IT intensified the suffering of Rauch in his want of sympathy with the friends of Napoleon in Rome, that he looked upon the emperor as the personal foe of his beloved queen ; and this, with every other feeling, united to inspire him with interest in the work of making a fitting monument of her. The bereaved husband had been his early and steady friend, and if the artist could now repay his kindness it would be by means of his own well-beloved art.

It was in Rome, July, 1810, that the intelligence of the death of the queen reached him. He had already modelled a bust of her as an expression of gratitude, and he finished it, and in September sent it to the king. It was placed in her empty room in Charlottenburg.

The king was fired with the idea of building a fitting mausoleum for the queen, and was so pleased with the bust that he wished to give the commission to Rauch.

He wrote to Von Humboldt to obtain sketches from Canova and Thorwaldsen and Rauch for a full-length figure of the queen, to be placed on a sarcophagus.

Rauch was overwhelmed at the idea of the king's proposing to him a competition with these two artists, so much his seniors in age and reputation ; but he felt bound to obey, and he prepared his sketch, which he sent to the king in November. "I cannot understand," he says, "why the king should pass by Schadow, and send to

Rome." Thorwaldsen became so much interested in Rauch's work that he wished him to make a bust of himself, and he resigned all claim to make the statue of the queen, saying that it belonged to Rauch to do it. Canova took the same position. Humboldt's letter to Rauch is full of interest, and enters into minute details in regard to the position of the sarcophagus in the Greek temple. He says, "Finally the king has come to the much happier conclusion to have the figure of the queen herself, of life-size, in a quiet position, draped, but with cloth of so soft a texture that the form of the body will appear through it."

Rauch was deeply affected by the trust reposed in him, and the generosity of the two great sculptors, who resigned their interests and recognized the propriety of his doing the work from his love and veneration for the queen.

Never did sculptor have a more stimulating task. He was not only inspired by his own tenderness, respect, and gratitude for the beautiful woman, but he found in her the ideal of his country, the German-hearted queen, who, in the midst of all the distress and excitement of the time, never despaired, but held up the fainting hearts of prince and peasant in the hour of humiliation.

And yet Rauch had some misgivings in turning to this work; for he was at that time so wholly wrapped up in classic art that a portrait statue, prescribed to order as to its treatment, seemed like a fetter to his genius. Yet he was to learn from it the truest lesson that Greek art has for us, how to make limitations a new source of success. Had he yielded to this, — I had almost said boyish feeling, — and remained in Rome, working under the influence of Canova and Thorwaldsen, and studying Greek art instead of universal nature, what a loss to himself, to German art, to the world! For in this statue he found the secret of the union of the Real and the Ideal, the Individual, the Characteristic, and the Universal. So beautifully, so nobly, does it portray the ideal womanhood, that every heart melts at its tender beauty, though the life of the heroic queen be wholly unknown to them; and not less the husband, whose very heart was bound up in her, so cherished it as bringing her back to him, even "in the very habit as she lived," that when Rauch made a second statue, improving upon some artistic points, the king was loath to look upon it, feeling it must be another, and not herself.

The king wished to have this work done under his own eyes at Berlin, but he forbore to press the point. Von Humboldt did not hesitate to urge it, however, and offered to Rauch every inducement and assistance in making the journey to Berlin. It was a hard struggle to leave Rome, and his work and his friends there; but he did not hesitate to do so, and on the second of February he travelled, as he says, "through a purgatory of ice" to Vienna, where he spent a week of paradise with the Humboldts, and went from there as a courier by Dresden to Berlin, where he arrived on the fifth of March, 1811.

He was warmly welcomed, not only by the king, but, which he felt more deeply at the moment, by his old master, Schadow, who felt no jealousy at the commission given him, but rejoiced at his success.

Rauch first made a sketch according to the wishes of the king, who desired the most simple treatment of the woman he loved. But Rauch, with his fine artistic sense, saw all the capabilities of the subject, and made another drawing of the queen in her majesty. This delighted the king, for it was a vain effort to restore to him the wife he had loved, but possible to preserve to him and to the world the lofty ideal of her character. The king called all his family together to see the sketches presented, but all, like the king, unhesitatingly preferred that of Rauch. Rauch himself was troubled lest Schadow should feel wronged; but he consoled himself with the thought that he had made no effort to obtain the commission, but had only obeyed the king. Humboldt reassured him on this point. Canova wrote to the king, saying that he had sent a sketch merely to comply with his wish, and that he considered the king's choice in every way the best.

Rauch made a small model in clay, half-size, which at first delighted the king; but when at evening he returned to study it alone, he objected to some classical figures of genii which Rauch had introduced into the bass-reliefs of the sarcophagus. He thought only Christian subjects suited the lofty character of the queen and the afflicted state of the country. Rauch accordingly modelled subjects from the New Testament, and Thorwaldsen asked that, out of special respect to the king and the blessed queen, he might be allowed to model one of the figures. The king was surprised and touched, and said that the work of so great an artist would add to the value of the monument and please him much, but owing to a change of plan the bass-reliefs were given up entirely, and this offer was not carried out.

Rauch had modelled the statue larger than life, but the king wished it of the exact size. He yielded gracefully, however, to his relations and friends, saying, " One must not dispute with artists and their followers ; laymen like me always come off second best." The poor king almost lived in this work, and it was hard for him to consent to its being taken to Rome to be put into marble. But Rauch felt that he could execute his task better in Italy, and had already given orders to have suitable marble selected for it. The king had a cast made from the model, and also from the bust, which he gave to dear friends. This work had been done in Charlottenburg, whither the king often came to see it.

Rauch left Berlin January 4, 1812, in company with Rudolf Schadow, and they spent two happy weeks together with the Von Humboldts at Vienna, and then, by invitation of the crown prince, went on to Munich.

Rauch remained a while at Florence, and then went to Carrara to examine the marble for the sarcophagus. Quite delighted with the result of his researches, he went on the ninth of March back to Florence to Salvetti & Co., to receive his packages.

Here he received a letter from the forwarding agents at Bologna, saying that, on opening the packages at the Dogana, at Bologna, they had found, not the plaster models in the chest, but only bits of plaster, and all in a thousand pieces, on account of bad packing. Rauch had already engaged a courier for the evening to go to Rome, but he borrowed twelve piastres, and mounts, without dinner, but with a heavy headache, into the courier wagon for Bologna. Arrived at Bologna, he hastened to the office of the agent, Benassi, and, on opening the chests, was relieved to find the damage not so great as he feared. The upper half of the statue was indeed broken into sixty pieces, but not so badly but that it could be restored to serve for a model. The joints were sharp, and the surface had not suffered. A professor of the academy offered him a room in which to do the work of restoration ; and he was enabled on the eighteenth to return to Florence and start from there on his way to Rome.

At Carrara, Rauch was engaged in many other works besides the statue of the queen; but he gave his most devoted attention to that, feeling as if he could not find marble pure and white enough for it, and rejoicing that he had already learned so much about working in marble. Tieck was of the greatest assistance to him, as he also had charge of the candelabra to be made after Schinkel's drawings. While the workmen were engaged on the first rough cutting of the marble, Rauch made a flying visit to Florence to make studies for the details of the sarcophagus from the antique. He then made a wholly nude model of the statue of the queen before clothing it with the soft drapery which modestly veils without concealing the graceful form beneath. He says, "It is a true character statue of her, and not an Adonis or generalized form of beauty." He watches with great interest all the mechanical processes, and takes great pains in the execution of the candelabra. His own intention was to finish the whole work at Carrara; but he yielded to the wish of the king that he should finish it at Rome, where he could have the advantage of the criticism and sympathy of other artists.

On the twenty-first of June the statue was unpacked in Rome, and Thorwaldsen saw it. He was extremely well pleased with the idea, as well as with the execution in marble. Rudolf Schadow expressed a surprise and admiration of the work that made Rauch feel that what he had heard before had not been favorable. "It is quite different in marble," he said. Rauch felt that he had gained a great deal from his work in Carrara, having learned the nature of marble and how to work it.

The artist finds consolation in his work for all that troubles him in politics, and his thoughts are constantly in Carrara, directing every part of the work on the sarcophagus, asking to which workman the buffalo-heads or other parts of the work are given. He has all so clearly in his mind that he can make minute changes without seeing it. Although he mixes up politics and sculpture in his letters to Tieck in a way which shows the disturbed state of his mind, as, "Do you believe in peace?" immediately following a question about the quality of the marble, yet he is thoroughly careful and exact in all his accounts with the workmen and with everybody.

At the close of the year 1813 he went to Carrara to see that all was right, but wished to keep his thirty-eighth birthday, January 2, in Rome. He changed his plans about the ornaments of the candelabra, and began to model the three Fates. On the eighth of January he exhibited the finished statue, which brought a crowd of visitors, and hindered his work.   He was most anxious for the judgment of Thorwaldsen and Canova.   Both showed themselves well satisfied, and Canova marked his appreciation by proposing the sculptor as a member of the senate of the Academy of St. Luke.   His heart was divided between his work in Carrara, his interests in Rome, and his desire to see the statue well placed in Berlin.

On the nineteenth of July, the anniversary of the queen's death, the last stroke was made on the sarcophagus in Carrara ; and chance willed that on the same day the statue in Rome was packed up to go to Guebhardt & Co. in Leghorn, who were to care for the shipment to Hamburg, and thence by land to Charlottenburg, as had been prescribed by a cabinet order.   On the fourth of August the atelier at Carrara was deserted, and Rauch hastened to Leghorn to oversee the departure for Hamburg.   An English brigantine was selected, carrying three hundred tons, and bound direct for Hamburg. Rauch was afraid of the equinoctial storms, and also of the American privateers, — it was during our second war with England, — and he had the whole lading insured for five thousand Roman scudi.   He decided to go to Berlin to receive and place the monument.

He stopped on his way at Vienna and Munich, and in the latter place on Christmas Eve he read in the *Allgemeinen Zeitung* that the ship that carried the queen had been seized by an American privateer in going out of the harbor of Lorient.

Rauch felt as if his forebodings of evil were fulfilled ; but then came a strife of feeling, for already he had become so conscious of greater artistic possibilities in his subject that he felt as if he would gladly begin it all anew, while he felt all the grief that the loss would cause the king.   With these conflicting feelings he travelled all Christmas week, and finally reached Berlin on Sylvester

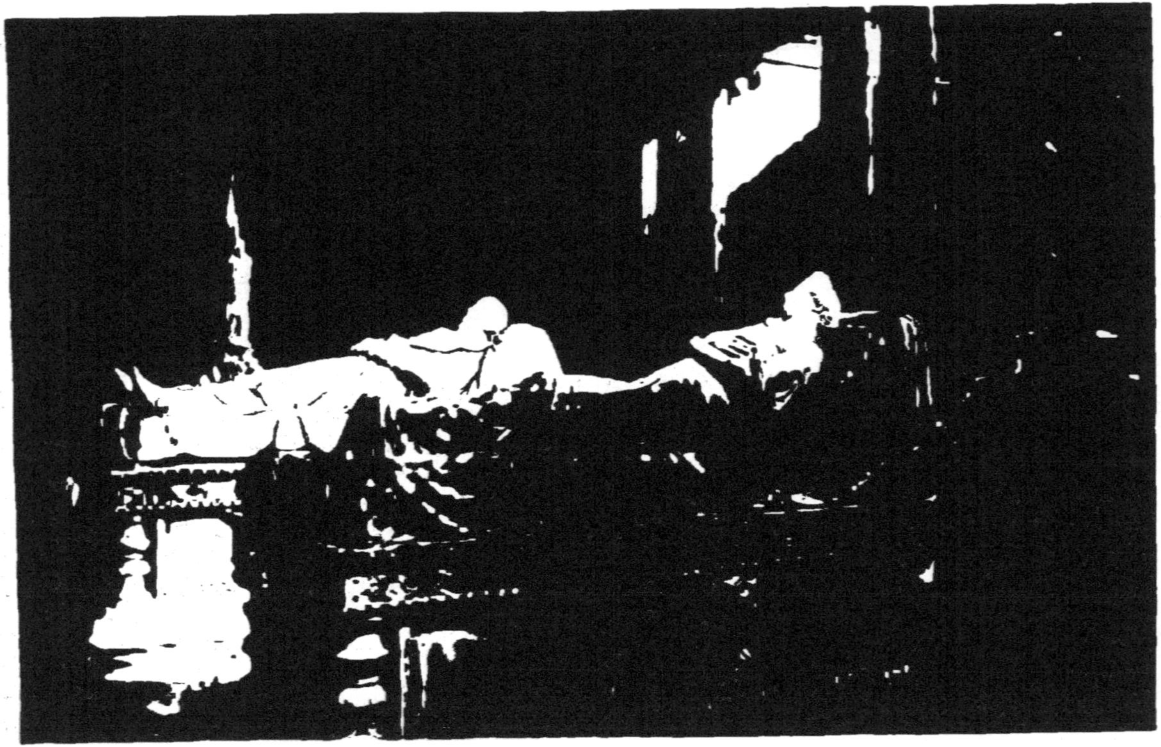

King William and Queen Louise, Charlottenburg

Day, at four o'clock. He was warmly welcomed at Berlin, and great was the excitement about the captured monument; but on the seventh of January came the news that the English privateer Eliza had taken the American ship, that the monument had arrived unharmed at Cherbourg, and from thence had been carried to Jersey. It arrived in Berlin May 22; and, although water had penetrated the folds on the bosom, it was but little injured, and was taken to Charlottenburg and cleaned. On the thirtieth of May the scaffolding was knocked away, and almost at the same moment, when, after its troubled voyage, the beautiful statue of the queen rested in the place she loved so well, the king returned from the Congress of Vienna.

That very evening, as he was busy with the last touches, Rauch was startled by the word that the king was coming with his family to see the statue. He drew back, not to disturb him in his first emotions.

Charlottenburg, built by Schlüuter under Friedrich I., enlarged by Knobelsdorf for Frederic the Great, has a large garden extending down to the river Spree. Trees a century old throw their shadows over the broad green meadows, where the king liked to pitch his tent, and where the queen had so loved to live that she hoped it would be her last resting-place. An avenue of dark green firs leads down to this favorite place, and at the end of this walk the mausoleum is placed. It is a simple Doric structure of dark-colored granite, on the steps of which are vases of red Hortensia, the queen's favorite flower.

This monument was not to minister to the vanity, but to satisfy the heart-longing, of the king, and hence the simple form he had chosen.

On a stand lies the couch, and on this the form of the queen. She does not lie stretched out as in death, but as if slumbering, with one foot softly lying over the other, her arms crossed on her bosom, and her head gently

turned to one side. Only the diadem in her hair marks
the queen, while the glory just perceptible on the bier-
cloth shows that they would willingly canonize her as a
saint.

No royal robes, but a softly flowing grass-cloth lightly
clothes the beautiful limbs down to the feet. In this
very simplicity the artist has expressed the nobility and
grace which filled her life. How truly he has preserved
her character is shown by the deep interest which the
countenance calls forth in the observer, though entirely a
stranger to her, and in the satisfaction it gave to the one
who knew her best and loved her so dearly.

The bier-cloth is ornamented with a border of eagles
and crowns, with German letters forming the inscription,
" Louise Königin von Preussen."

The long sides have a field of arms, of which one shows
the •Mecklenburg buffalo, the other the Prussian eagle.
The same armorial subject is repeated in the candelabra.
Both are alike in this, but the one finished by Tieck shows
the three Hours in relief, symbolizing life, while the other,
by Rauch, has the three Fates, indicating death.

The king visited the mausoleum again the next day ; but
Rauch, having a sick headache, waited in the city, and the
king would not excite him until he was better. June 9
he invited him to Charlottenburg, and gave him the most
complete and minute expression of his satisfaction, both
in the general result, and in every detail of the improvements he had made.

The crown prince was equally satisfied. Schinkel gave
his unqualified approval ; and the general public, while
their eyes filled with tears at the moving beauty of expression, " did not fail to wonder at the perfection of every
feather in the eagle's wings."

Although others were entirely delighted with the monument of the queen, Rauch, who held to an ideal with
extreme tenacity, was never wholly satisfied. Even when

working on the first statue, he had a longing to change the model, but did not feel at liberty to do so, and the thought constantly pursued him. In 1818 he had sought to gratify this artistic feeling; and after his work on the great military statues was finished, he felt impelled to take up anew the statue of the queen, who might rightly be regarded as the soul and inspiration of the War of Freedom.

He attempted to keep this work secret for some time, fearing that it would not please the king, but visitors to his atelier saw it, and he found that it had been spoken of in Berlin. He therefore confided its motive and history to Hofmarschall von Malzahn, who might explain it, if the king should hear of it.

His reason for secrecy was that he wished to work out this statue in artistic independence, unrestrained even by the veto of one who had commissioned it. He could not bear to give up this subject which so filled his heart and mind, and whose beauty was more perfect than he could hope to find in any model. So strong was Rauch's feeling for the beauty of the human form, that he never forgot one that had impressed his imagination. He writes to Tieck once of having seen at the theatre a child, perhaps ten years old, of such exquisite grace and beauty that he sits in his room lost in wonder and admiration while thinking of her. "Never in my life have I passed such an evening," he says; "nothing so beautiful ever affected me like this head, now and then looking up and down in changing movement, with the accompaniment of the little hands and waving locks." — "Years afterwards," says Eggers, "we perchance meet these waving locks in the master's works."

The thought of the queen's statue was ever with him, even when he could not work on the marble itself. He writes from Berlin to Carrara, "Is there not marble enough on the deltoid of the queen's statue to put in a

fine chemise in free folds? The naked shoulders trouble
me." In his sense of full freedom, he calls this the first
of his works that has satisfied him. But in the midst of his
other work it went on very slowly. In March, 1820, the
marble sketch was taken to Berlin with the granite bagna-
role bought in Rome, but not until four years after was
Rauch able to put his hand to the marble. In December
of that year he writes, "In eight days finished the head
and throat in marble." Then the work rests again for
more than two years.

Then an event which overwhelmed him with sorrow
drove him to his chisel for consolation.[1] He had rejoiced
in the hope that his daughter Agnes was about to have a
happy home of her own. Unexpectedly came the discovery that father and daughter were deceived by a villain,
and all her hopes were blighted. Rauch found comfort
only in the work that could fill his whole soul. While his
assistants worked on the monuments, he shut himself up
in his own atelier, and labored through August uninterruptedly in the completion of the statue. Gradually he
returned to other things, without giving this up, and at
the end of November he could note "the entire completion of this very detailed marble work."

Dec. 1, 1827, he wrote a long letter to the king, telling
him of the origin of his work on the statue, and the spirit
in which he had carried out his idea. He points out that
the position is more restful, the hands more natural, and
that the diligent study he gave to the first model has
enabled him to make the drapery of this one richer.

Rauch was not confident of the effect of his letter.
He asked the " Hofmarschall von Malzahn " to transmit
it to the king. The Marschall wrote him that he had
acquitted himself of his commission to the best of his
ability. " The king," he said, " was at first taken aback,
then he went over everything at great length, and finally

---

[1] See Rauch and Goethe.

said, 'I might say to you that he would come to see the work, but he could not deny that the matter surprised him ; and it was astonishing to him that you had already prepared the statue the size of life.' "

We cannot wonder at the momentary reluctance of the king to accept a new work. The first statue was made under his supervision, almost with his help. It delighted him and satisfied the artists of his court. What was the criticism that proposed changes in it ? It seemed to question his judgment. Moreover, having been made, it must belong to him and to no one else, and yet he had not asked or wished for it.

Until the close of the year the king delayed to see it. Only the queen's son and brother of the royal family, and Schadow and Wichmann among the artists, had a private view of it. Rauch was in a painful situation, because the secret had leaked out in social circles, so that William von Humboldt advised him to share it with his brother Alexander.

But when the king at last, January 21, came to the atelier, the work itself pleaded for the artist. The king expressed his satisfaction, and Rauch had the opportunity of explaining his criticism of the Charlottenburg statue. The king gave him a gracious permission to make a needful journey to Nuremberg, and so the dreaded interview passed off smoothly.

On his return from Nuremberg, the placing of the statue was arranged for, by a royal cabinet order, in the " Antique Cabinet " temple in the new palace at Potsdam, whose former contents, collected by Frederic the Great, had been sent to the museum just finished. Rauch was ill-pleased with the place, and tried, through the influence of Prince George of Mechlenburg-Strelitz, to have the statue placed in the square building which the great king had built for a cabinet of coins for his own private use. This request was granted ; but he was not allowed to open new windows, only to darken disturbing lights. The monument stands now in a simple mausoleum, an octagonal building whose lower roof rests on a raised platform under the beautiful trees of the castle garden, visible even to those without through the uncurtained glass doors. The interior room is simply draped with dark red velvet, and the whole lighted by a window opposite the door.

In comparing the two statues, Rauch himself claims more grace, dignity, and beauty for the second one, so that others, as well as connoisseurs, would at once recognize the first as a sketch, and the second as a solution of the problem. This effect is reached partly by richer drapery, and partly by the more perfect action of the form. The drapery is in freer and fuller folds, falling even to the tips of the feet. But "the deeper distinction between the two statues lies in the inward movement of the figure." This is seen even in the quiet, death-like slumber. The general attitude of the statues is the same. The upper part of the body is slightly raised by pillows, the head is inclined to the right, the hands rest one upon another on the breast, and the right leg is thrown over the left. Both forms appear to be in sweet slumber, and yet the artist makes it very clear that it is the sleep of death. "This," says Dr. Eggers, "is only possible when the perfect cessation of all muscular activity, which cannot appear anywhere in a living organism, is visible everywhere in a sleeping form. In the two works of Rauch this condition exists in the slight stiffness of the position of the upper portion of the body, of the throat and hands. In the second statue the head bends a little more to the right, the left hand leans less far and with slighter motion over the other, and the right foot is less stiffly crossed, so that the tip stands higher, by these slight touches bringing the queen a little nearer to life, and to our sympathetic feelings, without freeing her from the slumber of death, but suggesting the possible awakening."

Efforts were made both with King Friedrich Wilhelm at this time, and with his successor in 1846, to have an antique temple built to contain this precious memorial, but the stirring political events of the time prevented the design from being carried into execution.

In 1853 Rauch was modelling an eagle for it, and later, in 1856, Stützel was commissioned to prepare a sarcophagus; but Rauch's own death, as well as political disturbances, prevented the execution of the design.

Besides these full-length statues, Rauch repeatedly modelled the bust of Queen Louise with a veil or garland, of which copies were distributed to many of the princes and noblemen of Europe.

Some persons still prefer the first statue at Charlottenburg. It is more accessible to people from Berlin, and their familiarity with it endears it to their hearts.

The delight of the people in this statue was universal. Goethe wrote to the artist, " The second statue of the immortalized queen is received with the greatest sympathy, and the undertaking, memorable in many aspects, is crowned with universal applause, of which I wish you joy from my heart; for the first had won so much attachment, and so many remembrances clung about it, that it is saying much if the new statue keeps its place beside it, to say nothing of its being preferred to it."

It always remained the master's darling work, which he thought of again and again with new interest. The king gave him a gratuity of six thousand thalers gold out of his private purse.

In fact, this beautiful model of the queen, to whom he first owed his artistic success, occupied his heart and mind through the whole course of his life, from the time of making the first bust in 1815 until his last year of life, when he was again occupied in designing for it a suitable pedestal and surroundings, which we hope a happy future will not refuse to the ancestress of the German Empire.

Criticism of this beautiful work is needless. It is the meeting-point of the real and the ideal. It has won its way to the heart of the world. Republican America feels its charm, as well as United Germany. "The earth waits for its queen," said Margaret Fuller. She may find the prophecy of her in this woman, sovereign by purity, intelligence, and truth.

The artist worked not with his brain alone, but with the full glow of his warm and grateful heart ; and he worked for a king who forgot his state in the devoted affection of a husband. Nothing is more touching than the tenderness with which he hung upon the marble image of his lost love, to which he turned for consolation amid the wreck of his fortunes ; and his faults as a king are forgotten by us when we think of him as the beloved companion of this cherished and beautiful woman.

CHAPTER V

BERLIN AND LAGERHAUS
1815–1816

BERLIN at this time was full of joyous activity. Rauch was warmly welcomed, not only by the royal family, but by all artists and friends. Political hopes were at their height, and men's minds were active in science, literature, and architecture. Rauch led a merry, social life with the congenial companions he found in Berlin. He dined weekly with the crown prince, meeting the most distinguished military men, as well as scholars and architects. He dined with Schadow every Tuesday; and he never failed at the select circle at Burgsdorf, where after politics were settled they made themselves merry with gossip till late into the night. He supplied the print-shops with the·colored caricatures then in vogue, in which Napoleon came in for a large share of ridicule.

He was busy with many plans of work, when everybody was startled by the news of the escape of Napoleon from Elba and his return to the Tuilleries. When Rauch entered the rooms of Blücher, in order to model his bust, he found that no peaceful work was to be thought of. The rooms were already the headquarters of the Prussian army, and the hero would give only a few minutes to the work of the sculptor. When Rauch was invited to dine with him, he first took his dinner at an eating-house, and employed all the time of the meal in work on the bust, placing himself near the general while he ate. He finished the likeness, and at the quiet hour of coffee went over it again. The same evening came the order for Blücher to go to the army. On the tenth of April the bust was finished. Berlin was half emptied by the rush of men to the army, and Rauch would have gone with them if the monument of the queen had been placed in safety.

He followed the whole course of the campaign of the summer of 1815 with the most strained interest, seeing the enlisted men and volunteers troop through his city, where the crown prince held a perpetual review of gleaming bayonets, until, on St. John's Day, when twenty-four postilions brought the news from ·Waterloo in by the Brandenburg gate; and the next day all Berlin joined in the "*Nun danket alle Gott*" that sounded through the cathedral. Although the king was hurrying off to the army, he gave Rauch one or two sittings for his bust, still objecting to the colossal size.

Although the king's generosity opened the way for his return to Italy, it was a long time before Rauch went thither; for he became deeply interested not only in many projects of his own, but in plans for the general furtherance of art in his own country. Sometimes he wished to give up Carrara altogether, and have Tieck with him in Berlin. Then he planned for a "permanent great atelier, even if the water of Carrara did not run under its windows."

The boldness of Napoleon I. in coolly appropriating the works of art of all European nations, to bring them together in Paris, had some excellent results. As soon as peace was declared, artists and connoisseurs flocked to the French capital to see such an array of treasures of painting and sculpture as Europe had not seen before; and treasures, before known to but few, were brought to the light of day. Napoleon's generals certainly showed excellent taste in their selection. In 1815 Berlin had an exhibition of the restored works of art, and the result of it was the recognition of the need of a museum, in which not only to preserve valuable works already existing, but to stimulate the art of the present day.

Rauch was intensely interested in the project, and took great delight in the acquisition of paintings, as well as statues. The ministers consulted with him in regard to the plans for the foundation and support of the museum, asking him on his return to Rome to point out the statues and reliefs of which casts could be obtained, with information as to their cost. I will not here follow out the history of all the plans which were proposed at this busy and exciting time; but it is of great interest to see how the renewed life and hope of the nation longed to express itself in art, even while the necessity pressed so heavily upon it to repair the damages of war. Rauch saw his future before him as master of a large atelier with workmen and scholars, and he longed to return to Carrara and go on with the work which was to prepare the way for it. He was delayed in fulfilling this desire by the great number of busts that were demanded of him. These included generals, physicians, and beautiful women, whose friends longed to have their features perpetuated by the same hand which had so delicately moulded those of the beloved queen. The bust of Blücher became so popular that forty casts were made of it, and, the mould being almost worn out, Rauch asked permission to have it cast in bronze at the Royal Foundery.

Another popular hero now came upon the scene. Rauch writes to Tieck an eloquent account of the entry into Berlin of Alexander of Russia, and refers back to the early time when he accompanied the emperor by the king's command from Memel to the boundary, and saw his first meeting with the king. He then thought the Emperor looked like a beautiful brother of the antique disk-thrower, but now he thinks the king more blooming even than he. A few days after his entry, General Ostermann wrote him from Leipzig that he must move every stone to make a bust of the emperor for him. He must follow the emperor to Warsaw, even to the bounds of Russia if necessary. Rauch tried to enlist the king's assistance, but he flatly refused to urge his imperial guest. He even said to Alexander, " Look out for him ; he makes everybody colossal." The sight of the queen's monument at Charlottenburg first gave the emperor the idea that his former attendant at Tilsit amounted to something ; and he consented to give him a sitting of an hour and a half, during which the emperor wrote despatches. The emperor was very gracious to the artist, and the likeness was pronounced satisfactory.

This close study of life in portraiture was very interesting to Rauch ; but in the presence of life he felt the shortcomings of his art, and he longed for a renewed sight of the antique. He found help in the beautiful statue of Hygæia in Charlottenburg, which he modelled in clay after his day's work was over.

It was this conviction that he had something to learn which would complete his preparation for his life-work in art, that drew him back to Italy, in spite of the charms of his life at Berlin, where he had all the delights of friendship and society and abundant employment.

One of the busts that troubled him most was that of the Frau Hofmarschall von Maltzahn, a face of pure life and friendliness, " and one cannot make laughing busts," he said.

The rush for busts continued ; he had a dozen models to take to Carrara with him. Meantime, Tieck, busy in carrying on the work at Carrara, was seized with despair at his own bungling work, as he expresses it, in comparison with that of Rauch. He lays down the chisel with which he was making a repetition of the eagle for the sarcophagus of the queen, and declares that he must wait until Rauch comes ; while Rauch confesses that he is always plaguing himself to reach the grace and ideality which Tieck gave to his work.

Rauch was at last allowed to depart on the seventh of July, 1816. The journey was delightful, although solitary. Free from pressing cares, yet with his mind full of great plans for the future, both for himself and for art, he could give himself to the enjoyment of nature, even while he looked forward to a life of earnest and honorable activity. He always looked back to this journey as a sunny spot in his life.

Rauch found on his return to Italy that the revisiting of great works of art is a means of measuring one's own artistic progress. He is full of enthusiasm, and declares himself "mad with delight" over the Vatican Museum. He writes to Tieck, "Heaven can hardly grant to the blessed greater joys than are given by such works as the Torso, the Apollo, the Laocoön, and the Mercury, and still more the Venus of the Tribune, which are my newest experiences. I saw to-day for the first time the Transfiguration and the Madonna del Foligno. But why do I speak to you of them? How grieved I am that you are deprived of them, and I of you with them." He goes everywhere, and revisits the old places, and remarks that he has taken the minimum size, which the ancients ever employed on monuments, for the Berlin statues.

He finds Thorwaldsen busy with his Adonis; and he remarks upon it how little the workman has to do with the statue, and how the artist's own hand must be everywhere.

He has an interesting correspondence with Schinkel in regard to the desired purchase of the Boisserée collection; but I must pass over much which does not relate to his personal life.

In July he was again at work at Carrara. Everything speaks for the unusual regard in which he was held both at home and abroad.

On his return to Berlin, Rauch accomplished the realization of his long-cherished plan of a great royal atelier for sculpture, which should not only facilitate his own work, but become a permanent institution of the country. Schinkel had prepared a grand plan for such a building, which perhaps delayed its accomplishment. Rauch hoped it would be built during his two years' stay in Rome, but it was not, and Humboldt advised him not to return to Berlin until the atelier was ready for him. But in the spring of 1818 State Councillor Schutz wrote to him that he thought that his presence was necessary to advance the work. Since the Schinkel plan was not carried out they must find another place; and in May, Bussler announces that this was found in the Klosterstrasse, in a former storehouse.

This Lagerhaus, still standing, and still so called, is a solid, plain building erected in the fourteenth century to serve as a fortress for the elector. When the Elector Frederic II. built himself a castle at Cologne, the then so-called " high-house " was given as a fortress to knights of prominent families. Under the Great Elector it was the residence of the governor. Frederic established an academy for knights there, which was given up in 1712. Since 1713 the house has borne its present name, because in it the Privy Councillor Kraut established a depot for wool, which was given out to cloth manufacturers, who returned it in cloths. Later, a very considerable manufacture of fine and regimental cloths was there carried on, with a dye-house, and residences for the overseers and master-workmen.

Rauch was rather discouraged when he saw this old building, and found how much was to be done to put it in order, and to get a proper light. He thought of it as only temporary, and laid before the king a plan for a new building on the Wilhelmsstrasse. He got no encouragement, however, and could not send for his Italian workmen before the spring.

Meantime, Tieck writes him how impatient they all are to set out for Berlin, and how Gaetano and Giuseppe are studying the language with grammar and dictionary to be ready for the journey.

His artist friends were longing to join him; he was eager to go to work, and yet he had no place to begin. Even the friendly welcome he received increased his unrest, for he felt that he was doing nothing to justify it. Great works are planned for the new square of the Opera House. Where are his Bülow and Scharnhorst, which were from the beginning destined for it?

He misses Tieck, the careful, orderly friend, who smoothes every difficulty; and Tieck misses him when he wants the quick, resolute blow of the chisel to finish the work. "Work goes on quickly where Rauch is; the farther off he is, the more it lags." Tieck longed to be in Berlin, Rauch pined for the quiet work of Carrara: they needed to be together and to help each other.

Dannecker asks him to procure marble for some of his works. Rauch took great pains to fulfil the commission; and Dannecker "jumps with joy, like a boy," over his letter. He makes the acquaintance of the French painter, Wach, who was thoroughly instructed in the French methods, of which Rauch says, "It is not easy to see so excellent studies anywhere else." Even the French painters in Rome spoke with high respect of Rauch, and pitied him "that he had the misfortune to be a German." Rauch had refused to let his home and atelier to any one else, but he now allowed Wach to have the dwelling-house. Tieck and Rauch went to meet him and Humboldt at Florence, but unfortunately arrived too late. They consoled themselves, however, in the closer studies of the pictures, statues, and churches in Florence and Lucca. Eight times Rauch made little trips to Florence, Rome, and Pisa to keep himself acquainted with all that was being done in art.

The early part of this century saw that battle between the classic and the romantic, one phase of the eternal balancing of the old and the new, the spiritual and the natural, which ran into every department of thought, literature, and art. While Rauch never was an extreme partisan of either school, he was yet deeply interested in every phase of this question; and his admirable grasp of the spirit of classic studies, with his vivid interest in the political struggles and intellectual life of his own day, gave him that true sense of historic art which comes from not confining interest to any one nation, but which makes itself felt by all who understand the expression of human passions and actions.

Koch and Thorwaldsen stood on the side of classic art; and the figure of Hope which the latter modelled, after his studies in restoring the Æginetan marbles, is in strong archaic style.

The painters who went back to Fra Fiesole formed a colony in the cloister of San Isidoro, and Overbeck was the leader of this movement. Rauch gives generous and discriminating praise to both Cornelius and Overbeck.

A separation between the Catholic and Protestant influences had already become inevitable, and now the division was between Nazareth and Paganism. In the spring of 1817 the Nazarenes kept the birthday of Albert Dürer. Dürer was honored as Christ, Raphael as Madonna. Wach expresses himself freely over this "profanation," as Rauch calls it. He writes, " Thou great worthy soul of the immortal Albert Dürer, one shall not so mock thee; thou sawest so far about thee as thy clear eye permitted; thou knewest nothing of such wilful narrowness. . With discretion and true modesty wouldst thou consider what the art of the time produced, prove all, and keep what is good, and always turn again with reverence to the inexhaustible and ever new nature, and alone in her seek to divine the great world-soul. This monkish intolerance goes mortally against me, as this wholesale contempt of all which does not resemble their imaginary fixed idea. What woful poverty! What blindness for the great miracles of the world of nature! What narrowness where all should strive after the highest and noblest freedom! Can the German never be original? Shall the yoke of imitation always oppress them, even in the time of their greatest and most significant national uprising?"

The tendency of the painters, poets, and even architects, to go over to the Roman Church was very marked. From this faith they gained the charm of mysticism, the rich storehouse of legendary art, and the noble style of church architecture. Greek art had exalted the human body as capable of expressing all that is divine in gods and men. But Christianity prefers painting, which lends itself more freely to ecstasy and sentiment. So the sculptors did not readily yield to the tendency towards the Romish Church. A zealous friend wrote to Rauch, and sent him books assuring him that his salvation was in danger. Rauch put the letter among his papers and scarcely spoke of it to any one.

While Rome was full of good painters whose names are still dear to us, as Cornelius and Overbeck, Schnorr; von Carolsfeld, Philipp Veit, Karl Eggers, and others, the only Italian painter of that time to be named was Camuccini, whom Dr. Eggers calls "the last Italian painter." The new school belonged to the Germans.

These artists were deeply impressed with the importance of the mission of Germany, which was to conquer Rome in art, as her hordes had anciently overcome it in war; and no wonder that the coming of the young prince, whose whole soul was devoted to the fostering of art, seemed to them a presage of success. Rauch came to Rome, April 30, 1818, just in time to take part in the celebration of the birthday of the Crown Prince of Bavaria. Excepting ladies, the guests were exclusively artists,

ninety-seven in number, and all Germans.   For the moment all jealousies were forgotten.   Though the time for
preparation had been short, astonishing results were presented in allegorical representations, and all felt that the
triumphs of Germany thus portrayed were really to be
carried out on the grand stage of her art.   The prince
seemed the happiest of the guests.   As he took leave of
them, he gave the last pressure of his hand to Karl Fohr.
"We shall see each other again," he cried; "we belong to
each other."   Two months later the body of the unfortunate young artist was drawn out of the Tiber.   Rauch was
exerting himself to introduce the talented young man to
Humboldt, and his letters echo the thrill of sorrow that
ran through the whole artistic world.

In Thorwaldsen's studio Rauch thought his last work,
"Mercury killing Argus," the boldest and most beautiful
of his designs, the purest flower of his genius.   He was
delighted with the triumphs of his contemporaries, but
he turned again to the antique with fresh enthusiasm.

He went to Naples, Padua, and Venice, and was deeply
interested in the art of Mantegna and other Italians; but
he did not keep so full a note-book as formerly, and his
journey was a very hurried one.   He returned well and
happy to Berlin, July 28.

Among the works which had occupied Rauch during
the time of his absence from Berlin, were the candelabra
which a French gentleman had commissioned him to make
in commemoration of the rising in La Vendée.   Schinkel
assisted him in making the designs, and they were very
elaborate.   The base was to be formed of lion-skins, and
the shields of those honored in the war.   He left the execution of them very much to Tieck.

One of the light-bearers represents mourning, the other
the joy of victory, and half-concealed female figures bear
urns in their hands inscribed with the names of those who
had taken part in the struggle.   They were to be eight
feet high.

Rauch does not quite like to have these candelabra go to France, and wishes he might repeat them for Berlin, only he would make them three times as high! This boyish ebullition of patriotism is indicative of the state of feeling in Prussia. He closes to Schinkel, " Don't laugh over my marble projects, and let us cherish the pride of believing that these carved stones will point out in the future where men lived and fashioned the true and the beautiful." The life of Rauch's art is in that sentence.

After more than a year's work the candelabra finally went to Hamburg in twenty-four chests, and from thence were shipped to Paris. Here they found recognition and applause in the art exhibition of 1824. But owing to the various changes and revolutions in France, these monuments never found their place, and it is not known where the chests containing them are hidden. All that we have is a drawing of Schinkel's sketches, and a plaster cast in the Rauch Museum representing the forms of women in triumph.

Another plan which occupied Rauch's mind was a fulllength statue of the king. In regard to this, the question of modern costume arose which became so important. A bust of the Princess Charlotte, afterwards Empress of Russia, is mentioned for the peculiar turn of the head, bringing almost a three-quarters' view when seen in front, which characterizes the early bust work of the master. He also put the bust of Thorwaldsen in marble. It has no drapery but the beautiful flowing .hair, which is handled with great skill. "The charm of Thorwaldsen's face," says Dr. Eggers, "was the blue eye and the childlike, friendly look, which gave something divinely inspired to the whole expression. Rietschel had something of its inward friendliness." To express this, Rauch for the first time opened the eye, indicating the pupil, as he frequently did afterwards. As a change from the realism of portraiture, Rauch took up again the bass-relief of " Jason going in search of the Golden Fleece," and, after making some changes, cast it in plaster. It is in the Rauch Museum. The busts of Scharnhorst and Prince Blücher were made for the Walhalla. Marble busts of the three allied monarchs, King Frederic William III., and the Emperors Francis Joseph and Alexander of Russia, were finished in May, 1818, for the Minister von Stein. Besides many other busts, the models of the statues of Von Bülow and Scharnhorst were made in Carrara in 1818. The head of Scharnhorst was modelled after a picture by a painter, and a little profile drawing by an amateur. There was not even a death-mask.

While this work was going on, Rauch had turned his thoughts to the statue of Blücher. Silesia had already made a movement to secure this statue; and Rauch, on hearing of it, had written to the Countess Brandenberg to secure it for Tieck. She herself, however, was fully decided that Rauch should make the statue, while other influential persons wished to give the commission to Rudolf Schadow. The princess proposed a concurrence, which she thought would stimulate artistic production, and even Thorwaldsen was applied to for a sketch. On the twentieth of March, 1818, Rauch sent sketches for the statue to Breslau. The great warrior is conceived as "Marshal Forwards." But it is with a noble, firm step that he is represented as moving onwards. "It is almost possible," says Dr. Eggers, "to prefer this sketch to the one finally executed at Breslau."

A glance into Rauch's workshop at Carrara would show how closely Sculpture, on its material side, is allied to Architecture, Mechanics, and Business, and how necessary practical sagacity and sound judgment are to the success of the artist who undertakes great monumental works. Besides the thorough acquaintance with the materials of clay, stone, marble, bronze, etc., which are indispensable to the sculptor, and the direction and control of numerous workmen, the mere keeping of accounts, and making contracts on a large scale, is a work of no little responsibility.

Rauch writes to Lund, "I assure you that I seldom pass an evening without being busied at least two hours, or often the whole time, with accounts and correspondence." A busy scene was the workshop under the management of Tieck, who was eminently fitted for the position. Here Rauch found many of the workmen who were afterwards his helpers in his atelier. "Giuseppe, the son of Lazzarini, must hew out of the rough, and sketch; Ceccardo goes from bust to bust and points; now steps Lazzarini in with the file; here helps Tieck, who himself makes the eyes, or goes over what Lazzarini has not brought out delicately enough: the borer is Solari, and he also must make the hair; Tevi must polish bust after bust; Gaetano belongs to the finishers; Baba is the plinth-maker; but the young Cechino writes the names thereon. He has a specially fine hand for the ornamental, and must make the stars on the breast, the oak-leaf embroidery on the collar, the eagle on the mantle of Alexander, even the little tassels, when the others have cut them out too stiffly. Gaetano's son, the young and bright Franceschino, travels with the master, and wins great praise from him, so that he takes him to Berlin."

The relation to Tieck, which has sometimes been made a reproach to Rauch, was a union between two different natures, which, working in harmony, admirably completed each other; but Rauch was inevitably the bold, vigorous leader, while the other was the careful, painstaking executor of the work. At times Tieck longed for a more independent position, but he had not the courage to seize upon it when it was offered. Rauch used every effort to persuade him to accept the professorship at Düsseldorf, which would have been an advantageous position, as leading to still higher employment, and also very beneficial·

to German education in art ; but Tieck shrank from the difficulties of the position and the exertion necessary to secure it. Rauch was delighted to retain him as his co-worker at Carrara, Berlin, and Rome ; and when he let his workshop to Rudolf Schadow, he made the express condition that Tieck should have a room in it. Tender and sympathetic in his nature, he entered into all the interests and pleasures of the workmen, and kept the inner life of the atelier harmonious, while Rauch arranged the outer and larger part of the work. Dr. Eggers compares them to a married couple, Tieck being the good housewife, who cares for all the economics of the common welfare, engages the servants, and makes all around her pleasant and happy, living with the more active master in perfect concord and understanding.

Rauch evidently suffered from depression at this time. It was probably the reaction from his crowded and exciting life of work. Tieck writes him consolingly, " Who is there in Germany who does not speak your name with a kind of reverence, and rejoice in your personal acquaintance ? " He had great delight in his little daughter, enjoying her sports and caresses ; but how much his heart, so open to the charms of domestic life as he had seen it in his friend Humboldt's family, must have felt the want of a true, well-ordered home with an honored and beloved wife, which the artist above all men needs, to balance the excitement of his work ! This anxiety and restlessness at last laid him, in November, on a sick-bed, ill with nervous fever.

He was sleepless from restlessness and impatience. Kohlrausch and Hufeland attended him ; and Franceschino, with the peculiar gift of Italians for personal service, made an excellent nurse.

Tieck's weekly letter from the workshop, bringing violets which Teresina had plucked, lay unread. Finally, on the twelfth of December, he wrote to Tieck from his

bed that they were working day and night on the Lagerhaus, to get ready the two large ateliers and the small
one, a dwelling for himself and his people, and a lodging-
house for Tieck. A relapse followed, and he was not able
to write again until Christmas. He was much emaciated,
and the sense of want of vigor in his formerly stately
form brings out tears of pain.

Tieck wrote every Sunday; but as his letters were
fifteen days on the way, it was long before the echo of
Rauch's sickness came back. Then he cries, " For God's
sake calm your mind ; it is worrying that has brought you
low." He writes of affairs, and says he will be very
careful, and buy no clothes, and will not go to Leghorn
and Pisa. He reminds him how much money will be coming
in in the summer for busts, and closes with, "Would to
God that I were with you. If I had the means I would
leave everything and set off this night and travel night
and day until I reached you."

But now happiness and enjoyment began to return.
When the crown prince heard of the sickness of the
master, he ordered that everything should be sent him
from his table ; and now when Rauch could again sleep
and eat, he could choose among the freshest and sweetest
viands. Strengthening baths were taken, and he looked
forward to a ride on the ninth of January.

As soon as he counted himself well, he turned vigorously to the establishment of his finances, sending urgent
letters to the princely patrons for whom he had made
busts, and resolving that he would never take a commission for a bust again, except on condition of prepayment
of one-half the price ; for he holds it unjust to keep an
artist waiting three years for an outlay of three hundred
thalers, "to produce sharp noses." He orders the completion of his statue of Æsculapius at Carrara, as an
honorarium to his physician Kohlrausch. He is full of
delight over an Arab horse lately brought from Con-

stantinople, having in mind Apollo with his chariot for
Schinkel's theatre. Finding that not a stone is touched
for the atelier, he begins a series of strong, business-like
letters to the Oberfinanzrath Rothe, who begs him to be
patient four or five days longer, and to leave all to him.

Some relief from this wearisome condition was found
in a journey to Breslau. He was invited thither to a
conference of the Monument Commission on the sixth
of October, when many noblemen and landed proprietors
would assemble there. He went somewhat earlier, partly
to work on the bass-reliefs, and also to visit the Priebome
marble quarries, which had begun to attract attention.

Rauch at this time felt a little anxious about his own
finances, and his journey, which required a new travelling-
carriage costing two hundred and twenty-three thalers, did
not seem likely to improve them. But he put care behind
him as he began to feel the wonted charm of travelling ;
and his first great enjoyment was in passing a whole day
with Ludwig Tieck in Ziebingen, near Frankfort. Rauch
indeed knew him less as an author than as the brother of
his dear friend, but he found great delight in his conversation, and his pure and delicate feeling for art.

He reached Breslau on the eleventh, and dwelt in the
house of Herr von Stein. On the thirtieth he was presented to General York, that he might model his head.
The general received him at a handsome breakfast, and
Rauch was much impressed by his energy and power.

On the fourth of October the conference in regard to
the Blücher monument took place. It was agreed with
Baron von Stein and Langhans that, in order to show the
plan of the monument, a pedestal should be made of
boards, and a figure of canvas and pasteboard should be
painted. This shows how little the men of that time were
accustomed to the erection of statues.

While modelling the bust of the Duke of York, Rauch
made some interesting observations on the difficulty of

modelling any one part of a man without the rest. This is characteristic : he saw things in wholes, in the mutual relation of their parts, and the trunk and limbs are as expressive as the face. He says, "I have completed this head in four days, but I could have done it better in two, if it had been on a statue ; it is so much easier to fit the right expression to the action, and bring it out, even from the beginning, while a bust must be attacked in general, and so becomes insignificant."

He carefully investigated the Prieborne quarries, and in his letters to Tieck gives full particulars of the quality of the marble. He earnestly desired to find in his own fatherland the materials for work ; but he feels that he cannot wait for the development of the stone-work here, but must return to Carrara. Yet full of impatience and many cares as he was at this time, for he felt a stress for money which was unusual with him, he neither loses sight of the Congress at Aix-la-Chapelle, nor of the potato harvest in Carrara, which had been arranged according to German methods. And, in spite of his empty pockets, he must send to England for the " Stuart and Revett," which he wants. The book cost over a hundred and fifty-five thalers, but it was a treasury of the best engravings of France and England. He must have it. " What a splendid possession ! " he cries. Careful economist as he was, he knew how " to spend for his genius." His last days in Breslau were made very pleasant by social intercourse, and by a visit to Tieck's home, where he had a frolic with the children, whom he drew round in their little carriage.

CHAPTER VI

GERMAN ART. — SCHOOLS AND MUSEUMS
1819–1822

RAUCH's relations to the life of his time and to the development of art in Germany were so intimate, that it is impossible fully to understand him without some acquaintance with the drift of historic events, and the work of other artists in Germany. In his second volume, whose appearance was long delayed, in order to make use of new material in the correspondence of Rauch, Dr. Eggers gives an interesting sketch of this youthful bloom of art in Germany, when every tendency of thought and every phase of feeling seemed to find expression. I can give only a slight *résumé* of these influences as they especially influenced Rauch.

" The summer of 1819 was sultry in its physical and spiritual aspects. The reactionary spirit of the government shown in the Carlsbad decree against the associations of students had caused profound dissatisfaction, which broke forth in the murder of Kótzebue by young Sand, — a deed which distressed the friends of freedom more than it intimidated its foes." " Is that the spirit," writes Frau von Humboldt from Rome, " that animates our German youth ?".

Wilhelm von Humboldt retires from the ministry, since he cannot guide the state to constitutional freedom. The German thinkers withdrew from politics into the calmer regions of speculation and study. The armies of France had been driven out of the fatherland, but her ideas still held a strong sway in literature and art.

How much the intellectual life of Germany turned away from politics appears in the diaries of Rauch. He had followed with keen interest every detail of the War of Freedom, but now the most stirring events of the time receive scarcely a comment. The murder of the Duke de Berri in 1820 is briefly mentioned, followed by a note that Ceccardo has made the first point on a relief for the Bülow monument. As slightly are noted the Turin Revolution of 1823, the death of Pope Pius VII., and the accession of Leo. XII., and even the death of the Emperor Alexander, and the mutiny when Nicholas ascended the throne in 1826. He says of the Russian movement, " The issue of this tumult indicates the intention to overthrow the Russian dynasty, and to erect a republic; to repeat the madness of the Neapolitans, the Piedmontese, and the Spaniards; only with less humanity, and with less good fortune than the young emperor was able to secure for himself."

But the struggles of Greece for freedom, which awakened sympathy even in many conservative hearts, since reverence for antiquity united with interest in humanity, called renewed attention to the classics, and gave fresh meaning to old allegories. At the same time an excitement for the Christian church, which caused many reversions to Catholicism, led also to a renewed study of the history and mythology of the Middle Ages ; while the younger men, full of hope and patriotism, would hear of nothing but German religion, art, and science. Thus, while we see the same confusion and jarring of many different influences in the world of art and literature, as in the political world, we yet find rich activity and life, — a drinking anew from old historic sources, and an openness to new influences. History is no longer a dead letter, a dry record of facts, but a study of the evolution of humanity. Thus a history of art arises, and it is seen how art is related to the historic development and spiritual life of the people.

To this upheaving of life was added what was indeed necessary to give it solid success, — a great advance in the material means at command for the expression of thought.

Art could no longer be confined to a few wealthy patrons, or be at the command of an exclusive church, if it was to bear its part in this great uprising of the people ; and the arts of reproduction needed to be greatly extended to carry on the education of the masses. Albert Dürer and others had in the first time of Protestantism found the value of such means in influencing the people. We find Goethe deeply interested in the improved methods of engraving, and especially of lithography, which gives with so much truth the *chiaro-scuro* and feeling of the original work. Steel-engraving and printing in colors excited much attention in England. But most important of all was the wonderful invention of Daguerre, who began his experiments in photographic work in 1822, although it was nearly twenty years before he attained satisfactory results. This art has revolutionized methods of reproduction, and has proved a powerful ally, instead of a dangerous rival, to genuine art work. At the same time the art-unions began their work of mediating between the artist and the public by introducing the works of one to the other. Without denying that they have been capable of errors and even follies, we cannot but recognize the great service they have done in spreading the knowledge and enjoyment of art. There is a beneficent process of natural selection always going on in art, which, if it may possibly sweep away a few jewels, saves us from being overwhelmed with the rags of the garments we have outgrown.

In 1824, in Berlin, artists and friends of art united to obtain commissions for their countrymen studying in Rome. Humboldt was the soul of this little band, to which Rauch, Tieck, Schinkel, Wach, Schadow, and Begas belonged.   They now proposed to extend it under the name of "Union of Friends of Art in the Prussian State." At Rauch's request, the king examined the plan of the union, and consented to be its patron.   Goethe expressed warm interest in it.   In the spring of 1824 Rauch writes to Lund, "that the union is already in its desired path. There is money," he says, "but as yet no acceptable pictures ; this rouses up the good painters, and the public is very sympathetic."   It found less welcome in Rome. But the fruits of years of study of German artists in Rome were now appearing, and young artists were returning to their native land full of eagerness to ripen their talents in German air.   Finally all these tendencies towards activity in art found a concrete expression in King Ludwig of Bavaria, who esteemed the promotion of art the great object of government.   Alike devoted to classic art and German glory, he built his Walhalla with an eager haste and impatience corresponding to the spirit of the times.   "I don't treat art as a dessert," he said to Rauch ; "it must be our beefsteak."   He would gladly have drawn Rauch into his own exclusive service as a sculptor; but Rauch's early relations to the royal family of Prussia, and his strong attachment to them, made it impossible for him to leave his home in Berlin.   He had, however, frequent and pleasant relations with King Ludwig; but we agree with Dr. Eggers that it was most fortunate that he preserved his independent position, and was not drawn into the rapid current of the royal amateur's designs.   In Schwanthaler, King Ludwig found a man whose lively fancy and rapid execution suited him.   Rauch founded his school on the principle of thorough work, and spared neither time nor labor to carry out his ideas to the most perfect expression.

Rauch was not at all carried away by the romantic school, so far as it was represented by mysticism and Catholicism.   He always remained a liberal Protestant, and studied alike the lessons of antiquity and the needs of his own time.

At the same time Berlin was fast becoming, under the direction of Schinkel, a noble capital of art ; the painters were decorating the Opera House, and under the direction of Rauch a great school of sculpture was being rapidly established.

In the spring of 1819 Rauch was in the full tide of activity in the Lagerhaus, happy in the companionship of his friend Tieck and the skilful co-operation of his laborers. He writes to Frau von Humboldt, " Tieck has made a stepping Apollo in clay, — splendidly successful ! If it were only possible to get him an order for marble ! Do you know how beautifully he can work in that material ? "

The great demand for busts continued ; and Rauch writes in regard to the bust of Hardenberg, " The people have gone mad over the likeness, but I cannot find the least pleasure in it." Rauch began to model a colossal bust of Frederic the Great. Many other commissions poured in, some of which indeed came to naught ; but in a few months the atelier was crowded full, and all were busy and merry.

Now that his work was thus prosperously going on, Rauch indulged himself in the happiness of a visit to the home from which he had so long been absent. He had last seen his mother in 1797, when he accompanied King Frederic William on his journey. She had died in 1810. A very aged brother of hers, Johannes Hildebrandt, was yet living in Mengeringhausen ; and some distant cousins on his mother's side, and the widow Marhof Niggemannat Flechtdorf, to whom Rauch had given his mother's inheritance, remained. He found also a cousin, the court-physician Mundhenck, who was happily married, and had two charming daughters, living in Pyrmont. His own blooming young daughter Agnes accompanied him on the journey

He spent three refreshing weeks in this family life, and the intercourse thus renewed was always kept up. His relations delighted to send him sausages and other delicacies for the household. His daughter Agnes, who had been for the last five years at the Luisenstift, now took charge of his housekeeping, and made pleasant little social parties in the home. He had a visit from his relatives, and took pains to give his medical cousin every opportunity of professional observation in Berlin, and himself showed the party everything of interest in the world of art.

He afterwards went to Pyrmont in search of health. He writes to Humboldt, "Since the beginning of the year [1821], when the cold and wet weather began, I have suffered uninterruptedly from pains in the limbs, which were as good as cured by Kohlrausch. I pass the nights without sleep, sometimes when I am travelling, in wildest delirium. By day this bad condition hinders me from work, and drives me to hypochondria. I shall go to Pyrmont at the end of this month." These pains appear to have been caused by his habit, when absorbed in his work, of kneeling down in the damp clay, although he preferred rather to believe them to be a result of the severe nervous fever from which he had suffered. He spent the summer months at the baths, and made a few busts, among them one of his medical cousin.

Every journey afforded him opportunities of artistic study and pleasure. At Braunschweig he enjoyed the fine pictures, and at Hildesheim the rich old bronzes. He was much interested in studying the manner in which these were cast, as is plainly to be seen "in the Euripides, not over a model in '*cire perdue*,' but in the modern manner with a core." He was already interested in this method of casting, in relation to his Blücher statue.

He made comparisons between the antique and mediæval work, and spoke disparagingly of Peter Fischer's reliefs, saying they were coarse, like those of an ignorant founder. "How unhappy were we sculptors but for Greek art and its works!" he cries. He found reason to modify this judgment, however, when he saw more of Vischer's productions. Not only art, but nature, gave him the keenest delight. He noted every tree and stone, the form of the clouds, the lights and shadows, and was grieved when night came on and concealed the surroundings. If his daughter fell asleep from the heat of the day or motion of the carriage, he called out, "For shame! look about you!" But he could not bear the senseless chatter of admiration, and forbade the use of "*himmlisch schön*," or "*fürchterlich reizend*," even when passing through the wild, picturesque scenery of the Saxon Switzerland. He delighted to live over again with his daughter the lively feelings with which, in his first journey to Dresden, he had seen the beauties of his own land. Rauch's personal happiness centred more and more in his beloved Agnes. He took the younger, nine-year-old daughter Doris from school, and secured for her a governess, who for forty years acted as housekeeper, and took charge of his home and daughters most successfully. Agnes was old enough to enter society, and her own charming character and manners, as well as the regard for her father, secured her a cordial welcome in the best families of Berlin. He accompanied her to balls, masquerades, and receptions. She must always present herself in her ball-dress beforehand for his criticism, that she might not, in compliance with fashion, infringe on the real laws of beauty. She must leave the ball at the prescribed hour as punctually as Cinderella, and no entreaties served to prolong the time of amusement. She must give up the rich viands which her father despised, and enjoy the ham and potato soup whose fragrance always greeted her return home.

During his middle life Rauch was subject to severe

attacks of headache. He would continue at his work as long as possible, trying to drive off the attack ; but when sight failed him he would come up from the atelier, saying, "I am good for nothing." The pain was usually so severe that he must go to bed, often for some days, without eating anything, being almost unconscious until the attack wore off, usually about nightfall. Then he rose up, ate his potato soup and ham, and returned to take up his work where he had left it. These were black days in his calendar. He counted them every year on Sylvester Day, as, "Twenty-two headaches, of which eighteen were in bed." Sometimes with the addition, "The only interruption to work." One year, when he noted twenty-six, he says, "Except this fatality, I was never better in my life." The attacks grew less in later life, as he often remarked for the comfort of young people who suffered in a similar way.

He was very regular in his diet, and did not like to take anything but his usual meals, and he was never known to approach anything like a debauch on any occasion. He loved the society of cultivated men, and talked much and well on all subjects in which he was interested, but in the atelier he was perfectly silent. He shared in all the entertainments of the court, in concerts where Catalani and Sontag sang, and in the tableaux and private theatricals where Faust was acted by dukes and princesses. He rarely visited the theatre, except for some great work of dramatic art. He enjoyed Gluck's "Alceste ;" and often his sculptor's eye was delighted with the forms and movements of the actors. "Don Juan" was his favorite opera, while he cared little for the popular "Der Freischütz," and could not fix its melodies in his mind.

He was frank and generous in his judgment of other artists, even when their theories and methods differed greatly from his own. A touch of irony sometimes appears in his estimate of the "*genre*" painting of his day. He warmly recognized the genius of Leopold Robert, whom he had known in Rome, and introduced this leader of Realism to the Berlin Academy, and ordered a picture for his own gallery. He had great personal sympathy for artists, especially if they were earnest and laborious ; and for one who was sick he exerted himself to obtain commissions for copies. He gratefully remembered his old master, Ruhl, and endeavored to assist his sons, whose own merits would not give them the high places they coveted. For nothing else would have led him to take the painter, Ludwig Ruhl, under his personal care, and seek to introduce his pictures to Prince Charles. His pictures (of horses) were not indeed worthless; but, being a handsome man, he paid more attention to his clothes than to the canvas on his easel ; and was too eager for high society, where he might play the fine gentleman, to please Rauch, who had no attraction to the fool (*hausnarr*).

Rauch also assisted 'his old master when he was deprived of his office and work in Cassel, procured marble for him, and took an interest in his work, although his old master deprecates his employing his sharp, critical blade upon it. The younger son, Julius, became an excellent architect in Frankfort on the Main, and later the Hessian electoral court building director.

Rauch kept up his connection with Rome through occasional correspondence with Frau von Humboldt and other friends. He writes with delight that the king has ordered Rudolf Schadow's " Achilles and Penthesilea " in marble. But Schadow never finished the group.

On the twelfth of January, 1822, Frau Buti sent Rudolf's best greetings, and gave notice of a dinner which Signor Alberto (Thorwaldsen) had given to the household. They danced, and drank punch made from lemons from Rauch's garden, giving him a special "*Hoch*" as the patron of lemons. Schadow had planted lemons, apples, and palms in the garden in remembrance of Rauch. Fourteen days after the feast he was taken ill with an inflammation on the chest; and Rauch was startled with the news that, on the first of the next month, their friend had found his last resting-place in S. Andrea della Fratte. Frau Buti took charge of studio and garden until Emil Wolff was sent as a five-years' pensioner to Rome. He remained there in constant correspondence with Rauch until his death.

His correspondence and friendship with Lund was equally close and enduring. After making a rich student journey with Wach, in which he gathered treasures of sketches of Italian painters, Lund left the Eternal City, more than a year after Rauch. He accompanied Thorwaldsen, "who gave way to a new race in Rome," to his home, where a number of commissions awaited him for many altar pieces, and for painting the introduction of Christianity into Denmark for the royal castle. A pupil of David's, he had kept closely to classicism, and had belonged to the select Humboldt circle. He only agreed in the choice of subjects with "Nazareth," which he believed to be already dying out. To Lund the correspondence with Rauch was most precious, for he felt the want of artistic sympathy in Copenhagen very deeply; and his homesickness for Rome was not relieved until he became betrothed, and wrote joyfully to Rauch of his new-found happiness. He earnestly desired the same blessing for his friend.

With all his blessings Rauch had indeed often felt the want of a centre to his home, a partner of his joys and sorrows; but, as he had before said to Schinkel, he now answered to Lund, that, if he did not follow his example, "it lay not in his will." But he was now very happy in his work in the Lagerhaus, and his family life with his daughters.

His birthday was a standing festival at the Lagerhaus. Here his artistic friends assembled, accompanied by their wives, and filled up the hour in pleasant intercourse. One of the company unrolled a copy of verses an ell long, in which he recounted how the Great Elector made his legendary round on New Year's night to inspire the Rauch statues, and to secure the order for the statue of old Fritz.

But however gay and pleasant the social life, when Rauch returned to the atelier he was again the silent, earnest master, devoted to work himself, and requiring the same diligence from others. "I am again in my accustomed course of work," he says, on his return from a journey; "that is, to rise and go to bed with the lark, and between times to work eight or nine hours." From half-past five in the morning, when the neighbors in summer or winter saw him place the shaving-mirror so punctually at the window that they could set their clocks by it, until breakfast, he conducted his correspondence, in which his rule was of great punctuality. The time until one o'clock, when he took his noonday meal, was given to the atelier. Here the greatest order and neatness prevailed. It made him unhappy that an old measuring-circle that he had used in his years of study got mislaid. He disliked any interruption, and looked upon every one who came during his working-hours without great necessity as a thief. But he was very glad to receive those who were earnest to learn, and gave them the clear, frank criticism which he prized so much himself. When the king visited the studio, and criticised the long over-hose of the Blücher statue, Rauch said, "He is perfectly right." He showed the work of his pupils to the king, and was pleased that they gained his approbation.

A break in the enjoyment of the Lagerhaus came from the constant attempts of various persons to get possession of a part of it for other purposes. Every year some contest of this nature must be fought. Once he had to resist the letting of a hall for the exhibition of a sea monster;

and he obtained the promise of its castellan that "in future no cattle shall be brought into the neighborhood of your Excellency's atelier." He had to threaten an appeal to the king, which finally secured him in peaceable possession. He added an annex to the Lagerhaus for a marble-yard, in which he could store marbles sent from Carrara. The great cost of marble prevented the use of this stone, which Rauch considered the best adapted for ideal work. He was not satisfied that the artist should model only the soft clay; he felt that he should, with hammer and chisel, give the last touches to the hard stone. He stored up blocks of marble, which he carefully selected in Carrara, both for his own use and for sale to other artists, many of whom took advantage of the opportunity. It remained for many decades the chief source of supply for Germany. The English imitated his example until, finally, the price of marble rose so much, that in 1828, good Carrara marble was cheaper in Berlin than in Rome.

He had imported not only marble but marble-workers; and his example was followed by Thorwaldsen and others, until the supply of skilled workmen was exhausted, and Wolff found it very difficult to secure suitable assistants.

Rauch tried to secure a pension for the men he had brought from Carrara, to support them while there was a lack of work in marble, as their skill would soon be needed for the restoration of antique works for the museum. He succeeded in gaining an allowance of two hundred thalers. When, however, the hope of a permanent foundation for marble sculpture was given up, all the workmen but Ceccardo Gilli finally returned to their homes. He was a very young man, and he became devotedly attached to the master, and remained with him until his death.

Many of his German scholars were very helpful and dear to him; but dearest of all were Rietschel and Drake, who came to him in 1826 and 1827. Rietschel, indeed,

became bound to him in a friendship so close, tender, and
enduring, that Dr. Eggers compares it to that noble tie
between Goethe and Schiller, which Rietschel has immortalized in his statue.   He was at first repelled by Rauch's
earnest, even severe, manner.   But when Rauch had seen
Rietschel's drawings, and his model of a bust, and especially a sketch of Tyrolean singers, the Rainers, he was
so much struck with the character of the work, that he
gave it warm praise ; and it was quickly decided that
Rietschel should remain in the atelier.   Rauch was a
severe critic, but he was overflowing with delight when he
discovered new talent or excellence in any one.   He used
few words, but illustrated his meaning by actual work on
the object, cutting away or adding or changing with a
master-stroke.   An anecdote told by Rietschel shows his
manner of teaching.

Rauch asked him if he had modelled a relief.   Rietschel
had no idea about it, and thought a relief was only a figure
cut through the middle, with its flat side laid down.
Rauch told him to take a manikin, which was draped in
calico, and had served for a figure of an apostle, and make
a Paul, with a book under his arm and a sword in the other
hand.   Berghes showed him how to lay out the nude
figure ; and Rietschel, knowing nothing of the flat principles of relief, went on building it up higher and rounder,
until the outer arm stood almost free, and the drapery followed it with ever-increasing impossibility.   Rietschel
says, " Rauch came day after day, saw the work, and went
away without saying a word.   I thought that indicated
great satisfaction, and I went on encouraged.   Finally, on
the third day, he asked me for a wire, which I reached
him, full of expectation.   Then he cut down the height
of the figure almost one-half, till he left only a high outline, and said, ' How could you make such an infamous
tinker's work ? It should be only so high.' "   He laid down
the wire and went away.   Tears stood in the pupil's eyes

over his failure. But the friendly Berghes came to his aid ; and Rietschel, having given his mind to the subject, made a relief which must have satisfied his master, since he used it later as one of the ornaments of his staircase.

Rauch's principle of teaching was self-instruction, not only because he had gained his own knowledge in that way, but because he believed it was the only thorough one.

He expected pure love and a full surrender to art, and constant effort, after the best of which one is capable. Worldly ambition was offensive to him in others : he never felt it himself. As Rietschel was once trying to model a free figure that Rauch had given him as an exercise, Tieck found him in great despair over his own want of power. Tieck, who was often the consoler when Rauch had been severe in blame, relieved Rietschel by a playfulness which was in line with Rauch's thought. "What are you so troubled about ?" he said. "Do you wish to make a masterpiece? Never mind Rauch!" Rauch may be said to have known no other aim than striving for the best. Every finished exercise was only a stepping-stone to another ; and he struggled like a young man who exerted himself as if he had never done anything in his life. He was modest in the deepest sense of the word, and relentless towards himself. If anything displeased him in his work, he would destroy months of labor, and unweariedly begin anew. Thus he always remained young, because he always began every work with fresh ardor and zeal, as if he had accomplished nothing.

The closest relation existed between Rauch and his master, Gottfried Schadow, and his elder friend Thorwaldsen. Thorwaldsen had renewed the classic feeling in sculpture. He left to Greece itself its highest god, the Zeus ; but he used the beautiful circle of Greek forms to express the whole range of thought and feeling, of force, craft, and strength, but especially of love, — the master-passion of life, the all-conquering " Amor," which is alike his first and last work. By no means slavish in his imitation of the Greek masterpieces, but using their method of simplicity and repose to express new thoughts, his works seem almost a continuation of theirs, and to link themselves happily to a circle of plastic Christian representations. His Christ and his apostles express the modern feeling in fit harmony with the ancient form, showing that true art is not a fossilized but a progressive creation.

Thorwaldsen hardly belonged to any nation; and he does not express the life of his time even in his portrait and monumental statues. He avoids the question of modern costume, and uses either a wholly Roman costume, or a modification of the cloak, or a dress of the Middle Ages.

Gottfried Schadow works in quite a different direction. He does not shun the question of modern costume, but meets it directly.

On the twenty-eighth of July, 1781, at three o'clock in the morning, the master Tassaert sent his apprentice, Gottfried Schadow, seventeen years old, to draw the ruins of the tower of a church lately overthrown. Picturesque ruins had until then only been known by engravings and pictures ; and artists and *dilettanti* thronged to take advantage of this actual ruin for purposes of study. Schadow had the greatest success in his picture, and his artistic existence may be said to date from this event.

Penetrated by his love of reality, Schadow went to Rome, where he preferred the Roman art to the Greek, especially where, in the delineation of men of the period, it proved faithful to every detail, from the crown of the helmet to the rim of the sandal. But the delicate sense of beauty, and the true artistic feeling of Schadow, preserved him from the excesses of realism ; and although he has not the wide popularity of Thorwaldsen, whose tender sentiment is felt by all classes, he is equally prized by connoisseurs.

As Dr. Eggers has well expressed it, "From the Greeks flow the fountains for which men thirsted." This people dwelt close to art: art was to them nature, and Thorwaldsen drew from the natural source. But the springs of nature flow unceasingly in actual life, and to them Schadow turned.

So he went to the living world, and measured and drew hundreds of men of all ages and classes, to find the most beautiful proportions of the human figure, and in this laborious, empirical way to settle the question by his own standard whether the German human form corresponded to Greek laws.

He followed nature so closely, that he boldly represented the historic men in the clothing which they wore in life. Thus he unconsciously reached the Greek principle, on which he laid his foundation of portraiture ; for the Greeks held it to be a fundamental principle so to fashion the individual man as he was clothed in life. The character of a personality penetrates his clothing, and determines it. The truth of the kernel breaks through the shell. As the poet says, " Nature has neither kernel nor shell; both are alike." Therefore that clothing will be most natural to a man which he has worn all his life.

According to this idea, Schadow wished to represent Frederic the Great in the costume of his time, as he also modelled the beautiful group of the crown princess and her sister, not omitting the band around her throat. Rauch admired his work in this respect, and speaks of his Luther monument as " a naïve, true, and excellent work."

While Thorwaldsen and Schadow thus brought out with admirable skill and feeling the varying characteristics of classicism and realism, it was the special merit of a third artist, Rauch, to unite these differing tendencies in an organic unity. He gave full emphasis to the independence of individuality, but he escaped the fetters of bare naturalism and narrow actuality, while he rose in the region of the universal, and in the free world of thought, bringing out his noblest self. "This, his achievement, is the history of art; and for the development of sculpture we must unquestionably accept it as a fact, and as a method of work consciously dictated throughout."

Not that Rauch worked on a theory of eclecticism, taking so much of reality and so much of ideality, but that his whole perception of natural forms was so clear, and his thought was so vivid, that this method of conceiving art sprang out of his whole life. He was helped by Schadow and Thorwaldsen, as he also helped them; for it is not the prerogative of genius to stand isolated and alone, but to gather into itself the influences of his time, and give them out to others again in fresh organic life.

Schadow and Thorwaldsen were genial enough not to be uninfluenced by Rauch. The proof is in their works, while Rauch's constant recognition of his indebtedness to them fully appears in his diary.

If Schadow did not go so far as Thorwaldsen in his indifference to national interests and feelings, yet he did not feel the full influence of the modern life of the people, but recognized the grandeur of dynasties as a thing apart from the life of the people's heart. Although actually only thirteen years younger than Schadow, Rauch's artistic career really began much later; and almost at the very time of his recognized mastership at Berlin, Schadow was ready to lay down the chisel. Schadow had his struggles early in life in his efforts to marry the woman he loved, and to provide means of support. Rauch had his outward existence smoothed for him, and his struggle was to escape to his ideal life. But even the years in the queen's antechamber brought precious results, for the close tie which bound him to the king and queen gave him a deep personal affection for them, as well as a strong love of his country ; and he was born with the nation in her throes of agony, and rightly became her representative in art when she was again prosperous and happy. Neither the nation's foe nor the hand of death could conquer the noble Louise: she rose again in his art, more truly the queen of the nation than ever before ; and if she was the founder of the Unity of Germany, he helped to give form and substance to her work. Thus in art, as in life, he belonged to his own period ; and he most truly mirrors the life of his own time because he so deeply studied the whole life of the past ; and he is most true to his own people because he was so free from provincial narrowness, and recognized worth and loved goodness in every people. Germany must live in his spirit. She has achieved unity; she needs now to broaden her lines, and to enter into true relations of respect and mutual benefit with her neighbors, in order to develop a national life equal to the intellectual glory which her poets, artists, and philosophers have shed around her.

The formation of noble museums in her national capital is one of the benefits which Germany owes indirectly to the victorious career of the man whom she esteemed her greatest enemy, and is one of the ever-recurring proofs how life can bring good out of evil, and victory out of defeat.

The collection of ancient works, gathered from all Europe, and shown so freely at Paris, was a grand object-lesson, which led all men to consider the preciousness of these works of art, and the importance of placing them in proper care. Five and thirty statues stood in the antique gallery, labelled " Fruits of the Conquest of Germany." How many Germans then recorded a vow that these statues should be once more returned to their owners, and that the nation should become their guardians ! One of the articles of the proposed treaty of peace required their return. In September, 1815, the returned works of art were placed on exhibition, and all felt the need of a suitable, permanent place for them.

Perhaps for the first time in Europe it was felt that works of art should be the birthright of the people rather than the private delight of kings and nobles. All lovers of art knew that in the museum open to the people lay a powerful lever to raise the whole structure of art. The king entered warmly into these plans. A great impulse was given to the desire for a suitable museum building, by the purchase, in 1815, in Paris, of the celebrated Giustiniani Gallery, with which should be united what could be found in the royal palaces at Berlin, Potsdam, and Charlottenburg. One hundred and fifty-four pictures out of that gallery, and twenty single ones that the king had bought elsewhere, passed under Rauch's windows; and the king had also commanded many copies after Raphael, and his own full-length figure in life-size, by Gerard.

Rauch announces to Tieck in triumph, that on the fourteenth of February, 1816, one hundred and thirty-five pictures of the old German masters will come from Heidelberg, — the collection of the brothers Boisserée. He thinks the matter is all arranged that they are to pay ten thousand thalers, which will go for the finishing of the Cologne Cathedral, and so there is great joy all around. But, unfortunately for Berlin, the rejoicing was premature; and after Schinkel thought the matter all arranged, the pictures went to Munich, the decisive "yes" not having been said soon enough by the ministry.

In the year 1820 the great museum was planned, and Rauch took the warmest interest in Schinkel's plans for it, and in his struggle to carry them out. Schinkel went to Italy to study buildings, and also to procure casts from the antique and other works of art; and he constantly writes of them to Rauch. Already the museum project had influenced Rauch's artistic career, since it led to his being commissioned to purchase works of art in Italy, and to have casts made there; and he was also much employed in making restorations of ancient statues, which led him to a very careful study of classic art.

He secured the Barberini Faun, and casts of the Colossus of Monte Cavallo and other fine works; and Altenstein, the minister of state, approved of all, and adds, "You will oblige me very much if, during your residence in Italy, you will leave nothing unobserved which can be important to us in future for the progress of art." And Rauch replies, "I will, with the greatest zeal, do everything to secure for the Prussian state that pre-eminence in this department which it already enjoys through so many other scientific establishments."

Bunsen and Thorwaldsen assisted in this work, and Paris and London furnished objects of interest to add to the collections.

In 1819 a tourist gave such glowing accounts of discoveries in the land of Delos, that Wolff was sent to Greece, with an architect named Wessenburgh, at the cost of the state.

After an absence of six months, they reported to Rauch an almost total failure in attaining the object of their expedition; the representations of the tourists proving incorrect and false. They express their convictions that without further excavations there is nothing to be gained. Time seems to have justified their opinion.

But the work of the museum did not always run smoothly, and there was much difference of opinion between artists and connoisseurs. Rauch complained that "literary appointees did nothing right at the museum. Professor Gerhard has invented the convenient term 'apparatus,' and on these he works and fusses. He is now going again to Italy (where I and a thousand others might like to run every hour), to Greece, etc., while the work for making known the treasures of Berlin is at a stand. It is dreadful! Wilhelm von Humboldt plainly foresaw this sinecureship, and now a great deal of friction has occurred; for as the building of the museum approaches completion, the question of filling the rooms comes into the foreground, and it is necessary to decide what objects should be received, and to arrange the appointments of the administration." Important additions were made to the commission, which consisted of very able men, and Rauch was appointed as "one to be trusted for competent judgment, on account of the high position in which he stands in respect to art culture, by his acquaintance with the finest pictures that exist in foreign galleries, and especially in relation to antique sculpture."

Much controversy arose in regard to the additions to the committee; but Rauch was finally fully appointed, May 16, 1829, and in a month he presented a plan for placing the antique sculpture in the Rotunda, and for the hall, afterwards called that of "the gods and heroes." A year was passed in the necessary restorations, in framing, hanging, and placing the pictures, and at last Rauch had the satisfaction of seeing the result of eight years' care.

The building was finished in 1830, and Rauch writes to Rietschel, "The museum of statues and pictures is the most delightful which I have ever seen for similar purposes, and the great beauty of the whole pleases me yet more than the finest antique statue."

July 1, 1830, the king visited the new museum for the first time, with the Duke of Mecklenburg, and was received by Brühl, Schinkel, Tieck, Wach, Levezow, and Rauch. He expressed unconditional satisfaction with the work. The museum was opened to the public on the third of August, as an offering to the people, on the king's sixty-first birthday. On the same day the news of the Revolution of July in Paris was received at Berlin.

At the same time that Rauch was working so busily with others for the great museum, he was actively engaged in his atelier, that new institution of art which he controlled as governor and final authority. It would be interesting to follow in detail Rauch's work in the restoration of statues, but it would require too much space. He says that "from 1824 till 1829, five to seven workmen were uninterruptedly engaged in this exacting and weary business. Twenty-nine subjects were wholly, and nine others partly finished. As he was going to Munich, he left what further work remained in Tieck's hands."

Rauch urges the purchase of two bagnaroles from the ruins of the baths of Diocletian, although the restoration of the handles, with other repairs and polishing, will cost two thousand scudi, which Humboldt thinks very dear; but yet the finished vessels will be of great rarity and beauty; "for," he says, "besides the one intended for your majesty, there is only one similar, and that of less beauty, in the Vatican at Rome." The king approved the purchase, and in April, 1820, they arrived in Berlin, and were temporarily placed in the Art Academy. In connection with the Danish and Russian Museums, he procured casts of the Æginetan marbles, and thus was able to have the whole series for Berlin. By an exchange with the British museum he also obtained casts of some of the Elgin marbles, of which Caroline von Humboldt had written him glowing accounts.

Rauch took pains to arouse interest in every direction, in order to increase the collections. He tried to get casts of the statues in the Cologne Cathedral, and asks Beuth to procure anything possible in London.

October 12, 1820, a cabinet order was issued, by which the art treasures of royal palaces, gardens, and galleries were given to the public museums.

Rauch was much interested in the picture gallery, and all felt confidence not only in his taste, but in his skill in managing delicate business relations. Different museums eagerly contested for the different collections offered for sale from time to time. The Giustiniani collection, which formed the groundwork of the gallery, needed much revision and restoration, and an engagement was made with the painter Palmaroli to put the pictures in order. Rauch failed to get the fine Boisserée collection of pictures ; but, since it did not come to Berlin, he rejoiced that it went to Munich, and not out of the country. He succeeded in getting the Solly collection of three thousand and six pieces, which needed much careful selection. Many of the pictures obtained were copies, or of inferior merit ; some were injured, and some not wanted in the museum were reserved for exchanges, or to fill up empty spaces in the various palaces. One thousand one hundred and sixty-five were thought suitable for the gallery, but Rauch finally rejected many of these. From the various palaces Hirt had made a list of seven hundred, but he left out four hundred, for which the Solly collection made ample amends. With the addition of nine purchased pictures, among which were two pictures by Fiesole (Fra Angelico), and one by Giovanni Sanzio (the father of Raphael), in the year 1823 there were one thousand three hundred and forty-nine pictures as a foundation of the future gallery. Many pictures also were purchased from private sources. The restoration and framing of these pictures required much time and money, twelve thousand thalers being paid out for this purpose in five months.

The whole amount paid for restoration of pictures appears to have been about one hundred thousand thalers.

Count Ingenheim was a very active assistant in the purchase of pictures. He discovered that the Prince Lante had a Raphael for sale, for which he asked one thousand five hundred *Louis d'or*. Rauch must speak to the crown prince ; but, as he was just then interested in buying a Roger van der Weyden, he refused to give more than a thousand. Ingenheim was enthusiastic. "If we had that picture the king need not buy another for the museum." The King of England also was in treaty for the picture; but the zeal of purchasers was a little cooled by the opinion of Camuccini that it was not genuine, and was spoiled. However, neither Waagen nor Schinkel was convinced of this; and Waagen counselled the purchase, although he did not think it one of the finest easel pictures of the master.

Not until 1827 could Emil Wolff write to Rauch that the picture was secured, and then at the price of eight thousand five hundred scudi, besides a copy of the picture by Karl Eggers, and a portrait of the Princess Lante, to be made by Von Grahl. This was a purchase somewhat after the style of the Sibylline books, and even then the commission "*degli antichita e belle arti*" objected to the sale; but the Pope declared that "the friendship of the King of Prussia is more important to me than a picture."

In preparing the sculpture gallery, Rauch had the help and sympathy not only of his old friends Schinkel and Humboldt, but the active co-operation of Emil Wolff. Wolff went to Rome after the death of his cousin Rudolf Schadow in 1822. The inheritance of his cousin's work fell to him. He had been a pupil of the elder Schadow, and was under the powerful influence of Thorwaldsen. He occupied the apartment of Schadow, and took up the chisel to finish his group of "Achilles and Penthesilea." He became, as Schadow had been, Rauch's right-hand man in making purchases for the museum, and was full of glowing enthusiam; he was the Roman scholar of the German master.

In the Northern capital Wolff was engaged in working on one of Thorwaldsen's apostles, which were executed by young sculptors under his direction. His next original work was a monument to Rudolf Schadow. Schinkel writes of this to Rauch in 1824, "Wolff's little marble relief on Schadow's grave is most tenderly felt out and finely executed ; like himself, it makes no pretensions, and is on that account charming. This monument is remarkable for its successful blending of antique symbolism, in a laurel-crowned victory presenting a wreath, with a figure of Christ welcoming the parted soul. Rauch later failed in such an attempt in the Blücher Berlin monument, and only when an old man, in the monument of Frederic the Great, succeeded in the representation of such a union. Wolff sends his sketches to Rauch for criticism, and expresses the greatest gratitude for his advice, which he says he shall certainly follow ; unfortunately Rauch's share in the correspondence is lost.

Count Ingenheim was also a very important helper : he would often make a purchase with his own means, and trust to the king's taking the picture for the museum. Casts of many of the finest antique statues were thus procured, besides bronzes and collections of Etruscan remains. Ingenheim kept watch of all the excavations in Rome, partly to secure a quantity of seemingly worthless old fragments of weather-stained marble, which Rauch could use in his restorations. Wilhelm von Humboldt speaks with the highest praise of the restorations planned by Rauch, and during his absence carried on by Tieck. "I think I can say with perfect truth that they are models worthy of imitation, and that no other museum rejoices in such perfectly arranged, such carefully thought out, and beautifully executed restorations as these."

Rauch profited by his journey to Italy to obtain casts for increasing the collections in the museum. He sent to Berlin whatever casts he could get of Thorwaldsen's works. The minister, Altenstein, commissioned him to obtain at once casts of the Amazon of the Capitol, "A Daughter of Niobe," and the group of "Menelaus and Patroclus" in Florence, and also to inquire with regard to the cost of copies of the Ghiberti gates in the Baptistery at Florence. These last proved too costly to purchase.

A controversy now arose in regard to the comparative importance of art and science in the museum, and it was complained that much more money was spent for pictures and statues than for objects of scientific and archæological interest. Rauch, of course, took the artistic side very warmly, and Dr. Eggers allows that even his judgment was a little warped by strong personal feeling. He was anxious that his friend Ruscheweyh should be employed to engrave the treasures of the museum ; but he finds little co-operation from his colleagues. Later, when he thinks he has secured the consent of the commission, the death of the engraver puts an end to the plan. His greatest satisfaction is in the work of Wolff, who continues to send him word of whatever can be procured of value. In 1832 casts of the Arch of Constantine were sent to Berlin. Only a few original works of sculpture were bought at this time. The policy of purchasing casts of the best works every year has been steadily pursued, and now it is said that Berlin has the most complete collection of this nature in existence. It is of immense value to students, who have the masterpieces of different epochs and different schools, side by side, for comparison.

A little anecdote related to me by the son of Rauch's old friend, Chevalier von Bunsen, will give us a parting glimpse of the master in the enjoyment of the works of art that he had toiled so many years to collect. "I had not long been entered on the books of the Berlin University, in 1843," he writes, "when Rauch, an old friend of my father's, accosted the shy lad one evening at the house of an acquaintance. 'Have you seen any sights ?' he asked. 'Only the Museum of Antiquities,' was the answer. 'And what did you like best there ?' — 'I could look at nothing after the head of Julius Cæsar.' — 'Well,' he said, placing his mighty hand on my shoulder, 'let me tell you that I cannot live without it.   In my house there are three casts of it.' "

From the middle of January, 1819, Rauch's letters are full of jubilee over the final completion of the Lager-haus.   He is delighted with the arrangements, which he minutely describes.   "How fine the workshops are!   A foundation for a museum could not be nobler and more fitting.   There is an ornamental window case ; what splen-dor!"   It is his constant joy to watch the progress of the work ; and he calls all his friends to come and rejoice with him.   He wants Tieck ; but Tieck, formerly so impatient to come, now is not ready.   Rauch constantly urges him, and writes him every detail of preparation, and what to bring him : as fine paper from Florence, sponges for modelling, a cask of pumice-stone, etc.   He goes into the cost of sugar, coffee, meat, butter, but breaks off, saying, "What would people say if such an unartistic letter fell into other hands ?   But, after all, are we not striving for the general good of art, to place a god in his chariot and Blücher on his granite pedestal ; to say nothing of heroes, emperors, etc ?"   And then he con-siders the important political question whether Wilhelm von Humboldt will accept the call to the ministry of state.

Rauch was almost wild with impatience for Tieck's arrival.   Everything was ready ; even the troublesome disputes with the former occupants of the Lagerhaus (for an execution had to be served on the princesses to get them out) were settled, and he could, in a certain sense, now call the house his own.   Tieck's rooms were all ready, and even the watch-guard, which he had asked Agnes to work for him, lay on his table.   Franceschino is full of impatience to greet his father in the new Eng-lish coat which the master has given him for his faithful service.

Tieck writes that he has not the money for the journey,

and Rauch sends him an order on Leghorn; but Tieck has already started before this letter arrives, and on the twenty-seventh of April Rauch goes to Potsdam to meet him. Franceschino went also, embraced his father, and welcomed the Lazzarini, father and son, and Ceccardo. The last of July the moulder, Domenico Bianconi, was added to the company which formed the working force of the atelier.

All went busily to work. Rauch built up Bülow and Scharnhorst, and modelled on the reliefs, while Tieck took direction of the work for the theatre. The workmen, being well paid, were delighted with the change, and did wonders. In June Rauch could show the king the design for the Bülow statue.

Thus was Rauch's desire fulfilled, and he was established as the centre of the school of sculpture, which continued forty years under the direction of its founder, and brought forth the many noble works that have adorned his country, and given lustre to his name.

CHAPTER VII

RAUCH AND GOETHE

1797–1832

ONE of the most interesting circumstances of Rauch's artistic career is his relation to one "by whose spirit no one in this century has remained uninfluenced." Fortunately we have full record of this friendship.

The bust of Goethe, which Rauch began to model in 1820, when Goethe was seventy years old, led to a constantly increasing intimacy between the sculptor, then forty-three years old, and rapidly developing his powers, and the great leader in all national literature and art.

One of the earliest works of art that ever drew the attention of the boy sculptor was a bust of Goethe, by Trippels, in the castle at Arolsen; 'and he listened with eagerness in the atelier of Ruhl to all he could tell him of the man whom this masterpiece represented. And almost the last artistic thought of the dying sculptor was that he might yet improve his work, and finish the model for the group of the great poets Goethe and Schiller.

When at twenty years of age Rauch waited in the antechamber of Queen Louise, he had already in his evening studies taken for his guide into the region of art Goethe's Propylean, "where head and heart both entered into their rights." Later, the "second part of Faust took possession of his soul," and Schinkel was to him "the dearest interpreter of this wonderful poem." His diary gives frequent evidence of his interest in the poet, whom he often names, and at last he says his "understanding has increased through the circumstance that he has made Goethe's personal acquaintance, and has experienced the immediate influence of his speaking presence." He said to Lewes that "Goethe's talk on art had roused an enthusiasm which influenced his whole life." Already intimate with Schadow and Tieck, Goethe wished to come into relation with this artistic power, to give to, and receive from him.

Frau von Humboldt had written to him in 1812, speaking in high praise of the statue of the queen. The first meeting proposed on Rauch's return from Italy fell through on account of Goethe's absence in Carlsbad, and so in the summer of 1820 occurred the first personal introduction in Jena. On the twenty-fourth of September Rauch sent the first cast of the bust of Goethe, begun in Jena, to an academic exhibition. In October the crown prince received a cast for his birthday ; two were sent to Goethe, and one to Stein in Breslau. Stein writes of it thus : "One first rightly sees that a whole world lies in his eyes, when one has him quiet before him in a bust, and is not distracted by what he is saying, and there is not the space of an eyelash in the face wherein there is not character and likeness." The bust was sent to his old friend in Copenhagen, Frederika Brunn. She stood with Lund a half-hour before it, and exclaimed, "My God, it seems at last to breathe!" The bust was everywhere recognized and praised. This success led Goethe's friends to consider the idea of enlisting Rauch's co-operation in carrying out the plan of a monument in Frankfort, already suggested.

On Goethe's seventy-first birthday, 1819, Thorwaldsen took part in the festival at Frankfort. The inspiring hour gave to Sulpice Boisserée the idea of having a statue of the honored poet in his birthplace. Thorwaldsen agreed to it later, and a Denkmal Verein was formed. Boisserée, Staatsrath von Bethmann, and Herr Brentano, with others,

were on the committee, and to them was given the carrying out of the project.   It was planned to erect a temple
of marble and bronze in some beautiful spot in the neighborhood of Frankfort, and to have a statue by Dannecker.
The inner wall, lighted from above, should have a frieze
ornamented with subjects from Herrmann and Dorothea.

Thorwaldsen approved the plan in general, but suggested that the subjects should be more varied, and
drawn from other poems of Goethe.   Boisserée gives
the commission to Dannecker, and begs Goethe to allow
the necessary sittings.   Goethe consents to this, but
adds, "It is truly a serious matter to send a sculptor
where he no longer finds forms, where nature on her
retreat burdens herself with the necessary only."   He
therefore proposes a face mask taken by Gall six years
before as the foundation of the bust.   The committee,
however, insist on a new one ; but for a year no meeting
of the poet and sculptor can take place, on account of the
illness of Dannecker's wife.   This is a serious interruption, for Goethe thinks "the woodcock of life is whirring
by, and must be hit with a quick shot," and, speaking
under correction, he proposes Rauch as the maker of the
bust.   Dannecker has made the same proposal, on account
of the hindrance to his own work.   Scarcely four weeks
later the meeting between Goethe and Rauch took place,
among whose results was the bust.   Goethe declared the
handling of the bust "truly grandiose."

Much discussion took place about the proper position
for the monument, as the site first suggested was found
to be very costly.   Goethe proposed uniting the monument with the library, but others were unwilling to give
up the idea of its being an ornament to the city.

In the summer of 1821 the official commission was first
porposed to Rauch through Boisserée, who wished to know
the cost of a marble bust, and eventually of a marble
statue.

Rauch was not pleased with the plan. He wrote to Frau von Humboldt, "A colossal bust in a temple with closed doors, standing in an open space, does not please me. The façade of the house where Goethe was born, with a statue of him, would make a fitter monument. The confectionery temples on the islands and promenades are a horror to me; but I think the gentlemen will come to sounder thoughts, by which much expense will be saved." He replies to the committee, however, that a likeness of Goethe of the size of the Dannecker bust of Schiller, on an 8×9 foot-support, corresponding to the proposed plan, to be represented after the Greek manner as an undraped Hermes, or after the Roman manner, having the breast covered with folds, with a pedestal, would cost from about nine hundred to a thousand thalers. A standing or sitting figure, 3×4 inches over life-size, would cost thirty-eight hundred to four thousand thalers.

He did not conceal his opinion of the plan from Boisserée. A lively discussion of differing views followed, but at last, after eight months, a compromise was effected. Boisserée gave Rauch a commission for a statue, and asked for sketches for a standing or a sitting figure which, if not in a separate building, might be placed in an open, well-lighted room in some large public building.

Earnest discussion as to the costume then began. Rauch wished it to be either fully classical or entirely modern, while others thought the one too strange for the well-known poet, and the other too familiar for a stately monument. A mixture of Greek robes with necktie and boots seemed to be demanded. Rauch wanted a classically draped statue in the open air, Boisserée one in boots in a room. Achim von Arnim left no stone unturned to connect the statue with the library, as Rauch himself had once suggested. Then the local press took up the question. Rauch communicated to the papers his idea of uniting a building for the Stadel Museum with the library.

But there was dispute not only over the place, but over the statue itself. Bettina von Arnim had designed a group representing in antique costume the poet, whose lyre Psyche is tuning.

Bettina's design was a very fanciful and pleasing expression of her own sentiment; but as she herself expresses it, " I was thought capable of forming the idea, though at that time I had never interfered with the arts." But this "glorified production of her love" could not, of course, satisfy the thoroughly artistic demands of Rauch. Bettina mistook inspiration for creation. She had the fancy, but not the forming power of an artist. No opinion of her design was directly asked of Rauch, although it was hoped that he would give one; but although he preferred to keep silence in public regarding it, he expressed his views very frankly to Professor Ritter, in a letter which I am obliged to translate somewhat freely, as we have only a rough sketch of it.

RAUCH TO RITTER.

To Professor Herr Ritter in Berlin, — I have the honor to reply to the question of Herr von Bethmann of the seventeenth of January, sent to me by your excellency.

I have seen with pleasure the drawing of Frau Bettina von Arnim, representing Goethe grouped in a sitting attitude, with a naked young female figure, and lyre, and also later the small model wrought in clay after this drawing, by the help of the sculptor Wichmann.

The idyllish representation of Goethe on the Gothic seat richly ornamented with pictures, with the laurel crown in the right hand, and in the left the lyre, and the other accessories, may succeed in a picture or relief, as Michael Angelo has successfully shown in the Sistine Chapel,[1] keeping the principal subject uninjured, while making clear the desired image of the poet; but as a personal (*iconische*) statue, which should immortalize the characteristic personality of the one to be represented, it is thoroughly impossible; that should be done in a work of sculpture with the greatest possible simplicity of truth and breadth, as the Greek, the Roman, and even newer works, sufficiently teach us.

If a similar thought had been given to me in words or writing as the subject of this monument, I should not have hesitated a moment to carry it out according to my own arrangement. But I cannot undertake it after the

---

[1] This refers to the Daniel in the Sistine Chapel.

sketch of Frau von Arnim and Herr von Wichmann, since, as a round work of sculpture, the lines and forms are neither practicable nor beautiful, and its execution in marble would involve the greatest obstacles, which could only be overcome with great effort and skill, of which the sculptor would have the trouble and the designer the praise.

The execution in marble of the above-named model in full size may probably cost two thousand thalers more than than of a statue without such accompaniments. Other grounds against the taking of this design, even as weighty, I would wish to impart to you by word of mouth.

FEB. 10, 1825.

Rauch's zeal was not cooled by all this difficulty. He sent an estimate of five hundred and ten thalers, and made out an inventory of the sitting figures of antiquity from the bronzes and pictures of Herculaneum, the museum Pio Clementino, etc., and began his work. He sends his sketch first not to Frankfort, but to Weimar. Goethe prefers a standing figure. "The sitting figure," he says, "if not managed with great taste, has something heavy, but it is easy to know where to put a standing figure ; every niche-like recess in the wall is a suitable place." He also decidedly preferred the antique costume, and objected to the Psyche group as not at all suited to the round. In a small relief it might be a pretty idea. Rauch made new sketches to suit Goethe's ideas, and declared himself ready to go to Weimar, whither he accordingly went with his daughter Agnes, June 18, 1824. He was warmly welcomed by the Goethe family. He finds Goethe very little changed, full of life and health, wonderfully upright in person, his eyes full of life, and the color of his face of almost youthful bloom, so that he feels ashamed of his bust, that looks older than nature. The days were passed in delightful artistic discussions. The plans for the museum met Goethe's full approval, and the object of the journey, the Goethe statue, was not forgotten. Rauch measured Goethe's height, which was six feet, one and two-thirds inches, or one hundred and seventy-four centimetres.

The Frankfort people became impatient of delay, and

were anxious to have the statue for the celebration of Goethe's fifty years of service. The models are at last sent, and subjected to criticism. Dannecker praises them freely, and Boisserée says, " You have not only represented Goethe's traits with the greatest truth, but you have known how to breathe his spirit into the work, and there is no doubt that the statue executed after this bust will be a thoroughly worthy monument." He then makes some minute criticisms of the limbs, and the want of freedom in the sitting position. He suggests that the sandals should be exchanged for shoes, as approaching modern costume more nearly, but supposes that the bareness of the arm may demand a corresponding nakedness of the foot.

Bethmann now takes the matter into his own hands, and, having received from Rauch the contract for the price according to his sketches, he says, " To-day Goethe's fifty years of service are celebrated in Weimar. I believe the day cannot be better honored than by signing this contract." Nov. 7, 1825.

Rauch announces to Goethe that one of his dearest wishes is fulfilled, and that "with living interest he will go to hard work." Goethe responds in a very warm letter, expressing his delight that what he has wished and longed for is to take bodily shape. But a year later Bethmann died, and Boisserée took up the work with fresh interest, urging Rauch to its completion.

Rauch answers him, April, 1827, that the great model of the statue will be begun this spring, "at which, after so many '*herren Stadtholders*' '*en pantalon*,'" he says, "I am much delighted. I hope that my longing after nude arms and legs, at least after a costume that does not arbitrarily conceal the form, will be justified." Goethe also speaks of Bethmann's loss as a death-blow, but hopes that he himself may live to see the completion of this monument of Rauch's art and personal regard.

Yet this is the last that we hear of it for ten years.

Bethmann's heirs do nothing towards carrying out the commission, and Rauch had no disposition to touch the statue while it remained uncertain whether, according to his wish and Goethe's, it would ever be a public monument.

While this matter of the Frankfort monument was under consideration, a lively correspondence was kept up between Goethe and Rauch, who seemed to draw nearer together in affection as well as in interest in art. The artist Meyer acted as Goethe's pen. Rauch sent drawings and models of various sorts for Louise Seidler, the instructress in drawing of the young princesses; and Goethe often sent Rauch little poems, among them one on the unveiling of the Blücher statue in Rostock, 1819.

The next principal subject of consideration was a medal for the jubilee of the Grand Duke of Weimar. Rauch had taken a great interest in the stamping of coins by Brandt, and had especially admired a head of the king, with an eagle on the reverse. "We believe that even on Greek and Roman coins no finer image of an eagle is to be found." He hoped "that the royal Prussian coins in future would be distinguished as works of art among those of other cultivated nations, and that posterity would have through them a proof of the continued efforts and art-industry of their ancestors, as is the case with us in regard to Greek and Roman coins." Goethe was also much interested in this art, and, naturally, especially so in regard to the medal of the grand duke. He ordered a sketch of full size, the medallion having for the face the likeness of the prince in a wreath, and for the reverse a suitable symbolic figure. He wished Rauch to consult over the design with Tieck, as "the artist formerly connected with Wiemar," and with Brandt on the work of the cutting and the cost.

Three proofs of the medal were sent in May. The face with the likeness of the duke gave satisfaction, but for the reverse Goethe proposed the zodiac, so placed that the scales should be uppermost, as a symbol of the jubilee month of September, with the inscription : —

DER FUNFZIGSTEN WIEDERKEHR. MDCCCXXV.

From Berlin came some proposals of change; and discussions ensued as to the color of the bronze. The medal gave much satisfaction, and Rauch, Tieck, and Brandt each received a copy in silver and in bronze.

At this time Goethe sent to Rauch a letter introducing to him "Demoiselle Facius, daughter of a medal and stone cutter of this place, who has inherited a love of, and a capacity for, art from her father, and who is going with Herr Posch to Berlin, in that world of art to become aware of what is demanded of the artist, and to what she should educate herself." In April Rauch wrote that the young artist came to the atelier to work on medals. The correspondence on both sides shows great interest in the young woman's work. Goethe is delighted with some busts sent to him, "which plainly show that she has the good fortune to possess a rich art element, and to be enlightened and helped by the master's inspiring sunbeams." The young girl did credit to the interest they took in her, showing herself not unskilful, both in busts and bass-reliefs. In expressing to Rauch his satisfaction with the medal of the grand duke, Goethe had said that he hoped they might work together again; and a welcome opportunity soon came.

Ten weeks later the grand duke called Rauch to Weimar to arrange a fifty years' jubilee for Goethe. He proposed to have a medallion, whose front should bear Goethe's profile after Rauch's bust, and its reverse a flying eagle bearing a laurel crown. This plan was changed, however, and the medal was to bear on the reverse the united profile heads of the grand ducal pair. The work was committed to Brandt. But neither was the medal ready at the appointed time, nor was the work satisfactory ; and Rauch begs further time for the engraver, that important changes may be made, so that the work shall be equally good with that of the grand duke's medal. Goethe cordially consented to the delay, and the supervision of the whole work was given to Rauch. The medal, as finally executed in 1826, shows Goethe's head with laurel wreath and toga, and the inscription : —

KARL AUGUST UND LUISE. — GOETHEN ZUM VII. NOVEMBER MDCCCXXV.

On the other side are the profile heads of the duke and duchess draped with the toga.

Goethe wrote to Rauch a most cordial letter of thanks, recognizing Brandt's patient and faithful work, and rejoicing in his success after so many trials. He concludes: "May the reflection and conviction for which, in the course of this year, he has had opportunity, work right powerfully for good in his future career." Goethe expressed much pleasure in this recognition by his friends, although he had said that a more fitting memorial was the proposed edition of his works by Cotta, "which, from my own material, endeavors to raise for me an enduring monument."

About this time Rauch suffered severely from sympathy with his beloved daughter Agnes, who had formed a marriage engagement which proved most unfortunate, and was finally broken. We have not his own words regarding this matter, but we catch the echo of them in this beautiful letter of Goethe's, which shows such frankness of affection, and tenderness of sympathy, as make it the best memorial of this noble friendship.

GOETHE TO RAUCH.

"That you, dear, honored man, in the moment of a heavy grief turn your thoughts to me, confer with me, and feel some alleviation of your sorrow, gives me the grateful certainty of an inward, sincere, good feeling, of a tender, cordial relation such as I have ever felt towards you.

" You thus show that you are sure of my truest sympathy, of a real participation in that trouble which violates, in its worthiest activity, a relation rich in spiritual forces, a beautiful, noble exercise of the happiest talent, and injures it in its very depths. So to me, with the deepest sympathy in your grief, it is yet some comfort to answer you at once. Even so to me, during a long life, events have come which, out of seemingly bright conditions, have unfolded a train of misfortunes; and there are fearful moments in which one might hold a short life as the greatest blessing, that one need not bear an insupportable sorrow for an immeasurably long time. Many sufferers have gone before me, but on me was the duty laid to continue, and to bear a succession of joy and pain of which any single instance might well have been fatal.

" In such cases nothing remains but to call up once more, in the most earnest way, the activity that still remains possible, and, like one engaged in a deadly warfare, to continue the struggle as vigorously when it goes against us as when all is in our favor.

" And so have I fought my way through, even to the present day, when to the highest fortune which might ever raise a man above himself, so much that moderates it is added, that it admonishes and obliges me from hour to hour to be true to myself, and for myself, in order to remain indifferent to that which one is justified in calling 'tricks of fate.' If I knew how to find no other means, yet it must certainly be wholesome for every one, who by his nature is fitted for noble creative activity, to set aside the repulsive sense of unforeseen hindrance, and, in so far as it is given to men, aspire to reinstate himself.

" The foregoing thoughts, flowing out of my own experience, may show that, in connection with the sad event that has happened to you, the memory of earlier sorrow has become living in my soul, and that at the same time my spirit has called up all that has been helpful to me. While it cannot heal, may this heartfelt sympathy have power, at least for the moment, to soothe your pain !

" With return of all most friendly and sincere greetings.

" Let me soon speak to you of artists and works of art, of. masters, apprentices, and scholars, and in many questions, wishes, and hopes express my sympathy.

Most truly,

J. W. VON GOETHE.

WEIMAR, the twenty-first of October, 1827.

Rauch answered this affectionate letter a fortnight later, and his answer is again full of artistic themes. He says, " I may truly say that the only true satisfaction that yet remains to me is to quicken my life by plastic art." This correspondence was soon interrupted by a visit to Weimar in June. Rauch left Berlin to take Agnes away from the Pyrmont Cure, and to have a brief vacation for himself. He found his daughter restored to blooming health, and enjoyed eight days in visits to old friends and relations. At the old town of Soest, which he found very beautiful, he was much interested in the oldest church, the Wiesenkirke, where, among some twenty-four mostly worthless statues in stone and wood, he found those of Mary, of John, and of a bishop on the side entrance, of extraordinary beauty. They went on to Cologne, visiting churches and museums, to Wiesbaden, Mainz, Frankfort, etc., and thence to Weimar, where they spent two days with Goethe, whose kindness and attention were those of a father. Rauch stayed with the prince, but most of the time was spent at Goethe's house, the evenings in the society of his choicest friends, the mornings in working on a small statue of Goethe in his dressing-gown. This is the well-known statue of which Reimer said, " It is the old master in his gown, just as he walks and stands ;" and the same of which Thackeray spoke, when Goethe received him in 1830, " He held his hand on his back just as Rauch represented him." When Goethe was yet a young man he noted in his diary, "I can do nothing sitting. Good things always come to me while walking." This trait led to his habit of dictation. This likeness was for a statuette, not intended for a public place, and Rauch made no question of the propriety of a modern costume for this purpose.

In 1837, after Thorwaldsen had finished his statues of Schiller and Gutenberg, the Frankfort Union again recurred to the idea of a sitting statue of Goethe by Rauch. The old disputes arose again, some wishing that the statuette in the dressing-gown should be enlarged, and others going back to the Von Arnim design. It is said that Goethe himself liked none of the plans but the statuette, and he thought even that too stout. Rauch had been to Weimar at his pressing invitation, to make some change in it. Rietschel was with him, and worked on the back of the statue while Rauch worked on the front, " and the old master stood between us, and told us charming stories, or showed us engravings." They stayed through the noonings and evenings with Goethe, who, like a happy grandfather, took Rauch repeatedly to the cradle of Alma, his youngest grandchild, to see the lovely child asleep, "a sight truly worthy of rapture." This was Rauch's last visit to Goethe, and even their correspondence was interrupted for a while, as Rauch was busy with work and travel. At last he wrote to Goethe, and received from him a letter full of the warmest expressions of affection, and of commendation of the young woman artist whom he had recommended to his care. He makes many interesting inquiries about art, and speaks of his earnest desire for an institute of plastic anatomy at Berlin. He says, " I find myself, almost for the first time, a propagandist. I want to see my plans carried out. It appears to me old age is impatient where youth is slow." This was his last letter, written only four weeks before his death.

Twelve years later "the beautiful child in the cradle" came to Rauch's atelier, "a darling, blooming, beautiful maiden." She left for Vienna. Eight weeks passed, and the diary records the painful intelligence of the death of the beautiful girl by typhus-fever. So ended the personal relations of Rauch with Goethe and his family. Of all the statuesque designs by which the sculptor sought to give to posterity a worthy statue of Goethe, none came to monumental execution.

After the Frankfort Union had discussed and rejected many plans, the Goethe statue was finally erected by Schwanthaler.

After Goethe's death an International Monumental Committee was formed to erect a double monument to Goethe and Schiller. Rauch went to Weimar to consider the best position in which to place it. The plan was not, however, carried further for ten years, when the then Grand Duke of Weimar commissioned Rauch for the model of the two great poets. But the old disputes about costume arose. Rauch was quite unwilling to represent the two poets except in classic drapery. His model in this style may now be seen in plaster in the Rauch Museum. It was very highly praised; but money for the execution flowed in but sparingly, and the whole matter was delayed until the art-loving King of Bavaria took hold of it. He desired, however, that the statue should be cast at his own foundery at Munich, and that it should be in modern costume. Rauch objected to both these conditions. He was not willing to have his work taken away from the foundery he had taken so much pains to establish, and he could not accept the modern costume for a public monument. He wrote to the king, regretting that he could not comply with his wishes; but he said, "An artist's embodied ideals are a part of his life."

Attempts at reconciliation on these points met with no success, and Rauch definitely refused the commission, and recommended that it should be given to Rietschel. He took a warm interest in this work of his friend, and predicted its well-deserved success. This beautiful group of Rietschel's, in which the costume of the day is treated with such refinement and poetic beauty, and the model by Rauch, now in the museum at Berlin, in which the classic drapery is modelled with great breadth and simplicity, afford the student an admirable comparative study of the two methods of representation.

The influence of Goethe and Rauch was mutually beneficial. Rauch was, indeed, mainly the recipient, since his artistic life began when Goethe was in the perfection of his powers, and he drank in the teachings of Goethe as the flowers the rain. Goethe's devotion to classic culture gave inspiration to the young sculptor's thought and works. The true relation of the ideal and the real was with both the great problem of art ; and to Goethe, the embodiment of his theories in plastic art, through the hand of a younger artist, with whom he was in close and affectionate relations, was a joy such as seldom comes to old age ; and the order and self-poise and thorough love of perfection which distinguished Rauch, were qualities which the poet dearly prized. Not crushed by his grief, but animated by the ever-living thought of his friend, Rauch went on his way to carry out the principles of art, in which they both so firmly believed.

CHAPTER VIII

HISTORIC MONUMENTS.—POLISH PRINCES.—ALBERT DÜRER

1815-1840

THE heroes of the War of Freedom for Germany were
fortunate in having artists to build their monuments who
were penetrated with the spirit of that struggle, and
capable of preserving for us their personal characteristics,
as well as the general feeling of the time.

Rauch was well fitted to bear his part in this work; for
while he never forgot ideal truth, he had a great respect
for historic accuracy. We might claim his statue of Queen
Louise as the beginning of this historic cycle ; for she was
indeed its inspiration, though she did not live to witness
its triumph. It will be impossible for me to follow minutely the progress of these great works in which he was
engaged so many years. The most important ones in
relation to his own development and the progress of sculpture in Germany, are the statues of Bülow and of Scharnhorst, the two Blücher statues for Breslau and Berlin, and
the genii for the monument on the Kreuzberg, just out of
the city of Berlin. The statues of York and Gneisenau
belong to a later period.

When Rauch designed the candelabra for La Vendée,
he wished to make a grand monument for celebrating the
war, having a statue of the king, and two immense candelabra with allegoric figures. The king objected to that
plan ; but he now conceived the idea of a grand monument
on the hill overlooking the city, of which Schinkel should

make the design, while Rauch should contribute to its decoration.

There was a time when no stranger left Berlin without visiting the monument on the Kreuzberg, either from motives of patriotism, love of art, or the desire to enjoy the beautiful view from the summit of the hill. But even in 1844 Waagen complained "that this monument was not so much seen as its subject and its artistic worth deserved." The distance of the monument from the city, and the miserable sandy road that led to it, combined with the increasing number of attractive objects within the city, produced this neglect. But in our day, since the railroad has been extended to bring distant places near, the Kreuzberg is again within easy reach of Berlin, and the hill is being made into a public park. A basement twenty-six feet high has also been added to the monument, which will make it more conspicuous from afar, so that it may now attract its due share of public attention.

Schinkel's work forms an obelisk nineteen metres high, on the ground-plan of an equal-armed cross. In each arm of the cross are three niches, and in each of these niches a statue of one of the most important battles of the War of Freedom.

One of the most interesting points in this work was the employment of the allegoric genius to express the spirit of the persons or events to be commemorated. This conception of the ancient world, which had almost given place to the Christian angel, had been lately revived. It was variously represented; sometimes as a figure in a toga, with suggestive attributes; sometimes as a naked boy, with only a pair of wings. Rauch designed for the monument the "Genius of Dennewitz," in the costume of a young soldier, holding a sword and laurel wreath. To indicate the most decisive victory, the head of the Genius of the Leipzig battle is surrounded by a starry crown; he is clothed in old Greek armor, and rests

the left hand on a large shield, while the right points to
the three eagles representing the allies. In contrast to this
is the "Genius of Wartenburg." "To indicate the rash
and bold passage of the river," this genius steps on to a
boat, belonging to a bridge, whilst he swings a standard
with a Prussian eagle. "The Genius of La Rothière," to
which Blücher's features are given, is yet more in action.
He is "in Northern armor, stepping quickly forward, with
a laurel crown in the left hand, while the right is raised
to express his decided character, and the victory of Prussian intelligence." In his models for the female genii he
has indicated his own sympathetic feelings by giving to
the one (Paris) the features of the beloved Queen Louise,
and to the other (Waterloo) those of the Empress Alex-
andra Feodorowna. The king urged on the completion
of the monument; but it was impossible to have all the
statues ready as early as he wished, and finally it was unveiled on the thirty-first of March, 1821, Nicholas of Russia taking part in the programme; and the hall was
thereafter called the Kreuzberg.

As soon as these modern statues were proposed, the
question of costume became important, and Rauch gave
much attention to it. Until within a short time the antique drapery had been universally used as alone appropriate to heroic subjects, but Schadow had already treated
them with bold naturalism. Rauch sought to unite the
characteristic costume of the time with the ideal beauty
which his æsthetically trained sense demanded. He substituted the modern cloak for the ancient toga, but instead of trying to use it in precisely the old manner, he
endeavored to give the character of the cloak, and yet develop its artistic peculiarities. This is the true method
of art. Both generals are represented in their uniforms,
as their contemporaries saw them. Their cloaks are
thrown about their shoulders, but neither in a strange,
theatrical manner, nor in a silly, prosaic one, but with an

unconscious, ideal fitness, as will happen to men in some exalted moment of their lives. The forms thus enveloped are in accordance with the laws of beauty as exemplified in Greek art, and the general impression of heroic military character is united to the personality of the individual warrior. The monuments of Bülow and Scharnhorst gave ample field for such considerations. That of Scharnhorst represents the contemplation of an heroic deed ; the general thoughtfully leaning on an oaken staff, wrapped in his own thoughts, his left side quite concealed by the cloak. Bülow's monument presents the deed itself ; he stands brave and confident, holding back his cloak with his right arm, his left supported on his sword, and gazing fixedly at the struggle he is directing.

Rauch had very poor material to work from, merely death-masks and slight sketches, and the descriptions of those who had seen the generals. The reliefs on the monuments, in strict classic style, help to carry out the idea. On Scharnhorst's is the armed Minerva, instructing in the science of war. On Bülow's is the first representation of the Victory, in which Rauch afterwards achieved such brilliant success ; while the Prussian eagle on both expresses the patriotic cause to which they were devoted. The eagle is at rest, but his wings are widespread, as if prepared for action, while the body, turned to the left, with the head inclined to the right, indicates constant watchfulness. He is also the bearer of the tablet, on which is simply inscribed : —

FRIEDRICH WILHELM III.

DEM

GEN. von SCHARNHORST.

im JAHRE, 1822.

On Bülow's : —

FRIEDRICH WILHELM III.

DEM GEN. GRAFEN BULOW,

VON DENNEWITZ

im JAHRE, 1822.

Appropriate inscriptions of the victories won by the general in his conquering march through the Netherlands are placed on the Scharnhorst monument. Rauch never undertook an historical work without making himself as familiar as possible with all the biography of his hero, and the localities and circumstances of his deeds; and he studied even the lions from life. The architectural part of the support was designed by Schinkel.

Rauch was handsomely paid for this work, but he enjoyed much more the recognition as an artist which he received from the king. "Day before yesterday," he writes to Frau von Humboldt, July 22, 1822, " I received at noon, with a very gracious cabinet writing from the king, the decoration of the Red Eagle Order, III. Class. I used to know how to deal with eagles, but this little '*musje*' takes me aback, and makes me grow red and hot."

While still engaged on the Blücher statue at Breslau, Rauch was commissioned by the king to make a monument to Blücher for Berlin. He began to make sketches for it in August, 1819. His first sketch represented the hero in full action, his foot resting on a howitzer. His costume is more strictly realistic than in the Breslau statue, yet it is not a historic incident, but a *résumé* of his whole military career that the sculptor gives us. Stein wished him to exhibit his sketches publicly, and let the people express their preference in regard to them; but Rauch appears to have followed his own thought, which was of quiet determination of purpose, rather than action; and he kept pretty closely to his first sketch.

In February, 1824, he had completed a model in plaster, and in November the bronze casting was finished. One of the first persons to see the completed statue after the king was the Duke of Wellington, who visited the atelier February 19, 1826. Rauch describes the visit, saying, " In lively, short, and decided phrases of rather faulty French, the duke expressed his pleasure, and the king sent him a small copy of the bronze statue." On the eighteenth of June the statue was relieved from its casings, and on the anniversary of the battle of Waterloo the monument was given to the city. When Rauch went to see it at five o'clock in the morning, he found many persons gathered about it. Among them was Blücher's old comrade, Gneisenau, who wished Rauch joy, with eyes full of tears and a trembling voice, while he recalled the old heroic times with his general, and the glorious deeds which now, mirrored in bronze, shone in the light of the morning sun. But Rauch was too much preoccupied to feel the full meaning of the scene. The first sight in the public square of the statue on which he had worked four years with the greatest care was a terrible shock to him. From the castle-bridge even to the watch-house his first impression was of mistrust, even terror. "Too long, too broad, was my first thought; the statue stiff and clumsy." He thought he had gained nothing of the effect for which he had been striving for years. And as he continued his walk to the end of the university building, and turned back, he was only partially calmed down by the view on that side. "The first thing," he says, "that encouraged me to reconciling reflections was a comparison with the Bülow monument which, in comparison with that of Blücher, looked to me like an over-big disproportioned wooden chest." Dr. Eggers explains this feeling of the artist as a physiological effect of his high-wrought expectations, and the difficulty of seeing as a whole what he had wrought upon so earnestly in parts. Three weeks later he wrote to Schinkel, then in London, "The people seemed pleased with the monument, only the sheath of his sword is wanting; and the pedestal, seen from afar, is not broad enough, but it fills its place."

This incident gives a valuable lesson to young artists, who often feel bitter disappointment when they first look upon the results of long and faithful work. The more intensely they have labored, the more likely is this reaction to come. Rauch was always eager for improvement, but he was by no means a morbid detractor of his own work; yet he was utterly unfit to judge of this statue at first sight. Always appeal from an excited brain to a calm one !

Rauch has been censured for incongruity in making the bass-reliefs on the pedestal, representing the events of the war, in a realistic style not corresponding to the character of the statue; but Dr. Eggers maintains that, at the distance at which the whole monument must be seen to get its full architectural effect, the details are lost, and the sculptures only enrich the general appearance; while if the spectator is near enough to study the details of the bass-reliefs he cannot see the proportions of the statue, and therefore the one does not interfere with the other. These reliefs are extremely varied in character, and represent many different scenes. One of the original sketches represents Blücher as triumphing over his enemies in the person of Bonaparte ; and Rauch defends this design against the criticism of the Pole, Anton Waga, saying, " Blücher contended against Napoleon rather than the French people, and, as Bonaparte is now dethroned and imprisoned at St. Helena, they cannot take it unkindly that he is thus represented." He says that " Anton Waga does not seem to remember that on the column of Victory in the Place Vendome, a bass-relief represents Bonaparte, at whose feet the Emperor Francis kneels and sues for peace (after the battle of Austerlitz). Both are likenesses. This monument remained standing when the daughter of the emperor was the wife of Bonaparte, and while the allied armies twice entered Paris victorious, and yet stands to-day, though the Emperor Francis is still ruler of Austria." This is one of the few instances where Rauch expresses bitterness towards the French ; he usually treats them as fellow-artists, and does full justice to their work.

The reliefs on the lower part of the monument represent scenes in the life of the people during the war, — the young volunteers leaving their homes, and soldiers taking the oath of fidelity to the flag. The men are parting with their friends, while a shepherd boy looks on with astonishment. The army goes on its way watched by the curious boys, and refreshed with water drawn by the peasant maidens from the fountains. Scenes of triumph and of death appear. The army goes into the rich vineyards of France. Dragoons are cooking their food, resting in slumber, or chatting with the market-women. Finally the army passes through the gate St. Martin, preceded by the bearers of banners, while the hero of the monument, Blücher, with his staff of officers, leads them on. To meet them comes, rolled on cylinders, by workmen, the regained Victory of the Brandenburg, which appears at the end of the row of statues, as representing the object of the march to Paris. These reliefs are of the greatest interest, and deserve a thorough study, in which Dr. Eggers's book would be an excellent guide. He closes his account by saying, " The historic epic of the War of Freedom, from the call of the king, on the tenth of March, 1813, to the second Peace of Paris, which, after the repeated entry of the allies into the Enemy's capital at the end of the year 1815, restored the treasures of art, is sung by Rauch in a plastic hymn of victory."

A tone of humor runs through these representations, and Rauch has introduced portraits of well-known men whose influence was felt in this popular war. Theodor Körner and Wilhelm von Humboldt are easily recognized. A cast of one of the most stirring of these scenes, " The Bivouac," was sent as a present to Goethe. Dr. Eggers says " that the frieze of the Blücher monument, with its admirable treatment in relief of modern stuffs, was a new achievement of plastic art. The casting of the whole pedestal was also a novelty in the history of the art of our times, which, until then, was accustomed to place the bronze statue on a stone basis."

Rauch's pecuniary reward was a thousand *Friedrichs d'or.* The cost of the monument was forty-eight thousand six hundred and eighty-four thalers.

Other portrait statues of importance now occupied Rauch's attention. January 25, 1826, he received a commission, by a royal cabinet order, for a statue of King Frederic William I. for the city of Gumbinnen, founded by him. The costume was to be the military uniform. The citizens had asked this favor of the king on the centennial celebration of the founding of the city.

The king had a special regard for his predecessor, Frederic William I., with whose ideas of statesmanship and economy, as well as of religious toleration, he had much sympathy. The work of the statue was much delayed by political and other causes, and it was not unveiled until 1835. It stands in the marketplace at Gumbinnen. The statuesque representation of the king is excellent. He stands in an erect attitude, corresponding to his strong character, but with an earnest, benevolent expression on his face. He is the first of the princes of Europe represented in a simple soldier's cloak, — the military costume of his time.

Indeed, the whole of this series of monuments to the heroes of Germany marks the development of popular ideas. Up to this time it was a maxim that public monuments were erected only by princes; the people had played a passive *rôle.* They were the governed classes. The seed of national feeling had been sown by the War of Freedom; yet it was not all Germany, even all Prussia, which united to erect a monument to the popular warrior. Mecklenburg was the first to place a monument in Blücher's birthplace, Rostock, and then the Silesians followed. He was theirs, because he had set forth from Breslau with a conquering army of Silesians, who first gave the cutting sharpness to the sword of "Marshal Forwards." *Dem " Feldherrn Blücher und dem Herre die Schlesien,"* was the inscription, and the cost of its erection was furnished by this province.

I am inclined to doubt whether Rauch found full satisfaction even in this noble historic work. He loved not only beauty, but quiet grace and sentiment, and was always striving after an ideal which was not represented by the captains even of a righteous war. Dr. Eggers says, "Rauch's power did not lie in violent movement approaching the dramatic, but rather in quiet greatness and unity, resembling architecture more than painting."

One of the most interesting and beautiful of Rauch's historic groups, which happily combines the ideal and the realistic in its treatment, is the monument to the two old kings of Poland at Posen, and its progress is strongly related to the modern movements in Polish history. The story of this monument dates back to the year 1816. In consequence of the arrangements of the Congress of Vienna, the Emperor Alexander gave a constitution to the so-called kingdom of Poland, which first came into effect in the year 1818 by the calling of a Polish parliament. The aristocracy and clergy of Poland appear to have been impressed with the desire to represent their political position by an outward sign, and also to indicate the union of all the separate parts of Poland. The fittest means for this end appeared to be the erection of a monument to the Polish princes, Mieczyslaw and Boleslaw.

Duke Mieczyslaw of Poland, who was obliged by force of arms to hold his land as a *fief* from the German Emperor, Otto I., went over to Christianity, and towards the end of the tenth century established the first bishopric in Posen. His son, Boleslaw the Great, redeemed the land from its dependence on the German emperor, increased it by conquests in all directions, and allowed himself to be crowned by the Pope in 1024. No better representatives, therefore, could be found to express the wish of the aristocracy and clergy for national unity and independence. After Boleslaw's death a sarcophagus was erected in the cathedral at Posen as a common monument to the two princes. This sarcophagus was entirely destroyed by fire and the overthrow of the tower, and in the year 1814 the bishop of Gorzenski proposed the restoration of the monument, offering to give the tenth part of his income for the purpose. As this was insufficient, however, a general call was made upon Poles for the erection of a national monument. In 1818, when in Carrara, Rauch received a letter from the Abbot Wolicki, asking him to prepare designs for a monument to the two kings. He refers again to the subject in 1819, but in 1820 the political difficulties in Poland seemed to render the prosecution of the plan unadvisable.

But the patriotic excitement, which found violent expression in the bloody revolution of 1830, again offered opportunity for an appeal to popular feeling; and in November, 1828, when Rauch dined with Wolicki in Berlin, he records in his diary, " First agreement for the monument in Posen." Schinkel was to be joined with Rauch in the preparation of an architectural design, which was to be on a very grand scale. But the cost of this plan was so large that it was difficult to raise sufficient money for it, and it was proposed to narrow the design to a statue to be placed in one of the chapels of the Metropolitan Church. Before the year was out, Wolicki, the zealous promoter of the scheme, died, and Prince Radziwill took it up. In order to carry out Wolicki's plan, a committee was formed; but, as Rauch had asked too high a price, they wished to intrust the carrying out of the designs to Herr Tatarkiewicz, under the direction of Thorwaldsen, as they hoped, as their countryman, he would be more saving of money. But before a decision was reached new difficulties arose. The insurrection in Russian Poland absorbed the interest of everybody, and in the year 1833 Prince Radziwill died, before he had put matters in train for the monument. In the summer of 1833 the papers and money already collected were passed into the hands of Count Eduard Raczynski, rightly considered one of the best friends of the fatherland.

As Count Raczynski made up his mind that the re-establishment of Poland was not to be expected from Napoleon I., he endeavored to arouse the national feeling through literature, by the publication of a series of old historic works. He resumed the purpose of securing a monument by Rauch, and assisted him by furnishing him with many historic details.

With the help of Wolff and Bläser, Rauch prepared the help-model, and in 1837 the great clay model begun by them was finished by himself. He writes to Rietschel that he finds great difficulties in arranging the group to his satisfaction, and wishes for his help, for he cannot seek that of others, as he does not wish to show the model to anybody sooner than to the prince, who has the best right to see it first. Rauch was not at first interested in his subject, for he was not much attracted to the romantic side of the Middle Ages. Schinkel, on the contrary, delighted in them, and it is thought that his hand is perceptible in the sketches made by Rauch for this group. But when Rauch received genuine portraits of Poles and other rich historic material from Raczynski, he began to feel himself on firm ground, and he made many changes in his design. The two princes no longer both look to the symbolic cross, but one of them shows the cross which he has planted, to the other, who is the people's representative. A crown is placed on Boleslaw's head, instead of the laurel wreath.

Rauch felt very much chagrined that he did not have the full control of the casting; but in the end all difficulties were reconciled, and he was very much pleased with the manner in which the work was done. In November, 1839, he met Rietschel at Lauchhammer (where the casting had been made). The group was almost ready, and now they made trials of putting jewels as ornaments of the coverings of the heads, the girdles, the sword and its trappings. Thus gilded and richly ornamented, the group became the shining feature in the Berlin Exhibition in 1840, and in February the placing in the cathedral at Posen was accomplished. In a richly ornamented and beautiful chapel stands this noble group, which is full of majesty and grace. The noble couple, father and son, represent the highest sentiments of devotion and patriotism; the action is simple and manly, and the costume is rich and flowing. I cannot give a better idea of its merit than by quoting the words of the celebrated critic, Franz Kugler. "All these elements," he says, "of historic truth, of character, of truth to nature, move in an element of pure, plastic beauty. In every separate form, as well as in their union as a whole, there rules a proportion, a clearness, a harmony of lines and proportions, a thorough conformity to law, with great freedom in details, — in a word, a perfection of style which can be found only when art is 'raised to its highest point.'"

Successful as this monument was, from an æsthetic point of view, the story of its financial affairs closes very sadly. The money collected from more than fifteen hundred donors was used up in arranging the luxurious chapel; and Count Raczynski himself paid for the statues. The statues were inscribed to the count as his gift. An evil-disposed member of the Landtag brought up the charge that the count had claimed an honor not due to him, as the statues were a component part of the whole monument. The Landtag, when appealed to, declared itself incompetent to judge the case. This was a hard blow to the sensitive nobleman, as he could not endure that any of his countrymen should accuse him of appropriating to himself praise which was due to others. He appealed to the king to grant the competency of the Landtag to decide in the case. This being granted, he collected the original papers to present to the Landtag, to show the way in which the business of the monument had been conducted. But the sting of this charge had penetrated his soul. He had the inscription taken from the statues, then went home and shot himself. His son had the mournful duty of vindicating his father before the Landtag of 1845. It was partly accomplished; but the inscription was so framed as to indicate that the funds "raised for the monument by Wolicki, were largely increased by Raczynski." The widow of the count presented the proofs of the transaction to the Landtag, and asked for the restoration of the inscription, but in vain. "So," says Dr. Eggers, "the monument of the Polish princes has also become a monument of that partisan spirit which has had such an injurious influence in Polish history."

The original models in plaster were brought from Lauchhammer to Berlin in 1847, and are now in the Rauch Museum.

The venerable aspect of the father, and the vigorous, manly bearing of the son, are finely contrasted. No limitations of costume prevent the full, picturesque effect of the figures ; the full, flowing mantle of the one, and the rich armor of the other, lend grace and dignity to the erect yet easy attitude, while the noble features are rather brought out than concealed by the regal covering of the heads. The cross in the hand of the father, and the sword in that of the son, are full of historic significance. The mediæval character of the group makes it more romantically attractive than the monuments of our own times.

A noble transition from the warlike portraits to ideal work is afforded by the statue of Albert Dürer. The approach of the three hundredth anniversary of Dürer's death aroused a strong desire among his countrymen to erect a fitting monument to him. A plan was formed by engravers and artists for a collection of German works of art. But King Ludwig was not satisfied with this, and declared that the greatest of German sculptors, Rauch, must design a statue of the greatest of German artists, to be cast in the only great bronze foundery in South Germany, at Munich. Rauch took the commission, August, 1825, and proposed a statue of Dürer based on the likeness he has given of himself. He inquired into the place designed for it, saying " A small square is preferable ; and the statue ought to stand, not in the middle, but in a good position at the side, as we see in the historical works of the olden time ; not after the tedious Northern fashion, at the end of a long perspective, where the monument looks like a target, or a salt-cellar planted in the middle of the table."

But the Nurembergers protested loudly at the casting of the statues at Munich. They thought it could be equally well done at Nuremberg, and that was the fitting place for the work. Rauch went to the foundery to examine the quality of the casting, and he had a bronzed and painted model of the monument of full size made in wood, which was erected in the marketplace, that all might judge of the proposed site of the statue. Although this place was found satisfactory, another trial was made at the Burgfreiung, where it would stand finely against a clear horizon ; but the general preference was for the neighborhood of Dürer's dwelling.

Rauch gave some time to the churches and monuments of Nuremberg, and was greatly *fêted* by its inhabitants, who took leave of him with the words, "You will live here to all time united with Dürer." He delighted the citizens by obtaining the king's consent to have the statue cast at Nuremberg, if he was satisfied with the work. Rauch was unable to be present at the great festival of the laying of the corner-stone. He applied himself diligently to this work, and in ten days after the festival the whole monument stood before him in a bronzed cast. He wrote in his diary, "It seems to me that I have never projected anything better." The interest was not confined to Nuremberg ; all Germany wished to take part in the honor to the great artist ; and contributions flowed in from artists and art-societies, so that in November twelve thousand gülden of free-will offerings were counted.

A great festival was held in Berlin on the three hundredth anniversary of Dürer's death, at which this model was shown ; and among many other tributes offered was a symphony of Mendelssohn's. Rauch could not have had a finer subject for his art. The personal beauty of Dürer, his noble bearing and character, the deep universal feeling of the people, and the position of the statue in his native place, were all powerful 'stimulants to the artist's imagination. Rauch was named an honorary member of the Union of Artists of Nuremberg. He already planned to improve upon his sketches, not foreseeing that this constant effort for improvement would be made a handle of, in trying to take the monument entirely out of his hands. He was led by the difficulties he encountered in procuring good work to investigate the whole subject of bronze casting ; and Dr. Eggers gives a very interesting account of the history and development of this important art-industry ; but my limits will prevent my entering upon this discussion, except in so far as it directly affects Rauch's work.

The new method of casting introduced by the French, by which the original model was not destroyed, interested Rauch extremely, and he took pains to establish a foundery and school in Berlin. He tried to bring a celebrated founder, Hopfgarten, with whom he had formerly worked, from Rome ; but Hopfgarten was not inclined to adopt the new method. Leguire was invited by the king to take charge of the school and the casting of the Blücher statue. The school was not, however, wholly successful, and in three years only one founder was fully trained. Hopfgarten finally came to Berlin, and used the new method. After many difficulties, such as beset all industrial schools where the attempt is made to combine instruction and practical work, the school languished, and was closed in 1832. Rauch did not lose his interest in the subject, however; and he continued his efforts for improvement in the instruction of pupils, and in the style of work. The technical question was finally decided in favor of the French method, not only for Berlin, but for all Germany, for which the Berlin foundery served as the mother-school. At the same time King Ludwig of Bavaria was doing his utmost to establish the foundery at Munich; and he wished to cast Rauch's statue there. Rauch formed an intimate friendship with the master of the foundery, Stiglmaier, which was kept up by a happy interchange of gifts and correspondence for many years. Stiglmaier hopes soon to rival the French founders, as "they have no secret but practice." Soon came the practical question, Where should the statue of Dürer be cast? As the expense would be much less, Nuremberg was chosen; and Burgschmiedt, the teacher of the polytechnic school, agreed, with the help of his scholars, to perform the work in eighteen months; but Rauch made the condition that a trial statue should show that the work could be done to his satisfaction.

Nothing now seemed to stand in the way of the execution of the statue; but many difficulties arose about the pedestal, and the cost of different materials. It was proposed to give up the bass-reliefs, and have a very simple pedestal. Rauch consented to lessen his own price, "in order that an essential hindrance be set aside, and that such a praiseworthy, unique monument in our fatherland may be perfected." This description expressed the truth, for this monument really forms a landmark in German art, giving to the heroes of art and science the public, full-sized statue formerly appropriated only to crowned heads and heroes of the sword.

A curious effort was made to supersede Rauch in this work. His enemies even went so far as to employ Heideloff to make sketches for a different representation of Dürer. The various sketches were sent to the king, who must decide upon them. One is described as "the forward-striding hero and artist-prince," while the new one expressed "the master turned back to his own thoughts, without pretension, and scarcely conscious of his own greatness." Such was not Albert Dürer, who, while truly modest, had a just estimate of his own powers and success. I do not know whether his biographer, Tausing, had this controversy in his mind when he wrote his splendid paragraph on the portraits of Dürer, but it is singularly appropriate to it. He says, "The lofty self-consciousness which all these portraits breathe, the joy in his own splendid personality, might be taken in a wrong sense in any other than Dürer. He is in that wholly the child of his time." The decision of the king was delayed for half a year, and then was in Rauch's favor. He should make the standing figure ten feet high, and of the new designs by Heideloff for the pedestal, the first and simplest shall be carried out in Eberweiser bell-metal, thirteen feet high, on four steps. Yet so sharp was the opposition that it was yet another half-year before Rauch received the definite commission. At this time he was receiving very important commissions from King Louis to finish the Max Joseph monument, and to make the six Victories for the Walhalla; and this may have led his rivals to hope that he would himself give up the Dürer work, which had proved so annoying.

But he took the commission, and only considered that this accumulation of work freed him from the obligation to have the Dürer statue finished at any definite time. Even to his immense power of work, unequalled by that of any sculptor of his time, it was impossible to touch the model till the next year, 1834. The king, becoming impatient, required the magistrates to announce when the statue would be ready. Rauch set the time on his side for the first of May, 1836. He made this decision just before his summer journey to Munich for the unveiling of the Max Joseph monument, and hoped that by personal intercourse with the king the newly arisen difficulties might be smoothed away.

He had copies made of the Dürer portrait, with the tablet out of the "Allerheiligenbilde," and of Dürer with Pirkheimer, from the picture of the "Martyrdom of the Ten Thousand." The engraving of the former had served him for his first sketch of the statue.

Prince Metternich and other grandees invited him to dinner, but he did not much enjoy the princely feast. He says in his diary of the eighteenth of July, "At midday at dinner in Hietzing, near Schönbrunn, with the chancellor, Fürst von Metternich. Fürst Wenzel Lichtenstein and many diplomatic persons were at this princely table, but the entertainment was not very agreeable, and I never suffered from greater tediousness." On his return to Berlin he received copies of the Dürer picture from Vienna, etched with miniature-like delicacy by Albert Theer, who had acquired fame in this kind of work. The king claimed his promise to have the statue by the first of May, and Rauch put his hand to it in February, and appealed to Rietschel to let him have young Melz to help him, but Rietschel could not spare him. Rauch went to work with insufficient help, and before the first alarm-shot reached him from Nuremberg, he had written to Rietschel that he was working busily on the life-size model of Dürer, making some changes, such as the right hand resting with the style on the left, which he hopes will be advantageous." It was not unknown to him that his opponents held fast to the Burgschmiedt design, but he based this change on the authority of the portrait in the "Martyrdom of the Ten Thousand." He supported himself on this ground when, a few days later, the demand came from the Nuremberg magistrates to know whether he had finished the model according to his promise. He had to answer "No;" but he excuses himself on the ground of the great amount of work claimed by the king, and the changes he had made, and promises to finish it during the summer. The Nurembergers were furious, and wrote to the king that Rauch did not take any interest in the monument, and that he was only fitted for warlike statues, and could not succeed in other subjects. They prayed the king to give the work to the greatest of European sculptors ; viz., Thorwaldsen.

He would unquestionably take a great interest in Dürer ; and as he had generously made the busts of Gutenberg and Schiller for nothing, he probably would not charge so much for this as Rauch had done. A strong minority sided with Rauch ; but a majority, five of whom were members of the art-union, were so carried away by passion as to send to the king a proposal, which Dr. Eggers characterizes as "alike wanting in artistic sense, truth, reason, temper, and logic."

Without making reply to them, Rauch appealed directly to the king. I give in full his temperate but manly and respectful letter, —

"Your Majesty's grace and favor make me bold enough to appeal to your Excellency's protection and indulgence. Your Excellency was pleased to command that I should be commissioned to make a model for the statue of Albert Dürer for the city of Nuremberg. The words which your Majesty spoke at the same time, that I was the best of the now living sculptors of Germany, how much soever I may be convinced that these words are rather a proof of your Majesty's disposition than my services, yet laid upon me a double obligation to put forth all my strength, in order to produce something worthy in the model under consideration. I have, therefore, since the completion of the monument of his late Majesty Max Joseph, busied myself particularly with this work, and I hoped to finish it in the month of May of this year. But I have found greater difficulties than I expected, and my achievement has not kept pace with my wishes; so that, with my former experience, I can scarcely calculate to have the model in clay finished in six months.

" During this time I have received a letter from Nuremberg, in which it is pointed out that your Majesty has been pleased to command that the monument of Albert Dürer should be erected in the year 1837, and that it is therefore necessary that the model should be in Munich during the next month, August, in order that the bronze casting may be begun, or the whole work will be considered as given up, so far as regards my connection with it.

" Only your Majesty's lofty protection can turn away this mortification and injury from me, for it appears that your Majesty's commands and expressions offer the pretexts on which to break with me. Even if the model in clay were finished, these few weeks would not suffice to make the cast in plaster, and dry it so as to be fit for sending.

" On this account, I therefore respectfully venture to beg that your Excellency yourself may please to give command that proper time be allowed me for finishing the monument, since the delay of a few months cannot be considered, if the artistic worth of a work which should last for centuries should suffer from over haste. Besides which, the erection of the monument could only take place much later, if, as appears, it is desired to have the model made in Nuremberg by another sculptor, who must now begin anew, and certainly must finish it much later than I can mine, on which so much work has been already done.

" In hope of a gracious answer to my most respectful prayer, etc."

The king extended the time to December, intimating that any further delay would be considered as putting an end to the contract. Rauch refused an invitation to the Strelitzer Court, on account of this pressure, which annoyed him very much. The matter became publicly known, and caused much excitement, with a good deal of heat on both sides. Rauch refused an invitation to visit Rietschel at Dresden because " Ludwig had demanded the completion of the statue in a very short time, making no allowance for unexpected hindrances." These soon came. His trusty helper Wolff was sick, and a new, inexperienced workman must begin the drapery of the great statue. Fifty-five hundredweight of clay was needed, and this great weight caused a shrinking of the model, and changed the action of the legs. This caused Rauch much embarrassment ; but finally, November 12, the clay model was finished, and the manikin could be relieved from the thick gray woollen stuff which represented the fur mantle of the statue. With characteristic economy this cloth was made over into winter cloaks for the grandchildren. For long years it served under the name of the Dürer cloak. What the little ones had often looked at with reverence, as the dress of the high man which they saw the grandfather make in his workshop, now proudly clothed their own little bodies.

The clay model was publicly exhibited a few days, with a free-will entrance-fee for the benefit of a school of industry for poor children, and over two hundred gülden were received. The applause was as loud as universal. The model was then given to the cast-maker. Meanwhile, the king urged Rauch to name a definite time for the delivery of the statue. This question came very opportunely, for Rauch could now complain of the injurious conditions of a fixed term of delivery on the part of the Nuremberg magistrates. The drying of a plaster cast ten feet high, at this time of the year, even if hurried, could not be accomplished at a given day and hour, and sending it too early might destroy it. Therefore, he begged the king to command the Nuremberg magistrates to delay the delivery, that the model might dry, and be properly packed and forwarded, which might cause a difference of four weeks. The king gave the desired command, and Rauch again had his hands free. The casting took place in November, and December was consumed in the drying, which had to be done with great care, and the retouching and necessary finishing was not completed until January, and on the first day of February Rauch was relieved from his task by the actual delivery of the statue.

But the annoyances were not at an end. Reindel announced the arrival and the preliminary placing of the statue for judgment and exhibition in a place entirely unfit for it, and very badly lighted. But he himself was quite overpowered by the statue, even under these circumstances. Rauch's patience was exhausted. He found an intentional purpose to mortify him by this neglect. He had asked for a suitable location for the statue, and they had given him the worst one possible. He wrote angrily to the magistrates, proposing to build a wooden booth, properly lighted, at his own expense, and demanded that the exhibition should be closed until this was done. But fortunately this time his displeasure was needless. The committee themselves saw the unfitness of the place, and at the sight of the masterpiece the old jealousies and quarrels vanished. The view of this splendid work of art, ten feet eight inches high, filled the assembled spectators as well as the committee with an admiration which increased the longer they looked upon it. The verdict of the artists was equally favorable. They agreed that "the work as a whole, as in all its separate parts, was a perfect success, and nothing was left to desire." This speech suited the committee, and all left the hall well satisfied.

In March of this year Rauch made a small copy of this statue "in order to keep a remembrance in his neighborhood." A cast is in the Rauch Museum.

From all sides the position of the statue is grand and simple. The high houses of Nuremberg, with their rich lines of roofs, gables, balconies, and towers form the background. The rather small square has a decided slope, so that the monument looks down even to St. Sebald's Church. The pedestal of marble, which appears somewhat too light, gives weight to the dark mass of the draped figure. The stately form wears a cloak richly trimmed with fur over a damask under-garment. The long, broad sleeves hang down on both sides. The left hand holds back the cloak, and by this natural motion gives occasion for fine graceful folds, and the leg is shown from the knee down in hose and ribboned shoes. The right arm falls almost directly down, and the hand holds the style and a sprig of laurel.

But the statue is still more noble by its inward meaning and expression: it is Dürer's very self. The noble head with its flowing hair, the handsome, regular features, the earnest, deep expression of the eyes, and the beautiful brow are the same that we are familiar with in the portraits by his own hand, while the manly grace of his attitude is in keeping with the self-respect which always recognized his calling as an artist as high and ennobling. It fitly stands in his birthplace, making it dearer still to all pilgrims to this shrine of truth and beauty.

Much discussion took place in regard to the pedestal. Rauch was very earnest to have Heideloff's designs carried out for a bronze pedestal with rich bass-reliefs. He wrote earnestly to the magistrates, urging this point, and offering to give his own assistance in making models for the pedestal without remuneration. The Nurembergers seemed willing to bear the expense; but Reindel writes to Rauch, April 19, 1838, that it was some time before a decision came from the king. But now it is here, contrary to all expectation, it is that the pedestal shall be made according to a design sent, in the simplest manner, entirely of stone, with no bronze work, and must be executed as soon as possible, since the erection of the whole monument must take place without fail on the twentieth of May, 1839. On one side comes the inscription, and on the three others, in round Gothic ornament, Dürer's monogram, his arms, and the state arms.

This was after Ludwig's usual fashion, when he had done the utmost for a great work of art, to hurry up the conclusion for a definite time, at the risk of spoiling the whole effect. Gärtner was the architect of the simple

ALBERT DÜRER, NUREMBERG

pedestal, and Klenze, through whom Rauch heard of the plan, begged him to oppose it, pointing out how unsuitable the marble pedestal would be to a bronze statue. To avoid delay the king gave up the proposed ornaments on the side, having only an inscription on the front : —

ALBRECHT DÜRER.

and on the back : —

ERRICHTET AM XXI. MAI MDCCCXL.

It will be remembered with what difficulty the casting of the statue was secured to Burgschmiedt. He did it splendidly. He first made a trial of separate parts, as the sleeve, lock of hair, head, and right hand. Reindel says, "The trials of Burgschmiedt succeed beyond expectation. The surface is so thick and fine that it only needs to be cleaned in order to make the clear color of the material visible, and chiselling is quite superfluous." He also says of the casting of the whole statue, that those acquainted with the best French casting say they have seen nothing better. Even Schinkel, who saw the nearly finished monument when travelling through Germany, declared the casting to be extraordinarily fine, and as pure as the model. On the thirtieth of March, 1840, the magistrates made known that the casting was successful, and the monument would be unveiled on Dürer's birthday, the twenty-first of May.

This must, of course, be done with festivities worthy of the occasion, to which Rauch was invited. He started with his daughter Doris for Halle, where they were joined by Agnes. They gladly accepted the invitation of Platner, a member of the committee, to dwell with him in the Ægidienplatz.

All the dignitaries of the city were present, and the address was made by the first Burgomaster Binder. The covering fell off, and, deeply overcome by the emotion of the moment, the two masters, Rauch and Burgschmiedt, embraced amid a tumult of applause. After the feast in the Rathhaus came a torchlight procession in honor of the artist. Post-horses were ordered for the journey home; "but," says Rauch in his diary, "instead of the post-horses ordered, Herr Platner surprised us with his four black horses harnessed to the carriage. With hearts full of thanks and emotion we took leave of this love-worthy family. At the Erlanger Gate I was, to my great surprise, again greeted by my friendly host and my artist friends, Reindel, Heideloff, Dr. Zumpe, etc., and with a '*lebchoch*' wished a pleasant journey, wherewith, in inextinguishable remembrance of a joyous, happy day, with a thankful heart toward these friends and this city, I continued my journey."

Thus the wearisome delays and many anxieties that had hindered the progress of this monument came to a happy end; and Dr. Eggers considers this as the best of all Rauch's portrait statues, far surpassing any of his military ones.

Rauch had modelled the face of Dürer from several different pictures, but he took the profile from a medallion of Dürer. He used this head for the portrait of Dürer to be placed in the Walhalla, only being obliged to change the arrangement of hair to suit the prescribed Hermes form.

CHAPTER IX

KING LUDWIG OF BAVARIA

1812–1852

THE frequent mention of the King of Bavaria, which occurs in connection with the account of the Dürer statue, leads naturally to a review of Rauch's relations to that art-loving monarch, which led to the production of some of the most important, as well as most characteristic and beautiful, of Rauch's works.

Rauch had been in friendly relations with this prince since his visit to Munich in 1811, and had received many commissions for busts, which he put into marble in Carrara. In the beginning of his bust-work Rauch had received only five hundred and fifty gülden (one thousand marks, or two hundred and fifty dollars) for a bust; but in 1823 he found that this price hardly covered more than the outlay; and he announced that he could not even make the Scharnhorst, which he had already begun, for less than double that price. The crown prince was unpleasantly surprised at this announcement; but after two years, having become king, he promised to pay the increased price, but at the same time sought for sculptors in Berlin who would work cheaper, and gave some commissions to Tieck and Wichmann.

Ludwig had already conceived the magnificent project of the Walhalla, a monument to the heroes of Germany; and it was a delightful thing to Rauch, in his fever of patriotic excitement, to have commissions for the busts of Blücher and Schwarzenberg, to be placed in this new temple of glory. All the little feeling about the price of the busts soon vanished, and, as Ludwig said, "he was most anxious to confer with the sculptor Rauch." A peculiarity of Rauch's early work may be found in the busts in the Walhalla, in the turning of the head so that the front view gives almost a three-quarters' view of the face.

The prince soon found fitting opportunity to show his interest in the sculptor. When his father, Max Joseph, celebrated the festival of his five and twenty years' rule, the magistracy of the capital decided on a monument to him, and to invite the crown prince to take charge of it.

The exhaustion of the city treasure through the building of a theatre prevented the immediate execution of this work, and Max Joseph did not long survive this festival ; but King Ludwig seized the opportunity to carry out the work on a grand scale, and asked Rauch whether and on what conditions he would come to Munich to see the locality and arrange for a colossal statue to be cast by Stiglmaier. For Rauch there was no question in regard to this commission, honorable to any artist ; but the answer must depend upon his king. The king graciously gave permission for an absence of eighteen months. Rauch announced his plan to Klenze in November ; but the work on the Blücher statue delayed him until the following April, and then the journey was entered upon with somewhat changed conditions. Rauch made a sketch of Max Joseph in the manner prescribed, sitting on a throne in royal array ; but he thought it best to go to Munich only for the preparation, and to make the model in Berlin, doing only the last work on the colossal statue in Munich. He now, therefore, asked leave for only a short absence for this journey, which he wished to extend to Paris, as they proposed, according to his advice, to build a large new foundery at Munich, and he must, therefore, make himself acquainted with the French works.

April 25, 1825, Rauch went to Munich with the sketches, and was received by the young king as an old friend. It was plain to see how delighted he was to find himself in the sphere of activity for which he had longed, and how he enjoyed the long conversations with Rauch. On the seventh of May the king approved the design of the monument in all its parts. The exhibition of the sketches became a real festival, at which many royal and noble personages, both lords and ladies, assisted. Rauch also enjoyed the society of artists and collectors, and with a joyful mind took part in the performance of a festival play which commemorated the ascent to the throne by King Ludwig. It was carried out with great animation by amateurs in declamation, song, and dancing.

Rauch left Munich May 13, to satisfy his long-felt desire to visit Paris, which he felt to be necessary to the completion of his culture in art. Stiglmaier was chosen for his companion, on account of his knowledge of the Parisian bronze founderies.

At Stuttgart he had great pleasure in spending four rich hours in the study of the famous Boisserée collection ; and these pictures were to him, " next to Raphael's, the wonder of the world." Then he saw his old friend Dannecker again, after an interval of twelve years, and says that the Ariadne, which he had seen in the model, charmed him more than ever ; but a statue of Christ, and another of John, had little attraction for him. He sought in vain for the meaning as well as the form in them. Certainly Dannecker has in these works not only gone beyond the limits of his power, but the boundaries of art. When we meet him on the ground of the antique, or subjects approaching to it, then we see the old school-fellow of Schiller create plastic works in which he has done the best of his time. " It is doing Canova no wrong, but one is only fair to Dannecker, when one ascribes to him no little merit that he has essentially brought

about the turning away from the time of modern stupidity
(*Zopfzeit*), and the return to the antique." Rauch thought
that Dannecker had tried to express in the Christ the
words, " I go to my Father," and that this is impossible to
represent in sculpture without any action. " The wish,"
he says, " to say too much, and to characterize too strongly,
and to express too many details, leads to obscure speech,
and consequently to want of the characteristic, a fault
that we repeatedly meet with in the development of
plastic art." At Strasburg, Rauch enjoyed the magnificent cathedral, and paid his respects to the old Ohmacht,
to whom his own city is indebted for so much plastic
adornment, especially the bust of Klopstock. He tried
to engage Helmsdorf, a landscape painter, as a teacher
for the Berlin Art Academy, which did not yet satisfy
him.

A rapid journey of two days brought him to Paris,
where he wandered as in Elysian fields, or, as he says, "in
the happiest intoxication," at finding himself where he
had so long desired to be. Schinkel and Beuth, whom he
had hoped to meet, had gone to London. " Don't send
me a letter," he wrote to Schinkel, "but a long list of all
that I must see." Alexander von Humboldt introduced
him to Hittorf, and for two weeks both were his constant
and delightful guides.

First, the sculpture of the Louvre attracted him, next
to that of Rome the finest museum of ancient sculpture
in the world. After that came the works of the French
sculptors. He speaks with pleasant appreciation of all his
contemporaries. He calls Cortot's relief of the king of
Spain "a distinguished work of art." Of David D'An-
gier's statue of Racine, bust of Lafayette, and several
reliefs, he says, " They are portrayed with distinguished
talent and knowledge." The aged Houdon, eighty-five
years, calls forth his respect. In the Théâtre Français,
where he admired Talma and Mademoiselle Duchesnois in

Hamlet, he saw "Houdon's statue of Voltaire in marble, represented in living truth. Its living yet quiet invention and admirable execution are like the best Greek work." He is also delighted with Père la Chaise, its beautiful situation and its monuments, especially of General Lefebvre, of Prince Demidoff, Marshals Massena and Ney. Even the vegetation and the cypresses in the open air delight his northern eye. He saw David's first picture, the "Oath of the Horatii," and his last, "Venus and Mars," and says the beginning was certainly better than the conclusion. He visited Ingres, whom he had known in Rome, and Huyot and Cassas on account of their celebrated painted studies of Egypt, Greece, Rome, and Palmyra. He was delighted with Horace Vernet's charming house, and his atelier in the *Rue de la Tour des Dames;* and with the highest satisfaction he learned to know the Spanish masters in the collection of Marshal Soult.

Hittorf took charge of his architectural entertainment, taking him to the Italian opera to show him its interior and decoration, to the Garden Choiseul, where he saw a model of the Pandrosium of Athens in its actual size, and thence to Mount Calvary for a view of the whole city, to the new churches by Huyot, and to the unfinished Arc d'Étoile.

Rauch declared Nôtre Dame the finest cathedral known to him, especially in its interior, as by its whole impression it was worthy to stand by the Dom at Ulm. He went to St. Denis, St. Cloud, Meudon, and Versailles with Humboldt, who also introduced him to the royal library, to the cabinet of engravings, and into the choicest circle of his own acquaintance. At Gerard's, who kept open house on Wednesdays, he met Duvenet, former director of the French academy at Rome, and the sculptor Dupré, his old acquaintance. He learned to know the engraver Toschi, as well as Richomme. He made arrangements with them to receive pupils from the Berlin Academy; and Mandel and Lüderitz were sent to Paris, and Eichens to Toschi, at Parma, for a four-years' course. He visited the Jardin des Plantes, and was especially interested in a vulture on account of the power of his wings and body.

The evenings were spent at the theatre, or in delightful society; and on June 5 Humboldt gave him a farewell dinner, at which many distinguished artists were present, and then, hastening back without pause, after eight days he met his family at Potsdam, who accompanied him the same day to Berlin.

In this same month Rauch received the intelligence that the corner-stone of the Munich monument was laid; but it was a year and a half before the contract between him and the Munich magistrates was finally settled. There were questions in regard to changes in the sketches, and to the estimate of cost, which required careful consideration and much correspondence. Stiglmaier had mentioned that critics had found fault with the architectural effect of the union of the supporting lions with the upper sockel, and Rauch suggested to Klenze that candelabra should be introduced. The jealousy of Klenze, to whom the architectural design was committed, also caused delay and trouble; for he considered his the most important part of the work, and did not like it that the magistrates conferred exclusively with Rauch over its execution. He even caused an inscription to be placed on the finished monument, " Leo von Klenze invenit."

Before Rauch went on with the execution of the monument, he availed himself of a journey to Nuremberg, to make an excursion to Munich, in order to shorten the correspondence, and to bring the contract to a final conclusion. This came about with the representatives of the magistrates finally on the twelfth of February. According to this, Rauch was to make the life size help-model in Berlin, and in two years after its completion carry out the full-sized statue in Munich, for which purpose an atelier was to be provided for him. The items of cost were exactly calculated, and the whole sum of the monument was to be two hundred and thirteen thousand marks (fifty-three thousand two hundred and fifty dollars). He spent a week in Munich in the enjoyment of the society of his artist friends, and then hastened back to Berlin to work.

On his return to Berlin he was himself dissatisfied with the plan of the Max Joseph monument; and, to fill up a space which he thought looked empty, he introduced two figures. One of these, finally called "Felicitas Publica," became a very favorite statue for decoration, and has been repeated many times. It is a very rich, flowing, majestic figure. Even as late as 1852 a bronze copy was placed in the city hall at Breslau in remembrance of the queen's visit to the industrial exhibition.

After finishing this work Rauch turned to the life-sized model of the sitting statue. On December 18 the first naked ground-plan was made, and formed in plaster. He had an impression of this model made by Gropius in *papier-maché*, and draped it with the king's cassimere cloak, and modelled the drapery on the plaster. In scarcely seven weeks, on March 21, 1829, this work was finished, and his workmen were sent to Munich to prepare the iron skeleton for the colossal model, and to put upon it the first layer of clay. Four chests with the models of the lion pedestal had preceded them, and four more chests followed in the beginning of June, with the models of the king's statue, and of the Fortuna, with books and other articles.

Stiglmaier had long prayed and hoped for the sending of the model, which he burned with curiosity to see. March 2 he sees an exceedingly high wagon in the streets. That could only be the long-expected pedestal, and truly it was. It had travelled four weeks, through storm and snow, often with a team of eight or ten horses, having been obliged to go around many of the smaller towns whose gates were not high enough to admit it.

The city was in excitement; all the journals announced that the colossal statue had come. But much yet remained to be done in preparing an atelier, for which Stiglmaier had been working for a long time, and in finding suitable lodgings for the work-people. Rauch had his dwelling of two rooms in the neighborhood of the atelier. He sent careful directions for all the details of stoves, windows, etc. Three atelier rooms for Rauch, one large and two small, were connected with the foundery. In August, 1828, the dry-heating began, and all the steps of progress were reported to Rauch. Stiglmaier could hardly be satisfied that any place could be good enough for the master, and refused one of eight rooms at the price of a thousand gülden; but Rauch was more easily pleased, and took one at half the rent on Odeon platz. A housekeeper and servants were provided, and all was prepared for him, when Berghes and Sanguinetti announced that they were ready with the first foundation of the building up of the statue. Rauch left Berlin on the twenty-eighth of July, and to his great delight he had the companionship of his dear friend Rietschel, "who would be a companion and help" to him in the work before him. The friendship between these two brothers in art, of which I have already spoken, had gone on steadily increasing. From the pupil, Rietschel had become the cherished and beloved fellow-worker; and Rauch delighted as much in his artistic success as in his own, and constantly notes his progress in his diary. When Rietschel failed to get the allowance for a journey to Italy, Rauch took measures to make up the deficiency. Any one familiar with Rietschel's work, which may now be well studied in the Rietschel gallery at Dresden, and with his own beautiful face, as shown in the bass-relief, can readily understand how worthy he was of this affection. The friends made a short visit to Goethe at Weimar, and reached Munich on the second of July. July 11 Rauch first put his hand to the colossal model of the king. Soon after he designed a Bavaria for the other side of the pedestal, as a companion to the Felicitas. After about four weeks the last retouch was given to the nude model, and Rauch could begin on the drapery, which he hoped to have finished by the beginning of September, in order to carry out a favorite plan of again spending the winter in Italy.

Wilhelm von Humboldt writes him a warm letter of congratulation on the speed and skill with which he has executed this work. He says, "One sees clearly from this how all which people say about the rule of idea and feeling in art is a pure want of taste. Ideas, and much more genius, must indeed be there ; but without the hand both are inactive, weak, and slow, and the hand needs practice in working itself, and confidence in directing where it has the help of others. All does not take place without much mechanism. If seeing, feeling, and making do not lie in an artist as in one mould, it is only a half existence with him."

But Rauch did not finish his work as soon as he hoped, not because his work was hindered by occasional excursions with Klenze to Starnberg, and a visit to the widowed queen at Tegernsee, with pleasant enjoyment of the artistic society of Munich, but because he took a severe cold from the heavy rainstorms of the summer, and the dampness of the clay, which delayed him fully three weeks ; and it was not until the twenty-second of September that he could resume his work. During this illness Rietschel worked diligently on the figure of Bavaria, which Rauch had sketched.

A visit from his daughter and her husband cheered his convalescence, and he was able to show them some of the beauties of Munich and its vicinity. On the thirtieth of September Rauch received from Cornelius a diploma of honorary membership in the Munich Art Academy, and on the same day three great wagons with eighteen horses brought into Munich Thorwaldsen's monument of the Duke of Leuchtenberg, which was placed in the Frauen-kirche.   Three years earlier King Ludwig had the intention of giving this work to Rauch, because Thorwaldsen had not fulfilled his engagement as to the time of delivery.   Rauch declared himself willing to undertake the work if Thorwaldsen, with full knowledge of the circumstances, wished to give it up.   This led to the completion of the monument by Thorwaldsen.

On the twenty-fifth of September a festival was given by the artists, and on the twenty-seventh Rauch mounted the carriage with Rietschel which was to carry him south. Rietschel accompanied him as far as Innspruck, where he was obliged to take leave of him to return to Munich. Rietschel closes his youthful recollections with these words: "As Rauch the other morning at six o'clock went away from Innspruck, and I remained behind to return to Munich the same day, the parting was infinitely hard to me, and I saw that it was not easy to him.   My whole love, honor, and gratitude followed the excellent master and friend."   I will leave to another place the account of Rauch's journey, to complete now the history of the monument.   Rauch stayed in Italy until April. Rietschel kept him constantly informed of all that went on in Munich.   Rauch writes from Rome, "That the works of the Bianconi are making such good progress makes me very happy, and I am full of obligation to you ; for you have been helpful at my side in all parts of this heavy business.   For all, all my most hearty and undivided thanks."   As in January they are busy with the plaster, Rauch repeats how happy the news from the atelier makes him, although he says that he is only half happy, since he is not at the work himself.   "But I hope to make up for all, and to be very busy in Berlin.   For I see

better what I 'really should do myself." But soon after
Rietschel was obliged to return to Dresden, on account
of the work on the model of a statue of King Frederic
Augustus, and Rauch sent to Berlin for other help. He
left the matter to Tieck, and it was arranged that Drake
should go to Munich. Drake was a favorite pupil and a
most efficient helper, and he bore an important part in
the completion of the monument. During the absence of
Rauch in Italy they worked on the great model in plaster,
often under the eye of King Ludwig, who willingly praised
their work, but did not hesitate to scold them if he
thought they left off work too early before a holiday.

Rauch returned to Munich April 18, and gave three
weeks to working on the hand and head of the colossal
statue ; but his work was hindered by the same trouble in
the back and limbs from which he had suffered before. He
could work only in the forenoon ; the afternoon was given
to the cure. At night he suffered severe pain. Steam-
baths, leeches, blood-letting, were tried ; but nothing gave
him relief, and he left Munich to go to the baths of Gastein, from whence he returned to Munich on the twenty-
sixth of May. He had nothing more to do on the Munich
work, and could give it up to the casting. The casting
of the lion-pedestals, with the figures of Felicitas Publica
and the Bavaria, was successfully accomplished by Stiglmaier in 1831, and that of the statue itself in the year
1833.

In this statue Rauch has happily overcome many of the
difficulties of a sitting figure placed on a high pedestal.
The king, in his coronation mantle, sits on a throne with
his head lightly turned to the right, the right hand raised
in the act of blessing, while the left, leaning on a support,
seizes by the middle the sceptre lying on the upper arm.
The mantle, drawn over the right shoulder, opens itself to
the upraised right arm, which is clothed with a richly
embroidered uniform. A very good bust by Stiglmaier

served as the model for the head, and in the full face is the
expression of benevolent earnestness.

Not only does Rauch express the warmest gratitude for
Rietschel's assistance in this work, but he also learned to
prize another pupil, Drake, and he predicted his brilliant
future career. "Herr Drake is fully occupied with some
commissions in my atelier, and will soon gain a distinguished reputation. He is yet very young." And again,
"Drake is such a talent as only appears from century to
century."

When Rauch returned to Berlin, he found so many
claims upon him that he could not do anything more for
the monument for a whole year. But the bass-reliefs for
the upper pedestal were still wanting. Rietschel assisted
him in the work. I will give the description of the best
ones, which represent the relation of religion and art. He
has represented the two great branches of the Christian
church by the figures of its priests, with an angel between
them, extending her hands to the shoulder of each, while
the light of the Holy Ghost on her head illumines all
around. The Catholic has the features of the Court
Bishop von Straber, who was personally known to Rauch;
and the Protestant is modelled from the portrait of Von
Schmidt, cabinet preacher of Queen Caroline, and the
leading Protestant minister in Munich.

Equally interesting is the representation of art in the
second field. In the first sketch the figures were purely
allegorical, but Rauch finally took the portrait of Cornelius sitting at the easel for the principal figure. On the
left the sculptor is working and looking up to a plaster
group of Charity, while on the right sits the architect
taking measures for a ground-plan, and behind him, in the
background, are workmen raising stones.

As Rauch was considering the plan of this relief, he
expressed to Drake his wish that he had Klenze for a
model of the head of the architect. At that moment

Klenze walked in, and Rauch insisted that he must stand as a model. Impossible! He was on his way to Petersburg, and had only a half-hour to spare. "Just enough!" cried Rauch, while Drake, at a wink of his eye, at once prepared a form and the modelling-stick. Now Klenze must stand still, though on coals, and with watch in hand. In twenty-nine and one-half minutes Drake showed him the relief-portrait. Klenze took the stick and wrote on the rim of it, twenty-nine and one-half minutes, and then vanished. In that time the sculptor had seized all the strong peculiarities of the face, and the tangled, bushy hair. On the third side, with the inscription, is the representation of science by an astronomer, who investigates the heavens with his telescope, while a figure of Night discloses the constellations from under her veil; and on the other side, by the biologist, who gazes with wonder at the singular forms which Tellus reaches up from out of her depths. Thus Rauch paid honor to those scientific men, such as Oken, Schubert, Schelling, Fraunhofer, whom King Ludwig had welcomed to add to the glory of Munich. Dr. Eggers makes the criticism on this relief that "it is disturbing ; that the pillar, the laurel-tree, and the figure of Tellus are cut through by the line of the relief-field." For once Rauch seems to have confused the boundaries of the arts, and attempted a picturesque effect more appropriate to painting.

The king was now becoming very impatient, and wished to set the first of May as the time for the unveiling of the monument ; but even kings must wait. It was impossible to have the work done at that time, and it was finally only on September 5 that the colossal image, drawn by twelve horses, was brought from the foundery to its position. The last necessary work upon it filled up the rest of the month. The first Tuesday of the festival week, October 13, was decided on for the unveiling. Rauch was expected to be present, and Stiglmaier secured rooms for him just opposite to the monument. He started with his son-in-law, D'Alton, from Halle, September 30, in order to arrive in Munich on Sunday for the first day of the festival; but, owing to over-wearied post-horses, they arrived on the fifth day in the' Theresien Meadow, just as the train of wagons which represented the Alt-Bavarien's circle by the wearers of different costumes drew up before the royal tent. They saw everything; the shooters, the wrestlers, the beauty of the splendid beasts, — goats, steers, cows, horses, and swine. Ninety thousand men must have been present.

The next morning Rauch went with Stiglmaier to the monument, still in the booth, and on which the men were working. He was not entirely satisfied with the effect of the casting, and said he could not understand whether it was owing to the want of skill of the workmen, or the difficulty of the material, that the final effect of bronze leaves so much to be wished for, and that this material does not compare with marble in the capacity for expression.

The first general idea of the reliefs was to represent the giving of the constitution, and the blessings which flow from a well-ordered government.

The first relief, in the composition of which Rietschel assisted, represented law and agriculture. Both are treated allegorically.

Rietschel, who had become professor of the academy at Dresden, and established a household there, now came to join Rauch at Munich, and together they visited the studios, and examined many works of art.

On the twelfth the monument was shown to the king by Klenze. The king expressed high praise of it, and told Rauch that he felt he was right in the decision not to yield to his wish to retain him entirely in his service, but to remain in his home and true to his own king.

The day of unveiling at last arrived. Rauch had "a restless night from the very fulness of his prosperity."

The excitement of seeing his finished work in its abiding-place left him no peace. He hurried out of his house and found the morning cloudy. He hastened the passage of the morning hours by making some visits, and he went to the Art Exhibition to forget himself in the works of others. He was enthusiastic for the excellent Peter Hess' picture, "The Entrance of King Otto from Greece into Nauplia," as "a work of the most striking talent." "So I went," he notes, "through the wet, but by degrees animated, streets to my dwelling, where I found that the Maximilian Street was gradually filling up. Burgher guards on foot and on horseback, the trades with their flags each borne by two men, the boys with their leaders, and the maidens dressed in blue and white, formed two choirs near the monument. Towards half-past twelve came the persons of the ministry of the university and of the academy, in fine gala dress, and with uncovered heads, and then the clergy, with the archbishop and court bishop at their head. The magistrates went into the new palace, but soon returned, and after them the whole court in full array. The king came with a quick step, followed by the royal princes, the Field-Marshal Prince Wrede, the generalship, pages, etc. The choir-singing began, and the second burgomaster asked permission of the king to unveil the statue, which the king granted. The archbishop pronounced a blessing, and at a pull of the first burgomaster on the cord, the golden image stood free. A hymn sounded amid the ringing of all the bells in the city, and the thunder of one hundred and one cannon most powerfully accompanied the inward feeling and the outward expression. With Edouard" (d'Alton), "Stiglmaier and his family, with friend Rietschel, Preacher Trautschold, and other friends, I looked out from my dwelling at the spectacle, to which Heaven did not appear unkind, since the cloudy day cleared at the moment of unveiling, and lighted the monument and the scene for two seconds, which made a great impression on us all, and cleared my spirit so that I recovered from all the care and uncertainty of a nine-years' work, and was peaceful and happy over its success. All my earlier wishes were richly fulfilled." On that and the following day Rauch was constantly accompanied with ever-renewed good wishes and congratulations until the moment when he set foot into his carriage, which at noon stood at the door. The king took leave of him most graciously, and, after a short stay at Halle, he returned to his workshop at Berlin.

Before closing this chapter I must devote a page to Rauch's Italian journey, which I passed over lightly in order not to interrupt the story of the Max Joseph monument. It is chiefly important for his observations on ancient and modern art.

Rauch had long felt an earnest desire to revisit Italy, and his Italian friends constantly urged him to come there. His friend Humboldt encouraged him in these words : " To visit Italy, to travel through it quickly, and then with increased courage and fresh longing for work to come back, is the happiest thought that you could conceive."

He began his journey October 27, 1829. He went by Innspruck and the Italian lakes, and spent the Sunday at Milan. He wandered about the wonderful cathedral at evening, admiring the effect of its thousand statues. He met here "the interesting engraver" Longhi, and visited both painters and sculptors. He then went to Genoa, Spezzia, and Carrara, where he found his own work in good progress. His constant correspondence with Riet-schel, and his note-book, give full accounts of this journey. At Lucca he speaks of the pictures of Fra Bartolommeo, and then he came to his old friends at Florence.

November 20 he left Florence with a *vetturino*, and enjoyed the cold weather, which enabled him to go much on foot. He says, " Everything after my long absence has for me a closer, higher interest." He reached Rome on the twenty-fifth. He is constantly with Thorwaldsen, and speaks most tenderly of this old friend, and will delay his journey to Naples to be with him, as he was soon to leave for Munich. He is in his old home again with Frau Buti, and he finds the city cleaner and more friendly than before, and French and English more spoken.

He touches lightly on many artistic points, but says he stood two hours before the Transfiguration of Raphael, sunk in admiration and enjoyment, and could only look at the Madonna del Foligno, the morning was so dreamed away. The next day was given to the Raphael Stanze, of which he says, " It seems as if I had never seen anything so beautiful ; never this fulness and richness ; never the whole ; never the details seen and felt so carefully."

Thorwaldsen was to take possession of Rauch's house in Munich ; and Rauch writes, " Thorwaldsen will need no other accommodation than lodging, service, and breakfast, but especially your help not to miss the artists and good friends. Place my models skilfully in view in the atelier, but leave the large one of the king's statue where it is ; it will not interest him."

Rauch was deeply interested in the two-days' visit to Pompeii, and the other beauties of the Bay of Naples. His evenings were spent at the theatre. He was astonished and delighted at the Pompeian paintings, and says, " These days are the most satisfactory of my life. The works of painting especially busied my thought, and always repeated to me 'that with the end of the Greeks, painting disappeared from the world.' I always believed this as regards forms, but now that I have seen the colors on the wet walls I am astonished at their harmony. The workmen are now busied with the house of Meleager ; all which comes to light is of the highest richness and excellence : one house on this street even surpasses that in richness and beauty." He does not neglect the modern artists, and speaks with praise of Colantonio del Fiore (Il Zingaro), Antonio Solario, and the old Southern school.

But most exciting of all his excursions was that to Pæstum, where he saw the noblest of Greek ruins in Italy, which are still more impressive from the solemn loneliness of their surroundings. His keen eye detected in the stalls of the archbishops at Salerno ancient capitals in the stone of Pæstum, and he suspected their origin to be from a fourth temple at Pæstum, not yet brought to light. He was promised that immediate steps should be taken to excavate this temple; but the work was delayed by the unsuitable condition of the ground. This is what is now called the ruins of an amphitheatre. Official notice of his discovery was sent to Berlin in December. Pausing at Benevento on his way from Naples, he is so much excited by the Arch of Trajan, that he declares "that all which is most worthy of seeing from antiquity is less important than this."

On returning to Rome, as he had already written to Rietschel, Rauch felt a strong desire to remain and model and finish a statue there; but he was convinced by the wise advice of his friend Humboldt, who wrote him thus: "I thought that to see Italy, and above all Rome again, would be an unending enjoyment to you, and, more than that, a true elevation of the spirit, a new nourishment of the fancy, and a true encouragement to new efforts; and your letter tells me that it has entirely proved so. But I wish, not only for all our sakes, but hold it better for yourself, that you should return to Germany in the spring. The time of life for work passes very quickly, and if it be a charming plan to remain a year in Rome to finish a determined work, yet this appears to me practically unfeasible; since, especially for a sculptor, a great expenditure of time and cost goes to the bare erection. One

should then decide to choose either Rome or the fatherland for his work-place, and unite therewith visits to the
other, as you are now doing, which thus gives freedom to
the fancy, without her becoming one-sided and uniform
from continuous work."

He remained a month in his own villa, rejoicing in the
trees which he had planted, and modelled a bust of Prince
Henry of Prussia in clay. He speaks of his desire to
return home, as he is now a happy grandfather, and
Humboldt also wishes him to come back for the opening
of the Museum.

At Siena he remarks that the artists, more especially
Duccio, whose works in purity of form and execution
remind one of the fine pictures of Pompeii, must have
seen the ancient paintings. This dependence on the
antique was also evident in the sculpture of the celebrated
Niccolo Pisano.

A short stay was made in Florence with his old companions ; a day or two spent in Bologna, and the same in
Parma, where Toschi accompanied him on his art-excur-
sions ; and he proceeded over the Brenner Pass, and
reached Munich, April 9. Boisserée writes, " Rauch is
here and full of his Italian journey. He looks somewhat
thin, but right well ; and what he tells in his lively, spirited way raises my longing to go thither." He had been
at work on the king's monument only three weeks, however, when his health broke down, and he was ordered to
the baths at Gastein to recruit.

He gives a lively account of his journey and his annoyance from his servant's smoking bad tobacco. He never
forgets his art, but takes the opportunity of his ten-min-
utes' bath to study his own limbs in the water, as the
anatomy is more evident. He also notes the beautiful
color of the flesh, and wonders if Goethe ever took the
bath there, which must have given him heavenly pleasure.
He wishes that his feet had eyes, so that he could see the

upper part of the body equally well. He has plenty of chamois, grouse, and heathcock at table, but he says, " No nightingale rejoices the ear, no bird but the hawk ; never once the everywhere darling sparrow did I see, only a few redbreasts fly over the raging waterfall."

His mind is very active and full of projects, and he writes to Rietschel that he proposes to return the river Ache to its original bed, so that the warm springs may be protected from the noise of the waterfall, and the bath guests may sleep more peacefully.

He now learns, too, with great delight, that the *Land-tag* has at last decided to erect the statue of King Frederic Augustus in Berlin, and that the commission will be given to his dear pupil Rietschel. He writes to him most warmly, and rejoices that he will have his society in Berlin, as the statue will be made there. He is anxious to return, but thinks the water is helping the nervous affection, and believes now that the trouble in his prudent head has gone to his stupid limbs ; "he wishes the head had kept it." He returns to Berlin in May with great joy, and hopes never to be away from his atelier so long again.

Among the results of this work for King Ludwig was Rauch's great interest in the subject of casting in bronze. He studied it earnestly in Paris, and made very interesting comparisons with the work of the ancients, and of the old Italians and Germans. Founderies were established at Munich, at Berlin, and at Nuremberg, at all which places Rauch had work done ; and, as we shall see, there was a wholesome rivalry between them to do the best work, and obtain the employment on his statues.

I will not attempt to follow out all the technical details of this work. The story of it was extremely interesting to Rauch. To Benvenuto Cellini appears to belong the merit of first using the modern method of casting by piece moulds instead of the destruction of the original model, as was necessary by the old method of "*la cire perdue.*" Gottfried Schadow in 1791–1792 learned this *technique* in Petersburg, Stockholm, Copenhagen, and Paris, and introduced it into Prussia. Forty years later Schadow again brought forward the subject in regard to the Blücher monument at Rostock. Objection being made to Goethe's proposal that it should be made by Pflug and his son in copper, a bronze cast was decided on, which was confided to the founder Lequine, of Paris, to be cast in the Royal Cannon Foundery at Berlin. The cast of tne statue gave satisfaction, but the brass plate of the pedestal had to be helped by the hammer as it was bent in casting. This was in 1818. To this followed a second casting of one of Schadow's works, the Luther at Wittenberg, which succeeded well in 1819.

Meanwhile, Rauch was busy with preparations for the Blücher monument at Breslau, which was to be cast in bronze. He therefore set himself diligently to work, according to his usual habit, to learn everything he could, not only about the practical work, but of the history of the subject. The results were meagre, but historic research has since brought out much more. He found in Germany sporadic cases of work in metal, such as the equestrian statue of Frederic Augustus II. in Dresden, which gave an idea of the difficulties encountered a hundred years before. Frederic the Great, some twenty-five years later, at the building of the new palace at Potsdam, established an atelier for metal work. Here the group of the three women supporting a crown, for the great middle dome, was cast, and also the Atlas with the globe, on the little cupola of the council-house in Potsdam.

From France, Rauch received some data regarding the cost of the work, which convinced him of the advantages of the new method.

Rauch tried to bring his old friend Hopfgarten from Rome to cast the Blücher statue, and to establish a workshop and school there. But Hopfgarten was averse to trying the French method, maintaining that the results from the old one were equally good.

It was proposed to send workmen to Russia to learn the work, but as Lequine applied for the position of founder for the Royal Art Academy and the work of casting the Blücher statue, this was judged to be unnecessary. The king appointed Lequine to establish a school for founding in bronze, and for a yearly stipend of five hundred gülden he was to instruct two pupils, to be selected by Rauch.

In spite of Rauch's careful oversight and earnest effort, this school was not wholly successful, and only one founder, Kastner, was really fitted for the work. Three learned the art of coining. But he never gave up his efforts to get the best workmen to Berlin, and build up the foundery there. Hopfgarten finally accepted the new method, and came to Berlin, where he was engaged on work for the king.

While Rauch was thus struggling to establish this branch of art industry in Berlin, King Ludwig was deeply interested in establishing his foundery, and the first product of it was to be the statue designed by Rauch. Thus he came into direct personal relations with the Munich Bronze Foundery, which were facilitated by his former interest in Stiglmaier, the director of the new institute, who had been introduced to him by Klenze in 1824.

Stiglmaier's history recalls that of Benvenuto Cellini. He began life as a goldsmith, but soon developed an ambition for larger works, and, having gained the recommendation of Canova, went to Naples in order to study his art by seeing the casting of Canova's statue of Charles III. Righetti's kindness allowed him to see the whole process, but the eager young man lost the favor of the older founder by his zeal. Righetti had a secret process of casting. This was really no other than the before-named "other process" of Benvenuto Cellini, by which the original model is preserved. Whether Righetti had learned it from Cellini, or had found it out for himself, he was not pleased when Stiglmaier, who had heard of this method, but had not seen it with Righetti, found out all the technical methods for himself.

He made the experiment on a statuette of Venus, two feet high, modelled by his friend Haller. In his day-book he details with great minuteness the result of his efforts. From September 22 to October 14, 1820, was employed in preparation. Many unavoidable delays occurred, and the excitement increased as the end drew near. By some mistake one of the assistants poured his molten metal into the air-hole. The casting was broken off, and came to a standstill. "The crowd of lookers-on," says the poor founder, "stood first dumb about me, then slipped out one by one and left me alone with my pain." On the seventh of November a second casting was begun and failed. With unbroken courage he began the third cast, and on Christmas Eve the metal was again poured in. It ran into the mould and spurted joyfully out at the airhole. "Our joy knew no bounds; we raised a loud cry of joy, and embraced and kissed each other. Pasquale the helper kissed the head of Phidias coming out of the broken form, and burnt his mouth, for it had not had time to cool."

From this time a close acquaintance and correspondence followed between Stiglmaier and Rauch, not only in relation to artistic matters, but in friendly intercourse. Rauch writes of the marriage of Agnes, and Stiglmaier tells of his own nuptials.

The account of the difficulties in regard to the Dürer statue with King Ludwig need not be repeated. They sprang from the king's royal impatience, which did not like to be opposed even by the inevitable conditions of art. The same spirit was apparent in regard to the work for the Walhalla, including the victories; but although Rauch was somewhat fettered by the wishes of the king, yet he was too grateful to him for the splendid opportunities he had opened to him not to rejoice in all that he had done for the promotion of art in Germany. Unfortunately, the king's haste led him to prefer the dashing, bold Schwanthaler, who, as Klenze writes, "contents himself with dictating statues and reliefs. The king knows that something is wanting, but he lets it go, led on by the same haste of creation."

Rauch says of the pressure brought to bear upon him to hasten work on the Victories, "I was never in my life more disturbed, and never had worse hypochondriacal nights than now, when King Ludwig urges so hard, and I have no means to do more than I am doing."

King Ludwig offered five thousand thalers for the proposed Goethe and Schiller group, if it were cast at Munich; but he differed seriously from Rauch in regard to the costume of the statue, and Rauch objected to his plan of the two wreaths.

King Ludwig showed his full appreciation of Rauch by the position he has given him in his great temples of art. Kaulbach painted his portrait in the seventh field of the frescoes on the new Pinakothek, with the other sculptors engaged in his work, and Rauch used his own portrait in the representation of sculptors on the relief on the Max Joseph monument. Ludwig writes to him, "I wish to receive your best likeness, that your statue may be prepared, which I wish to place, with six of the best sculptors of my own time, in the east niche of the Glyptothek. That Rauch should not fail there, goes without saying. Since the Glyptothek is in antique style, it follows, of course, that the costume should be the same for harmony. This determines me, little as I like the new in antique dress. How high I hold you is known to you far better than to a generation. With this feeling, I am your most appreciative Ludwig."

King Ludwig was anxious to retain Rauch in his constant service, and invited him to Munich. It was a tempting proposal, for Bavaria was then the kingdom of art, while Prussia was still struggling with poverty and sorrow ; but Rauch's nature was essentially loyal, and he could not leave the king who had befriended him from boyhood. The marriage of his daughter also made a strong tie to her home, where he knew the best joys of family life. We must rejoice that he decided to remain in Berlin, where he worked in greater freedom and with that devotion to thorough perfection which made his influence on art so precious. He gained from Munich an impulse in art, and to Ludwig we are indebted for the production of his most original works; but we are not sorry that his life and his fame belong to Prussia.

CHAPTER X

HOME AND FRIENDS. — SCHOOL AND ATELIER

1830–1840

ON May 26, 1829, Rauch's oldest daughter, Agnes, married Dr. Eduard d'Alton, a son of the celebrated writer on comparative osteology, who, having already made a reputation in Paris, had been appointed professor of anatomy in Berlin. The married pair remained in the Lagerhaus in Berlin, while Rauch went to Munich, and thence to Italy.

The birth of his first grandchild, a girl, on the same day that he discovered the ruins of the fourth temple at Pæstum, was a great delight to him. On his return home he found great satisfaction in the child; and writing to his friend Rietschel on the birth of his first daughter, he betrays the grandfatherly feeling by his anxious injunctions to him in regard to the care of the child. "Take care," he says, "for the most anxious watching and observation of the child, even pedantic foresight, — this is our earnest prayer." His diary records all the little illnesses and other slight events in the lives of his grandchildren, and informs us that he gave his granddaughter Eugenie on her first birthday a carnelian ring, engraved with two children's heads. He expresses his joy to Lund: "For you know," he says, "my daughter's well-being makes my earthly heaven and my best refreshment after the labors of the atelier." The little family was successively increased by the birth of Marie and Bertha, and then of Guido. In 1834 Professor D'Alton received an appointment at Halle, which occasioned the removal of his family thither a little later. The separation was very painful to Rauch. He wrote to Rietschel, "In the spring begins my solitude, which, if I could go back to Carrara, would not be so heavy as here."

This change, however, finally gave him a new interest; for in 1835 he determined to build a house in Halle for the family, after his own ideas, "not in the mason-and-carpenter style," but suited to home-life. He proposed to decorate the house, especially the interior, and hoped to introduce a new and better style of house architecture, in conformity with the ideas of Schinkel. This "*D'Alton-isch Hauschen*" was long a unique specimen of the modern villa. The architect was Strack, a pupil of Schinkel. The grounds were about five acres in extent, affording space for gardens in both front and rear, and the view was both extensive and beautiful. One noble elm has outlived all the changes the house has seen. In December the house was roofed in, young trees having been already planted. At Whitsuntide, Rauch saw it for the first time, and said that "both house and garden surpassed his expectations." He found beauty and convenience united in an admirable whole.

Rauch employed himself during this visit in modelling in profile his three granddaughters, now three to six years old; Eugenie with braided hair, the others with short, straight locks. They are charming, simple pictures of childhood, and have often been repeated for the family. Later in the same year he modelled Guido, and he made use of these models in the decoration of the staircase. Rauch planned to decorate the corridor and staircases with the work of his contemporary artists, Tieck, Drake, etc., and he writes to Rietschel begging him to have his profile portrait sketched by Metz, and to send him also, if possible, a bit of his relief-work, that he may have "you and your hand forever united there." He says, "I prepare for myself the pleasantest rest, in passing my last days with my own people and among these bass-reliefs, remembrances of my most active days, and of the society of friends so dear in themselves. Our friend Strack exerts himself with his fine talent and our small means to care for everything, to satisfy our needs as well as our eyes."

The house-warming took place at Christmas. The grandfather and his daughter Doris and the four children made the winter journey, passing two nights on the way, and Agnes and Eduard received them with tears of joy in the brilliantly lighted house.

Almost every year Rauch made two visits to Halle, in spring and autumn, until the opening of the railroad shortened the time of the journey, so that frequent re-unions with the growing family were possible. He took pleasure in the care of the gardens, and especially in what he called his "*Wandstammbuches*," or collection of bass-reliefs on the walls. These were plastic mementoes of the present and the past time, a mingling of fragments, sketches, and finished work in an album-like manner, the large and the little mixed in pleasing confusion. The collection of sixty pieces first planned was afterwards more than doubled. The setting of these reliefs began about six feet from the floor, and sometimes reached the ceiling. He was eager to fill up every blank spot with portraits of his friends, especially of artists. Rietschel holds an honored place as a mark of old and tender friendship. Rauch tried to keep some symmetry in the arrangement, and therefore sends exact measurements for portraits which he wishes to place in relation with his own or others.

The spaces between the reliefs were filled with Pompeian colors, and Wach painted the figures and decorations which were to unite them.

The D'Alton family often visited their grandfather in Berlin, the children staying with their Aunt Doris, under

the care of Fräulein Lieberkuhn, the good house-dame
who had been so long with them. The grandfather did
not fail to enforce his principles of education. His great
motto was, "Poverty is a blessing; it rouses us to self-
reliance, to activity, to independent thought." Even with
the children he suffered no idle lingering : they must busy
themselves with something. The utmost which he allowed was, that they might sit as quiet observers of the
work, of whose worth and meaning they might thus learn
to think ; a permission of which they respectfully availed
themselves. The parents came regularly at Christmas-
time, thus uniting that festival with Rauch's birthday on
the second of January, when he was accustomed to gather
his Berlin friends to meet his family. The grandchildren
took part in this festivity, playing duets for their sixty-
one-years-old birthday-child.

Rauch had but few relations, and had not seen them
since the death of his cousin Dr. Mundhenck ; but he corresponded kindly with those who remained, and sent them
money according to their needs. Some of his country
friends sent him the home-made sausages dear to his
German heart, while Frau Engelhardt added the pickled
brawn, of which he was fond. Rauch could always add to
his thanks the remark that the contents of the packages
were consumed in health and enjoyment with friends and
fellow-laborers. According to his frequent expressions,
these years were the most healthy of his life ; his attacks
of headache constantly decreased, and only occasional re-
currence of pain made summer journeys to Aix necessary.

On one of these journeys he made a long stay in Munich, on account of the works in process for the Walhalla.

His journey by Darmstadt, Bonn, etc., was full of interest,
giving him the opportunity of seeing Schepeler's fine collection of Spanish pictures, which he compared with those
of Marshal Soult in Paris.

Herr Schepeler was his companion at Aix in his walks

and observations. Rauch's eager desire for knowledge always led him to inspect industries as well as works of art; so he visited cloth-factories, coal-mines, and great elevators, and a steam-engine of one hundred and twenty horse-power, and did not fail to observe with human interest the condition of the work-people.

On his return he gave a glance at Düsseldorf, and was much impressed by Lessing, then a young man of thirty-one, whose first fresco, the battle of Iconium, he much admired. Rauch kept a note-book with careful details of routes; and his habits of method and order on his journeys, as everywhere else, enabled him to accomplish a great deal in a short time.

He gained strength from his journey; but the sciatic pains returned the next year with so much severity that he repeated the experiment, but the weather was so bad that he said "that on the whole he returned worse than he went, a distressing result for so much loss of expense and time." The final conclusion was more satisfactory, however; for after these pains had passed, another journey was not necessary.

His next journey was purely one of pleasure. He had long held the kindest relations with the brother of Queen Louise, the Duke of Mechlenburg-Strelitz, ever since the time when the young duke had gone on his tour of study to Rome, with Rauch as his artistic guide. The duke now recommends to Rauch young Wolff as a pupil, and Rauch's answer gives us a fine idea of his plan of education for an artist. The duke's letters are full of affectionate remembrance of his early intimacy with Rauch, and of recommendations of this young aspirant to art.

Rauch answers after the usual compliments, saying,—

"I can only repeat how dangerous it is for a young man destined to the pursuit of art to begin his life-course with studying its theory, instead of practising the *technique* of eye and hand, in which the greatest part of sculpture consists, and with which as a last resource the most necessary means of subsistence can be gained.

"On this account I advise placing the young Wolff with a sculptor with whom he may pass four or five years, not as a student, but as an apprentice, reserving two half-days in the week for visiting the academy for instruction in drawing. Evenings and Sundays he can consecrate wholly to the study of art.

"If there is a true impulse and vocation for art, it will show itself clearly in the years so spent; if it does not exist, he will remain, with the *technique*, a skilful workman, having a well-paid and honorable existence, of which in our modern times there is great need; for the world swarms with sighing, lazy young artists wandering about, burdening their parents and the state."

Young Wolff, and another pupil recommended by the duke, proved very able scholars. Rauch took them to his studio, and on Sunday to his table, and the duke was delighted with their progress. Rauch made repeated visits to the duke, and modelled many busts, among them those of the Duke and Duchess of Cambridge. The society was delightful, and much time was spent in excursions by water and land. A favorite amusement was found in performing living tableaux, in one of which Rauch figured as the Father in Bendemann's picture of "The Mourning Jews."

At a later visit to the duke, Rauch had much pleasure in the society of some of the court-dames, especially with Fräulein Dewitz, in whom he found much artistic sympathy. She sent him the second part of "Faust," which took possession of his whole soul, although, as he says, "without being able to follow the bold flight of this world-soul who belongs to the race of Titans," and so he reads again this "*Helena-jagd*" from the beginning. Invitations from the duke, accompanied by kind words from these gracious ladies, are more frequent than the busy artist can accept, and he answers that the "hard, weighty *must* is more powerful than the *will*." But in the hot days of July he is again there, and they find relief and refreshment in excursions to Hohenzieritz. At this time Rauch places the bust of Queen Louise in the room where she died. "It is the most beautiful marble that I have ever worked," he wrote.

This pleasant interchange of thought and letters continued until Fräulein Dewitz became the wife of Von
Bernstoff, the minister of state, in 1845, when Rauch
wrote, " I need not describe to you how happy the union
of our dear friend the Fräulein Augusta has made me."
The pleasant friendship continued unchanged.

Another old friend of the Roman days, Alexander von
Rennenkampf, who had long been a member of Alexander von Humboldt's household, now recalled himself
to Rauch's remembrance. A correspondence full of
interest followed. Rauch waited a year to answer his
first letter, that he might send him full particulars of himself and his work. Out of this correspondence grew
Rauch's interest in the nuptials of the young King Otho
of Greece, and the re-opening of the Penthelicon marble-
quarries, with the suggestion of what an inspiration it
would be to make a lovely statue of the same marble in
which Phidias and Praxiteles wrought.

One incident of this friendship was the visit to Rauch's
atelier of Rennenkampf's twelve-year-old daughter, who
writes, " I have been with my aunt to your friend Rauch's.
What an artistic man he is! with his splendid statues and
his gray hair, — a fine old man ! I like him awfully !
(*Ich habe ihm schrecklich gern an !* ")

Two blocks of Greek marble reached Rauch's workshop
in 1838 ; and he writes thus to his friend, " Now look at
me, dear friend : I bend my broad back deep down into a
right angle ; both arms sink perpendicularly to the ground,
and lips and fingers tingle with pure gratitude ; and now
having risen up you meet a stream, yea, a waterfall, of
resounding words of warmest thanks for two blocks of
marble from the holy Penthelicon, which by your suggestion and the great distinguishing favor of King Otho
have come into my atelier. One shall be used for an
ideal head which I shall begin in a few days. For the
larger one I will make a statue four feet high. I am

very proud of this royal present, since it is the first Athenian sculptors' marble which has come here for centuries.   But it will also excite me to lay my hand upon it. This marble appears to me to have different life-sap from that which is quarried at Carrara."

Out of the smaller block Rauch worked a Victory in 1843, and offered it to King Friedrich Wilhelm IV.   It bears the inscription, "Gebrochen, 1838, am Pentelikon. C. R. fec., 1843."   It stands now in the red-silk saloon in the castle of that king in Berlin.   The head is taken essentially from the second of the Victories made for the Walhalla.

On the death of Prince Radziwill, Dr. Eggers remarks that he was the only person who called out any love of music in Rauch.   This art had too little of the plastic character to interest him fully.   He became conscious of its artistic value only when it was united with dramatic expression.   When he on a Sunday dined with the prince, with Schinkel, Beuth, Wach, and Tieck, and single scenes from Goethe's "Faust" were given with only the accompaniment of the piano and violoncello, Rauch remarked, "This true, noble beauty in such a simple setting has taken hold of me wonderfully."   The new musical influence which came in with the romantic tendency of the young Mendelssohn went through circles with which Rauch had no affinity.   It was the same in literature ; the new politically colored romances had no attraction for him.   Only Immermann was sympathetic to him, and that more from his personal acquaintance than from his writings.   He sent his collected works to Rauch, which were allowed a place beside the translation of the romances of "Boz"[1] in his library.   Except these no romances had a charm for him.   Goethe, Shakspeare, Burger, Körner ; and out of the antique world Æschylus, Sophocles, and Ovid, represent the national literatures.   History had its place in the

<hr>

[1] Dickens.

collection,—Plutarch's Lives, Becker's World History, and later Ranke's History and a number of special histories, particularly that of Prussia and her military affairs, found place. But science and archæology were represented in illustrated works and innumerable maps, with more than a thousand sheets of illustrations of ancient and modern art, ornamentation, landscape, portraits, and anatomy, as well as a collection of original drawings. He also took a deep personal interest in the work of Franz Kugler in the history of art.

Rauch's social life was rich and gay. His presence was very welcome at court, and he took part in all festivities, and in theatricals and tableaux. He was interested in the representations of Wallenstein's camp, and the meeting of Richard and Saladin, with their rich costumes. All new works of art were freely discussed. Next perhaps to Schinkel, Rauch was the favorite of this circle. Science could not be neglected in a company of which Humboldt was a member; and among many new discoveries discussed was the newly invented daguerrotype, of which Humboldt gave a full explanation. In the summer months Rauch often visited the royal residences of Sans-Souci and Charlottenhof; but, while he enjoyed this social gayety, he always returned with delight and fresh vigor to his school and his work.

The old age of his master Schadow was duly honored. He had laid down the chisel, and as director of the academy served the cause of art with his pen. Shortly before his seventieth birthday his celebrated "Polyklet" was published; and on that day, in May, 1834, Rauch greeted him in the name of the Academic Senate, and presented him with a medal.

Four years later his fifty-years' connection with the academy was fitly celebrated. The venerable master received calls from seven o'clock in the morning, and was bright and happy at the evening feast.

Another of his oldest friends, the great architect Schinkel, had been suddenly attacked with illness, accompanied with difficulty of speech, in 1838 ; but for two years, by occasional resort to curative baths, he had maintained his literary activity. On the tenth of September, 1841, he visited Rauch's atelier, two days after his return from a journey to a " Cur," apparently in better health than when he left Berlin. He complained only that he saw everything double, and in rainbow colors. As Rauch went to return his call on the eleventh, he learned to his dismay that he was speechless and senseless from palsy. Most feelingly Rauch notes in his diary the progress of the disease, and the close of the life of his true friend of forty years, whose course was so glorious for art, and who was unequalled as a man and a friend.

The castle of Tegel, the residence of the minister Wilhelm von Humboldt, was always one of Rauch's happiest homes. It was built by Schinkel, and he himself aided largely in its decoration. In a letter to Frau von Humboldt he says, "Tegel looks like a marble altar set in green." It was full of beautiful works of art, some of them antiques which Rauch had restored, and others of his own designs. He finished with his own hand the marble bust of the lovely grandchild, Thérèse von Bülow, who had died at twelve years of age. Frau von Humboldt was his dear and constant friend, looking after his physical comfort when he was with her, and when he was absent writing constantly to him, even from a sick-bed, and taking the deepest interest in all his artistic plans.

Not less constant and friendly was his correspondence with her husband. Humboldt's letters are full of artistic news; and from London he writes that the king wishes him to sit to Lawrence for his portrait, and he tells of the palaces that are building, and of the statues ordered from Westmacott, Bailey, Chantrey, and others.

We can hardly imagine a happier and more beautiful

life of art and culture than existed under this friendly roof. It was only saddened by the illness of its beloved mistress, "which brought general mourning into the house."

Before this irreparable loss took place Rauch had already formed a close friendship with the distinguished brother, Alexander von Humboldt. He had long been interested in Rauch, who had modelled his bust; but when he returned from his celebrated journey to America, and took up his residence in Berlin, the intimacy grew closer, and the sculptor was included in that circle of the finest minds of Germany, to whom he expounded his grand views of the Cosmos. The delighted listeners wished to present to Humboldt a medal to "commemorate this feast of thought." It should, according to Leopold von Buch, "express that Humboldt had first brought a soul into the face of the world, and had exercised such beneficent influence over the earth as no mortal had ever done before him, unveiling one half of the globe to the other half."

On one side of the memorial was a spirited portrait in profile, with the inscription:—

ALEXANDER AB HUMBOLDT.

executed by Tieck; the reverse was an allegorical representation by Rauch.

Apollo surrounded by beams of light comes with his four span out of the background towards the spectator. Under the horses is arched the zodiac with its signs: the land and the water are represented by two reclining figures turned towards each other; the one on the right a bearded man with an urn of water and an oar, and near him the head of a sea-monster; and on the left a female figure with a horn of plenty, near which a lion rests. The circle of beams about Apollo is surmounted by the inscription:—

ILLUSTRANS TOTUM RADIIS FULGENTIBUS ORBEM.

Humboldt expressed his thanks to Rauch in writing, adding, "After such a comparison there is nothing left but to die."

Rauch often met Humboldt at Tegel, and he never forgot one beautiful Sunday morning in May. Wandering for hours in the open air with his friend, he listened to his speech with that feeling of perfect accord that we feel only in the enjoyment of nature with a kindred soul. Rauch writes in his journal, "Would I could give to every friend such enjoyment! I believe I could wish for them nothing more splendid than to hear the discourse of this man, who carries the creation of the world in his own mind, and has the talent to give it back to us all harmonized and made clear." Rauch assisted in the preparation of the funeral monument for Frau von Humboldt, and during his visit in Rome he procured statues to fill the niches on the outside of the palace. Wilhelm von Humboldt's greatest pleasure seemed to lie in the completion of his wife's favorite residence. When Rauch visited him in 1833 he found him visibly failing in health, and the next April he mourned the death of this friend of forty years. He describes his going to Tegel to visit his sick friend, accompanied by Wach : "On leaving we went," he says, "into the alley to walk to our carriages. Alexander went with us : from the height of the trellis they called to him, and we feared the worst. He wished to hasten, and he could not; he must stand still to gain strength to take the next step. This was also a grief, to see this strong, vigorous body and mind bowed down. The minister Wilhelm von Humboldt departed at this moment, six o'clock in the evening. Earlier he was my dearest support, my all; later, the most sympathizing friend, even to the last." He then recalls how tenderly Humboldt always treated him, when he felt so keenly the deficiency of his early education, and was troubled to approach so nearly to such an exalted personage. "Humboldt was always friendly, indirectly forbearing, correcting; never did I experience a mortification from him. His brother came that summer with Parisian friends from America, and I remember my astonishment over everything which I saw and heard every hour; in the room, as in the open air, in the collections, or on the old walls, and how much I wished to learn from it all, if my capacity of reception had allowed it. I enjoyed from that time even to the present, without interruption, the favor and friendship of this distinguished man and his family."

It would be hard to imagine a greater blessing for a young student than the friendship of such a man as Wilhelm von Humboldt, and the privilege of sharing the home of such a woman as his wife. It is one of the most delightful pictures of noble public service combined with domestic happiness that we find in history.

During the last year of his life Rauch's diary contains frequent notices of meetings with his friend Alexander von Humboldt, who survived him a year and a half.

Wilhelm von Humboldt was never forgotten by Rauch, as he wrote to Rennenkampf in 1835, and he loved to linger, about Tegel, where he had enjoyed such happy intercourse with him and his family. Two years later Alexander von Humboldt wrote him, inviting him to pass his sixty-eighth birthday with him, saying, "Since my brother's death you are to me the most refreshing, most charming presence in this world, which has now become almost a desert to me."

Wilhelm's oldest daughter, Caroline, had retained her home at Tegel; but after living there about two years, ill health obliged her to go to Berlin, where Rauch visited her, and when leaving her, he was struck with dismay by the emaciated hand which she reached to him from beneath the beautiful silken covering. She saw his look, and smiling turned to a picture of the young Humboldt girls, saying, "Such was Fräulein Caroline's once plump hand,

and now she reaches it to you in this state." Two weeks later Rauch went with her uncle to Tegel to her burial.

In its fourth decade, what may fitly be called the "Berlin school of plastic art" was still living. Dr. Eggers counts among the products of this school not only those artists who had grown immediately out of Rauch's school and his leadership, but also those who, although working independently, were yet inspired by his spirit, — Tieck, Wichmann, and their followers ; for their nearness to Rauch, and the weight of his mind and character, had opened to them the same wide range in which he worked.

It is not strange, however, that an artist of such a decided character, and so frank in his expression of both praise and blame, and at the same time so remarkably successful in his career, so favored by the court, as well as beloved by the people, and so prominently before the public, should have encountered some enmity, springing from rivalry and jealousy. The course of his life, as it has been traced for us from most ample sources in his private diary and letters, shows him to have been capable of the warmest friendship and most generous appreciation both for his compeers in art, and for those who sought his instruction. His life affords one of the most charming pictures of social life to be found in the history of artists; but,

> "Be thou pure as ice, as chaste as snow,
> Thou shalt not escape calumny."

Accordingly, murmurs arose of his engrossing an undue share of work and public fame, to the neglect of other artists of equal merit. Many of those whose talent he did not rate as high as their own estimate, and, still more strangely, some even of those whom he warmly appreciated, have thought that he stood in their way, instead of giving them assistance. The expression of this feeling has found its way into the artistic literature of his time and country.   Let us look the charges fairly in the face, and see what ground we can find for them.

Rauch, it is said, wished to bring all the work of his own time into his own atelier; he seized it as much as possible for himself, even snatching it out of the hands of others.   He did not suffer any one to come near him, and had not that friendliness with his scholars that Thorwaldsen had, who, without grudging, gave them his works to execute; especially he was jealous of every budding genius, if it threatened to surpass his own.   Such talent had appeared in his lifetime (and here before all Rietschel is named), and the superiority became so unquestioned after his death, that his artistic position has to be considered as entirely surpassed by that of others.

Dr. Eggers says, "So many complaints, so many errors about Rauch."   The question about his final position in art he considers later; now Rauch's personal relations to his school are to be considered.   He has been compared disadvantageously with Thorwaldsen; he might have been contrasted with Schwanthaler, whose greed and jealousy were notorious, yet interesting anecdotes can be given of Schwanthaler's generosity; and Thorwaldsen took away the work on the Frauenkirche, even after the contract was made to secure it for his own pupils.   In fact, the desire to secure great works for his own atelier is a natural one, by which all are influenced.   Competition is a stimulus in art as well as in commerce.   As Goethe said, "Mastership often passes for egotism."   The master has a right to do what he can do better than others. True artists know the difference between this genuine effort for recognition and jealous envy of others' success. Surely, Rauch's whole relations with Thorwaldsen, Tieck, and especially Rietschel, show how far he was from any such mean jealousy, and how he rejoiced in their merit and success.   We have Rietschel's own testimony in his youthful recollections.

Rauch's own letters and diaries are filled with notices of his fellow artists and pupils. He writes of them to Wolff, to Rennenkampf, and specially to Rietschel, and keeps his distant friends acquainted with all the personalities of his atelier. When he saw in Rome one of his most distinguished scholars, August Wredow, who was for thirty years in his atelier, he writes, "Wredow's statue of Ganymede is one of the finest and best-finished in Rome." He speaks in the same strain of high commendation of both Emil and Albert Wolff, of Kiss, Berges, and Drake. After speaking in praise of Kalide's work, he adds, "His moral purity makes me prize him still higher, both as a man and an artist." He mourns for Drake's sickness as involving the loss of such an excellent artist, a born sculptor, the only friend in the atelier whom I can trust and also find an answer from. Wredow is one whom he is accused of throwing into the shade; but he writes, "Wredow's model of the Paris statue is one of the finest statues of the last thirty years. Neither Thorwaldsen nor Canova have made one equal to it." But why multiply instances of a disposition which is so evident in all his life?

But was there not some ground for this tradition? Rauch did not lavish praise on crude, unfinished work, however promising; he was exacting of thorough work from himself and from his pupils, and was equally ready to give full, appreciative criticism as soon as the pupil gave signs of capacity for real mastership in art. So he watched carefully the early work of Kiss, and gladly acknowledged his ability when he began to produce the works that have since given him fame. He speaks enthusiastically of his "Amazon Tamer," even in the first sketch and model, and in his note-book he follows every step of its progress to the successful public exhibition, when it so pleased not only the artists but the public, that the Lagerhaus could not contain the numbers that flocked to see it.

Five years before, Rauch had made a sketch of a fighting lion, which he now put into the hands of his pupil Albert Wolff, with whom he worked it over and sent it to the king, and finally, in 1849, after Wolff had made seven different sketches, he gave it wholly up to him. The king was not willing to give the execution to Wolff until he had again seen Rauch's original drawing; but to Rauch's satisfaction he decided for Wolff's last sketch.

Similar proof is given by Rauch's relations to Rietschel and Drake, for thirty years his dearest scholars. He was greatly interested in the commission to Rietschel for the monument to Moser in Osnabruck, and to the King Frederic Augustus for Dresden. By Rauch's advice Rietschel made his journey to Rome before beginning this work, he having a commission to make a new model of the king's statue under the eyes of the artists of Rome, especially Thorwaldsen. But Rauch counselled him during his short stay in Rome to make nothing new of his own, but to study the works of others, making sketches of what interested him; and he advised him not to begin a new model of the king's statue, but only to make retouches on a cast, "In which I hope you will have the advantage of Thorwaldsen's counsel, and gladly remember it all in the life-sized model." He followed this work with a constant interest, which changed the pupil into an equal brother in art.

Rietschel was soon after appointed professor in the Academy of Art in Dresden, and he writes freely to his old master of the difficulties he anticipates in his new position, and adds, "How gladly would I personally share my work with you, look at my work with your eyes, and hear strong blame and good counsel from your mouth!" He dwells on his lack of good criticism, saying that of painters is the most useless of all. In this love of strict criticism we probably find the secret of Rauch's unpopularity with pupils, so far as there is any truth in it.   He was undoubtedly a strict and even severe master, and those who could not be as grateful for his strong blame as for his good counsel and generous praise turned away from him.

Another charge against him is part of the heated controversy then going on between realists and classicists. It is said that he did not give sufficient detail in his drapery, but only generalized folds.   His classic taste might well lead him in this direction, but he never followed it without careful study of his subject and of the material he intended to represent ; and if the realistic feeling of drapery is overlooked, it is because he is seeking to bring out more important meanings.   He says, —

"Do away with all superfluous folds : marble cannot endure them, much less opaque bronze."   He was much interested in bronze casting, and has high praise for the founder Fischer.

Rauch counselled Rietschel not to accept the offers of King Ludwig, but to remain in his own country ; and experience confirmed the wisdom of his advice.   Rietschel remained in Dresden, and its nearness to Berlin enabled the brother artists to have frequent personal communication.   Their correspondence shows how close their relation was, and how deeply the elder sympathized with every joy and sorrow of his former pupil.   He writes him most tenderly on the death of his cherished wife, yet tries to brace him up to seek consolation in work : " Since life is work alone, and this is the only joy in life, you will again be restored to health, and give undivided thanks to Heaven that you can look forward to so much more in this direction."

Thus Rauch was the life of the workshop and school ; judging strictly, inspiring others by his own creative work, and upholding them by counsel and sympathy.   He had always in view not alone the production of his own conceptions, but the education of others, and the development of art in Germany; and therefore he deserves to be considered as the founder of a school, and an epoch-making artist.

He was always interested in the improvement of the reproductive arts, knowing that they are essential to a broad diffusion of artistic taste and knowledge.

He had met the celebrated engravers Toschi and Richomme in Paris in 1826, and had arranged with them to receive pupils, in order to build up a school of engraving in connection with the academy of Prussia. As his own master-works began to excite attention, not only in Germany, but in other lands, he felt an interest in engraving on his own account, that those who could not see the original statues might share in the knowledge of his work.

By the command of the king lithographic reproductions had been made in 1824, by Luderitz, of the statues of the warriors Scharnhorst, Bülow, and the two Blüchers; but they were not very satisfactory. Rauch then considered the publication of engravings of his works, and took advantage of a brief correspondence with Boisserée in regard to the Goethe statue to ask his advice about it. Boisserée applied to Cotta in Stuttgart; but he at first refused to undertake it, and Boisserée advised Rauch to print a first sheet at his own cost, as a feeler which might lead to the publication by Cotta. He had drawings made from seventeen subjects, and had eight of them engraved by Berger, the son of the professor of the Royal Academy. As he had to pay ten *Friedrichs d'or* for the engraving of each plate, the outlay had already grown to nearly seven hundred thalers, when he once more made an effort to find a publisher for the nine new plates which meanwhile had been engraved by Buchhorn, also a professor of the Berlin Academy. Many attempts failed. Of Roman engravings after Thorwaldsen only one hundred and thirty copies were sold. The house of Gerstacker & Schenk finally undertook the commission. Waagen wrote the text for it. A French translation was so poor, that the state minister Ancillon, who undertook the revision of the proof-sheets, wrote to Rauch, "I know not what barbarian has ventured in this gibberish to make the pride of the fatherland known to strangers : I don't want to know him ; but it grieves me that your friendship did not trust me from the beginning with this work, and I willingly offer myself as a translator of the following sheets. Your name is a national possession, and it is the duty of every Prussian to bring it before foreigners in proper form."

The result was not satisfactory. Rauch writes to Boissérée commending the engravings to his attention, that he may see what is the condition of the art of engraving, for which the government is doing nothing. Sixty-six copies were sold in two years.

Rauch was not discouraged, however, but had the Queen Louise monument and the higher reliefs of the Blücher statue engraved by Caspar, and the lower, the expedition to France, by Eichens, who, as previously mentioned, became by Rauch's recommendation the pupil of Toschi, the celebrated engraver of Correggio's works. But these engravings did not prove good, and now by Rietschel's advice he turned to Thaeter.

This engraver has left valuable autobiographical notes and letters, from which his own interesting history and the story of his connection with Rauch can be learned. He was an early friend of Rietschel, and had a hard struggle in his artistic career. He now came to Berlin, and engraved a plate from a drawing by Rietschel of Rauch's new monument to Francke, at Halle, to the satisfaction of Rauch. Thorwaldsen was also greatly pleased with it. Thaeter, however, left Berlin for want of employment, and in 1830 we hear of him in Munich, and then in Dresden, and again busied with work for Rauch, in drawings and engravings of the Max Joseph monument and the reliefs of the Blücher monument.

Rauch writes to Rietschel in 1830, praising his work highly, and then follow special directions for the improvement of the engravings of the Max Joseph monument. "But," he adds, "do not think that I wish to find any fault with you or Thaeter ; but it is always my desire to make the thing as good as possible. If I am wrong, that is my harm and shame." So careful was he in criticism ! To further expressions of praise and slight criticism Thaeter answers with expressions of thanks, January 2, 1831 : "I can never forget that the first day that I took hold of your work was the birthday of my good luck." The work continued with frequent expressions of satisfaction and gratitude on the part of the engraver for two years. But with all his admiration for the engraving, Rauch was not quite satisfied with the representation of his conception of the statues. He gives an instance of his meaning in regard to the statue of King Max. Perhaps an explanation of this want of comprehension of the statues may be found in a remark which Thaeter made in his diary when he first began to work for Schnorr. "I must confess, also, that the Rauch subjects, on which I worked constantly, wearied me more and more," and he gave practical expression to this feeling ; for Rauch writes in 1837 to Rietschel, "I have seen or heard nothing of Thaeter since 1835, although he has yet a drawing of mine to engrave." He says also that the engravings have been rather severely criticised, which he fears Thaeter will not find pleasant ; and he has withdrawn several of the plates, and is inclined to withdraw them all, since he thinks they will not help his reputation ; and he will try to have only light sketches from Gropius. Rauch had written Thaeter four letters, asking him to make some changes in his work, before he received an answer. It was not a pleasant one. Thaeter refused to make the desired changes, and asked that his name be left off the plate if they were made by another. Rauch says, "I must, therefore, have the plates engraved as they are, and bear the injury; but I can get this satisfaction out of it, that Thaeter now is a good engraver, and can serve others better than he has served me, on which account I am not sorry, and consign my deceived hopes with the plates to oblivion."[1]   So ended Rauch's relations with Thaeter.

But some writers in encyclopædias have blamed Rauch for his treatment of Thaeter, and accused him of inviting the engraver to Berlin, and then neglecting him.   Rauch's justification can easily be found in the autobiography and letters of Thaeter, and his own letters to Rietschel.

Rauch made other experiments with different engravers, but was discouraged to find that he was left with a balance of three thousand six hundred thalers against him, and he writes to Rietschel, "What shall I do?"   He has been advised to try etching; but as a last hope he gives a single sheet of the Dürer statue to an art-house in Nuremberg, and succeeds in getting back half of the cost.   He mourns over his lost ideal of the noble German *technique*.

However, he was correct in his predictions of the success of Thaeter, who profited by the criticisms he had received, and who became the foremost artist in what was called *gezeichneten Kupferstitches*, in opposition to the *farbiger Stitch*, which strives after the effects of color.[2]

---

[1] This recital of the difficulties which Rauch encountered in the effort to obtain a worthy reproduction of his works, gives us a vivid sense of gratitude for the invention of the daguerrotype and photograph, which have placed such ample means at the command of the artist, and which instead of superseding the more permanent forms of engraving have proved themselves valuable allies.

[2] By his thorough study of drawing Thaeter did great service to the school of color, which has proved so successful in Germany; and the greatest master of this school, William Unger, confesses that he owes much to the three-years' teaching of Thaeter; and he is not the only one of his scholars who have become distinguished in the field of colored engravings.

CHAPTER XI

PORTRAIT AND MISCELLANEOUS SCULPTURE

1821-1844

THE combination of a strong sense of personal characteristics in his subjects, united with an appreciation of ïdeal representation which he never lost sight of, especially fitted Rauch for portraiture ; and accordingly we find his work in that line, both in monumental statues and in busts of living men, of great interest and value.

The sudden death of General Gneisenau from cholera stimulated the desire for a monument to this popular general, and Rauch was commissioned to make a statue. His second sketch was approved, and he confided the execution of it to Drake. The marble was embarked on the brig Fortuna from Leghorn, which was stranded, and only the crew saved, thus giving Rauch the always coveted opportunity of improving upon his work. The pecuniary loss was only the insurance premium, and he went to work at once on a new sketch. The new design was simpler and more unpretending. The cast was sent to Carrara in 1838, and was finished in January, 1841. It was unveiled with great festivities at Magdeburg, at which the king commanded the sculptor's attendance.

I must pass over many projects of work, some of which were given up, and some only carried out at a later period, in order to speak of the busts which now occupied much of his time. This work was not entirely to Rauch's taste ; for he felt the expression of the whole figure, and was not contented with that of the head alone.

He writes to Rietschel in warm praise of his bust of Prince John, saying that he has himself spent much time in such work, and he knows how much is needed, from the first blocking out of the clay to the last stroke of the chisel, in order to give satisfaction to one's self or the spectator. But fears arise in his mind that this success will lead to great business of this kind for Rietschel, instead of which he wishes him to turn to greater works.

To Lund he calls the demands for likenesses an "everlasting plague," especially when he has to work from insufficient material, death-masks, or poor pictures; "always new stuff for hypochondria and dark hours; a work of necessity, of dislike, and without prospect of success, which is unfortunately unavoidable, and so often repeated and so burdensome that it makes me tired." This last expression in the diary refers to the bust of the minister of foreign affairs, Count von Bernstoff, which the king had commanded, and which he had to make from the death-mask. In spite of all difficulties he succeeded to the perfect satisfaction of the king. Among the many busts which he had to make from death-masks, we are interested in one taken of August Ernst, the Count Voss, who died in 1832, and who was the grandson of the well-known Countess Voss, who was sixty-nine years at the Prussian court, "*eine Hofmeisterin, wie sie sein soll.*" The face of this count, scarcely entered into his sixtieth year, is of winning, friendly sweetness, and reminds one partly in the form, but still more in the expression, of the portrait of his grandmother, which is given in the " Remembrances of Her Life." Among these many busts, more or less wearisome, Rauch had genuine satisfaction in making one of Stägemann, which was ordered by his friends for a festival commemoration of his fifty years of official life. " I shall finish to-morrow," he writes, "the bust of the councillor Stägemann, in which no common face or form of head appears, but only a right living physiognomy seventy-five years old; what a work!   The splendid man is so dear to me that I am going to do this work *gratis*, as a memorial."

Schadow prized Rauch's work in portrait busts very highly; in no other branch does he praise him more fully. In 1810 he said of a bust by Thorwaldsen, "Just in this line he stands after our Professor Rauch."   This judgment may be justified by comparing the busts by Rauch of Alexander von Humboldt and the children, Gustav and Louise, with the busts of Wilhelm von Humboldt and his wife, by Thorwaldsen.   " Every one recognizes the feeling of a ' speaking likeness ' which we have in looking at a good portrait, even when we do not know the original; but Thorwaldsen's busts gives us the impression of unlikeness.   Did Caroline von Humboldt look so ? asks one, doubting, and those who knew her aver that she did not. The effects seem labored, and the marble remains cold and impassive."   This seems to me to point out by contrast the especial technical merit of Rauch's busts, in the exquisite flexibility of the muscles, so that the face seems sensitive and ready to express any emotion, while it is full of present dignity and repose.

Rauch continued to justify this favorable judgment of his old master in increasing measure.   He never did any careless work.   Even if he did not willingly undertake a bust, he gave the same conscientious attention to it as if it were his own choice; and he always examined every copy of his often-repeated works in marble.   His busts in marble seem to have been a favorite present from one prince to another.   In May, 1821, Rauch modelled the Crown Prince Nicholas of Russia, who was then on a visit to Berlin.   When he came again in 1829 as emperor, the bust was remodelled from nature, the face made somewhat fuller, the hair of the head less abundant, and the beard stronger.

1822 was a very busy year for busts.   In February he finished the model of his daughter Agnes, begun in the previous November. He began putting it in marble in 1837, and changed the style of hair to a wavy crown. I have not seen the criticism elsewhere, but it seems to me that Rauch was a little over-fond of this style of a crowned or wreathed head in his female busts, and that it gives an over-weight to the top of the head, which disturbs the symmetry and lessens the force of character. He continued this work in 1844, and added an ivy wreath, whose berries hung down on the side. In the following year he received the bust blocked out in Carrara marble by Sanguinetti; but it was not finished until thirty years later, in 1850, when only a little change of the mouth was needed.

In 1826 the Duke of Wellington ordered the bust of King Friedrich Wilhelm III., which Rauch modelled in his full uniform. This bust was repeated, with changes in drapery, many times for distinguished princes and generals.

In 1828, having no outside commissions for busts, he modelled one of himself. He made it without drapery, and slightly turned to the left ; and he says others thought the likeness good. This bust went to his friend Lund, in Copenhagen, who uncovered it on festal occasions. Caroline von Fouqué, the wife of the poet, writes enthusiastically of it to Rauch, and concludes, "Of your clear, good eye, which shines out so life-like from the white plaster, and of the smiling mouth which trembles with a jest, and smiles within and without, I might say many things, and yet not say enough." In 1829 Rauch made a bust of his friend Schleiermacher. Schleiermacher had confirmed Rauch's daughters in their early years ; and now while his bust was in progress came the joyful espousal feast of the eldest daughter, Agnes, to Dr. Eduard d'Alton. The wedding was celebrated by Schleiermacher in a circle of friends of distinction, including Humboldt, Schinkel, Wach, Tieck, Bunsen, Schadow, Schlesinger, Rietschel, and many others.

Schleiermacher's bust was put in marble by contributions from members of his congregation and other friends.
He is clothed in a preacher's gown ; the face is slightly
turned to the left, and expresses the mild, eloquent character of the great preacher.   The execution is masterly, and
this is perhaps the best bust of that period.   Since 1869
it has stood in bronze at the foot of Lubeck's Height in
Breslau, Schleiermacher's birthplace.   The same summer
Rauch modelled the young Prince Alexander, afterward
Emperor of Russia, which was repeatedly copied in marble ;
and finally he took in hand the portrait of Frederic the
Great, begun two years before.

The number of busts executed in ten years, between
1819 and 1829, most of which are now in the Rauch Museum, amounts to about forty.   I condense slightly Dr.
Egger's admirable account of Rauch's work in busts : —

" A comparison of the busts in their chronological order
shows, besides an increasing care and skill in the execution, a continual development of the master in recognizing the demands the bust makes as a subject of plastic
art.   Originally Rauch was led by the feeling that the
bust is the head of an imaginary statue.   It was on this
account placed in sympathetic action in position and expression, even in excited action, since from such a point of
view the head alone represents the action of the body and
the limbs ; hence the energetic turn of the head, the
expression of a determined thought in the countenance.
This decided character shown in the Blücher busts by the
grim, decided turning to the left ; in the Scharnhorst by
the inclination of the head turned sharply to the right, in the
expression of energetic reflection turned to a single point,
is decidedly weakened in the following period of ten years.
The strong turning of the head appears only as a movement of a general character.   We know only two heads
strongly turned to the side ; those of the Count Ingenheim and the Grand Duke Nicholas.   In the latter it be-

comes almost a profile view, and expresses very happily the quick, energetic character of the duke, without indicating any action of the moment. The decided turn has become a very slight inclination, so that the spectator does not see an entirely front face, in which the characteristic modelling of the forehead and nose are not so well shown as on the side.

"In the expression of the bust, momentary action is less and less given, and the general character, the ideal content of expression, put in its place, as the model statues of the antique teach us ; and as this has become a leading art principle with the old master Schadow, when he gives the rule, ' It is not wise to show the expression of emotions in a bust.' In keeping with these views Rauch generally puts the head on a pedestal without drapery, or, if he uses it, it is in the antique style ; the Ionic chiton for women, the toga for men. In rare cases he uses the military uniform or cloak, or the gown of a preacher, as in the case of Schleiermacher.

"Opposed to this approach to the ideal stands the single realistic movement, to enliven the physiognomic expression by emphasizing the pupils of the eyes through depression, and a deepened circle to produce an effect like painting, a plastic untruth which (it must be modestly said, since Rauch did it), if it does not overpass the bounds of art, at least comes very near the edge."

"Until the year 1822 only two busts, those of the Princess Charlotte and of General Scharnhorst, are known with the indication of the pupil ; in the time from 1823 to 1826 we find very many without this indication, and from that time till 1830 we see none of the busts without it, and after that only in special cases, in which this mark is left out for evident reasons."

I may add here an account of the portrait statue of Friedrich Wilhelm I. at Gumbinnen. This royal ancestor was a great favorite of Friedrich Wilhelm III., who found in him the pacific virtues which he sought to emulate, — energy, order, and economy, with religious tolerance and the encouragement of industry, while he had also won military renown by the establishment of the *Landwehr* and the extension of Prussian territory. He was protector of the Protestants, who were oppressed by Austria. Nearly eighteen thousand of the citizens of the archbishopric of Salzburg left their old homes to accept those offered by Friedrich Wilhelm. The lands desolated by the plague offered room enough, and so Gumbinnen became a city. The king cared for this colony till his death. Six cities, over three hundred villages, and some six thousand houses were built up, and the impoverished land became blooming and prosperous. On the centennial anniversary of the founding of their city, the people of Gumbinnen were very anxious to erect a statue of their founder. Rauch was engaged to make a sketch. His first sketch pleased the king; but the execution of it was long delayed, waiting for Schinkel's plans for the pedestal. Many details then vexed the sculptor, such as questions in regard to the cost of the inscriptions, which now are left to the stone-cutter.

The king saw the statue in 1838, at the same time as the second one of Queen Louise. He was satisfied on the whole, but made some criticisms on the buttons and ornaments, and thought the head too youthful. After some difficulties in the casting were overcome, Rauch was at last able to show the finished statue to the magistrates of Gumbinnen in 1830.

But the placing of the statue was long delayed. The rising in Poland, the spread of the cholera, and finally a destructive fire, made it hard to pay the cost of the work, which was about fifteen hundred thalers; and the king, in consequence of a petition from the city magistrates, finally paid it in 1835, so that on his birthday the unveiling could take place. It now stands in the marketplace at Gumbinnen.

The representation of the king is excellent.   The bearing is sturdy, corresponding to his simple, vigorous character; and he has an earnest, benevolent expression. Being the first among the princes of Europe to wear the simple soldier's coat instead of a court-dress, he is clothed in the military dress of his time, in pointed boots, close-fitting trousers, long vest, and an open embroidered overcoat, with stiff collar and facings, out of which appear the ruffs and cuffs.   The ermine cloak is closed on the right shoulder, and the right hand is raised as in blessing.   The right side of the body is free, while the other side of the cloak is raised half way up the body by the left hand leaning on the sword.

We have, fortunately, one fine specimen of the portrait bust in America, which will reward the study of those who have become interested in the work of the German sculptor.

Rauch's bust of Alexander von Humboldt in the Corcoran Gallery is a beautiful specimen of his portrait work. It was made especially for Mr. Corcoran, at Humboldt's request.   The quality that most struck me was the exquisite flexibility of the muscles, which seemed to quiver with changes of thought, as seems very characteristic of the man.   The whole expression is very tender and sweet, while the fine brow and clear outlook indicate his intellectual power.   A man of affection and thought one would be inclined to say, rather than of extreme willpower, and yet he knew well how and when to act.   The dimpling effect around the mouth gives a feminine beauty to the face; but the fine modelling of the muscles of the neck shows that Rauch did not seek beauty at the expense of firmness.

This bust is slightly changed in the turn of the head from the one for which Humboldt sat in 1851.   This well-known early bust had ceased to resemble him, and, at the command of the king, Rauch, in four sittings, made the bust of the gray-haired author of the " Cosmos " which has become the typical likeness. It was given to the king in marble in 1854, and in 1856 it was repeated for Mr. Corcoran, it is said at the special request of Humboldt.

In 1825 Rauch received a commission for a monument to August Hermann Francke, the founder of an orphan asylum in Halle. This was a happy departure from the old custom of raising statues only to princes and warriors. Rauch felt that in this statue the beautiful, modest, humane spirit of the man was to be shown, and this could be done only in a group, and he placed Francke between two of his orphan boys. This design being presented to the committee, Chancellor Nemeyer said, " In order to build a monument to the humane Francke, one must himself be a man as humane as the excellent Rauch." The sketches and casts were subjected to severe and even unfriendly criticism, and there was much dispute about a place for the statue ; but the contract was finally executed in July, 1826. The original design was changed by making one of the side figures a little girl, a happy idea, which must have touched Rauch's feelings. The children wear shoes, and are draped in sleeveless shirts, girded at the waists, — an ideal costume, which unites well with the quiet handling of the spiritual robe. This happy idea of the children opened to Rauch a whole new plastic activity, which he repeated in marble and bronze, and which led to the later forms of children in which he personified Faith, Love, and Hope.

In the monument of the Princess of Darmstadt, as in the Psyche image of Adelaide von Humboldt, Rauch found an opportunity for uniting ideal expression with portraiture. The reliefs connected with the portrait gave this opportunity, and Rauch could never feel satisfied with any work of art that did not unite these two characters. At this same time he was engaged on the monument to Maximilian Joseph of Bavaria, the sides of which were to be ornamented with reliefs. " This was a busy time in his atelier, both busts and monumental works in various stages of relief being found there.   Scarcely was the last touch put upon the reliefs of the Blücher monument, when already the clay was being formed into sketches which in nine years grew into the colossal monument for the Bavarian capital ; and the immense figure of Friedrich Wilhelm I. was built up near the almost finished models of the three figures of the Francke monument.   The marble dust flew under the chisel and file which were finishing the evangelists and the baptismal font, the Cooper monument and the marble image of the Psyche.   Dazzling lights played on the deep-colored clay sketches of the Goethe statue, and the designs in antique style for Cassel ; while their progenitors, the muses Urania and Polyhymnia, looked earnestly at these followers ; for Rauch had given to these antique forms the head and face which an envious fate had hidden from their discoverers.   What forms of creative fancy were here !   Along the walls, on ledges and stands they stood ready ; on tripods they awaited their final destiny ; while in a separate hidden work-room the hand of the master lightly raised the last veil from the second marble image of Queen Louise." From the queenly woman, Rauch passed to the representation of a beautiful child, also in the sleep of death.   In 1821 the Princess Elizabeth, daughter of the Arch-Duke Ludwig of Bavaria, died in her sixth year.   Moller, a celebrated architect, was commissioned to build a mausoleum, for which Rauch was to model the sleeping child. He accepted the commission with such zeal that at the end of the week he sent three sketches, of which he recommended the last one.   Only a slight change in hair and drapery was desired by the mother.   He afterwards sent the cast, asking for further instructions.   The princess gave suggestions for improving the likeness, but was so pleased with the design that she begged Rauch to exe-

cute it with his own hand, saying that she would willingly
wait longer for his own work. Rauch needed no urging
to do this work so dear to his feelings ; but he was unable
to finish and send it until August, 1831. By Rauch's wish,
Moller made some changes in the mausoleum, especially
softening the contrasts of color by the use of *giallo antico*,
and by having the window painted with flowers and leaves,
so that the burial-place might appear like a summer bower
lighted by the morning sun.

The lovely child lies in slumber, the curly head turned
to the right, the soft drapery leaving the arm and head
bare, while the little foot and ankle are shod with a laced
boot. The right hand holds an unfinished wreath, into
which the loose flowers in the left hand were to have been
woven. She has fallen asleep, weaving a garland for her
young life. The mausoleum is no longer as Moller built
it, and in 1878 a larger building was in progress, under the
direction of Professor Wagner of Darmstadt.

He also received a commission for a funeral monument
to the wife of Count Schulenburg. The plan was for a
standing figure whose left hand, perhaps holding a tear-
cloth, rests on an urn of ashes, while with the other she
expresses thankfulness. It was to stand on an altar decorated with snakes, reversed torches, cypress branches,
and other emblems of death. Rauch made several sketches,
and this monument was finally completed and placed on
the grave ; but there is some doubt as to the part which
Rauch took in the execution. His interest in the work
was not sufficient to make him anxious to finish every
detail of the work himself, and the many allegorical accessories seemed to him too much in the expiring Rococo
style. Dr. Eggers thinks it most probable that Tieck had
a large share in the work. The statue itself is thoroughly
classic in style, and reminds one " of that priestess who, .
banished to the altar of Diana in Tauris, stands long
days on the shore, seeking the land of Greece with her

soul. But the action of this hand and face points not to a land beyond the seas, but to another beyond, to which the soul is turned."

Whether in connection with this work, or from other causes, we know not, but differences of temperament and methods of work brought about a little coolness of feeling between these two artists who had long worked so harmoniously together. While Rauch was excessively methodical and punctual, virtues or faults which are not apt to lessen with age, Tieck on the other hand had no consideration for time, and would linger over his books and his favorite studies far into the night, and unfit himself for work on the following day. His pecuniary affairs were also in disorder from his constantly lavishing money on his sister's family. Rauch writes to Humboldt in 1822 that it is hopeless, since what can Tieck do when he works only to pay off debts? Owing to these differences of habits the artists separated their households. But so soon as Rauch went away for a summer trip of a few weeks, Tieck resumed his old habit of writing constantly to him, and begins one of his letters, "Although it is no longer probable, dearest friend, that you can receive this letter, yet I cannot bring my heart to let the post-day go by, even although I have nothing to write." The little division of feeling was temporary, and although Tieck's pecuniary embarrassments continued, Rauch did not weary in his efforts to procure him suitable work. It is quite probable that this motive led to his work on the Schulenburg monument.

Another very interesting work of this period, about 1822, was the adaptation of the figures of the apostles of Peter Vischer from St. Sebald's Church at Nuremberg. In preparation for the celebration of the three hundredth anniversary of the Reformation, Schinkel was commissioned to prepare a new design in classical style to conceal the tasteless appearance of the old cathedral built by Frederic

the Great in 1747. Before the high altar he arranged a
screen, for which he designed a bronze grating. It opened
through three doors ornamented with rich arabesques in
Schinkel's style of Greek renaissance. Fluted pillars,
with simply composed capitals, form the supports of the
grating, and they are so far apart that between each two
is the statuette of an apostle, the adaptation of which was
committed to Rauch. Schinkel had for this purpose determined on bronze casts of the celebrated twelve apostles
of St. Sebald's monument by Peter Vischer, and he committed to Rauch's atelier the restoration of the forms,
with the necessary proportions, and also the revision of
them to correct formal faults, in order that the *technique*
might be brought into harmony with the style of Schinkel.
Little change of this kind was needed, on account of the
excellence of this work of the flowering time of German
renaissance.

The best of Vischer's figures are copied exactly, or
with very slight variations. So the well-known Paul, the
Thomas, the elder James, and Bartholomæus are unchanged. The robe of Peter is a little shortened, and
with John and Philip the position of the right hand is somewhat changed, and the same is the case with some features of Andrew and Matthew. All these changes which
seemed necessary to the harmony of the general effect were
carried out under Rauch's direction by his helper Peter
Kaufmann.

But he reserved for himself and Tieck two statues
which seemed to require more essential changes. Tieck
altered the awkward position of the left arm, stretched
forwards with the book in Simon Xelotes, and changed
somewhat the position of the saw and drapery.

Rauch himself undertook what he thought to be the
weakest figure, the Thaddeus. In the general position of
the body, only the left leg is changed, so that it turns a
little more to the left, with the foot turned outwards. He

has also changed the left arm ; and the club which Vischer's figure held in a painful position, perpendicular to the body, he has placed on 'the ground near the left foot, so that it is easily supported by the arm.   The drapery is entirely altered.   In harmony with the other statues Rauch has given him an under-garment reaching to the ground, while Vischer left the lower half of the thigh bare, and covered the upper part with breeches.   The cloak which Vischer had drawn smoothly about the body like an apron, Rauch has thrown like a toga over the shoulder, with beautiful folds under the left arm.   The classic taste of the modern sculptor appears in strong contrast to the simple directness of the old German art.   Although I can readily believe that Rauch's dignified and impressive figure is more in harmony with Schinkel's architecture than Vischer's own work would have been, I cannot think with complacency of thus using another artist's work.   It seems like forcing on him a dress he might not willingly wear.

Tieck also prepared the angels in copper for the niches, and Rauch presented the marble baptismal font, which was decorated with fishes and palms in a simple and pleasing manner.   It was not wholly finished until 1831, which Rauch thinks was fortunate, as he executed it in a more thorough manner than he could have done before.

Dr. Eggers makes an interesting comparison between the representations of the apostles by Thorwaldsen and by Vischer ; but I can only call attention to the superior robustness and energy of the latter.

Rauch knew the statues of Vischer only by casts, until a short time before the work was completed ; but in the winter of 1828 he spent four weeks in a journey to Nuremberg and Munich.   He saw the statues in company with Reindel, the engraver in copper, and he says of them that all the figures are conceived with fine invention, and with especial boldness, character, and lightness.   The heads are modelled and finished with great care.   All the upper figures and groups are the most spirited sketches of modern sculpture, and the heads are noble masterpieces in their position and expression. The children are beautiful in form, and certainly must have been modelled from observation in a nursery. The architecture may be well conceived for the time, but it is rough in execution, and the reliefs are excellent in every respect. Each apostle weighs between sixty and eighty pounds. What a valuable influence on Rauch this study of the genuine old German art must have had at a time when his tendency to classicism was so strong.

The tender feeling shown by Rauch in the mausoleum of the queen led many to desire to have their beloved dead as beautifully portrayed, and many commissions came to him for monumental works. In 1823 he received one from the Duchess of Cumberland, the sister of Queen Louise, to make a reclining statue of a still-born child, of which Westmacott (the English sculptor) had made a death-mask. Rauch made a beautiful design of a portrait head with the little body fully draped resting on extended Psyche wings. It is an exquisite creation, which might suggest a soul so pure that it needed not the discipline of mortal life.

A monument for the wife of Sir Edward Cooper occupied him many years. Sir Edward wished the harp of Erin and other emblems introduced, which conflicted with the taste of the sculptor, who had hard work to make his ideas conform to the exacting requirements of Sir Edward. He says it was a great test of his perseverance, and he did not get his usual vacation, which nearly brought on hypochondria. "The remembrance of such art," he says, "will make him turn with more delight to the work on the Victory for the Walhalla." The statue was successful in England.

Rauch worked more cheerfully, we may believe, with Schinkel and Tieck on the monument to General Scharn-

horst in the Invalid Church in Berlin.   Tieck represented
the life of the hero on the surface of the sarcophagus,
while to Rauch was intrusted the modelling of the lions,
which he studied first from the antique, and afterwards
from nature, for which a menagerie at Berlin gave him
opportunity.   His attention being thus called to the study
of lions, he did not rest until he had become able to represent them according to his own thought.   He has modelled not only the lion in deep sleep, but the lion in battle;
and in 1829 he designed the group of lion conquerors,
which he executed thirty years later for the staircase of
the museum.

He gave similar careful study to the monarch of the
air, the eagle.   He carved it on the Bülow monument,
both sitting and flying.   In 1820 he attempted the heral-
dic representation of the armorial eagle according to the
arms of Friedrich I., which three years later was finely
executed in cast iron, and placed on the gates of all the
fortresses of the Prussian states.   In 1823 he modelled a
free-standing eagle with the crown for the gate-posts of
Coblenz and Ehrenbreitstein.   This standing eagle he
has modelled again life-size after fresh studies from nature,
and finally he has made it in smaller size, in order to have
it cast in bronze for an ornament for a bookcase.   Then
in 1844 he modelled for the finance-minister an eagle in
relief; and even in the last year of his life he made that
majestic eagle crowned with laurel which in the native
land of the Prussian dynasty adorns the royal buildings
in Sigmaringen.   It is the same eagle that we have
already met on the monuments of Bülow and Scharnhorst, but carried to the highest perfection by the continual study of nature.

In connection with these accounts of the lions and
eagles, which have something of an allegorical character,
I may mention the two life-sized stags ordered by the
Grand Duke of Mecklenburg-Strelitz in 1827.   The duke,

who was a passionate hunter, wished for these stags as
ornaments for the pillars at the entrance of his park.
Rauch had little opportunity to make the necessary studies, and was obliged to rely mainly on the engravings in
the grand duke's library. The stags are represented as
counterparts, the heads turned towards each other, and
without essential differences. The duke was pleased,
and Rauch was the only one dissatisfied; for he always
desired to make thorough work. As he visited New Strelitz his dissatisfaction with the stags increased, and at last
found expression. The duke promised him a stag's head,
with its crown of horns ; and when he at last killed a stag
of ten, he sent it to Rauch wrapped in a cloth dipped in
brandy. Rauch writes September 21, 1835, "It came to
me so promptly and so fresh that there were two nice
roasting-pieces for the share of the moulders, who drank
your highness's health in chorus, and thankfully sounded
forth the merits of the fine present ; they loudest for the
meat, and I, more inwardly, for the bones, each happy
according to his taste. Before the banquet the head was
modelled and cast in plaster, and the 'Royal Anatomy'
cared for the curing and bleaching of the bones."
Rauch placed the cast and the whitened skeleton, with
the antlers attached, in his atelier for his own instruction,
and as a perpetual model to others, "so that in future in
collections we may see the antlers suitably placed, and
not stuck on like goats' horns." Rauch repeatedly received from his princely patron other parts of stags, which
are now preserved in the collection of models at the Rauch
Museum. But when the duke, many years later (in 1844),
spoke of putting the stags on the castle in Strelitz, and
the king also ordered them for himself, Rauch began the
thorough revision of his model ; and he found that he had
to change almost everything. The heads, the breasts,
even to the withers, were to be made smaller, and the legs
had to be remodelled. With the help of his assistant

Devaranne, he finished the first model in February of that year, but not according to his wish; and he worked two months longer on the careful touching up before he declared the model finished. Two years later they were cast in bronze, to guard the last entrance of the Wild Park in Potsdam. Casts of these stags are in many private grounds.

A very pleasing design of Rauch's, which showed more sympathy with the romantic spirit of the time than he often yielded to, is the *Yungfrau Lorenz* and the stag. This pleasing legend relates that the maiden, being lost in a wood, prayed earnestly for deliverance, when a stag appeared, by whom she was carried to her home. This subject was partly suggested by an old carving in the church of Tangermunde representing the maiden hanging between the antlers of a stag. The religious expression of the subject harmonized with the feeling of the moment, when the people were praying for deliverance from the cholera.

Rauch's religious feelings were direct and simple, and he loved this expression of confident trust. But as the ideal and real were always present in his mind, he also enjoyed the representation of the stag which he had formerly studied so carefully, when carving them for his friend the duke. Rauch's representation of the original as riding on the stag may have been taken from ancient coins. The ease with which she rides the wild creature gives a hint of the miraculous character of the event. This group was cast in bronze, and plaster casts were made and sold all over Europe ; for it gratified the longing of the people for romantic and sentimental devotion.

Rauch was also very much interested in the art of relief in the stamping of coins and medallions. He tried to establish a school for this work, but did not receive much encouragement from the government. He succeeded, however, in interesting Beuth of the Gemeinde

Institute in the plan, and he secured the instruction of three pupils for three years in stone-cutting. As early as 1826 he had received a commission for a medallion to commemorate the introduction of vaccination. He has treated this somewhat prosaic subject with great simplicity and beauty.

An old physician sits on a low bench, while a young mother brings her two babes for the protecting ministry, at which she looks with some awe. The older child, nearly nude, hardly shrinks from the touch, but looks with curiosity on the operation, while the little one clings timidly to the mother's knees. The cow in the background adds to the picturesqueness of the group, while it suggests the meaning of the whole.

A bass-relief of Christ crowned with thorns (I believe his only attempt at that subject) is full of health and sweetness, but it has hardly the depth of expression of Him who bore the sorrows of the world.

Rauch's desire for ideal work had not as yet been satisfied. As early as 1820 he had in his mind the conception of a Danaid, and his day-book notes, "Modelled the sketches for a nymph for the long bridge." This work was never forgotten, although many interruptions and delays occurred in carrying out his conception. It is said that a very beautiful flower-girl, whom Rauch often saw sitting in an archway selling her flowers, was the model of his first sketch. Rauch was unwearied in the study of a subject that had seized on his imagination. He often felt as if his past work were fruitless, but this feeling stimulated him to fresh exertion; for he was too broad and healthy to yield to despondency.

But while at work on the Danaid, fortune had most welcome commissions in store for him. The Count of Hohenthal, at Priessnitz, ordered a marble statue of an Apollo Musagetes for the monument to his son; and scarcely had he designed the sketch for this, when a commission came from the Countess Reichenbach to adorn the staircase of the Electoral palace with ten marble statues and candelabra. The subjects were to be mythological, and of his own choice; "By which," he writes to Lund, "the noblest nude shall be predominant. . . . Thou canst not feel," he says, "how this word strikes my ear, which for so many years has heard only *pantalono*, and the which saw nature only *en pantalon*. I need not assure you how much more freely I shall design under these auspices."

In September, 1826, he went to Cassel for an interview in regard to these works. Agnes accompanied him. He was received by the court director, the elector, and the countess, on the staircase he was to decorate; and all the splendors of the palace and gardens were shown to him. The contract was made for ten marble statues, to be finished in five years, for forty thousand gülden; and four groups, three feet high, for the ornament of the splendid fireplace. Rauch joyfully wrote to Lund that he was delighted with his reception. Lund replied to him, "I understand how joyfully you go to such work, and sansculottism is allowable in art; but one who solved the hard riddle of representing modern clothing in plastic art so well as you have, must not be too hostile to pantaloons." In the winter of 1837 two sketches in clay of Hero and Leander, and one of Psyche, were finished, and preparations for placing them were already made, when political troubles prevented the elector from continuing the work. He left ungrateful Cassel in anger, and there was no more talk of the work for the palace. Even the sketches are lost, and nothing remains of that dream of a future of ideal creation.

Although Rauch's taste inclined so strongly to the classic in art, and he did not enter fully into the romantic sentiment of his time and country, and besides was even somewhat severe in his manners, and strict in his discipline, he was yet full of affection and religious feeling. Early in life he had promised to give a work of art to the church in his native place, Arolsen ; and, being reminded of his promise in 1831, he sent sketches of three charming statues of boys, representing Faith, Hope, and Love, for the use of the church.

After some correspondence in regard to the placing of the statues, Rauch decided to revisit his native place, where he had not been for thirty-two years. He was received with the greatest enthusiasm by his fellow-townsmen, who were proud of his renown and grateful for the affection he had shown them. His own beautiful letter will give the best idea of his feelings in making this visit : —

AROLSEN, June 2, 1844.

"Could I make a statue of the longing, as I have felt it for years, and now the joyful realization of seeing again our dear native town, then could I paint to you, most worthy friend, the state of soul, and all that moved me at the side of our friend Schuhmacher, as mine eyes found again the wooded hills, the meadows, the whole view of the long-desired dear native town ; but the pen cannot do it, and so I must leave it to your own feelings to carry out these hints. And then in the neighborhood of the first houses, this unexpected amphitheatre of images, welcomed by a crowd of every age, the nodding of groups and single men, that truly greeted me like a friend who had been absent only a day !

"How with wet cheek my heart beat in joyful gratitude he only can feel with me who, born in the quiet country, educated with narrow means, — I must say it loud and clear, — through God's blessing alone, has reached to that which blesses me. With torchlight procession and swelling song ended this joyful day of the welcome to art in the artist of the fatherland, so that I felt with true emotion that every shake of the hand was like a hoppity-skip to a child. All which love can offer I drained. I have on this evening given thanks aloud to Heaven.

"And high honors were repeatedly given me, and even the city accepts me, joyfully among her citizens. I might assure you each one of my fulness of thanks for so many proofs of love on this joyful day in the fatherland, but I cannot speak it in words. Every one must be convinced that I shall keep gratefully these precious hours in my heart, as the most beautiful picture of my life."

If he could not do it in words, he has most beautifully expressed it in these lovely childish figures, in which we feel his religious and affectionate nature so fully, and which have so entirely the simplicity of antique representation. They became exceedingly popular, and he repeated them in many ways. He made several sketches of the figures of Hope, one of which he designed for his own grave, and one for that of his brother.

Kugler said of the statue of Love, "Who could refuse that boy anything ?"

The praying maiden was another favorite subject of this class. Dr. Eggers says "that he for the first time in plastic art expressed the true spirit of the Protestant religion, and opened a path for art that has been only very rarely trodden since." This again was accomplished by his rare power of combining the ideal and the real; for the best spirit of Protestantism blends fidelity to the duties of this world with the hope of the future.

There is something very touching in the thought of this circle of youthful figures in which the gray-haired man has expressed the love and faith of his soul, after he had completed the grand monument of the stormy days of his youth, in which the conquests of the sword rather than of the spirit are celebrated. It shows how in passing on towards the kingdom of heaven he was becoming again as a little child in his love of tender and beautiful themes, yet losing nothing of his skill and expression.

This class of work fitly began with the Francke monument, and his progress is shown in the beautiful boy with the shell. It seemed as if the antique spirit, which does not seek to express an unreal sentimentality, but the natural, healthy life of childhood, had again returned to us. The well-known antique group of the boy and goose is a happy instance of this feeling. The children of the Francke group are not wholly free from sentimentality, perhaps because they are charity children. But the " noble three " are fully in the Greek style. Rauch has given them only the simplest attributes, letting them tell their own story in attitude and expression. His Protestant simplicity is shown in this, and also in the fact that, instead of the cross, Faith holds the open Bible. Hope only is winged : she bears us upward. In one nude sketch the upraised arms alone express the outreaching to that which is beyond.

These childlike expressions of great truths forcibly recall to us William Blake's exquisitely simple verses, one of which might form a fitting motto for Rauch's statues : —

> " For Mercy has a human heart,
>   Pity a human face ;
> And Love the human form divine,
>   And Peace the human dress."

CHAPTER XII

CONDITION OF ART IN GERMANY. — WALHALLA AND VICTORIES

1830–1857

BEFORE continuing the account of Rauch's great works in sculpture, I must, under the lead of our accomplished guide, Dr. Eggers, take a brief survey of the conditions of politics, literature, and art in Germany and Europe. This will be the more interesting to us as we now come upon familiar ground, when German art began to attract attention in this country.

Europe was in a state of great unrest. "The news of misfortunes in France press one upon another," wrote Rauch in his day-book on the fifth of August. At a tea-party at the house of the crown princess, at which Rauch was present, he heard the event of the Revolution of July, the dethronement of the king, the unfolding of the tri-color, and the appointment of the Duke of Orleans as lieutenant-general of the kingdom.

The uneasiness in the higher circles increased, as the symptoms of excitement among the lower orders on that side of the Rhine might prove kindling sparks in Germany. Belgium at the same time had violently separated from Holland. Disturbances of the work-people were taking place, and the contagion was spreading over the German border. Even Berlin, on the seventeenth of September, had its tailors' uproarious feast, in which the Field-Marshal Diebitsch-Sabalkanski, whose bust Rauch was then making for the Walhalla, with difficulty escaped the sabre blows of the armed crowd who went out of the palace yard, which he had unsuspiciously entered in common citizen's dress.

There was a general uproar and fear throughout Germany and Europe. "The great states were in fear of a general war, and the little ones of a powerful inward convulsion."

These events acted differently on the French and German minds. While the French sought to express their ideas in action, and an immediate change of institutions, the Germans found expression in songs, speeches, and processions; working less violently, but quite as powerfully through all literature and life. "The struggle," says Dr. Eggers, "was less bloody, but not less bitter." Unlike the French the Germans delayed long between a decision and an action. Deeds of violence are not conformable to the spirit of the German people, and the July Revolution of France was re-echoed by May festivals and songs and shouts.

Political feelings found their expression in national literature, as it had already prepared the way for them. How rich was the French romance-writing of the epoch of the July Revolution which, indeed, such writers as Victor Hugo, George Sand, Dumas, Sue, and others had largely helped to produce. In Germany political events had not yet come to their ripeness, and much of the popular writing was vague and formless. But one word came into prominence which was more than a whole book. Men began to talk about Young Germany; and although the growing boy was often as noisy, inconsequent, and obstreperous as boys are apt to be, yet they are after all good stuff to make men of; and it was from this new, young, rich life that a strong, manly national spirit might be hoped for.

It is almost impossible to give in brief space an idea of the intense feeling between the romanticists and the classicists, which under differing forms now agitated the literary and artistic world. Rauch, whose temperament was calm and healthy, and whose great merit was the admirable balance of the spiritual and the natural in his thought, had not looked without interest on this new phase of art, and had even "paid tribute to it" in the statue of the "*Jungfrau Lorenz.*" But he was shocked at the extravagances of the times, and especially at the suicide of Charlotte Stieglitz, who killed herself in a fanciful belief that it would restore her husband's mental health. The husband appears to have been a countryman of Rauch, and he exclaimed, "What a disgusting delusion!" But romanticism appeared in a better light in French art, in throwing off the dry classicism of David and his school for the fresh, vigorous life of Géricault, as shown in his great picture of "The Shipwreck of the Medusa." Escaping the worst extremes, the French romantic school in Delacroix took a new and noble direction in historic art.

While the lyrical and subjective movement predominated in German art, the French romanticists devoted themselves to portraying the real, passionate movements of human nature in the actual events of history and of life.

We may date from Wilhelm von Schadow's appointment as director of the Dusseldorf Academy the rise of that school which some years later aroused so much interest in America, and exercised an evident influence on our artists of that period. Eggers calls it "the turning-point whence the new German art began to unfold in all directions." He traces its birthplace to that room in Rome which Cornelius, Overbeck, Veit, and Schadow adorned with biblical frescos. At this time the movement was decidedly of a religious character, according to the general interpretation. Cornelius was ambitious of the title of Christian painter. And it is said that Veit, the director of the "Stadel Institute," resigned his office because the institute had bought Lessing's " Martyrdom, of Huss." Cornelius was about to leave Munich, where he had some friction with Klenze, when the king again bound him there by the commission for the frescos of the Ludwig Church, which were in his own line. The royal patron, whose motto was, " The painter must know how to paint," cared for no particular school ; but he was anxious to have the decorations finished that year. Numerous helpers were engaged. Some of them united with Cornelius in thinking that only the ideal meaning of a picture was the true measure of its worth. So Schnorr von Carolsfelt, Kaulbach, Genelli, Schwind, and even Preller, worked with Cornelius, even if the personal relation was not close. Lund writes to Rauch "that he cannot think that Cornelius is in his true place as director of an academy ; that in which his superiority consists he cannot impart to others, and that which can be taught he does not understand thoroughly." On the other hand, Wilhelm Schadow valued correctness of drawing and color. " Schadow is not the hero," said Rauch ; " but those he leads become so."

With the increase of *genre*-painting, and the representation of familiar scenes in life, a sense of humor came in, which helped to extend the influence of art in various ranks of life. Schrödter and Hasenclever became popular from this cause. Rauch speaks warmly of many of the new pictures as, " Sohn's ' Hylas with the Nymphs '[1] is one of the most beautiful late works I have seen." He praises Lessing's " Uhland's King," both for its grandeur and its technical excellence ; and he also speaks of the excellent landscapes of some of the Dusseldorf school. The French claimed the Dusseldorf school as French, and the German artists blamed the Schadowish works as "too French ;" but they excited great interest in Berlin, and Rauch said of Begas, " I believe that nobody paints a better picture."

[1] In the Berlin Museum.

To understand Rauch's work thoroughly, and the great service he rendered to modern, and especially plastic art, it is necessary to go a little way into the history and philosophy of this subject; for it was his great merit that he united the true idealism, which he gained from his profound study of Greek art, with the genuine realism won from his keen eye for all natural beauty, and with his hearty sympathy with human life. His own healthy, manly nature expresses itself in his work, which is both robust and tender, full of the strength and joy of existence, and yet not deformed by servile imitation, even of life.

The terms idealism, realism, naturalism, etc., must be used ; a definition of them given by Dr. Eggers seems sufficient to guide us in our further study of Rauch's sculpture.

"Realism can boast of very old recognition as the principle of art. No less men than Plato and Aristotle place the essential of art in imitation. Leaving aside the æsthetic worth of this principle, what interests us now is the main idea. Imitation is the determining point ; in as far as in an artistic creation somewhat is imitated, it is realistic ; in as far as something is added to it out of the creative fancy, it is idealistic ; but if we have the most exact copy conceivable of the naked fact, indifferent whether it be beautiful or ugly, charming or disagreeable, then we stand before naturalism." He goes on to illustrate this point by showing how realism and idealism are combined in the works of Dürer, Paul Veronese, etc. He shows how their works are realistic in their treatment, and yet ideal in their conception ; and he concludes by saying, "We must not treat these ideas like drawers in which to sort out different men and schools ; but we must use them as measuring-rods to determine the æsthetic value of an artistic production."

This controversy in art, which raged so wildly both in

France and Germany, was coincident with, and indeed a part of, the great revolutionary struggle which ended the triumph of reaction and placed the citizen-king on the throne of France. Rauch was deeply interested in all these events. David d'Angiers was the great leader in modern French sculpture. An early *protégé* of David, and a pensioner of the academy at Rome, his early course was in favor of classicism, and he was a strong opponent of realism. He could not escape the strong impulse of the time, however, and in 1830, for the first time, he consented to the use of the modern costume in sculpture. D'Angiers had known Rauch in the student days at Rome. In 1829, having heard that Goethe was beginning to grow old, D'Angiers hastened to Weimar to make a bust of the poet. He was thus brought into comparison with Rauch. D'Angiers himself had no doubt of his triumph, both as regards the likeness and the ideal conception of the work. This is the astonishing bust in the library at Weimar, of which the old master Gottfried Schadow said, "The high raised skull, and some other to us very strange handling of the features and of the hair, excited in us German artists more astonishment than admiration;" and Rietschel said, "What has D'Angiers made out of this head? It is hard to get free from the impression that it may not trouble one's nights." In 1833 Rauch entered into new relations with D'Angiers, as he sent him his sketches for the monument of General Foy. Rauch was especially pleased with the idea of representing the epoch by the individual forms of the general's friends, who were continually about him, even until his death. He afterwards used this plan in his monument to Frederic the Great. He asked D'Angiers to contribute to the Berlin Exhibition, and sent him his own reliefs for the Blücher monument, whose originality pleased the French artist so much, that he interested himself to get a representation of Rauch's work in the Paris Salon.

" *Der betende Knabe* " was chosen for this purpose, and it was well placed in Madame Baudin's salon, which was consecrated to his works. This was a marble reproduction of the praying child of the Francke monument.

D'Angiers is astonished that Rauch does not put his name on his works. " *Votre nom doit tenir une place trop honorable dans la mémoire des hommes, pour en priver quelques uns de vos ouvrages.* " A year later D'Angiers visited Berlin, and made a bust of Rauch, on which he spent eighteen hours out of his three weeks in Berlin.[1] " It has very strong peculiarities, especially in the over-height of the brow, and in the *corners*[2] of the hair. The expression has something austere, which Rauch had not even in his most earnest moments." Rauch writes to Rietschel : " D'Angiers has to-day finished my bust : it is more than life-size ; like and characteristic, and of great interest to all of us. It is going to Paris to be executed in Pyrenean marble. I am really ashamed of this ; such a distinction from friends in a strange land I could not expect. I think I have learned something from him about the working of the skin." D'Angiers makes free comment on all he sees in Berlin, and he wrote to Alexander von Humboldt : " *Croyez moi pour reunir le style et l'expression de la vie, votre Rauch, je le dis partout, est bien supérieur à Thorwaldsen.* "

A correspondence of twenty years shows how much artistic sympathy there was between these two men ; yet however closely they agreed in their high aims, D'Angiers's manner of expression remained always foreign to Rauch, and had no other effect on him than to make him cling still closer to his own conception of the ideal in plastic art.

The recognition of Rauch's merit by the French is shown not only by his election as associate member of the *Académie Royale des Beaux Arts* in 1830, and his full

---

[1] This interesting bust, given by Rauch by will to Prince George Victor of Waldeck, stands now in the princely library of the residence castle at Cassel.

[2] The so-called " poets' corner."

election in 1883, but also by the fact that Ingres asks his judgment of his latest work, and that Lemaire, who had lately won the victory in a concurrence for the frieze of the Madeleine, thought it necessary to ask for Rauch's recommendation in order to secure his presentation to the membership made vacant by the death of Cortot.

Another tendency in art which appeared at this time, and which was very distasteful to Rauch, was represented by Schwanthaler, who gained the name of "Fa-Presto" for his celerity in producing large works of sculpture. Rauch writes, "King Ludwig was the intellectual author of this style of *plastique*, with whom the principal demand was, much and quick." Rauch could readily see how the desire to ornament his capital speedily should have led the king in this direction; but he was thorough in his own work, and abhorred anything like slurring it over. He could not understand giving the marble entirely into strange hands. Thirty assistants were kept busy on the gable-ends of the Walhalla, and the work was almost entirely given up to them. Abundance of money spent in this way seemed only to hasten art in its downward course, while Rauch was carefully building up a school of young sculptors at Berlin, "who," says Dr. Eggers, "with their master, for more than a generation led not the German alone, but the finest plastic art of our times."

The course of sculpture had been different from that of painting; for under the lead of Thorwaldsen and Canova the influence of classicism was very strong. But it was impossible that such a great change in the political world should take place, such an uprising of the people and recognition of their life as of superior importance to that of thrones and dynasties, without affecting every art. This appeared in sculpture in the demand for the use of modern drapery instead of the old Greek costume, to which even Thorwaldsen had sometimes to yield. Rauch accepted the situation, although with some reluctance, and devoted much thought to the solution of this problem, how to unite truth to history with grace and beauty. He thus became the creator of this school of national plastic art, which took its meaning from the national life, while its form retained the purity and beauty of the Greek art. The slow ripening of Rauch's own artistic powers had fitted him to meet the influences of the time without being carried away by them. He never lost his power of receiving new impressions and thoughts; but he had learned to judge them wisely in the light of wide knowledge and long experience. While he shows very little of national prejudice against the French, and eagerly learns from their artists, whose great merit he often acknowledges, he was very little influenced by the French movements in art. His own direction became clear to him; and, while he gathered from others, he never lost his own personality. On the other hand, the French artists gave him generous sympathy and appreciation.

As little was he swept out of his course by the eagerness of his early friend King Ludwig for rapid work. He could not understand Schwanthaler's willingness to make a new model for the Walhalla every six weeks, and then commit the execution entirely to others.

In his atelier the law of moderation prevailed, and the most thorough execution was held to be essential to the true development of the ideal thought of a statue.

At this period Rauch had arrived at a point in his art when his acknowledged successes in the works he had already made, his clear convictions of the true principles of art which he had learned from his classic studies, and his wide acquaintance with the best work and life of his own time, fitted him for new achievements, — for the grand circle of Victories with which he adorned the Walhalla, and for many other noble works which add glory to his native land.

Having lived through the disastrous period of the

Napoleonic wars, and sympathized deeply with his king and his country, having entered with his whole soul into the war for freedom, and consecrated his best powers through middle-life to the commemoration of its great heroes, Rauch now had an opportunity of illustrating his beautiful faith, "that what one wishes in youth, one has the fulness of in old age," by the opportunity for a great work, which should combine his never-faltering love of classic art with his joy in the reviving life of his country. He found the expression of all this feeling in the ancient Nike, "the Victory which wakens the heroic spirit, encourages the combatant, and gives wreaths and palms to the victor."

But Rauch did not merely copy the Greek : he infused into this Greek form the modern spirit, and his Victories have the life of the great deliverance which his country had just passed through. He has used this form of representation more than thirty times, and especially fine are the splendid forms which adorn the German Temple of Fame, the Walhalla at Regensburg.

With all his strong classical leanings, Rauch was not insensible to the spirit of the age in which he lived; and now he saw how he could unite the spirit of classic art with the reviving life of his country, which for a century had been dominated by foreign influences in literature, art, and even politics.

Here Dr. Eggers finds the strong contrast with Thorwaldsen, whose mission was essentially to restore the spirit of Greek art. No strong national feeling gave him a new ideal, and love is the subject of his creative power from the beginning to the end of his career. As Thorwaldsen has given us more than sixty representations of Love, so Rauch, who found his inspiration in national feeling, has expressed this over and over again in his Victories, in reliefs, busts, and statues.

As early as 1811 the young Prince of Bavaria had conceived the idea of the great national Temple of Fame, the Walhalla, and had given to Rauch a commission for a bust. When Ludwig became king, he wished to take Rauch into his service, and to establish a great school of plastic art in Munich; but Rauch wisely preferred to remain in Berlin.

On Rauch's return from Italy, King Ludwig wished him to make six figures for the interior of the Walhalla, some partly sitting, some standing, which should be wholly his own work. But Rauch could not meet the eager wishes of the king, feeling obliged to return at once to Berlin. However, he had an interview with Klenze, the architect in Bologna, and agreed with him for the work he would do for the Walhalla.

He agreed upon the style and design of the group for the front gable, so that it could be safely finished by younger men, also for the six marble statues, of which one was to be finished each year, and that the whole should be ready by October 1, 1836.

Rauch, who was full of delight at the idea of being able to express his ideal of womanly beauty in nude figures, made a sketch of a Victory, which he sent to the king. It was a sitting figure, almost entirely nude, and holding in her right hand a laurel wreath, and in her left a palm branch. But the king objected "that the nude, however it might suit antiquity, did not fit in here;" and Klenze wished Rauch to consider the relation to the general architecture, and to the places designed for the statues. The details of the contract caused much discussion, and the king unwillingly consented to having the work done in Berlin, as he was in great haste to have it finished. Rauch began the work in 1831. The first sketch of the gable group, of which Rauch himself speaks with satisfaction, pleased the king. The principal figure is the Germania, with the throne and sword; the side figures consist of two groups of warriors, representing Prussia and Hannover, Austria, and Bavaria, swearing fealty to Germany, with female figures indicating the fortresses of Cologne, Luxembourg, Mainz, and Landau. Two other groups of sitting female figures represent Würtemberg on one side, and on the other, Hesse and the other small states.

The king consented that the execution of the statues should be confided to Rietschel, on the condition that one of the groups should be made in Rauch's atelier.

But the chamber of deputies objected to giving this important commission to a foreigner, and in the following year refused, by a large majority, to grant the money for the building of the Walhalla and the finishing of the Pinakothek. The king, however, was able to take the necessary sums from the civil list so that the work could go on.'

As Rauch proceeded with the modelling of the statues, there was much discussion in regard to the drapery and accessories. The fourth Victory was very much admired, and considered the finest yet made. It was draped except on the arm and breast, but the king objected even to this degree of nudity, and Rauch was almost in despair over his persistency on this point. Yet the king had the authority of Greek coins; and even the coin of Terina, from which Rauch seems to have drawn the idea of his wreath-throwing Victory, is represented as fully draped. In 1834 the first sitting Victory is put into marble. The block for the second is brought to the workshop; but while the marble is spotless, it has been cut away full six inches too much above the heel, so that there is not material enough for the limb, and Rauch is greatly troubled; but by skilful management he makes up for the defect, and as usual is jubilant over a difficulty conquered.

When King Friedrich Wilhelm visited the atelier in 1835, Rauch was able to show him four Victories in different stages of completion, and to tell him of their destination for Munich. "That's a king," said the monarch

VICTORY, VALHALLA

jokingly, "that orders something that gets done." These winged marble figures fortunately made a pleasant impression on the king, which to Rauch's great joy brought similar orders from him. But for two years Rauch laid aside almost entirely the work for the Walhalla, because he was engaged on the Dürer monument; but he took it up again in the year 1837. Klenze calls his attention to the wings of the Victories, which stand out too far from the wall and thus hurt the architectural effect. He also hints that a northern Victory should suggest the Walkyrie, and that the oak branch might be substituted for the palm. Rauch accepts this suggestion, and the next two Victories bear oak wreaths and branches. The king was constantly urging expedition in completing the work, although Klenze said that such haste was not necessary, for the Walhalla could not be consecrated until October 18, 1842. In July the six marble statues were exhibited in Berlin for three weeks, for the benefit of the restoration of the Cologne Cathedral; and in August a load of marble weighing a hundred and seventy hundred-weight passed through the streets of Berlin towards Regensburg.

On the first of September, Rauch, with his daughter Agnes and her husband, went to Donaustauf. In the afternoon they went to the Walhalla. Here they were received by the builder Estner, who had kept charge of the work for fifteen years; and the splendid bronze doors were opened to them. Rauch says in his diary: "I found the six statues on their stagings near the place of erection, all freed from the boxes, and not injured in the least. The impression of the whole on us was above all magnificent, such as was never seen; the novelty and beauty of the materials, the finished work, praising alike the builder and the architect, such as has never been accomplished in Germany in any time."

"So, then," says Dr. Eggers, "the cycle of victory of the Walhalla remained as it was created in eleven years' work, not as it was formed out of the free thought of the artist's fancy, but bound by conditions which showed themselves in the results, not as fetters, but as fruitful elements of creative activity." This was truly working in the Greek spirit, making limitations the sources of new power. His majesty was so well pleased with the statues that he wished no change in them. Rauch was unable to remain until the ceremony of dedication, which took place on the eighteenth of October.

Rauch had wished for free creation, based indeed on Greek models, but infused with the national feeling. Klenze on the contrary wished only decorative figures in strict relation to the architecture. The king finally took a middle course. The bounds, which according to Klenze were prescribed by the laws of architecture, should not fetter, but guide the artist's fancy, and indeed should lead back to the antique, in which the master-pieces of plastic art were created. Hence, on the side of architecture, he demanded the repose of the figures, whether sitting or standing; and he refused to permit nude figures, constantly demanding more drapery, and objecting to all characteristic attributes, except the garland and the laurel branch.

The more Rauch was thus circumscribed in the outer form of his ideas, the more powerfully did he turn to the expression of the inner life; and thus arose the forms of the Victory, mighty in their beauty, which "fill the temple with a grand hymn of victory, sung in strophes and antistrophes."

The difficulties of the task were overcome in many ways. It was a question how to unite the wings with the draped figures. As the statues were seen only in front, or in profile, the wings appeared behind the figure as a symbol, and awakened no question of organic connection; and where the statue was more fully seen, the folds were so arranged as not to interfere with the placing of the wings.

He composed the statues without the wings, and could thus use each of his Victories among his wingless Nikes. He wrote to Lund, to whom he sent a cast of his wreath-throwing Victory: "I leave out the wings: they are only an embarrassment."

It would seem almost impossible to make six repetitions of so simple a subject with so little variation in the accessories, without making them monotonous; but these bright, lithe, graceful Victories have each their own charm, and it is difficult to prefer one to another. In the middle of the right wall sits the grand figure, with the legs lightly crossed, the drapery falling in long folds, and the head crowned with laurel, looking thoughtfully into the distance, while the light, elastic arm holds a laurel wreath. As Rauch said, "In her, waiting is expressed." The way to her is steep: she is ready to give the prize; but the prize is costly, and she waits till the last struggle is over, and the brow is ready for the royal crown.

Opposite sits the wreath-throwing sister, in whom "attentive looking down from the height into the immediate struggle is indicated." She has paused a moment in her flight, and alighted on a rock, while she follows the battle with her eyes, and is ready to throw the wreath to the victor. She is a beautiful picture of joy in victory. The companion on the other side has flown down from Olympus, and has touched the ground with sure feet, stretching her right hand to the victor's brow. All is beauty, grace, and life.

On the farthest side is that sister who has entered with slow step and sunken head. Her beautiful head is bent by the oak wreath. A budding oak twig rests against her right shoulder, and the left hand holds her drapery a little raised, to give freer motion. She appears to think of the sacrifice which the conquest has cost: it is a victory, but dearly bought.

Opposite her, on the same wall, is the splendid form of

the self-crowning Victory, who is putting the wreath on her own head, as if for joy in the conquest.

On the left stands a more thoughtful sister. She has risen from her seat, and, holding the wreaths in both hands, she approaches the conqueror, a beautiful picture of victorious joy.

These six models were used also on the gables of the Royal Opera House in Berlin, after the old house was burned, and the king wished to hurry on their restoration. Tragic masks were put in their hands, and they were made to serve as muses. They were also used with modifications for other buildings.

In 1837 King Friedrich Wilhelm visited Rauch's atelier, and ordered two Victories in bronze for Charlottenburg. Rauch had freer play with these models than with those for the Walhalla. These statues were to be placed on high granite pillars. This position gave opportunity for more action, and the forms are not entirely draped. In 1840 the king celebrated the twenty-fifth anniversary of the peace, and wishing to erect a monument on the "*Belle Alliance Platz*" in Berlin, he had the Victory cast in bronze. She is holding an olive branch outstretched towards the city.

Again, in 1847, Rauch reproduced the Victories for the staircase of the Prince of Prussia ; but, with the welcome change of celebrating the victories of peace, he added to the laurel wreaths the olive and the horn of plenty.

Finally, for the fourth time, the old master must make a crowning Victory, and this time it must be colossal, three metres high. The sixth army corps wished to erect a monument on the battle-field of Leuthen to the memory of Frederic the Great. It was to be placed on the only hillock on the plain, from which Frederic had watched the battle. A colossal image of Victory was chosen, and Friedrich Wilhelm IV. gave a granite pillar, from which the figure could be seen far and wide. The wreath was gilded.   The statue has unfortunately suffered much, and needs restoration.

The king had given a copy of the Victory to the Grand Duke of Mecklenburg-Strelitz, to be placed in the garden of Neu-Strelitz.   It is touching to read the letter of the gray-haired prince to his still older artist friend, aged seventy-seven, who was then preparing for his visit to Rome.   He begins : " You have by your Victory for the battle-field of Leuthen, given a proof to the rightly astonished world that even in your old age it is possible to make progress ; and since this is established, how can it be doubted that Rome will refresh and strengthen you anew, as a man growing old is refreshed by the breath of a young maiden ? "

Rauch also prepared several marble busts of the Victories.   If his workers in Italian marble had nothing to do, he let them make a bust of Victory, which he finished with his own hands.   He had no fear in regard to the disposition of them.   In 1857 he sent a bust with his good wishes to his friend Strack on his forty-ninth birthday, recalling the days when they had worked together, and acknowledging artistic obligations to him.   Finally, America received her memorial of the great sculptor. The last notice of the completion of a work by his own hand is of a Victory.   As he returned from his last journey to Karlsbad, June 22, 1857, he wrote in his diary : " I found in the atelier the model of the statue of Kant in such good condition that I only had to go over it with Hagen.   On the marble bust of Victory for Mr. Lenox I had more to do : it was finished on the eighteenth of July." [1]   This is the last notice in the day-book of the completion of a work by his own hand.

Rauch did not recover from the sickness which the last bath journey had caused.   A few months later he passed

[1] This Victory is now in the Lenox Library in New York.   It is a beautiful classic head crowned with the oak wreath.

to quiet rest. A Victory was the boundary stone of his earthly creations. His Victory remains a most characteristic and beautiful expression of the most poetic side of his nature. While the Queen Louise is at once a tribute of affection and a true portrait, it is also a beautiful ideal ; but the Victory is a pure conception of his joy in the regeneration of his country, which he has made a universal symbol of the grand conquests of life.

CHAPTER XIII

MONUMENT TO FREDERIC THE GREAT

1780–1850

THE work by which Rauch is most generally known is
, the statue of Frederic the Great at Berlin, which is the
grand conclusion of his long series of monuments to
heroes and warriors. And yet this reveals to us far less
of his thought and nature than the memorials of his beloved queen and king with whom his whole life was asso-
ciated, or the beautiful circle of Victories which were the
joy of his heart. This great monument illustrates his
sad remark to Bunsen that "two-thirds of all an artist
thinks and executes is prescribed by the age he lives in."
We shall see how much he had to contend with in this
age.

Dr. Eggers considers this statue as Rauch's greatest
work.

Rauch was only three years old when the proposition
was first made to build a monument to Frederic II. In
1779, after the close of the last campaign against the
Kaiser Joseph, in response to the desire of the Prussian
Army, General Möllendorf proposed the appropriation of
two hundred thousand thalers for the purpose of erecting
a monument to the king. But the king declared it to be
improper to erect a monument to a commander who was
still living. For sixty years this project was discussed,
and not less than fifty-eight sketches for it made by
various persons.

After the death of Frederic it was proposed that not

the army alone, but the whole people, should take part in
the erection of this monument. In 1791 King Frederic
William II. wished a concurrence of artists to make
sketches, and he prescribed the general character of the
statue, which was to be in Roman costume. The most
extreme and *bizarre* sketches were offered, Chodowiecki
sending his with the note: "I have placed a sun on the
housings of the horse, to express the enlightenment
he [Frederic the Great] has spread through the world."
Many were very strenuous for the modern costume ; and
it marks the spirit of the times that the argument was
used that the antique costume would carry the king back
a thousand years, to the time when the human race was
divided into lords and slaves, while Frederic held fast the
thought of the unity of the human race, and taught that
kings exist for the good of the people.

The fearful events of 1792 put a stop for a time to the
discussions in regard to the monument, and they were
not renewed until 1797. Afterwards, the death of the
king delayed the execution of the plan, and on the accession of Friedrich Wilhelm III. he did not at once find himself in a position to carry on the work, of which, however,
he did not lose sight. Both the king and queen held Schadow's views in regard to the costume, and now determined
on a colossal equestrian statue, and Schadow received a commission to make estimates for a bronze statue with a granite
pedestal. Little did he think that in the queen's antechamber was the young man who was to carry the work into
execution. But long years of political troubles lay between
this plan and the final result. In 1822 notes from Rauch's
diary refer to suggestions from Schinkel in regard to
a renewal of the project. About 1829 the plan of a
Trajan's pillar was much discussed, and, a general sub-
scription being proposed, it was suggested that those provinces which had been conquered by Frederic might take
part in it if they chose, but that no demand should be
made upon them.

At last, in 1830, the affair seemed to take a definite turn in a proposal to Schinkel; but he objected on artistic grounds to the plan of a Trajan's pillar, saying that the extent of the bass-reliefs made it impossible to see the unity of the design, and that the statue of the hero himself with his head one hundred and fourteen feet in the air could not impress the beholder with his personality in its finer traits. Schinkel offered several other designs, representing the hero on horseback or in a chariot. In February the king gave Schinkel a cabinet order directing him to communicate with Rauch in regard to the details of the work, but he still adhered to the idea of the pillar, which was so unacceptable to Schinkel that he appealed to Rauch to help him in trying to effect a change.

Rauch was then on his return from Italy. He did not answer Schinkel's letter for some time, hoping to find some one who would help him to influence the king.

Rauch proposed a new plan for a monument, consisting of a statue of Frederic with six of his generals placed in a horizontal row below him, and of smaller size. But George of Mecklenburg objected to this, that as the great King Frederic was so immeasurably above all his subjects, they ought not to be represented on the same monument, even on a lower plane.

The king was not moved by Rauch's objections, and postponed the decision until he should return. Rauch now proposed that the pillar should be crowned by a Victory, and that the statue of the king should be placed on a lower pedestal. Bunsen writes that it seems impossible to move the king from his determination, and that "it appears to be written in the stars that we shall have to see the great king on the top of a steeple."

Rauch continued to make sketches for the monument, hoping that the king's plans might be changed by seeing them carried into execution. In 1835 the king began to

weaken in his determination, and directed Rauch to make
designs for a monument to Frederic, to be placed on a
pillar or a pedestal.   Soon after he sent to Rauch to make
a drawing of an equestrian statue of the great king in
his own costume, with royal mantle, staff of command, and
even the hat.   Rauch feared a new controversy, since he
objected strongly to any covering of the head which would
conceal the brow and shade the eyes.   Duke George supported him in this objection ; but the king neither wished
to give up his own idea, nor to give an explicit order
against the judgment of the sculptor and his artistic
counsellor.

Rauch then suggested a sitting statue of the great
king as he sat on the well at Nienburg weaving together
the torn threads of his fate, after the battle of Kollin.
This called forth an admirable letter of criticism from the
grand duke, showing that a great monarch should not be
represented at the moment when his fate trembled in the
balance, however nobly he rose from the depression, but
in the hour of victory.   He suggested that such a subject
would only be appropriate in a cycle of bass-reliefs where
it would be followed by victory, and the dissonance, as in
music, would heighten the resulting harmony.   Rauch
carefully preserved this letter, and followed out its suggestions in the bass-reliefs of his monument.   The king
finally called a new commission to consider the subject,
and they reported in favor of an equestrian statue, and
against the pillar.   March, 1836, the king gave Rauch an
order to make a model for the equestrian statue.   He
went eagerly to work, and in two months produced a
sketch of a statue with a rich pedestal.   The bass-reliefs
form a succession, showing the progress of the conflict,
from the first drawing of the sword to the final victory,
and the peace and the joy of the citizens.

He made a double model of the statue, with and without the head-covering, and was so well pleased with his

own work as to hope that he might carry it into execution. Although the duke, Humboldt, and other connoisseurs warmly received and praised these sketches, the king kept the artist waiting for two months without a word as to his opinion, or the final acceptance of the designs, while the excitement of the sculptor was such as to unfit him for work or enjoyment. At the end of that time the king criticised the representations of the generals, and wished allegorical figures substituted for them. Encouraged by the duke, Rauch patiently went to work again, and designed a circle of allegorical figures. Still the king delayed, and Rauch notes that he visited the atelier many times without saying a word about the monument. But Rauch had not been idly waiting during these years, and finally it was with surprise that he received an order from the king to go on with the statue. Congratulations came to him from all sides, and he felt that he was to give his best and his last powers to the work. Finally the order was given to him in the most flattering terms, December 8, 1839.

Now began the difficulties of the execution. He was obliged to enlarge his atelier to accommodate all the work. Next came the study of the horse, which must not be a typical Arab or Greek horse, but one of the sturdy English breed which Frederic actually used. Rauch used for a model an old horse of this race named Talbot, which was said to resemble strongly Frederic's favorite horse Condé. He also made journeys to various places to study the characteristics of different races and breeds of horses. Grave questions arose among critics even as to the representation of the horse's tail, and Rauch corresponded with the English sculptors Westmacott and Wyatt on the subject. His visit to Russia afforded him opportunities which he eagerly seized upon for further study. Many were the difficulties in modelling the horse and his rider of corresponding size, and it was only after five years' labor that the artist could put his model into the hands of the founder for casting.

Rauch had never been satisfied with the allegorical figures which Friedrich Wilhelm III. had suggested in the place of the heroes whom he had designed to surround the king; and now he arranged a modification of these groups, in the earnest hope that his successor, Friedrich Wilhelm IV., might see the appropriateness of his original idea.

It was an anxious day for Rauch when the king visited the atelier to view the completed model; and when at last he expressed his entire concurrence in Rauch's new plan, it seemed to the artist the culminating joy of his life. He must pour out his soul to his friends. The grand duke, although plunged into sudden grief by the death of his daughter, gave him the warmest sympathy.

But his joy was not complete until Rietschel shared it. He writes to him March 27, 1842: "You can clearly imagine with what other and new courage I now put my hand to the execution of the whole, than if the duty of moulding the allegorical forms in their insipidity were laid upon me. This day was, if not the happiest, one of the very happiest of my life. Praying God my former health and strength may keep fresh ten years more, I am yet modest, and really mean only half that time." This prayer was not dispersed in empty air. Rauch had still much difficulty in the choice of the generals and companions of Frederic who were to be represented on the monument, and also in arranging the names to be placed on it, so as to meet the king's wishes, and suit all parties, without violating his own artistic taste. He was obliged to change field-officers and generals about, as if he were manœuvring an army. "You hardly realize," he wrote to Rietschel, "how hard it is to represent these personalities as hussars, all with the same number of curls arranged over the ears by the same barber, and with no other attributes than the dagger and sword."

It was refreshing to change to the civic side and model the citizen's dress. But this side brought out almost greater difficulties in the choice of subjects. Each critic had his word to say, and when Preuss had proposed his idea of the representation of classes, everybody was suggested, from Voltaire and the Marquis D'Argens to the opera-singers Salimbeni and the Barberina.

It is difficult in brief space to give an idea of the variety and richness of the whole work.

On the lower part of the pedestal the events of Frederic's life were represented. The longer side was divided into three fields of nearly equal size ; those on the south side were to be consecrated to his birth and childhood, and his instruction in history and science and the forging of arms. As the lower part of this pedestal was decorated with the knights and officers and heroic deeds of Frederic's military career, it was enough to represent him as a warrior led by victory. The other three great fields represent him after the war was over, as the promoter of industry, the protector of art, and the philosopher of Sans-Souci. On the reverse was his apotheosis beyond the bounds of earthly life.

His childhood is represented on the fourth side. Two angels in long clothes, one swinging a palm branch, the other holding the little babe in its arms, bring him down to the royal pair, the mother holding out her arms to receive him, while the king's hands are folded in prayer. In the left corner is the rush-crowned nymph of the Spree with her swan, leaning on an urn. In the second field at a table sits Duhan, the instructor of Frederic, a book in his right hand ; before him stands the royal boy, and behind him a globe.

By Rietschel's advice he changed his first sketches, in order to bring them into greater unity with the rest of the work, by substituting allegorical figures ; so he put the muse of history in the place of Duhan, while the globe and a lighted candelabrum make a school of science. In the third field the teacher is replaced by a helmeted Minerva, who offers a sword to the youthful hero.

Indeed, he made so many changes in his designs that I will not attempt to give them. The bass-reliefs can now be studied in their final form on the finished monument, or more conveniently in the casts at the Rauch Museum. The general effect is very rich and animated.

After the completion of the model, the preparation for the casting in bronze and its erection caused yet another year's delay. Rauch had indeed made preparations for the casting six years before, when he summoned to Berlin, Friebel, who had shown himself a skilful founder for the Polish kings in the cathedral at Posen. He came to Berlin in 1845, and established his workshop in the new mint. With the erection of this foundry, Rauch did not escape the usual struggle for the means of existence. He had already spent more than five thousand thalers for the necessary preparations ; but the minister of finance would not repay him, because the administration of the mint belonged to the department of religious worship and instruction ; and the minister of religious worship also refused, because the outlay was made for the monument to Frederic. Rauch, already threatened with legal measures, declared to the king that under these conditions he could no longer work with cheerfulness. Then a cabinet order on the minister of finance, with a draft on the monument funds, freed him from his unpleasant position. Kings are convenient sometimes to cut knots.

The process of casting is as interesting as it is difficult, and at times Rauch was very anxious about the result ; but, as he gratefully tells his assistants, it was happily accomplished through their skill. But to Rauch himself his work did not seem a success, for the horse appeared too short in the trunk, and too long-legged — "no comforting sight." He was never reconciled to those

FREDERICK THE GREAT, BERLIN

long, or rather slender legs, as we learn from a letter which, many years after the monument was erected, he addressed to Councillor Schöll at Weimar. This letter is full of instruction to the technical sculptor, but is too long to insert here.

New discussions arose in regard to the inscription, and Rauch appealed to Preuss, who wished for one in German. But the king appointed a commission to decide the matter. The inscription is enclosed in a deep setting decorated with palms, on which are the king's crown, sword, sceptre, and imperial globe, and a cross, with laurel and palm branches.

FRIEDRICH DEM GROSSEN,
FRIEDRICH WILHELM DER DRITTE
MDCCCXXXX.
VOLLENDET UNTER FRIEDRICH WILHELM DEM VIERTEN.
MDCCCLI.

The colossal granite pedestal was also a great work, consisting of thirty-two blocks. Rauch wrote to Rietschel : "No time of work has been harder to me than this delay in finding these granite blocks. These will stand, the sure monument of Frederic the Great, when time shall have melted the bronze."

On the fifteenth of May began the moving of the great statue out of the foundry over the Haakschen Markt, the Spandau bridge, the new Friedrichs bridge, by the cathedral, to the booth before the destined station. Forty carpenters accomplished this removal on rollers in twice twenty-four hours.

Then the walls of the scaffoldings were taken down ; and Rauch now saw the statue in the early morning of the twenty-fifth of May on a level with the height of the pedestal, raising itself towards the free heaven, and rising high over the highest lindens. It gave to him an unexpected impression of powerful effect.

Great preparations were made for the unveiling of the monument. All Rauch's own family were present, his daughters and grandchildren. As guests of the royal family came the young nephew Friedrich Franz of Mecklenburg-Schwerin, and the venerable Uncle George of Strelitz, who arrived on the twenty-eighth "because he had no peace at home;" the Dukes of Braunschweig and of Genoa, and the young nobility of Saxony, Schwarzburg, and Würtemberg, and finally the whole of Prussia in countless deputations of all ranks and classes from every province in the kingdom. There came also merchants and mechanics, and representatives of art and science, and above all of the Prussian Army. Two of her veterans, old men of one hundred and six and one hundred and two years, appeared, as well as a hussar eighty-five years old, in his genuine old uniform. Besides these, came the future promise of the army, the young figures of the cadet corps.

On a warm spring day, May 31, 1851, the one hundred and eleventh anniversary of Frederic's ascension of the throne, the splendid procession passed through the files of soldiers drawn up like living walls along the streets.

Foremost appeared the great master, Rauch, adorned with the order of civil service, to which had been added the night before the star of the Red Order of the Eagle. He was preceded by the commission of unveiling, and surrounded by the artists, head workmen, and helpers who had been engaged in the great work. Dr. Eggers says, "None of the thousands whom Berlin assembled to this feast will ever forget the moment when the old artist, in all his majestic beauty, stepped on the broad square at the head of this festal train. The joyful greeting of those nearest him swelled into a jubilant cry of the countless multitude which surrounded the square like mountain walls."

The Prince of Prussia rode up to the artist, giving him his hand in greeting, and the ladies of the court came out on the balcony of the palace. The square being cleared, the march of Frederic the Great announced the arrival of the king. He came on horseback at the head of an immense crowd. Halting before the monument, after listening to a short speech from the president, he drew his sword and commanded the troops to present arms. Immediately thousands of voices, the thunder of artillery, the lowering of standards, the clang of bells, and the swell of the Hohenfriedberger March greeted the statue unveiled in the glorious sunlight of the day. A sacred silence followed the outburst of joy and astonishment; then from behind the statue sounded the clear voices of the choir of the cathedral, accompanied by the sonorous swell of the trumpets in the grand old choral, "*Nun danket alle Gott.*"

At the close of the song the king spoke to the army, and then to the burgomasters of the city. He then turned to Master Rauch, whose hand he repeatedly pressed, and gave him three memorial coins, struck in gold, silver, and bronze, from his own designs, in memory of the unveiling of the statue.

Festivities were continued through the week; but none could have been more grateful to the artist's feelings than the social meeting in the old Lagerhaus, followed by a feast given by the artists of the Royal Academy. Rauch was greeted by the festal hymn written by Kopisch and composed by Meyerbeer: —

> "Steht auf und empfangt mit Feiergesang
> Lobpreisend den Mann der die Stadt, der das Land
> Durch belebtes Gebild
> In Erz wie in Marmor verherrlicht."

The vice-director of the academy, Professor Herberg, said, "The day before belonged to the fatherland, but this hour is ours; the companions in art greet the artist, and are proud to name him theirs."

Music specially composed for the occasion filled the evening; a medal was given to Rauch, and the king kissed

him amid the applause of the company, who felt "that no
favor was too great for him who had been able to speak
out of his soul in enduring brass to the souls of all."

Finally the festivities closed with a grand reunion of
artists, with tableaux and dramatic representations. Many
of the greatest artists of the time were present, among
whom his old friends Kaulbach of Munich, Bendemann of
Dresden, Felsing of Darmstadt, and Schöll of Weimar,
are probably the best known to us. The press teemed
with poems in honor of the artist and the work. When
after a few weeks the temporary supports were taken away,
the whole beauty of the monument was revealed. Then
was recognized the architect Rauch in the whole structure ;
the painter in the composition of the groups ; the poet in
the conception of the whole, and in the character of the
details ; and, above all, the sculptor in the fashioning of
all the portraits, so that the greater part of them with few
changes were available for single statues, as was actually
the case with that of Kant. The whole cost of the monument was, in round numbers, two hundred and fifty
thousand thalers. Rauch made a copy one-fourth of the
size of the original for the Emperor of Russia.

I must refer my readers to Dr. Eggers for a full analy-
sis of the artistic qualities of this great work. It is certainly one of the finest large monumental statues of
modern times, and resumes in itself Rauch's life-long
studies in this direction.

An incident of a more private nature may close the
history of this great undertaking. Rauch had long wished
to present to the church of Arolsen casts of the four
cardinal virtues, from the designs on the Frederic monument. He communicated his intention to his friend
August Speyer, and made his preparations quietly for the
execution of the statues. The place for the casts was
selected, and the work was going on well, when Rauch
received through Speier the intelligence that the placing

of the four cardinal virtues in the church would not be agreeable to the consistorium, since they did not conform to the Christian standpoint, and would give offence to orthodox minds, and at this time such a conflict was especially to be avoided.

Rauch replied that this unexpected and unreasonable refusal of his gift had wounded him very deeply, and he begged that there might be no further mention of the subject in any way, as he did not wish to be reminded of it.

But afterwards Rauch received an address signed by nearly a hundred of the citizens of Arolsen, deeply mourning the decision of the ecclesiastical authorities, and expressing the hope that he would not blame his native city for this event.

Three years later Rauch heard that the magistrates of Arolsen had purchased his birthplace on a perpetual foundation, as a refuge for worthy citizens. Rauch sent to this establishment a gift of five hundred thalers, but at the same time gave the casts of the four virtues, for his castle, to the prince, who received the gift in the most friendly manner.

The mother of the prince commissioned Speier "to say to my dear Rauch, with a thousand greetings, how much I rejoice in his continued goodness; but especially tell him how I, as an old woman, am pleased to hear that his old home has become an asylum for aged women, and that he has given to this noble charity such a noteworthy gift. Express this all properly!"

In 1841 Rauch received a commission from King Friedrich Wilhelm IV., which must have been most welcome to him, to prepare for the mausoleum at Charlottenburg a companion monument to the "king of blessed memory," the husband of Queen Louise, to be placed beside her. The king wished the costume to be very simple, to correspond with that of the queen, and suggested the military cloak instead of the ermine mantle. Rauch made four different sketches. At first he endeavored to make the position of the figure balance that of the queen by the arrangement of the hands and feet ; but he abandoned that idea, and placed the king in a simple horizontal position. By the wish of Friedrich Wilhelm IV., many little orders were added, and the cloak was thrown back to show the epaulets.

In the summer of 1846, on the birthday of the dead king, the whole monument was finished in marble ; and Rauch writes to Rietschel : " I· intend to place the grave-statue of the king for a couple of days in the first of August in the atelier in a good light, before it goes into the worst light I ever saw. Nobody could do worse for me than to build such a miserable building for this work."

When the monument was placed in the mausoleum, Rauch was almost frantic over the injury to his work. The light came in on both sides, and destroyed the effect of the modelling. Friedrich Wilhelm IV. consented to darken one side of the room, and finally the trees as they grew up contributed to the same effect.

Great as was the success of the statue of Queen Louise, made more than thirty years before, now that this monument of the king was placed by its side, Rauch's progress in art was evident.

"The king lies stretched out in an almost stiff position, suggesting the death-sleep as well as the simple, soldierly character of the king, whose expression is of mild earnestness. Still more his artistic progress is shown in the fine lines which control the general form and give it a monumental character. Only in comparison with this later work was it seen how much the grand lines in the statue of the queen were broken up by the *genre*-like details of the drapery. One need only compare the bier-cloths to feel this contrast in all its sharpness."

I fully indorse this view given by Dr. Eggers. The exquisite charm of beauty and sentiment prevents one from remarking these defects in the statue of the queen ;

but when the comparison is made, one might almost say that one is the work of a young lover of art, as well as of his subject, and the other is the achievement of a master. Herein Rauch did a great service to the royal family, who were to become so important to Germany, by bringing out the ideal of a king, even in this likeness of a monarch of whom the country had little reason to be proud.

Rauch also modelled for the King of Hanover a statue of his lately deceased wife, a sister of Queen Louise.

Rauch enjoyed very much his visits to Hanover to witness the placing of the statue; not only because of his friendly reception, but because of the frankness with which the king, Ernst August, spoke with him on the exciting politics of the times. The calling of the united *Landtages* did not please him at all, especially within the royal palace. "Without giving room in it to such churls, he believed that he could make his subjects perfectly happy and contented: such representative assemblies should never rule, especially in Germany!" However little Rauch shared the political opinions of the king, who was obliged within a year to recall his words, he yet felt sympathy with the energetic, tense character of the man, and the unreserved openness of his speech.

When Ernst August died in November, 1851, and Rauch, according to his express wish, was asked to make his statue, these peculiarities came to his mind. He wrote to Frau von Bernstoff, "Although a dead form can afford little charm to the sculptor, yet the 'character-man' of our day, with his splendidly formed head, has something interesting in the highest degree, and calls out full interest for this monument." Already, when making the statue of the queen, Rauch had taken the exact measure of the king, in preparation for a later day; and the time came when King George, in December, 1851, commanded the companion to the monument of the queen. These two monuments rank with the best of Rauch's portrait statues.

CHAPTER XIV

POLITICAL CHANGES. — VISITS TO ST. PETERSBURG,[1] COPEN-
HAGEN, ANTWERP, AND LONDON

1840–1852

NOTHING could have given Rauch more delight than
the commission from the Emperor of Russia, through
the hands of his friend Humboldt, whose letter is full
of the warmest expressions of admiration and friendship.
It was dated February 3, 1830. Humboldt says, " On
my return from the Caspian Sea, and in the first days of
the convalescence of the beloved emperor, he has commissioned me to procure from Professor Rauch, as a proof
of the high regard which such a talent merits, a marble
mythological statue, nude, of the size of the Apollo Belvi-
dere, or, if he prefers it, somewhat smaller. You shall

---

[1] My German authority calls this city Petersburg only, and the same form is found
in many, but not all, German books. As this fact has caused discussion, I have tried
to obtain decided authority for one or the other expression. The report of the
" Petersburger Gesellschaft " uses Petersburg only, even when speaking of the court,
while the catalogue of the Berlin Exhibition uses the prefix St. Some English writers
use both forms indiscriminately, but the earliest authority that I have found, "A History
of Peter the Great by John Motley of London," published in 1703, never gives the prefix, although he fully describes the building of the city. A Russian friend has, however,
made special inquiry for me in Russia, and gives the following statement, which seems
to set the question at rest, as showing that the city was named for the Apostle rather
than the King : —

" When Peter the Great took possession of the river Neva in 1703 he decided to build
a fort and a city there. On the sixteenth of May of the same year, foundation was laid
for the city, and he named it St. Petersburg, in honor of the Apostle Peter, whose day
with the Greek Church is on the sixteenth of May. Peter himself was christened after
the Apostle, and that was another reason why he named the city after his patron saint.

choose the subject freely, a male or female figure. If I said mythological, I wished only to express that all belonging to modern times is excluded." In 1831 is found an entry in the diary, " Sketches for a statue of Narcissus begun." This was probably a suggestion for the emperor's statue. In the end of the year Rauch notes that he has finished the sketches of a statue of a Danaid and a sitting Eurydice. The following year he sends both to the minister of the imperial house. He names the second sketch, "Expectations in the form of Eurydice at the moment when she listens to the distant tone of Orpheus, who is lulling Cerberus to sleep." Rauch had long before taken an interest in the idea of the Danaid, as expressing unsatisfied longing ; but the thought of Eurydice was much nearer to him, as indicating the triumph of art. He says that he chooses this subject because the whole form is capable of a determined expression which, especially in the head, can be brought out in a charming manner. Goethe had suggested this subject to David d'Angiers, "because the cause and effect would be easily seized, as in the Laocoön." In the sketch in the Rauch Museum, Rauch has represented the Eurydice sitting on a rock, in whose hollow at her left lies the Cerberus watching her. She hears the song of Orpheus from that side, and looks thither, full of expectation. We cannot help regretting that this sketch, which seems full of promise, was not carried out.

The Danaid sketch represents the maiden as she empties the sieve with both hands.

Rather against Rauch's wishes the emperor at once chose the Danaid as pleasanter for a room. Rauch himself worked on the clay model, and made a special study for the head from Mademoiselle Louise Engel, who was celebrated for her beauty. But he could not get the real Danaid expression into the beautiful head, and he changed it into a Flora, which he sent to the empress as a fore-

runner of the great work. A ring of diamonds with the
cipher of the empress was sent him in recognition of this
gift. After many disappointments in the quality of the
marble, and other hindrances, the work was finished in '
1839. Rauch saw many details which he felt he could
improve, but the spectators were fully satisfied. The
model received great applause for years, and Kugler wrote
this pointed epigram upon it : —

> " Traurig blickest Du her, der endlos währenden Arbeit
> Suchst Du lange ein Ziel : — nimmer doch gehe zur Rast,
> Setze den Fuss nicht ab von Stein und erhebe den Krug nicht !
> Denn gleich lieblich wie jetzt wärest Du nimmer zu schau'n."

King Friedrich Wilhelm was so much pleased with the
statue that he commanded a *replica* in marble. In 1840
the emperor came to Berlin at the time of the death of
the king, and renewed his invitation of ten years' standing
to Rauch to visit St. Petersburg and see his statue placed
in the beautiful palace of the empress. The emperor not
only paid him five thousand thalers, but gave him the
insignia of the Wladimir Order, Fourth Class, and a commission for a second female statue of the same size.

A note in the day-book may refer to this commission :
" The sketches for the Danaid, executed for the Emperor
of Russia, changed to a nymph of Bacchus, with the young
Bacchus on her knee." Both these sketches are now in
the Rauch Museum, and are reproduced in the fifth volume of Dr. Eggers's book ; and it is interesting to compare
them, and see how much difference of meaning and effect
can be produced by slight changes. The attitude and
position of the body and the leg remain the same in the
nymph as in the Danaid. On the right hip, instead of the
water-jug, rests the young Bacchus, throwing his arms and
legs about in childish pleasure, while in the left hand he
holds a bunch of grapes. The position of the arms is
only just so far changed as the difference of the object
supported, in the one case an urn, in the other a child,

makes necessary. The head of the nymph is turned to the right, looking kindly at the child, while the Danaid looks sadly at the opening of the jug ; the drapery, which covered only the right hip and forearm of the Danaid, is drawn away from the arm of the nymph, and gathered into a knot in her lap. The difference in the clothing, the opposite turn of the head, and the slight change in the hands, are sufficient to change the whole figure from a Danaid into a very opposite subject, full of the expression of joy.

The repetition of the Danaid was not yet begun when the king died, but his successor renewed the commission, and after long delays it was finished in 1852, and was one of the last great works in marble by the master. It now stands in an excellent position in the Orangery, where the whole beauty of the statue appears. She stands in her full beauty, between girlhood and womanhood, with her bowed head, emptying the unhappy urn. The delicate head and the deep sadness of the face mark the Danaid. The companion of the Danaid, the Eurydice, had also a life-history of ten years. In 1836 Rauch received a commission for two statues for the Duke of Orleans, to be placed in the Tuileries. As the Duke of Orleans a few weeks later stopped in Berlin on his bridal-tour, he came to Rauch's atelier, and remained three-quarters of an hour carefully examining the works. The duke chose for his own room a sketch of a sitting Eurydice, to be executed life-size in marble, and ordered it with the most flattering expressions of hope of a speedy execution. In 1839 Rauch worked on the clay model which Blaser had prepared. It remained, however, until 1843, almost fifteen months after the violent death of the Duke of Orleans, when at Rietschel's entreaty Rauch had the model again brought into the lower workroom, in order to continue the work. "*Grace à Dieu et Mitsching*," he writes to Rietschel, "that it is not fallen to pieces." Mitsching, the true servant of the atelier, had taken so much pleasure in the model found abandoned in the upper workshop, that with his own hand he had kept the clay moist all these years. "All the woodwork, even the pegs in the tripod (as a natural consequence), were rotted away, and yet the figure was preserved, although in fact only the iron and the clay remained; and she now stands screwed into a new plinth, as if she were imprisoned." Once Rauch set his hand to the continuance of the work. But since Mitsching dared no longer continue his peculiar method of preservation under the eyes of the master of the atelier, Eurydice succumbed to her fate, and was one day found fallen into dust.

When Rauch returned from the glorious unveiling of the Dürer monument at Nuremberg, he found preparations making for the ceremony of laying the corner-stone of the monument to Frederic the Great, of which I have spoken already. The king was so sick that he could only look out of the window in his night-robe for five minutes at the pageant, with which he expressed his satisfaction. Rauch writes in his diary: "It was an exciting, poetic, tragic moment as the conclusion of the good king's life. From this hour until that of his decease, the surrounding of his dwelling by sympathizing friends only ceased when the body was taken to Charlottenburg to its last rest." There, thirty years before, at the king's command, Rauch had awakened his lost queen to life in marble, and therewith laid the foundation of his artist's fame.

We can imagine how deeply the parting with the king, who had been so generous and kind a master to the young artist, affected the old sculptor. History is severe upon Wilhelm Friedrich III. It is good, therefore, to have seen him in his private relations, and know him as Lessing says God does :—

> "Der du allein den Menschen nicht
> Nach seinen Thaten brauchst zu richten, die
> So selten seine Thaten sind, O Gott!"

King Wilhelm IV. mounted the Prussian throne, and not only Prussia, but all Germany, turned its eyes to him with earnest desire and expectation. Rauch remarks in his diary, " Friedrich Wilhelm IV. can mark the beginning of his reign by no finer act than by the publication of two documents which were given to him on the day of his father's death." These were the last will of the dead king, and his admonition to his "dear Fritz in undertaking the office of ruling, with the whole weight of its responsibility."

I cannot follow out the history of the stormy times after the ascent of Friedrich Wilhelm IV. to the throne. The people were in a ferment of hope and expectation that the new reign was to bring all they desired of freedom and prosperity, and every form of wild scheme and visionary plan found enthusiastic followers. The king shared many of the feelings of the time, but he had not the wisdom and strength needed to lead the country. We may now see how the noblest feeling and thought of that time was striving to bring about national unity and constitutional freedom ; but in the midst of the struggle it was not always easy to recognize what was the wisest and truest statesmanship. I shall only try to show how Rauch was affected by the changes.

While he certainly was not a bigoted opponent of progress, and always belonged to the people in sympathy of feeling, he had yet been brought up, and lived, we may say, all his life in affectionate relations with royalty. He loved peace and order ; and if he were an idealist in his love of beauty in art, he was not an extremist in his devotion to theory in politics. He loved his country as an actual personality, and was, as we have seen, thrilled by her danger, and most happy in her salvation ; but he was not a statesman with far-reaching views of her future destiny. The confusion in church and state, arising from the half-way measures and weak action of the government, was

distressing to him. He writes to Rietschel, " How irri-
tating is this drift of events ! " and asks him if it is the
same in Dresden. He cannot be enthusiastic even for
the gift of the constitution, longed for since 1815, and
now called *Landtag*, which was established on thoroughly stable grounds in 1847 : the artists were not represented, even at the opening of the *Landtag*, at which
only the outward appearance, the extraordinary display in
the church and the " White Hall," seem to him worthy
of mention.

Sooner than was expected the constitution was overthrown in that fearful night of March, 1848, whose hor-
rors in the immediate neighborhood of the Lagerhaus he
lived through with his people. What troubled him most in
this fierce outbreak of political passion was the deliberate
conspiracy in imitation of the Parisians. The seventy-one
years' veteran did not withdraw from active participation
in the measures taken to calm the raging waves : he
helped in the organization of the artist troop to join the
Burgerwehr and the student-corps ; and he writes to his
Rietschel, " A week of distress, of uncertainty, in which
we spent our nights, is indeed over, but not the impression
of what we have lived through, and what is before us in
the near future. Who could have believed this movement to be so colossal, and the downfall of the existing
conditions so irresistible ? Where is counsel, where is an
outlet to good to be found? " The only comfort to him
and his people is, " that the worst has not happened : our
king lived, and was active in all that the event demanded
of him. God can now help further. What the government have delayed to do for three and thirty years will
now arise in a new form for Germany. The Hohen-
staufens desired it : may we live to see it ! "

He feared that the worst excesses of communism would
prevail, if the good sense of the burghers and land-holders
did not hold them back from the abyss of a German re-

public, to which the eloquence of all sorts of vagrants seemed to be driving them. He believes that future generations will see better days, but that first of all princes and people will be lost in distress and rudeness, through the "trinity of universal arming of the people, direct suffrage, and free press." If these expressions seem extravagant to us, we must remember the excitement of the times; that Rauch's politics were very much matters of feeling, and that in a diary and familiar letters one does not always choose his words very carefully.

Towards the end of the year he indeed saw guaranties of a more hopeful future in the calling back of the Berlin garrison under Wrangel, in the disarming of the *Burgerwehr*, and breaking up of the state of siege; and on the sixth of December he wrote in his diary: "The news of the day brings great joy to all right-thinking people, on account of the constitution long desired from the king, which the nation has been kept out of through the most infamous hindrances, caused by the deputies themselves, until no hope was felt of its realization; and now at last the king himself has made an end to the matter. God bless him!"

This was indeed the crowning glory of poor Friedrich Wilhelm IV.'s reign, by which alone he holds a place in history.

Rauch now took again a lively interest in politics, seeking to promote the election of conservative delegates. He had already joined the *Preussen Verein*, and stood with his whole soul on the Prussian side of the great question: "Shall Germany disappear in Prussia, or Prussia in Germany?"

He felt very deeply about all the questions of the relations with Austria, and thought a great opportunity for Germany was lost by the refusal of the king to accept the *rôle* of emperor.

But whatever bitter feelings Rauch had towards the king's public policy, they did not disturb their private relations. Rauch's personal dependence on, even his admiration for the king, increased as he recognized the industry, the patience, the depth of good-will which he brought to the solution of these problems, which not the call of his heart, but of his position, put before him in a way that stirred the depths of his nature. His hope was to lead his people by the way of peace and ideal creation to higher civilization. For that he felt a royal vocation and enduring power. But the movement of the times demanded struggles, especially on the political field, which the king had been obliged to enter, and indeed with many far-working happy results, but without his ever finding inward satisfaction and peace in them.

The king could see the importance of the encouragement of art, especially of architecture, to the full development of the nation, and herein he felt at home in the exercise of his royal functions. He was always in close relation with Rauch ; and in the midst of the stormiest days of 1848 he sent for the sculptor, to talk with him of artistic subjects, or to discourse of ancient Babylon with Humboldt. Sometimes he was called away from his harmless enjoyment of such discourse, to trying business of state ; but he either seized the first opportunity to return to artistic or literary conversation, or he took up the pencil himself to sketch a plan and divert his mind from painful topics.

Believing that a long and peaceful reign was before him, the king at once began to consult Rauch about great projects for filling the vacant places with statues, and especially for carrying out the idea of the great equestrian statue of Frederic the Great. Schinkel's incurable sickness was a great trial to him, for in his classic tendencies he found a refreshing counterpoise to the prevailing romanticism.

Rauch at this time took a warm interest in the development of German painting. When the frescos of the museum were unveiled in 1844, he wrote in his diary : "I never experienced such a powerful impression from a work of art as from this. God bless the artists and princes through whom arise such genuine works of art for the joy and satisfaction of the present and the future !"

He writes also to Rietschel very warmly of two Belgian painters who exhibited their work in Berlin. "What will you, what will the painters say when they see the two Belgian painters? So I think should colors, stuffs, so also the light and shadows, so also the flesh be painted on a flat surface, — what dead paints does Dusseldorf give us on the contrary !" He also speaks in high praise of Cornelius's powerful cartoon of the Apocalyptic Horse. He recognizes Kaulbach's merit, and speaks of one of his pictures as "thoroughly beautiful in spiritual meaning, as well as in finished art." He calls Kaulbach spirited as a composer, draughtsman, and painter, and hopes from him the desired leadership of art in Berlin.

Rauch always regarded art in its widest relations, and was not fettered by any school or form of art, however strong his own preferences might have been. The awakened mind of Germany was then expressing itself nobly in painting, architecture, and music, and Rauch rejoiced in it all; but, as Dr. Eggers says, "The plastic art of that time was in Rauch and his school."

The change in the Prussian throne, so important to Rauch, happened in a summer otherwise full of interesting events. He had long ago been invited by the czar to visit St. Petersburg, and he now decided to undertake the journey. He embarked for the city in 1840, on the steamship Hercules, with his statue of the Danaid, and he arrived there July 4. The voyage was made pleasant by the society of Russian officers, and although he could not forget his experience of sea-sickness in 1804, yet the sight of the Russian fleet brought back more inspiring recollections, of which he says, " An indescribable youthful im-

pression was that which, in the year 1804, on my voyage
to Italy, I felt in the roadstead of Toulon, where the
French fleet was stationed which was beaten under Admiral Villeneuve by Nelson at Trafalgar.   From the
admiral's ship on a Sunday morning I enjoyed this novel
and wonderful scene with the Count Karl von Sandrecki."
His first impression of St. Petersburg was bewildering.   He
says, "About six o'clock in the evening I went with Captain
Mertens and a young Dessauer Gartner to St. Petersburg,
whose splendid appearance with the ferries on the Newa
filled me with astonishment; but yet more, as before
the statue of Peter the Great I looked over the immensity
of the splendid square, even to the Alexander pillar with
its wonderfully bold, rich architecture; my mind was so
stunned I could not take it in, and I had a feeling of being
overpowered that I never experienced before, and that I
felt again more or less every time I took a walk there."
Four weeks passed away in rich artistic enjoyment.   He
was especially interested in the equestrian sculpture of
Baron von Clodt, the most distinguished artist in that line
in Europe, "whose talent," he says, "after centuries has
given us the form of the horse, as perhaps the Greek art
fashioned it, and as they could bring forth only by severe
study of nature."   This interest had a very practical side
for Rauch, as he was already engaged in modelling the
equestrian statue of Frederic the Great.   He spent much
time in Clodt's atelier, and was constantly excited to admiration by his thorough knowledge of his subject.   He
bought casts of different parts of the horse, as well as of
Clodt's newest works.   These casts are in universal use
at the present day as material for the study of horses.
He also saw in Clodt's studio the original model in wax of
the horse-tamers, designed for the pavilion at Peterhof.
Clodt brought repetitions of this group to Berlin, as a gift
for Friedrich Wilhelm IV.   Rauch says, "Here before the
castle, placed eight feet high, they have gained in size and

life, and give this terrace a beautiful appearance. The model of the Tscherkess horse which Clodt sent to the academy, Herr von Olfers has had cast for the museum. The whole front of this horse is the finest which the art has brought forth for a thousand years. All my paths now lead through the castle in order to enjoy it." Rauch modelled Clodt's bust while he was in Berlin.

But this was not the only pleasure that St. Petersburg gave him. While Rauch was staying as his guest at Peterhof, the emperor ordered from him a bust of the Princess Marie, Duchess of Leuchtenberg.

At one of the sittings the Emperor Nicholas sat at the same time to Madame Robertson for a full-sized portrait. What a stimulating artistic pleasure was this rivalry! Another time it did not work so well. The sitting was delayed about an hour ; Rauch was out of tune from the long waiting, and the model sat very uneasily. "Besides," says the diary, "we had the company of many persons, and a French reader with a resonant voice, who read Victor Hugo's 'Louis XI.' in his best pathos. I believed my last hour had come, and about half-past four I was in a condition that I cannot describe." Yet, in spite of all this annoyance, the bust was a very beautiful work. It was finished on the day of his departure, and immediately ordered to be put in marble.

The emperor took pleasure in accompanying Rauch to the beautiful villas and palaces, but he enjoyed most of all the fine collections of works of art. On the birthday of the emperor, at the Cathedral of the Mother of God at Kasan, he heard for the first time the celebrated Russian church song, which may be fitly compared with the *Miserere* at Rome. "A song of the highest edification."

Largely enriched, not only in experiences referring to his own art, but in the fuller acquaintance with all art and history, Rauch took a regretful leave of the city and all the friends he had made there. He thought St. Petersburg, as an art station, equally if not more important than Munich, Vienna, Dresden, or Berlin.   The Duke and Duchess of Leuchtenberg urgently invited him to spend a year with them, as a guide to art, in Italy.   The empress expressed a similar wish some years later, but Rauch could not leave his accumulated work.   The emperor ordered a four-foot-high knightly statue of the blessed king, as well as a similar representation of the Frederic monument in bronze.   "If I were only a forty-year-old," cried Rauch, "what might I not now begin?   But such an old dry stick!"   The emperor, after urgent invitations to renew his visit, took an affectionate leave of him, and on the first of August he again stepped on board the Hercules; and, after a pleasant voyage and a short visit at Heringsdorf by the way, he arrived in Berlin on Sunday, the eighth of August, and on Monday morning, with fresh courage, he began to set up his St. Petersburg study of horses at the atelier.

For the next five years he made no more journeys, but found his recreation in visiting his daughter and her increasing family at Halle.   The family festivals of birthdays, baptisms, etc., frequently tempted him thither.   The introduction of railroads at this time brought a great increase of activity in all the large German cities, and Rauch exclaims with delight : "To Halle in five and a half hours!"   It had been a two-days' journey.   But Rauch had a lively desire for a yet closer union with his family, to secure which a professorship in the Berlin University was desired for Professor D'Alton.   All difficulties seemed to have been smoothed away, for the king himself congratulated him on the prospect of having his son-in-law so near him, that the old artist might gain refreshment daily in the family circle, and rejoice in the sunshine of old age. But a few weeks later these hopes were shattered by the opposition of the medical faculty.   "A very dark, critical, decisive day."   A few years later and a yet darker day brought the desired living together, but with a most painful void. It was in the summer of 1854. Rauch had just returned from his last Roman journey, on which we have yet to accompany him, when fourteen days later the telegraph brought the unexpected news of his son-in-law's death. Rauch took his final journey to the much-beloved homestead which he had created for his family. The estate was settled, house and garden sold,[1] and the widowed daughter went with her children back to Berlin.

Rauch still enjoyed his visits to his friend Rietschel, who was his companion on many a journey of business or pleasure. Rietschel was invited to accompany him when he wished to show his younger daughter, Doris, the beauties of Saxon Switzerland. He was very anxious to bring Rietschel to Berlin, as his successor at the academy, since he thought no one so well fitted for the place; but Rietschel was already first at Dresden, which was not a village, and he did not care to change, to be second at Berlin, which was hardly Rome. Rauch was delighted at the many and important works in which Rietschel was engaged, and he thus prettily congratulates him : " Never have I taken in hand with greater joy the little pine-tree (the water-mark of the paper) sheet and pen than at this moment when I rejoice with you, my dearest friend, on the good taste and friendly will of our dear king, who has given to you the execution of the group of the Pietà, for the Friedenskirche in Sans-Souci.

Rietschel also refused a call to Vienna; but Rauch never ceased to urge him to come to Berlin. He urged him on the ground of the great field opened for religious sculpture, which he alone was well fitted to occupy. He calls Rietschel his "master;" "for," he says, "I often stand in the greatest admiration before your model of Lessing, and especially before the Giotto, and call for your counsel and help."

[1] It passed into the possession of the well-known historian Dümmler.

The king rewarded Rauch's loyal affection with every mark of confidence and honor. Rauch notes in his diary of May 31, 1842 : "Morning, six o'clock. To my great surprise, and without the least suspicion, I received through the general-order commission the insignia and the order of the statute of peace, '*pour le mérite*,' from his majesty the king." In the Jasper Hall, at Sans-Souci, nineteen knights of the order were on that day, for the first time, received and regaled by the king, who, in honor of the hundred and second anniversary of the death of the great king, had established this order of peace for science and art. For native knights he had elected : Cornelius, Lessing, Mendelssohn, Bartholdy, Meyerbeer, Rauch, Schadow, Schnorr von Karolsfeld, and Schwanthaler. Rauch was present at the banquet, and Dr. Eggers says, "He was distinguished in this circle, not only as the first sculptor in all Germany, but for his own statuesque beauty of person and his courtly grace of manner." He felt, indeed, the claims which society now made upon him as a severe tax on his time and strength, and he asks Rietschel whether it had been as bad in Dresden this winter as in Berlin, and he says, " It is hastening my end, and is physically and morally destructive to the rest of my life, which is fast growing *old*." He notes in his diary the names of many titled visitors to his atelier, sometimes with an affectionate word of comment ; but dearest of all to him are the visits of artists, among which that of the Nestor of sculpture, Thorwaldsen, is especially welcome.

In his diary he gives an account of the festivities of his seventieth birthday, January 1, 1847. After giving a full account of the music, speeches, etc., he wrote, " This was the most beautiful day of my life ; " and adds, to complete his felicity he had the hope of his daughter's family being reunited to him in Berlin. We have seen how sad was the fulfilment of this hope.

On his eightieth birthday the king received him with a

hearty embrace at Potsdam, as the only guest at the midday meal of the royal pair, his majesty drinking his health, and giving him the highest class-ribbon and order of the red eagle.

It may be pleasant to know that the dinner-cards for the birthday feast were etched by Menzel. In the foreground were a number of Victories in a row, dancing with Blücher, Dürer, and the Polish princes; in the middle ground were the old Fritz with Seidlitz and Zieten, while the Queen Louise in the background floated down from the monument on the Kreuzberg.

Another joy was added to the family life. This was the marriage of his first grandchild, Eugenie d'Alton, to Felix Schadow, the youngest son of his old friend Gottfried Schadow, an excellent historical painter. Rauch wished the ceremony to be performed in the Lagerhaus, on the same spot where twenty-two years before Schleiermacher had held her at the baptismal font. The marriage was happy but short-lived, for the bridegroom survived his father-in-law only a few years. The birth of a great-grandson increased his joy, — a Gottfried Schadow, who, at eleven months, was already delighted with the Christmas-tree and what hung upon it!

Travelling had always been one of Rauch's great pleasures. His habits of quick and careful observation, and his deep interest both in the world of nature and in all that concerns the life of man, were constant sources of novelty and entertainment. Although an ardent patriot, he was cosmopolitan in his tastes and feelings, and could enjoy a good thing wherever he found it. In the summer, Rauch's desire to visit Copenhagen was quickened by the offer of delightful companionship; for the general director of the museum, Von Olfers, and his young friend Strack, wished to visit Copenhagen and the Thorwaldsen Museum. He could no longer see his dear old friend, for a year had passed since he had written sadly of the death of Thorwaldsen ; but he recalls the fourteen years which he had passed under the same roof with him, and he writes, "Thorwaldsen's vicinity, his activity, his teaching, formed the basis of my later culture ; and through this I have to thank him for the success of my life."

The thought of Thorwaldsen's death may have urged him to delay no longer the fulfilment of his plan to see his friend Lund once more, and to make a closer acquaintance with Copenhagen, which he considered one of the important art-stations.   They arrived in Copenhagen August 2, and took Lund by surprise.   Under his intelligent guidance the travellers saw all that was interesting in art and archæology in the city, and among other things one of the earliest of Rauch's busts, modelled when he was in Naples.

His deepest emotions were called forth by seeing the works of his friend brought together in the Thorwaldsen Museum.   At the reception given at the royal court to the distinguished guests, Rauch learned to know the splendid young poet Andersen, who presented to him, on the following day, his biography of Thorwaldsen.   This was the last time that he ever saw his friend Lund.   He left him happy in doing good work, and in the most affectionate family relations ; and their correspondence lasted ten years longer.

In 1846 Rauch went only to Halle, but in 1847 he went on a journey of technical interest.   He had long had an earnest desire to find in his native country marble that would be suitable for sculpture.   Prince Albert of Prussia, the owner of Castle Camenz and larger territories in the earlship of Glatz, had communicated with him in May, 1844, in regard to his efforts to make the marble found in the Seitenberger Valley profitable.   Rauch gave him advice as to plans for quarrying it, and in 1847 he decided on a visit to Dresden, to extend his journey and examine the spot for himself.   He was warmly received, and saw the quarries. He found one vein of marble of a fine crystallization, equal to the best Greek ; but it was only in thin sheets, two to three feet broad, and two to three inches thick. He hoped, however, that on going deeper it might be found in larger blocks, and he thought that it would be very suitable for the restoration of the antiques.

Rauch did not lose his interest in the mechanical progress of his art, and he continued his work in the academy. As a teacher for many years he was punctual at the hour, in order to pose the model. Even in the year of his death this activity continued ; he notes in his diary, July 27, "The model placed in the *Art Saal*. Great heat." Schadow notes how for a month Rauch worked on a model in presence of his scholars, and he says, " It were much to be wished that all professors and teachers would work thus, since nothing is better for pupils than to watch the work of the master."

For academic instruction Rauch laid all the stress on the elements, on the instruction in *technique*, as we have seen in his treatment of Albert Wolff, and he wished all other academic studies to be kept only for Sunday enjoyment. He always gave his vote in this direction when questions of academic reform came up in the council. In 1838 he was a member of three unions for securing the rights of property in works of art, and preventing unauthorized copying.

With the ascent of the throne by Friedrich Wilhelm IV. the plans for completing the cathedral of Cologne began. The *Dombau Verein* was formed, of which the king was patron ; and a committee was appointed, of which Rauch, Beuth, Stüler, Von Olfers, Krausnick, and the two preachers Ehrenberg and Strauss were chosen members. The king's speech at the laying of the corner-stone of the south portal in 1842 met the liveliest response from the whole German people, who united in the popular refrain :—

> " Was will des Teufels Witz und Spott?
> Es kehret schon der rechte Gott
>   Auch bei den Deutschen ein;
> Nur frisch, Gesellen, frisch zur Hand!
> Macht Platz fur's ganze Vaterland
>   Im Dom zu Köln am Rhein."

The six hundredth jubilee of the cathedral gave occasion to fresh expression of the longing for German unity. Rauch and Von Olfers went as delegates to the Cologne Festival, which lasted two days.

He was tempted to go on to Belgium, and enjoyed its many works of art, especially with Verboeckhoven, who accompanied him. He was very much interested in the great feast at the unveiling of Simon's equestrian statue of Godfrey de Bouillon, the first great work of the artist, good in its totality, but less so in plastic correctness. He rejoices with the happy Brusselers over the promise in it.

In company with Gallait, the painter of "The Last Moments of Egmont," he visited the exhibition, where he found all the richness of the Belgian, Dutch, French, and German schools, of which he "never saw a finer, more characteristic collection." He admires the boldness of the sculpture, and the freedom and beauty of costume, to which, he says, "the neighborhood of Paris may have contributed."

By Mechlin, Ghent, and Bruges, he went to the sea at Ostend, and then back to Bruges, in the company of his old friend Prince Peter of Ahremberg. He saw all the works of the Van Eycks and Memling, in which he found no end of enjoyment. At last he reached Antwerp, and had the fulfilment of his life-long wish, as in the earliest morning he saw "the greatest, most beautiful masterpiece of Rubens, the 'Taking Down from the Cross,'" and once more by evening light, at the song of the vespers. Writing to Rietschel, he says he is like a dry plant refreshed with the dew, and he longs to go again to Antwerp in the company of this dear friend.

But one longing still remained unsatisfied. The Elgin marbles had roused his soul's desire thirty years ago, and the more he studied the casts, the more earnest he was to see the originals, for he had important questions to ask them.

As far back as 1838 he had bought an English grammar, to learn enough of this tongue for the cooks and the coachmen ; and, as the grammar alone was not sufficient, he notes, January 31, 1838, " Received the first lesson in English from Professor Buckhardt." But it was not until the year 1850, when he was seventy-three years old, that he was at last able to take what we may well call his " student journey." As soon as he reached London, where he was warmly welcomed by his friend Bunsen and others, he hastened to see the great masterpieces of Greek art, the Elgin marbles.

He writes in his diary only : " Towards evening, in the company of Bunsen and Dr. Meyer, the private physician to his highness Prince Albert, I visited the first wonder-works of antique sculpture at the British Museum, the Elgin marbles, taking but flying notice of the other art treasures." His friends seem to have done their duty most thoroughly in showing him all the sights of London, including also visits to Oxford and the Isle of Wight, where he saw Prince Albert, Queen Victoria, and Barclay's brewery. He speaks of many artists, and specially of Chantrey and Westmacott. It is impossible to recount all the interesting places he visited, and the works of art he mentions ; but he was most deeply stirred when he stood with the Duke of Wellington before the marble statue of Napoleon, which he had seen Canova model in clay when Bonaparte was at the height of his glory. He saw it executed in marble and sent to Paris, and now he found it at the foot of the staircase of his great conqueror, shown as a trophy, and surrounded by his own busts of Friedrich Wilhelm III., the Emperors Alexander and Nicholas, and Prince Blücher.

In the harbor of Portsmouth he saw the ship Victory on which Nelson met his death-wound.   The British Museum was his constant study, and he consecrated his last as his first day to the Elgin marbles.

The son of Chevalier Bunsen, Herr George von Bunsen of Berlin, has most kindly written for me an account of two very interesting incidents of this memorable visit, which make us feel almost as if we stood in the sculptor's presence.   He says, "In 1851 Rauch was invited by my father, with Francis Lieber and many another friend of his younger days, to spend some time at the Prussian Legation in London during the first great exhibition.   I had the honor of being appointed his cicerone. Insolently critical, according to the fashion of that age, I presumed to speak disrespectfully of many a work of art among the monuments in Westminster Abbey.   Contrary to his habit, for Rauch was a ready converser, he remained absolutely silent, except to draw my attention to some finely carved arm or telling attitude.   Before we quitted the Abbey, however, he expatiated to me on the life of bondage peculiar to artists.   'Two-thirds of all an artist thinks and executes,' such was, I think, the substance of what he said, 'is prescribed by the age he lives in.   We may ask the question, What has he added of his own?   We may admire the subtle diversities which raise him above his age.'

"During that same visit to London he was one day taken by me to the medal room of the British Museum. I well remember the eagerness with which Mr. Vaux and his colleagues complied with my request that Rauch should be shown not necessarily the rarest, but the most beautiful specimens of Greek coins.   He looked at each lovingly.   He praised with eloquence.   Then of a sudden he became silent, and I could observe tears running down his cheeks.   It was not until he was outside that wonderful museum that Rauch opened his mouth.   'You must have wondered,' he said meekly.   'But all my life have

I hoped against hope that the boon might be bestowed on me of seeing a great work of Greek art in the state in which the artist left it. This day the blessing was conferred. It was too much for me.' "

Herr von Bunsen thinks it may be needful to remind us of the more emotional nature of the German to explain these tears ; but if I have been successful in making my readers feel the sensibility to the sacredness of art that distinguished Rauch, and at the same time his strong desire for completeness and perfection in all its works, I think they will sympathize with' the old artist, who was at last brought face to face with the dream of his youth.

He returned home with only a brief stay at Bonn, and with his family at Halle.

Under a picture of his atelier drawn by Ludwig Pietsch he wrote, " *Meine Werkstatt, meine Heimath.*" He was yet to send forth from it the crowning works of his life.

CHAPTER XV

LAST JOURNEYS AND LAST WORKS

1853-1857

AFTER the finishing of the monument to Frederic the Great, only a few works remained in commission, such as the statues of York and Gneisenau, the group of Moses in prayer, and the projected Thaer monument for Berlin. This comparative leisure awakened a desire for travelling, and on the fourth of August, 1853, in company with his daughter Doris, his granddaughter Marie, and a servant, Rauch started for a journey to the Rhine and Switzerland.

He is full of delight at everything; the finished cathedral at Freiburg, the noble one at Basel, and the fine pictures of Holbein. He enjoys all the works of art, and the meeting with old friends, as keenly as he does the beautiful scenery of Switzerland. He writes to Rietschel that the three subjects of art which through their magnificence have most filled and blessed his journey, are the Lion at Lucerne, many cartoons of Veit at Carlsruhe, and the eight study-heads of the apostles, by Leonardo, at Weimar, as living and impressive as the Vindication of Huss, by Lessing, at Frankfort. Every step on this journey appears to have offered either new objects of interest, or sweet reminiscences of the time when he saw these places in the company of dear friends forty-nine years before. The following year brought a yet more delightful journey. By the marriage of his granddaughter Eugenie with Felix Schadow, the son of his old master and friend, the union of the families of the two greatest German sculptors was happily completed, and Rauch decided in the evening of his artistic life to go again to Rome with his young friends in their morning of joy. He began the journey May 1, going by Leipzig, Bamberg, and Nuremberg, to Splügen and the Italian lakes. On the ninth of May they reached Milan. Here, on a rainy day, he saw the beautiful cathedral, which made even more impression on him than ever before; and he was also deeply interested in the cartoon of Raphael's school of Athens. At Genoa he admires the beauty of the city by sea and land, and then he goes through a wonderfully rich valley to his old work-place at Carrara, which he found greatly changed but full of life and business. Here he spent four days in visiting the workshops. He saw and admired the work of many modern sculptors, as Tenerani, Franco Franchia and his son Giacomino. An interesting day was spent at Siena, and at last, on the twenty-seventh of May, the travellers arrived at Rome, and took up their quarters at the Grand Hotel d'Amérique in Strada Babuino. The next day very early came many visits to friends. He went through the rain to the Secretary Von Arnim's and other places, and dined at Wolff's with the sculptor Wittig from Dresden. "In the afternoon to St. Peter's through the sacristy. Vespers in the Chapel of the Canons. Rained all day."

Another day Tenerani was his guide. We are specially interested in his visit to the studio of Crawford. He is severe on the equestrian model of Washington, which he calls "frivolous, without form, without truth," but likes his reclining children "much better." He mentions also four clay models for an allegorical group for Boston. May 31, among other places, he visits the studio of the English sculptor Gibson. He names some of his works, especially a beautiful Venus in marble polychromatic, but does not give his opinion of the use of color. He adds to this account of the English master, "Works of the American Miss Hosmer, twenty-two years old, a prodigy for sculpture, very fine heads and sketches for a Magdalene." Many visits to sculptors and to painters (including Cornelius and Overbeck) are noted, and then a visit to the Quirinal, lately put in order by Pius IX., and decorated with the Italian colors, red, green, and white. After all these visits the old man went through the Columbaria, the circus of Maxentius, and to the monument of Cecelia Metella. On June 11, after he had spent the morning in the usual manner in visiting studios, he attended a feast made in his honor by the artists at the Villa Freeborn, the home of the English consul, opposite Ponte Molle. English, Belgians, Americans, Dutch, and Italians were all present. He returned home at eight o'clock.

But what gave him most delight was to compare the present with the past half a century before, and to recognize the great progress that had been made. "To see this again in its whole circle, and to enjoy the new with it, surpassed in exciting reality even the most ideal pictures which twenty-five years of longing had painted, and it cannot be told in words." He gladly recognized the improvement in the city. "Rome is more cheerful, renewed by cleaner streets and squares." He notes the improvements at every step of the way, and speaks of the delightful afternoon passed with his friend coming across the Campagna back to Rome. "What never-imagined precious moments inspired my grateful heart and soul with the feelings of the present, and the memories of the earlier time. I dwelt in the same room of the Casa Buti as fifty years ago, heard the rush of the fountain of Trevi. Even the same chimneys smoked as then; but Signora Laura looked no more out of the Zoega window." But all joys must end. On the sixteenth of June a rich company of artists accompanied the departing guest out of Porta del Popolo. The diary briefly notes the summer beauty, the oak woods of Nepi and Narni, the cypress wood behind Foligno, and, oh, anti-climax! the sorrows of the hot season, "Fleas, fleas, and everywhere fleas!" Of his three-days' residence in Florence I note his few words of our own Powers: "A pretty statue of a woman, Washington, modern, a dreary work in marble; very interesting in the mechanism, key and spatula of gutta-percha." Of Dupré he says only, "A model bust in clay, in French *allongé periwig*, handled with much taste."

Fortunately we have in Dupré's own memoirs an account of this visit, which gives us a vivid sketch of our hero : —

"One morning a gentleman came to my studio, who said he wished to see me. He was tall of person, dignified and benevolent of aspect; his eyes were blue, and over his handsome forehead his white hair was parted and carried behind the ear in two masses, which fell over the collar of his coat. He extended his hand to me, and said, —

"'For some time I have heard you much spoken of; but as fame is frequently mendacious, in coming to Florence I wished, first of all, to verify by an examination of your works the truth of all I have heard of you; and as I find them not inferior to your high reputation, I wish to have the pleasure of shaking your hand,' and he then took both my hands in his.

"'You are an artist?' I asked.

"'Yes,' he replied; 'a sculptor.'

"I wondered who he could be. He spoke Italian admirably, but with a slight foreign accent. 'Excuse me, are you living in Rome?'

"'Oh, no,' he answered; 'I lived there thirty years ago, but now for some time I have been in Berlin. I am Rauch.'

"I bowed to him, and he embraced me and kissed me, and accompanying me into my private room, we sat down.

I shall never forget his quiet conversation, which was
calm and full of benevolence. While he was speaking I
went over in my memory the beautiful works of this great
German artist, his fine monument to Frederic the Great,
his remarkable statue of Victory, and many others. I
recalled the sharp passages between him and Bartolini,
and, without knowing why, I could not help contrasting
his gentleness with the caustic vivacity of our master.
Their disagreements have long been over: the peace of
the tomb has united them; and now the busts of both
stand opposite to each other in the drawing-room of my
villa of Lampeggi." Dupré then gives at length their discussion in regard to the proposed removal of the David
of Michael Angelo to the Loggia. Rauch used his influence with the grand duke so effectually that he sent for
Dupré, and said to him : " Rauch is entirely of your opinion
in regard to the David, and he is a man who, on such a
ground, deserves entire confidence ; and I wish to say this
to you, because it ought to give you pleasure, and because
it proves that you were right."

Rauch wrote from Berlin expressing his pleasure at
this decision, and urging the arrangement of a proper
place for the group of Ajax and Patroclus, "to receive
worthily this work of sculpture, divinely composed, and
executed by Greek hands."

Rauch continued his way to Bologna, Mantua, Verona,
Triest, and Innspruck to Munich, which he reached on
July 4. He had not seen Munich for twenty years, and he
visited all the monuments with the zeal of a young man.
Many were quite new to him. A friend writes from
Munich : "How have we rejoiced in his blooming health
and youthful, glowing soul !" He was greatly interested
in visiting the foundry established by himself, where
among other works he found Crawford's statues of Henry
and Jefferson. The same day he visited Herr von Klenze
in the glass-house, saw the front of the Propylean by

Schwanthaler, went to Schwanthaler's atelier, of which he notes only "much indifferent," and then went to see the Bavaria.

The next day Frau von Kaulbach, whose husband was then in Berlin, invited him to a feast, at which many artists were present, and the evening was closed at the artists' beer-house in a select circle of artists and their companions.

From Munich he went by Bamberg and Würzburg and Halle towards Berlin, "which I entered about eleven o'clock, and all, glad and well, welcomed me." He writes to Rietschel: "A thousand times I thought of you on my truly refreshing, beautiful journey. I have enjoyed two spring months, May and June, as I never enjoyed these spring-days in my life; and were a repetition of such enjoyment with you, dearest friend, possible, I would willingly give a good bit of the remains of my life to make it actual. Felix was my loving, splendid companion, and we enjoyed each other immensely; but with a good sculptor friend one enjoys one's self on common ground differently." Thus successful and happy was this last journey of the silver-haired man to the land of his youthful dreams: it shows the perennial youth of his soul, that he found it richer and dearer than ever before.

Yet a few more works remain to be briefly noted. Even as early as 1831 it was suggested that statues of two other generals should be placed on either side of the Blücher monument, and in 1842 Rauch writes in his diary: "The king again recalls the sketches of the statues for the two sides of the proud Blücher; one of the always forward General Gneisenau on the right, and the other of the always morose, opposing, but yet boldly acting, General York on the left." Rauch did not finally begin the statues until 1844. Both were ready in 1845. Rauch had designed them smaller than Blücher, but the king thought it more fitting that they should be of the same size. In April, 1855, after a delay of six years, the king ordered them to be carried out. Various changes were made in the representation, but the differing character of the two men was preserved. In 1852 preparations were begun for the bass-reliefs of the pedestals. It was finally decided to make them of plain granite, the reverse side showing the arms of the heroes, while Victories with writing-tablets were to be placed on the front.

These monuments were given to the city of Berlin in a festive ceremony, with a brilliant show of military.

In the summer of 1853 Rauch received from Professor Hagen in Königsberg a commission for a statue of Kant eight feet high, and requests for an estimate of the cost. The place designated for the statue was the so-called *Philosophendamm*, on which Kant was accustomed to take his daily walk. The great model was begun in March, 1855, and Rauch again experienced the old difficulties about costume. He complains to Rietschel of the naturalistic ideas of costume which have come into the life of art. There was also a change in the location, as the telegraph poles would interfere with it on the proposed walk, and it would also be dangerously exposed in war.

Rauch expressed himself well satisfied with Gladenbeck's cast, but did not live to see the completion of the work. It was not unveiled until 1862, after the consecration of the new university building at Königsberg. Its final place was near the northwest corner of the palace, in the square since then named Kant Place, a few steps from Kant's former dwelling-place in Prinzenstrasse.

The last work of portrait sculpture, at the very close of his career, is a noble statue of Thaer for Berlin. Far back in the twenties, when Rauch had first achieved the degree of mastership with his military statues, and was, in consequence, besieged by commissions on all sides, he wrote to Caroline von Humboldt, then in London (June

28, 1828), that he had been asked in reference to a public monument to the States-councillor Thaer, then living, which should be erected in Berlin, and should consist of his statue and many bass-reliefs. It is considered one of his grandest conceptions. Alexander von Humboldt writes of it in his enthusiastic style, "that he had no idea that such naturalism could so bring the worth of the man and his employment into harmony with the demands of art ;" and he adds in his glowing panegyric : " A quarto volume might be written over the possibility that it was given to one spirit to create the Victories, the Sleeping Queen, Frederic the Great, Moses, Kant, and Thaer. *Vous nous expliquerez tout cela*, Mr. Schadow, Mr. Kugler, Mr. Giorgio Vasari !" This confusion of tongues seems to be necessary to the cosmopolitan Humboldt to express his feelings.

While we cannot withhold our tribute of admiration to the long series of Rauch's military portrait statues, on which he labored with a heart full of patriotic devotion, and which have undoubtedly contributed much to that growth of national feeling which has been the new life of his country, we may yet rejoice that his very last works were in that province of ideal and religious art which he most deeply loved. He had already made beautiful expressions of his religious feeling in the statues for Arolsen, and he had said that "the future of German sculpture would lie on the religious ground, and that Rietschel would be its pioneer." This was said after the completion of Rietschel's Pietà, and Rauch was already busy with his group of Moses.

Rauch had also received a commission from Sulpice Boisserée for a funeral monument with a head of Christ on it. But as Boisserée had suggested the Christ of Memling as a model, Dr. Eggers thinks that Rauch was somewhat fettered by the old German manner, and that this Christ is not so satisfactory as that on the monument of Niebuhr.

Rauch's best-known and greatest work in religious art

is the group of Moses and his friends, in Potsdam. Fortunately this is placed in the vestibule of the Friedenskirche, and is easily accessible to strangers. The group
illustrates the well-known passage which tells that while
Moses held up his hands in prayer, the battle went in
favor of Israel, but, when they sank from weariness,
Amalek prevailed. Therefore Aaron and Hur held up
his hands on either side, until the victory was won.
Moses has the typical emblems of the two bundles of rays
about his head, and the veil falling back, and he holds in
the left hand the rod which the Lord·had commanded
him to take. The costume is biblical, a lower skirt with
talus-like overdress with short sleeves. Aaron kneeling
at the left of Moses, and looking up at him, has a mantle
thrown over his dress, and supports Moses' left arm with
his own right. Besides the mantle, Hur wears a leathern
collar, or breast protector, and, while looking down at the
battle, he supports Moses' right arm with both his hands.

Rauch found great difficulties in the treatment of this
subject, and it has been subjected to many and various
criticisms more severe than any of the works of his youth
encountered. It may be questioned whether the subject
is fitted for historic representation in sculpture, as the
battle, the cause of the action, does not appear. Others
have considered it purely as a symbolic expression of the
power of prayer, or an allegoric treatment of the thought
that the army and church are the support of the state.
He himself calls it his " swan-song," and says it "goes out
in sighs." He tells of the long, weary winter nights when
he lay sleepless from two o'clock, and thought over this
work, and closes, "*Aelter werden, und schaffend arbeiten,
geht nicht.*"

In spite of all the criticisms, Eggers finds "in this
statue wonderful life and harmony in the movement, in
the drapery, and in the contrasting expressions of Hur
and Aaron ; everywhere the repose of beauty and sculpture."

It is certainly an earnest and noble expression of that mingling of patriotic and religious feeling which makes the peculiar power of Hebrew history, and which Rauch was so well fitted to understand and express.

While Rauch was engaged on this great work, he turned again to the early conception of the child, the Hope, which in 1848 he had modelled for the church of his native city. This was carefully executed as a nude figure, and then draped and winged for the final work in marble. At the end of the year 1854 Rauch allowed Medem, a pupil of Rietschel, who had lately come to his atelier, to begin a model in clay of this nude figure. The action was a little changed, and the hand held a lotus bud. A toga-like dress was laid on, and Rauch worked with his own hand on the clay model. The lotus flower was full of meaning to Rauch. The bud was the essential thing with him. "What miracles," he said, "are there not within the closed flower-cup!" It was the emblem of hope.

This was recreative work to him. The whole fashioning of the charming child, the significance of the action, and, above all, the soulful, confident expression of the countenance, make this one of the most beautiful forms which this master has left us.

Rauch had destined the Hope for the grave in the churchyard at Potsdam of his brother Friedrich, whose death almost sixty years before had opened the way which, seeming to lead him at first away from art, had brought him later to its highest summit. But before the model was put in permanent material, and the sixty years were fulfilled, the master himself was committed to earth, and the Hope cast in bronze now crowns the tomb of brown-red granite which marks his resting-place in the Dorothy city churchyard in Berlin.

The last work which Rauch finished, four months before his death, and after which no new work is mentioned in

his diary, is the eagle, in high relief, destined for the
ornament of the government building in Sigmaringen.
It resembles the eagle with the lightnings and the wide-
open wings, but this one, folding the wings more to rest,
sits on two laurel twigs that close behind him in a wreath.
" So fate has willed that the master of the plastic art of
his time has stamped the last work of his creative hand
with a symbol of his mortal pilgrimage, — the eagle rests
on the conquered laurel."

CHAPTER XVI

THE CLOSE OF LIFE

1857

ALTHOUGH Rauch in the later years often refers to feeling old and weary, he really retained his vigor wonderfully, and in his last years his health was better than it had been at an earlier period when he suffered from headache and sciatica.

"As he remained young, so also was he still beautiful. Nothing could be more impressive and venerable, and at the same time more truly friendly, than his bodily presence. His healthy countenance, his clear blue eyes, full of earnestness, goodness, and majesty, his silver hair flowing about his head, reminded one of Olympian Jove." Even to the last he was constantly to be seen in his atelier, clad in his dark clay-colored loose coat and fine white cravat. Somebody called him a "wandering work of art." He would listen to no urgency of friends to lessen his work when symptoms of old trouble reappeared. Work seemed to him the indispensable companion of his daily existence, his comforter, friend, and teacher ; how could it hurt him ? He attributed his strength to the fact that his daily work called out so much physical force. He used no bodily exercises, neither danced, rode, nor practised gymnastics, and rarely took a walk. These things seemed to him idleness. He never sat at his work, so that in his old age his feet were sore from standing. The only refreshment taken during his hours of labor was a glass of water, which Mitsching, the servant of the atelier, would often hand him, saying, " Quite fresh, Herr Professor." When he was much hurried in the atelier, and came to dinner quite exhausted, he took a half glass of wine. He would smell of it, and say, "Divine and refreshing," and later drink it, and feel his spirits revive.

From the royal table he would go at once to the atelier, take his working-garment from the servant, and give him his court-suit. "Work was his life; he prized nothing but beauty more highly."

His constant interchange of thought and feeling with his friends kept his spirits always fresh, and he had the rare power of gathering the results of others' investigations and making them his own. His conversation was lively and attractive, and, although not a learned man, he stood at the height of the culture of his time. In his diary he once wrote, "Humboldt said of Welcher, 'He writes too much and too diffusely; one sees that he does not think until he writes,' which frightened me very much, since I often find myself in the same case with my work."

He always wished to give the last touches even to copies of his work, and objected to bronze, because he had to leave the finishing to another. In 1855 he went to Karlsbad with his daughter, and after the treatment, to Dresden to visit his granddaughter, Marie d'Alton, and to see Rietschel and Bendemann. Accompanied by these and other artists he visited the new museum, all parts of which the king ordered to be opened to him, and where he was delighted to see the old works in their new position. The young artists gave him a brilliant reception. He saw the model of Rietschel's group of Schiller and Goethe, and the frescos of Bendemann in the dancing-hall of the royal palace.

He was very much interested in building a summer residence at Charlottenburg, and had the happiness of passing Whitsuntide there with his family. His love of nature was still a continual source of pleasure. He notes all the aspects of the weather, and the earth and sky, and rejoices at waking at three o'clock in the morning to see Venus in her beauty very near to the earth. He delights in animals, and yet more in the human form, and says of Madame Schröder-Devrient as Romeo, "What a wonder of genuine artistic representation combined with truth and grace!"

Through the union by marriage of his family and Schadow's, it came about that he kept his birthday in 1853 in his old master's dwelling-house, in which festival the Bendemann family joined.

Rauch kept his eightieth anniversary quietly with his beloved daughter Agnes, and in the evening had a great feast with his pupils and workmen. Rietschel came to the feast, and modelled his friend's bust. His diary, faithfully kept, gives us brief notes of his last year of life. It contains affectionate mention of his old friends Humboldt and Rietschel; speaks of social enjoyments and kind attentions from the king, and of short excursions for health and pleasure. On the fourteenth of October his diary closes. A few letters followed of a later date. By the advice of physicians Rauch decided to submit to an operation. He went to the Hotel de Rome in Dresden for this purpose, and Agnes d'Alton and her daughter followed him thither. The anxious friends waited a week for further intelligence. An acute attack threatened his life, but it passed off without fatal results, and the operation was delayed. His physicians objecting to a hotel, he was removed to a private dwelling. Here he revived so much as to be able to take short walks in the garden with his granddaughter. Every day he wished to hear from his atelier in Berlin, and he gave orders about the Moses group. Dr. Carus gave them hope that his strong constitution would yet triumph over disease. His careful daughter Doris was earnest to have him return home, but she was invited to Dresden to see for herself that it was better for him to remain where he was. Before she arrived an attack of

Bright's disease reduced him very much. It was very hard for him to keep patient in his inactive state. In the sleepless nights he missed the clock of the parish church, which he was wont to hear from the Lagerhaus, and a striking clock was procured for him. In the morning he liked to watch the kindling of the light in a baker's shop opposite, showing that the active day was beginning. It was hard to yield day by day, to rise later, and go from bed to couch only, and even to sleep in the daytime. There was a lessening of the fever and slight improvement when Doris came; but the attacks soon returned, the brain was affected, and illusions spread over the clear consciousness. These clung around the block for the Moses. He directed its raising and moving, when he meant his own body weighted with pain. The physicians had no longer hope. Felix Schadow came on the twenty-fifth of November, but did not feel sure that Rauch recognized him.

A moment of returning consciousness reawakened hope, and Rauch said, "I must try my strength;" but it soon passed away. The next day fatal symptoms appeared; but, supported by Felix Schadow, he was able to speak with clear sense. Almost the last words which he spoke were, "O my Saviour, must I then die here?" Then his senses darkened. The third of December, 1857, a despatch was sent: "This morning toward seven o'clock softly slumbered. The last forty-eight hours without pain or clear consciousness."

His earthly course was ended. In the Lagerhaus, which had been so long his true home, where he lived the life of work that he loved, his friends and fellow-workers silently awaited his lifeless remains, the statue-like image of the soul; and here most fitly were the funeral rites celebrated. Not the funereal hangings, but the unfinished works around, spoke most eloquently of what was to be no more.

His coffin was surrounded by all classes of men, from the Prince of Prussia, the royal household, the ministers, the members of the Royal Academy of Art, the associates of the university, the artists, the city magistrates, and the troop of pupils and friends, among whom might be seen the bowed form of Alexander von Humboldt, coming to take leave of his friend.

After the service of the church, the preacher, Doctor Jonas, unrolled the picture of his life and work, and Mendelssohn's song of *"Scheiden und Wiedersehen"* was sung, and the procession moved over the Königsstrasse and the Schlossplatz, and then took the same way that we saw Rauch tread in the height of his glory to the great monument of Frederic. Loving hands had covered his statues with wreaths, and the Prince and Princess of Prussia waited at their residence, as before, to greet the master. But now the train moved on to the place of peace, where his old beloved teacher Schadow and so many friends rested, — the church-yard before the Oranienburgh gate.

" But before the laurels and palms thrown by reverent hands mingled with the earth, Lieutenant-General von Weber, the old gray warrior, after giving the military benediction,[1] prayed for the fatherland, that it may have men and heroes worthy to be immortalized in stone and bronze, and artists who may know how to do it as Rauch has done. So the heroes live through him, and so lives Rauch."

In the spring of the following year the academy held a solemn memorial feast on the twentieth of March. It began at midday, daylight being excluded, and a clear candle-light shining on the brilliant company. The highest rank

---

[1] " Den Kugelsegen nach." We may well imagine the old general standing by the grave of the artist who had immortalized in stone so many of his old masters and companions in arms, moved to the deepest excitement, and feeling that no blessing could be so fitting as the salute of cannon that he had so often heard ring over the graves of heroes.

of scientific and artistic culture was present.   In the background were the busts of both kings under whom he had worked, and in the foreground his own life-size statue by Drake.   A beautiful · *adagio* opened the festival.   The memorial speech of the secretary of the academy, Councillor Tölken, reminded his hearers that this was not the festival of the dead, but of the immortal; and he drew a sketch of the great artist's life.   It was followed by a poem by Dr. Eggers, set to music by Taubert, which resounded festally through the hall in prayer and thanksgiving : —

> " Die Brücke zwischen beiden Welten,
>   O Herr lass aufgerichtet steh'n,
> Zum Trost, wenn deine Auserwählten
>   Den Weg zu dir zurücke geh'n ; —
> Du gabst ihn, er bezeugte Dich,
> Du nahmst ihn, — wir verehren Dich ! "

" So was the close of the earthly career of the master fitly sealed, and Rauch given over to history."

Occupying an important social position as Rauch did for so many years, and living in the closest intimacy with most of the best artists of his time, as well as possessing a remarkably handsome face and figure, it is not surprising that a large number of portraits of him remain, taken at all periods of his life, and in many various styles. I can mention only the most important.

One of the last items in his diary, January 12, 1857, speaks of the feast which he gave to his scholars and workmen, to which Rietschel came from Dresden, "and it became a right pleasant supper. With my daughters and grandchildren there were thirty-eight covers at table."

"Thirteenth. Rietschel, making use of a rough plan of my earlier bust, began to model the new bust after life."

"January 25, and to-day has finished it in masterly execution."

This is the beautiful bust of which there is a cast in the Rauch Museum, which, executed in marble in Rietschel's splendid manner, adorned the jubilee exhibition in 1886. The finished cast was sent to Rauch the second day of the Easter festival, April 13, and was placed in the red chamber before breakfast, to surprise him. He wrote to Rietschel: "Your hand prepared a second feast full of admiration and gratitude, including all our common friends, who delighted in your skill, and rejoiced with me in this work for immortality. It was a great festival!

"A chorus of our academic colleagues sounded yesterday a note of applause of the likeness, of the splendid handling of the whole, from the base even to the crown of the head, and the harmony of the single parts with the general effect."

This bust gives the most perfect representation of the beautiful artist head, whose traits will always be remembered, since it was taken at the highest period of his life, the loveliest, the most spiritual; and a descent from this height was never perceptible. As Rietschel said, "Rauch always remained young because he began every work with fresh enterprise and zeal, as if he had never accomplished anything before."

His friend Drake has also preserved this power of youth in his statue of the master. On the day after the unveiling of the Frederic monument, Olfers wrote to Rauch: "I have just come from Potsdam, and have to tell you that the king, our master, wishes to see your statue by Drake carried out in marble. It is of no use to object to it." In November of the next year Rauch writes to Rietschel: "Drake has to-day finished the model of my unworthy self with spiritual and technical artistic ability, in which you may see the most excellent work of art, as very few have been able to create such an iconic statue." The critics of that day fully indorsed this praise, and especially ten years later by placing it in the hall of the institution for which Rauch worked so long and lovingly, the Museum of Art. Drake also made a profile likeness of Rauch in a barret-cap, which was cast in bronze and placed in the home at Halle.

Bruges made a colossal bust in 1852, and Vischer a round profile for the medallion for the unveiling of the Frederic monument, and Afinger one for a circle of heads of Cornelius, Humboldt, and Kaulbach. Gustav Richter made use of this for a colossal medallion, and Hübner for a drawing published in Wilhelm von Schadow's "*Der Moderne Vasari*," and also engraved by Fr. Wagner. In 1859, after his death, Wolff modelled a profile of Rauch, which was set in his monument in the Dorothy Church at Berlin, as well as on a cenotaph in the church at Arolsen. Later a tablet of black marble, with the profile inlaid, was given by Doris Rauch, and placed on the right side of the church, not far from her father's statue of Faith. The portraits painted in his last days are less satisfactory.

Emma Gaggiotti, who was much admired by Alexander von Humboldt, painted an oil portrait, which hung in the villa at Halle; but Dr. Eggers thinks it is only decorative, and does not give truly either the outward appearance or the inward character of the artist. A life-sized drawing made by Gigoux for David d'Angiers is in the David Museum at Angiers. The representation of Rauch as a sculptor, by Kaulbach, in the fresco at Munich, as well as the one on the staircase at Berlin, is hardly intended as a portrait. Representing an earlier period is an excellent bust by Tieck, made in 1827. From this bust a medallion was cut for Rauch's sixty-third birthday, on the reverse of which was the wreath-throwing Victory, with the inscription in Greek, which I translate, " O majestic Victory, thou wilt never cease to crown him ! " Rauch was surprised and touched by this honor, and praises the medal and the likeness very highly, as well as the idea of the Victory, and the motto from Euripides.

But the execution of the Victory did not satisfy him, and he thinks it was engraved from a poor drawing of the statue, so that when he wishes to make a present of it to his friend Rennenkampf, he has it set as a paper-weight, so that the reverse does not show. Other statuettes were made by Drake, Blaser, and others.

An oil portrait was painted by Magnus in 1831, and one half-size by Senf. A pencil drawing was made by Gottfried Schadow in 1812, and engraved by Caspar in 1830, and also as a wood-cut for the first volume of Dr. Eggers's biography, from which it has been reproduced for this volume. Many others were made by different persons, of which we will only name two little portrait medallions in bronze by Vischer, which the fond father had set in gold bracelets for his two daughters, and a drawing in black and white chalk by Schneller for Goethe's album of his friends, taken during his visit to Weimar in 1834. Edward Bendemann also painted him in 1838.

In the last years photography gave us a faithful representation of Rauch's person ; but as visiting-cards were not then in fashion, these pictures are usually of large size, and only one copy was taken. Three excellent pictures were taken by Schmidt of Berlin a few months before Rauch's death, and are in the possession of his granddaughters Eugenie Schadow and Bertha Bunsen, and two also taken in Munich by Haufstagl belong to his grandsons Eduard and Alfred d'Alton Rauch.

At earlier dates, 1845 and 1847, are excellent daguerrotypes, and a drawing by L'Allemand has been lithographed and widely circulated. There is also a painting by Karl Begas in the Hohenzollern Museum.

After his death his statue was modelled several times

among those of distinguished sculptors, as ornaments for galleries, and finally, as late as 1882, his bust was painted in a *lunette* in the hall of the ministry of Cultus at Berlin, in correspondence with those of Goethe, Beethoven, and Dürer, representing poetry, music, painting, and sculpture.

A noble company in which to preserve an earthly immortality!

CHAPTER XVII.

RAUCH'S SCHOOL AND INFLUENCE ON MODERN ART.

WHEN two decades after Rauch's death the centenary of his birth arrived in 1877, the Academy of Art called his friends to a new festival of remembrance. It took place in the Cornelius Hall of the National Gallery. The representatives of the highest ranks of the state were present, the Emperor and Empress of Germany at their head. The bust of Cornelius gave place to Drake's statue of Rauch, surrounded by golden flowers; and the relations of Rauch who were still living, and his friends of the old time, and of the younger generation, filled the room. A sonata of old Giovanni Gabrielli, and a thanksgiving of Haydn, preceded the oration of Professor Dobbert, who with a full brush painted him as "the great artist who opened new paths for the plastic art of the century; but before all as the historian of the royal house of Brandenburg in marble and brass, singer of the freedom of Germany in the monuments of Queen Louise and the generals of that time, and by the creation of the forms of Victory, as the ideals of German popular spirit."

This naturally leads to the consideration of Rauch's position in art. In the last half of the eighteenth century monumental art, which had found a grand but solitary representation in Schlüter, had sunk to mere meaningless decoration, in which it mirrored the life of the time. A change was inevitable. It took place on the other side of the Alps through Canova; on the German side through Dannecker; in France through Houdon and

Chaudet. It reached its climax in Thorwaldsen, Schadow, and Rauch. Thorwaldsen developed the classic side ; Schadow brought out a noble realism; while Rauch, as we have seen, united these two influences in their best development on the realistic side by his monumental statues, on the ideal by his circle of Victories, and in rich combination in his statues of Queen Louise, the Polish princes, the Albert Dürer, and many minor works. He followed the path opened by Thorwaldsen in the use of bass-reliefs, and developed the true principles of realistic expression in this important branch.

To this service Rauch added great value by introducing into Germany the skill in the casting of bronze, which was then flourishing in France, through which was directly established the foundery in Munich, and, by the interest and rivalry thus excited, those in Nuremberg, Berlin, and Lauchhammer. The wholesome competition thus aroused led to an improvement in this industry, which has made great strides in half a century.

Rauch's art was a continual progress upward, and the descent did not appear in his time. It was a constant development, free from all greed for originality, that "search for the new which appears as the first sign of decay in art." Rauch's activity was in constant relation with that which was around him, with the ideas of the national history, as well as of those of art and culture, in which the first half of our century was rich, — a genuine son of his time, and that with full consciousness. When in 1845 he learned that Rietschel had finished the clay model of Thaer, he expressed the wish that he could see it before it was cast, and added, " That which has arisen living before us can only, yes only, strengthen us to new life-power; every creation has the atmosphere of its day. Ours can only live in that which surrounds us."

Dr. Eggers relates that when in Rome he heard of Rauch's death, an Italian sculptor asked, "Who will now make your statues?" for the feeling was strong that no one could continue his work.

A sense of the importance of a collection of his works, wherein artists could study his principles, was strongly felt. Kugler wrote, "Not because Copenhagen has its Thorwaldsen, and Munich its Schwanthaler Museum, but because Rauch's great artistic activity demands it of itself, it appears to me time that the foundation of a Rauch. Museum should be projected." This wish was stimulated by the remembrance that Rauch himself had deeply regretted the want of a collection of the works of the former masters, Schlüter, Tassaert, and Schadow.

This purpose has been well carried out, and the Rauch Museum now affords even the hasty traveller an opportunity to study this master.[1]

To few artists can the term founder of a school be more truly applied than to Rauch, for he actually created a great atelier, into which came students from north, south, east, and west, and even from beyond the bounds of Germany. He was the teacher as well as the exemplar, a strict master, and yet one who developed the individuality of his pupils; as Dr. Eggers says, "An educated soul,[2] which knew how to be a master among disciples and a disciple among masters."

Among Rauch's pupils Rietschel stands at the head. We cannot speak of these two in connection without recalling the tender affection, the entire trust, the profound respect, and the delight in each other's work, which they constantly manifested, without ever trenching on each other's individuality. Perhaps I have sufficiently celebrated this relation in the course of my narrative; but I

---

[1] It is hoped that at some future time Rauch's wishes will be fulfilled by adding to this museum the works of his predecessors, Schlüter, Tassaert, and Schadow, as far as they can now be procured. A collection of his pupil Drake's works is already in possession of the government, and will be placed near those of his master.

[2] Who will give us a good English word for *gebildete*? Did Paul have the same thought in "fashioned in his likeness"?

must add this word of Rietschel's, written to Rauch in 1854. "I have seen with admiration Merten's work on the small reliefs.[1] That is, indeed, the finest thing that has been done in art, and must afford you the highest satisfaction.   Above all, how much excellent work has been done here! how great is the number of skilled pupils!   What a reward for you! to be the founder of such an artistic development of sculpture, and, which is equally important, even of the industrial progress.   What a rich fruit of your spirit and your activity!"   When these two artists first met, Rauch was already forty-nine years of age, and Rietschel but twenty-two; but they recognized each other at once, and the relation of master and pupil soon changed to that of friendship.   Within a few days of Rietschel's entrance to the atelier, Rauch wrote in substance, " I have received young Rietschel into the atelier, although there was really no vacant place; for his beautiful drawings from the nude pleased me so much that I must make a place for him. If he learns to make half as good studies in clay, he will be a skilful sculptor, and I do not doubt that he will succeed.   I beg His Excellency to leave him three years with me."   Six months later he regrets that Rietschel had not had earlier acquaintance with work in stone, and adds, " Dresden will be proud of this man."[2]   A year later he is moved almost to tears by Rietschel's success, and adds, " When so much geniality and quick, active perception, united with high morality, shine in him, how much may we not expect from him!"   And again, in 1837, in speaking of his bust of Prince Johann, Rauch writes, " After such a work I must call you no longer pupil, but master;" saying that Rietschel surpasses him "on one ground, and that the highest, — religious sculpture."

Yet Rietschel gladly acknowledged everywhere the

---

[1] On the Frederic monument.

[2] The noble Rietschel Gallery, which I unfortunately saw only amid the confusion of cleaning, testifies how proud his city is of her promising boy.

influence of Rauch, which saved him from the extravagances of the Nazarene school, and led him to that recognition of antiquity which has given the repose and beauty of the Greek to works full of Christian feeling. He relates that he once entered the atelier without noticing a beautiful Niobe which had just arrived, when Rauch called out somewhat sharply, " Have you nothing to say ?" —" About what ?" I asked.   " Have you not then seen the beautiful Niobe out there ?" asked Rauch in excitement. " If it had been a Madonna would it not have charmed your eyes ?" This incident gave the young man an impulse to the closer study of the antique.

Rauch's teaching was always directed to developing the individuality of his pupils, rather than to impressing his own methods upon them ; and the effect is most evident in the work of Rietschel. Constant as was the intimacy between them, each speaks his own thoughts in his own language. It is indeed difficult to analyze the difference between them, but it is easily felt. If we are tempted to say that there is a more delicate grace, a sweeter religious feeling, a greater depth of soul, in Rietschel, the statues of Faith, Hope, and Love, the heavenly calmness of the Queen Louise, the tender protecting care in the Francke, the bright joy of the Victories, rise up in rebuke against us ; if we would ascribe more boldness, freedom, and historic life to the monumental works of Rauch, the majesty of Rietschel's Luther,[1] and the vitality of his " Goethe and Schiller," make us hesitate to utter our thought ; and yet the difference exists, and we have a true double star, differing more in color than in glory.

Dr. Eggers mentions many other sculptors who were pupils both of Rauch and of Rietschel ; but as their works are not known to myself or the American public I pass them by.

---

[1] Rauch did not live to see the crowning work of Rietschel's art, the Luther, which might be considered the finest fruit of his school ; and even Rietschel did not see the whole monument finished.

Next to Rietschel in Rauch's affections was Albert Wolff. As he was nearly forty years younger than Rauch, and the son of an old friend, the elder artist's relation was a fatherly one.

Wolff was introduced to Rauch by George von Strelitz ; and Rauch took a constant interest in his studies, and carefully prepared him to profit by his journey to Rome. He prepared for him a guide to everything best worth studying in Italy, and also proposed many subjects which he wished him to investigate for him, such as the process of oxydation in bronze casting, or the material of the pillars in the dome at Genoa, or the succession of frescos in the Campo Santo at Pisa. He worked on many of the most important statues, and has followed Rauch's methods very closely.

Drake is the third of Rauch's pupils. He was a fellow-countryman, born in 1805, and he entered the atelier at the age of twenty-two. He worked on the Max Joseph monument ; and his own beautiful Schlossbrücken group of "Victory crowning the Conqueror" was declared by Rauch to be a most original and well-executed work. Rauch frequently praises him, and finally writes in his diary, March 26, 1853, "Professor Drake sent me the portrait statue in plaster of the poet Scheerenberg, a plastic wonder of originality which I place higher in this line than anything which has appeared before." [1]

Bredow, who was three years in Rauch's atelier, was also very dear to Rauch. He sympathized with the younger sculptor in his classic taste, and says that he has solved the difficult Homeric problem of blending in the representation of Paris the voluptuary and the hero, in a way which neither Canova nor Thorwaldsen, and still less any other sculptor, has succeeded in.

---

[1] Drake has produced a number of masterly statuettes of Humboldt, Schiller, Rauch, Schinkel, Beethoven. A group of singing and playing children for the portal of the Castle Church in Wittenberg, and the lovely statuette of the butterfly-catcher, which was exhibited in the Jubilee Exhibition of the year 1886, are spoken of as among his most charming works.

Kiss, Bläser, and Afinger were also highly prized pupils of the master. The statue of Ernst Moritz Arndt in Bonn, by Afinger, takes a very high rank. Bläser excelled in historic portrait sculpture. He helped Rauch on the Dürer statue, on that of the Polish kings, and on the Frederic monument. Many excellent portraits of his are well-known, while the ideal figure of Hospitality in the National Gallery proves him a worthy disciple of the master. Finally Kiss, who was twenty-two years in Rauch's atelier, has won European fame by his group of the "Amazon struggling with the Tiger." Kiss represents the sculpture of animals in Rauch's school, in which the master himself took great delight.

Many other names, even, as Dr. Eggers says, to the half-hundred, might be given of Rauch's scholars who have taken an honorable part in the development of German sculpture; but instead of attempting to name them all, I will rather speak of a few who were more his companions than his pupils, and yet who are properly considered as representatives of the Berlin school.

Emil Wolff, when twenty-one years old, came to Rome just as his cousin Rudolf Schadow died after a short illness, and entered into the inheritance of his activity, and worked earnestly with Rauch for the museum. In 1878 he was still working at Rome in a vigorous old age.

The brothers Karl and Ludwig Wichmann, one two years older, and the other seven years younger, than Rauch, were pupils of Schadow, and fellow-students with Rauch in Rome. Their merit was chiefly in portrait busts. Wichmann made eight of the twelve statues for the Kreuzberg: two after Rauch's designs, two after Tieck's, and four from his own.

But I must especially name Frederic Tieck, who, if Rauch's intentions had been carried out, would have become with him truly a founder of the school. He died on the twelfth of May, 1851. In Rauch's day-book we find, " On

Monday evening at half-past eleven o'clock ended, in the peculiar weakness which has for a year made him incapable of work, the life of the friend of many years and companion of my workshop, Professor F. Tieck, — a life thoroughly devoted to art and science. From the year 1812, when I learned to know him in Rome, and again when after many years I found him again at Carrara, I shared my workshop with him, according to my changing residence, until July, 1818. Then I came to Berlin, where I made a place for him in the royal atelier, and also gave up to him the works of the new opera house under Schinkel. He was always to me a true, dear friend. What his indolence, dislike of work, and pressure of debt made of him in the last years, when he ended his days in every kind of increasing degradation of outward need and poverty, I leave to the reflection and explanation of the clear judgment of others." The explanation is easily given. Tieck was the victim of his weakness of character and his extreme good nature. Inconsiderate relations used him and his credit in such a manner that all personal assistance to him became impossible. On this weakness was shattered the plan of a common atelier. Rauch recognized his superiority not less in scientific training than in the *technique* of art. He divided with him his work on the candelabra for the queen's monument and for La Vendée, and on the monument at Kreuzberg ; and they worked together on the monument to Scharnhorst, and the medallions of Humboldt and Goethe. But Rauch was the driving power, and Tieck the one continually driven ; and so the desired co-operation was not established. Rauch soon surpassed him in skill as a sculptor. The work on the theatre, and that on the fifteen half statuettes for the crown princess, show him at his best in art.

Without entering into further details we may accept Dr. Eggers's statement that the first half of our century witnessed a real advance in art, the greatest since the

Italian renaissance. "If it was one-sided and violent in its action, its energy surpassing its technical ability; if the new wine was put into old sacks which spoilt the taste of the wine, and the present has done wisely to turn its attention to making new sacks; still we must remember that the sack is one thing and the wine is another, and if a wine is yet produced out of this fermentation of art theories and art execution, its grapes will have to be ripened by the same old sun of Homer, which brought out the bloom of the renaissance of art after a thousand years' sleep, and roused the spirit of Germany in the beginning of the century, and which is destined to lead the spirit of the German nation towards its ideal.

"And if the quickening sunbeams shall arouse again the sense of plastic art, above all in her monumental creations, it may again bind itself to Rauch, and may strive towards its highest aim on the way of Rauch and his school."

One final word of the man Rauch, and the character that he builded through his life and work. The first thing that strikes us is his rare good fortune. I have had no thrilling tale to tell of the struggle with poverty, enmity, and, worst of all, neglect, which has made dreary the lives of so many artists. His career seemed one of almost constant progress, for he had the wonderful alchemy which could turn difficulties into triumphs, and failures into success.

He was well-born, beautiful in form and feature, vigorous and healthy. Reared in humble circumstances, he never lost his sympathy with the people, but looked upon work as his birthright, and a good workman as his companion and friend. Withal, he had the great blessing of a decided vocation, which was clear to him from his earliest years, and in which his nature could find full expression.

His first trials, the death of his father and brother, seemed to cut him off from his work, and force him through filial duty into the life of the court. A weaker nature would have succumbed to its temptations, and in later life lamented his talents wasted, and longings unfulfilled; but while faithfully performing the duties of a servant in the queen's antechamber, he was laying the foundations of his future fame; and the tender relation thus formed with the royal family smoothed all his future career.

Unlike many artists, he was firm, exact, self-controlled, and orderly, and was rarely troubled by pecuniary difficulties; for his wants were simple, and his economy exact. With a passionate love of beauty, he found delight in nature and art at every step; and with tender sensibility of feeling, he had a rich life of friendship and parental joy. The one great want in his life did not make him cold and hard; if it gave a touch of bitterness to the sweet waters of affection, they were still pure and invigorating. As a master he was strict and critical, but he stimulated his pupils' powers, recognized their skill, and rejoiced in their fame.

Honor and length of days to the full measure of human life, and success which was fairly earned, were gifts frankly and modestly enjoyed. He grew more beautiful, more sweet and tender, with advancing years; for his nature was healthy and true, and he gave and received with equal directness and simplicity.

His patriotism was intense, but his thought was cosmopolitan, and he recognized merit in every nation. His religion was not speculative nor dogmatic, but sincere and loyal, and content with the forms in which he first received it.

If he had not the very highest range of mind, the intensity of Dante, the comprehensive grasp of Michel Angelo, the spirituality of Fra Angelico, the far-reaching imagination of Shakspeare, he was fitted to do the work needed in his time, — the renewed expression of the great thoughts of humanity in broad lines of artistic beauty which would impress them upon the minds and hearts of the people.

If he has not led modern art up to the very highest point, he has placed it on a firm and broad basis ; and on his shoulders others may climb still nearer to the heavens.

In writing this volume I feel that I have done what I could to carry out the prophecy with which Dr. Eggers closes the volume of correspondence between Rauch and Goethe. After comparing their mutual work and their influence on each other to that of the great linked names of Homer and Phidias, and Dante and Michel Angelo, poets and sculptors singing and chiselling their country's thought, he ends by saying, "So may Goethe's productions and Rauch's works be transmitted to distant races, and the track of their earthly days may lead into times, in places, and among people, who late, very late, may be called to enter into the rich inheritance of German art and culture, as well as all the well-guarded treasures of primitive days and of hoary antiquity."

Rauch's first great work, the Queen Louise, was once in American hands, and was near coming to our shores : one of his last busts of Victory was made for an American. Let us hold our claim upon him by carrying on his work for art. America, the heir of all the nations, should accept the good and reject the evil of all.

LIST OF WORKS

INSTEAD of a list of 378 works of various kinds executed by Rauch during his long life, I have thought it would be more interesting to have a chronological table indicating the date of his more important statues and busts, especially those mentioned in this book. The dates usually indicate the beginning of the work, but it is not always so.

1795. Stag's head for Wilhelmshohe Cassel.
1798. A bust of Hofrath Lenz, unfinished.
       A bust of Castellan Meister.
1799. Seven busts, including one of the prince's huntsman and a young
           maiden.
1800. Wach (the painter) as a boy, bust.
1802. Artemis and Endymion, first work exhibited.
1804. Ariadne.
       First model of Queen Louise, bust.
       Profile relief of Frederic the Great.
1805. Jason.
1806. Venus and Mars, relief.
1807. Amor.
1808. Caroline von Humboldt, bust.
       Gustav von Humboldt, bust.
1809. Luise von Humboldt, bust.
       Teresa Calderani, bust.
1810. Adelheid von Humboldt as Psyche
       Zacharias Werner, bust.
       Theodore von Humboldt, bust.
       Monsignor Capecelatro, bust.
       Queen Louise, bust.
1811. Queen Louise, sleeping, second model, bust.
       Thorwaldsen, bust.
       Franz Snyders, bust.

1811. Hans Sachs, bust.
        Admiral Tromp, bust.
        Van Dyck, bust.
        Gottfried Schadow, bust.
        Princess Wilhelm of Prussia, bust.
        Friedrich Wilhelm III., bust.
        Countess Brandenburg, first model, bust.
1812. Monument of Queen Louise.
1813. Work on the monument in marble.
1814. Profile portrait of Friederich Wilhelm III., relief.
1815. Martin Sehön, bust.
        Prince Blücher.
        Emperor Francis of Austria.
        Emperor Alexander of Russia.
        Candelabra for the Mausoleum at Charlottenburg.
        Æsculapius.
1816. Friederich Wilhelm III., bust.
        Frau von Maltzahn, bust.
        Prince Wilhelm of Prussia, bust.
        Prince Hardenberg, bust.
        Princess Charlotte, bust.
        Queen Louise with crown and veil, third model, bust.
1817. Funeral statue of Queen Louise, second model.
        Emperor Alexander.
        Bülow von Dennewitz.
        Candelabra for the soldiers of La Vendée.
1818. Scharnhorst.
        Count York of Wartenburg.
1819.• Apollo.
        Genelli, bust.
        Count Ingenheim, bust.
        Frederic II.
1820. Nymph for the long bridge in Berlin.
        Genii for Wartenburg, Leipzig.
        Dennewitz and La Rothière on the Kreuzberg monument at Berlin.
        Blücher for Breslau.
        Goethe, bust.
        Armorial Eagle.
        Victories, with the Dragon, Lion, Eagle, reliefs.
1821. Apostle Thaddeus, statuette.
        Statue for the monument of Countess Schulenburg.
        Grand-duke Nicholas, bust.
        Minerva — teaching,
                        fighting, } reliefs.
                        arming,

1822.   Agnes Rauch, bust.
        Count of Brandenburg, bust.
        Arms of Blücher, relief.
        Sleeping Lion, relief.
1823.   One sketch for Goethe statue, standing.
        Blücher for Berlin.
        Princess of Cumberland.
        Victory.
        Alexander von Humboldt, bust.
        Dr. Mundhenck, bust.
        Crown-Prince Friedrich Wilhelm of Prussia, first model, bust.
1824.   Companion to antique Danaid.
        Genius for Paris on the Kreuzberg monument.
        Wieland, bust.
        Elizabeth, Crown-Princess of Prussia, bust.
        Resting Stag, first model.
1825.   Genius for Belle Alliance for Kreuzberg.
        Professor Friedrich Tieck, bust.
        Professor Zelter, bust.
1826.   Striding Apollo.
        Max Joseph, King of Bavaria, bust.
        Blücher monument in Berlin, decorative.
        Reliefs on Blücher monument.
        Friedrich Wilhelm III. of Prussia.
1827.   Hero
        Leander } for the Elector of Hesse.
        Psyche
        Francke monument in Halle.
        Friedrich Wilhelm I. in Gumbinnen.
        Prince Wilhelm of Prussia, first model, bust.
        Stags.
1828.   Funeral statue of Princess of Darmstadt.
        Goethe in the House-gown.
        Rauch's own portrait, bust.
        Design for medal to Humboldt, relief.
        Design for medal to Emperor Nicholas, relief.
        Design of a pedestal for Dürer monument, relief.
        Font for the cathedral at Berlin, relief.
        Felicitas Publica for the Max Joseph monument.
1829.   Sketch for a Lion-tamer.
        Nicholas, Emperor of Russia, remodelled bust.
        Max Joseph, sitting portrait for Munich.
        Schleiermacher, bust.
        Frederic II. for Aix, bust.
        Monument for Frau Cooper, relief.

1829. Bavaria for Max Joseph monument, relief.
      Pedestal to Goethe statuette, relief.
1830. Praying Maiden.
      Prince Henry of Prussia, bust.
      Count Diebitsch-Sabalkanski, bust.
      Design for the medal to vaccination, relief.
      Striding Lion, decorative.
1831. Sketch of Narcissus.
      Gable-field of Walhalla.
      Reliefs of Max Joseph monument.
1832. Maiden Lorenz von Tangermünde.
      Sitting Victory, holding a wreath.
      Son of Prince Demidoff, bust.
      Count Voss, bust.
      Dr. Olfers, bust.
      General von Schack, bust.
1833. Expectation as Eurydice, sketch.
      Stepping Victory.
      Second stepping Victory.
      Dr. Hufeland, bust.
      George, Grand Duke of Mechlenburg-Strelitz, bust.
      Duke and Duchess of Cambridge.
1834. Design for a medal for Hufeland, relief.
      Bacchic scene, relief.
      Religion, art, science, for Max Joseph monument, relief.
      Medal to Hufeland.
1835. Boy with the cup. (Liebe.)
      Boy with the book. (Faith.)
      Fraülein Engel as Flora, bust.
      For the Max Joseph monument, giving the constitution, relief.
1836. Danaid.
      Profile portrait of architect Strack, relief.
      Profile portrait of the grandchildren of Rauch, — Eugenie, Marie,
          Bertha, Guido d'Alton.
1837. Albert Dürer for Nuremberg.
      Minister Count von Bernstoff, bust.
      Profile portrait of Bendemann.
1838. Group of Polish kings.
      Gneisenau for Sommerschenburg.
      Sitting Victory throwing a wreath.
      Profile portrait of Agnes d'Alton, relief.
1839. First Victory for Charlottenburg.
      Second Victory for Charlottenburg.
      State's Minister of Ladenberg, bust.

1839.   Monument of Niebuhr in Bonn, relief.
           Profile portrait of Friedrich Wilhelm III., relief.
1840.   Victory for the Belle Alliance Platz in Berlin.
           Prince Frederic of Prussia, bust.
           Profile portrait of Baron von Clodt, relief.
           Life-sized Eagle with the Lightning.
1841.   Victory crowning Herself.
           Victory mourning.
           Horse for the Frederic monument.
           Frederic II., bust.
1842.   Equestrian figure, Frederic II.
           Funeral statue, Friedrich Wilhelm III.
           King William of the Netherlands, bust.
1843.   Funeral statue of Queen Frederika of Denmark.
           Baron von Clodt, bust.
           ·Victory of Penthelicon, marble bust.
1844.   Monument for Memel and Oels.
           Corner figure for Frederic monument.
           Eagle for the Minister of Finance in Berlin.
1845.   Minister of State Von Rother, bust.
           Thérèse von Bülow, bust.
1846.   Paul Friedrich, Grand Duke of Mecklenburg-Schwerin.
           Beuth, Councillor of Finance, bust.
           Mercury, bust.
           Profile portrait of Eduard d'Alton, relief.
1847.   Pillar with Apotheosis of Frederic, sketch.
           Monument of Frederic.
1848.   Hope, undraped.
           Hope, draped.
1849.   One and two sketches for Goethe and Schiller group.
           Eugenie d'Alton, bust.
           Profile likeness of George Franks.
           Reliefs on Frederic monument.
1850.   Reliefs on Frederic monument.
1851.   Alexander von Humboldt, bust.
1852.   Count York of Wartenburg.
           Funeral statue of Ernst.
           August of Hannover.
           Designs for the pedestal of the Thaer statue.
1853.   Gneisenau for Berlin.
           Gneisenau's Arms, relief.
           Head of Christ for monument of Boisserée, relief.
           Eagle for sarcophagus.
1854.   Victory with tablet for Gneisenau relief, statue.
           Victory with tablet for York relief, statue.

1854.   York Arms, relief.
1855.   Hope.
        Kant (statuette).
        Sulpice Boisserée, bust.
1856.   Equestrian statue, Frederic, sketch.
        Wilhelm III., with pedestal.
        Moses group.
        Emperor Nicholas sleeping, third model, bust.
        Design of a Victory on the battle-field at Roubach, relief.
1857.   Thaer for Berlin.
        Bust of Victory, bust.
        Eagle in the laurel wreath.

INDEX

Verlag von F. Fontane in Berlin W.

Christian Daniel Rauch

von

Friedrich und Karl Eggers.

5 Bde. gr. 8°. Preis geheftet M. 63,—; geb. M. 73,—.

Jeder Band ist einzeln käuflich. Bd. V auch unter dem Separattitel:

Christian Daniel Rauch's Leben und Werke

von

Karl Eggers.

Mit 2 Bildnissen Rauch's, der Phototypie eines Briefes und 127 Lichtdrucktafeln mit Abbildungen seiner Werke.

Preis geh. M. 30,—; in Prachtband m. Goldschn. geb. M. 34,—.

Briefwechsel zwischen Rauch und Rietschel,

herausgegeben von

Karl Eggers.

2 starke Bände. Lex. 8°. Preis geh. M. 20,—
in Halbfranz geb. M. 25,—.

Mit 2 Lichtdrucktafeln, mehreren Hochätzungen und 2 Schreiben in
Facsimile.

Rauch und Goethe.

Urkundliche Mittheilungen von

Karl Eggers.

1. Band. Preis geh. M. 5,—; geb. M. 6,—; Liebh. Ausg. geh.
M. 6,—; geb. M. 8,—.

Mit 6 Lichtdrucktafeln und 1 Holzschnitt.